EASEFUL DEATH

EASEFUL DEATH

Cynthia Harrod-Eagles

**SEVERN
HOUSE**

First world edition published in Great Britain and the USA in 2025
by Severn House, an imprint of Canongate Books Ltd,
14 High Street, Edinburgh EH1 1TE.

severnhouse.com

British Library Cataloguing-in-Publication Data
A CIP catalogue record for this title is available from the British Library.

ISBN-13: 978-1-4483-1460-0 (cased)
ISBN-13: 978-1-4483-1464-5 (e-book)

All Severn House titles are printed on acid-free paper.

MIX
Paper | Supporting
responsible forestry
FSC® C013056

Typeset by Palimpsest Book Production Ltd.,
Falkirk, Stirlingshire, Scotland.
Printed and bound in Great Britain by TJ Books,
Padstow, Cornwall.

Praise for the Detective Inspector Slider mysteries

"Gripping . . . A fine read for procedural fans"
Booklist on *Before I Sleep*

"Another delightful mystery for fans of unconventional police teams, witty dialogue and excellent procedurals"
Library Journal on *Before I Sleep*

"Another satisfying mystery starring one of Britain's most engaging coppers"
Booklist on *Dying Fall*

"[This series is in] a league of its own . . . Will garner new readers and delight loyal fans"
Publishers Weekly Starred Review of *Cruel as the Grave*

"Outstanding . . . Harrod-Eagles' latest DCI Bill Slider novel brings the series to a new level"
Booklist Starred Review of *Cruel as the Grave*

"A witty, thoughtful mystery"
Library Journal Starred Review of *Headlong*

"Dialogue sparkling with wit and humor . . . Readers will wish for Slider's career to continue for many years to come"
Publishers Weekly Starred Review of *Headlong*

About the author

Cynthia Harrod-Eagles was born and educated in London and had a variety of jobs in the commercial world before becoming a full-time writer. She is the author of the internationally acclaimed Bill Slider mysteries, and the historical Morland Dynasty and War at Home series. She lives in London, is married with three children and enjoys music, wine, gardening, horses and the English countryside.

www.cynthiaharrodeagles.com

I have been half in love with easeful death

— John Keats

ONE
Poultry in Motion

Atherton stopped in the CID room doorway, ran a finger round his collar and said, 'Phew, is it handsome in here, or is it just me?'

Swilley didn't look up. 'Nobody missed you, Jim. Nobody at all.'

Gascoyne said, 'How was Portofino?'

'Transcendental,' said Atherton.

'He means nice,' Jenrich translated.

'No, I mean we contemplated our navels. Or, to be accurate, each other's.'

'TMI,' Swilley grunted.

'You're not very brown,' Fathom complained.

'We didn't go outside much. Anything interesting happen while I was away?'

'The coffee machine broke down,' Fathom said thoughtfully. 'But it turned out it was the fuse in the plug.'

'And I missed that! I'm never taking a holiday again.'

'Nat and me are thinking of going to Las Vegas,' McLaren said, unwrapping the foil from a salami sandwich from home.

'Why? You hate gambling,' Atherton said.

'He bets on the ponies all the time,' Fathom objected.

'That's not gambling; that's science,' McLaren corrected him. 'Anyway, Nat's always wanted to go. She wants to play the slots.'

'It's very uxorious of you to agree,' Atherton said. 'There's not much else to do there, you know. Apart from eat. The casinos give out free food to tempt you to play.'

McLaren brightened. 'Free food?'

'But mostly fried stuff. No vegetables. Just meat, bread and chips, generally covered in gloopy cheese. What am I saying? Go! You can comfort-eat to your heart's content. Though of course your heart's *cont*ent is likely to be the problem.'

'What are you *talking* about?' McLaren asked, baffled.

'I'll go and speak to the boss now,' Atherton excused himself.

The door from the CID room to DCI Slider's office was open, and Slider was at his desk working his way through a mountain of paperwork – or at least the foothills. He looked up as Atherton appeared in the doorway. 'I heard,' he said. 'Portofino was nice. Like the zen dentist who refused novocaine, you managed to transcend dental medication.'

'Ah, that's what I've missed about this place,' Atherton said. 'The zippy come-back. The ready wit. So nothing's happened?'

'It's August. I'm actually catching up,' Slider said, gesturing at the files on his desk. 'I've reached the Cameron years. How many PMs ago was that?'

Atherton took his usual position, sitting on the windowsill above the cold radiator. It hadn't worked since the first moon landings. Some religious sects believed that if it ever came on again, the world would end. 'Everything all right at home? No major traumas?'

He had left his Siameses, Sredni Vashtar and Tiglath Pileser, with Slider while he and Stephanie went on holiday.

'Apart from doing the Wall of Death round and round the house at two in the morning? And pulling the pelmet off the wall?'

Atherton clutched his cheeks. 'They're hooligans, I know. I'll pay.'

'No need. Dad screwed it back up. George has enjoyed having them. They do more interesting things than Jumper.'

'Interesting? That's one way to put it. How did Jumper cope in the end?' Jumper was Slider's ordinary, common cat. When Atherton had brought his two round, there had been bristling and hissing and tails in bloom.

'When they come into the room, he moulds himself into a square, closes his eyes and pretends they're not there,' said Slider. 'A technique he apparently learned from the tortoise.'

The tortoise was a newish accidental acquisition. George had brought it home from school for the Easter holidays, but when school resumed they'd said they couldn't have it back – some parent had complained about hygiene or allergies or possibly religious sensibilities, it wasn't entirely clear – and asked if the Sliders would keep it.

'Poor thing,' Joanna had said. 'Rejected at such a young age. Of course we'll keep it. I always wanted a tortoise.'

'*Did* you?' Slider was amazed.

'They're very restful. And long-lived.'

'Ah. Good point.'

'I should also mention that I wanted a pet pig,' she said.

'We'll take the tortoise,' Slider said hastily. It had been called, unimaginatively, Tortie, and he'd insisted on a name change if it was going to take up permanent residence. Fortunately, George was sufficiently beguiled by the new name, Habeus, not to object.

'Well, I'm glad they haven't entirely wrecked the place,' Atherton said, 'because I was hoping you might be willing to keep them for another day. I was thinking of staying at Steph's place tonight.'

'Of course,' Slider said. 'They're no trouble.'

'Thanks,' Atherton stood up to look out of the window. The sun shone down from a hazy sky, traffic was Tuesday-light, and no pedestrians were in sight. 'It's quiet out there.'

'What have I told you about not saying that? You'll jinx us.' Slider eyed the elegant back view of his sergeant, bagman and friend, and read studied insouciance. 'What's going on?' he said.

'Nothing.' Atherton turned, hesitated, picked an imaginary piece of fluff from his sleeve. 'I was just thinking—'

'Yes?' Slider prompted.

He looked at Slider and away again. He lowered his voice confidentially. 'I'm thinking of asking Stephanie to marry me.'

'Oh?' Slider said. This was momentous. Atherton, the serial hound, proposing? He didn't know how to react.

'So I thought – at hers, where she's comfortable, without the cats to interrupt . . .'

'What's brought that on, then?' Slider asked tentatively.

'Portofino. It was so easy. Just us, alone. Not doing anything in particular. Just talking. Not always even talking. You'd think we'd get on each other's nerves, but no. Anyway.'

'I see,' Slider said gravely. The lack of his usual fluency told more than words.

'I suppose *you* do.'

Slider was so famously happily married there was little danger
he would be mistaken for the stereotypical moody, troubled TV
detective.

'Well, anyway, I'm just thinking about it,' Atherton went on
briskly, heading away from the rocky shores of emotional sharing.
'You won't say anything to anyone, will you?'

'Why would I?' Slider said simply. Time for a change of
subject. 'Is anyone going for refs?'

'I'll go, since I've still got my shoes on,' Atherton said.

'I should hope everyone's got shoes on.'

'Figure of speech. Bacon sarnie?'

'Please.'

The call came in the afternoon, late enough for Atherton to claim
it was nothing to do with his incontinent invocation at Slider's
window.

Slider, however, still blamed him. 'You had to go and say it,'
he grumbled. 'Now some poor soul's paid the price.'

'Until the doctor's been it's just a suspicious death,' Atherton
pointed out. 'That needn't mean foul play.'

'Nutty Nicholls spoke to Renker after he spoke to despatch,
and he said Renker reckoned it was homicide. You play "chicken"
with the Fates, you're going to get fowl play.'

'So I cocked up,' Atherton said, looking out of the window.
Most of Shepherd's Bush consisted of Victorian terraced housing
of various sizes and degrees of poshness, but in the area known
as Wendell Park, there was this little 1930s pocket of semis with
the typical bay-window-and-gable-with-fake-beams. 'Look at it!
More mock Tudor than *Blackadder*,' he said.

'It's sound, decent housing,' Slider said. 'Nothing wrong with
it. What's the address?'

'Acacia Avenue, number 15.'

'Acacia Avenue!' Slider marvelled.

'Betjeman-esque irony.'

'Except that the streets on either side are Laburnum and Lilac,
so it might just be flowering tree names.'

'I like my explanation better.'

Wendell Park took its name from the eponymous small green
space, an area of grassy lawn with winding paths and benches,

some big old trees, a fringe of shrubbery and a few flower beds. It was one of those hidden treasures, the 'lungs' that made London more pleasant to live in, and was much valued by the locals. The streets around the park were quiet, just far enough from the main road for the traffic to be a distant hum; the houses were well-kept, and the parked cars to either side were those of modestly prosperous people, not a rust bucket in sight. Built before the war, none of the houses had a garage, but so far blessedly few had dug up their front gardens for hard standing. It was – well, there was no other word for it – nice.

'It's not right,' Slider said. 'You shouldn't have a murder in a place like this.'

'Aren't we always told suburbia is an unstable cauldron of repressed and seething emotions?' Atherton said.

'Are we? But this is hardly suburbia. Shepherd's Bush is still inner London.' Atherton's eyes and thumbs were busy with his mobile. 'It's like living with a fifteen-year-old,' Slider said testily. 'Put it away, for God's sake.'

'Just clearing the deck, given we're going to be busy for days,' Atherton said, holstering the phone in his pocket like a hot shootin' iron. 'This is it – left here.'

The departing ambulance passed them as they turned in, and the driver lifted a comradely hand. They acquired the reversion of his space, luckily, as the residents-only parking was already full with the usual circus: the original squad car, the Department Sprinter, the SOC van, wheels belonging to the photographer and the SOC chief, and an elderly powder-blue Toyota which he recognized as that of Dr Gupta, presumably the police doctor on call.

PC Renker was keeping the log at the side gate. Number 15 was a semi, adjoining number 17, and with no garage there was only a three-foot gap between the house and the boundary fence. There was a tall, stout wooden gate which gave access to the back garden and was standing open. Number 13 had a similar arrangement except that its gate was of metal bars. There was a three-foot-high wall between the front garden and the street, topped with privet hedge, and a curving path to the front door with a patch of lawn, neatly cut. Slider noted that the wall-and-hedge combination screened the front door from the road and the houses opposite, which was a nuisance. These days, doorbell cams could be a useful resource.

'Victim's name is Rhianne Morgan, guv,' Renker reported. He pronounced it *Ree*-ann and spelled it for them. 'Just eighteen. Dad discovered her this afternoon around half past four. He's David Arthur Morgan, age forty-nine. Unfortunately, he called the ambulance first, so there wasn't much crime scene to preserve by the time I got here. Luckily, one of the paramedics decided something was off and called it in. DS Jenrich took the para's statement.'

DC Fathom joined them. 'Body's in the kitchen at the back, guv,' he said. 'Safe route's through here.' He gestured to the side gate.

'Was it open when you arrived here?' Slider asked Renker.

'Yes, guv. The paras went in that way. They said it was open when they arrived. I don't know if it's normally closed.'

The garden was about thirty feet long and surrounded on all sides by a seven-foot fence and laid entirely to lawn. The Morgans were obviously not gardeners. At the back of the house was a concrete patio, over which SOC had already erected a tent. On it stood a foldable metal-and-canvas lounger. Next to that was a plastic picnic tumbler containing a twisty plastic straw, a number of glossy magazines and a pair of kitchen scissors.

The body was lying supine on the kitchen floor just inside the French windows to the patio. She was wearing a mini-dress, pale pink with a swirly pattern in darker pinks, and from this angle Slider could see a glimpse of pink cotton panties. He felt a rush of relief that they were in place. Statistically, most homicides were young male on young male and heat-of-the-moment, and that was bad enough. He hated it when the victim was female and still more when it was a young one. As the father of two girls, he couldn't bear to think about it.

Dr Gupta was just leaving. His job was only to pronounce life extinct. Even if the head and body were on opposite sides of the room, a policeman couldn't do it, nor, in the case of suspected crime, could a paramedic. Gupta was a tiny man, thin, bent and shabby-looking, who gave the impression of being desperately over-worked and under-paid. Slider had always felt sorry for him, until he happened to drive past his house one day and was reminded of how much doctors made.

As always, Gupta was dashing off, no time to spare. 'Strangulation. With a ligature,' he threw out, free of charge, as he hurried past.

'Ligature?' Slider queried.

'Not present.' And he was gone.

'Why, his time is worth a thousand pounds a minute!' Atherton said.

'Eh?' said Slider.

'Alice. *Through the Looking Glass.*' Slider looked blank. 'Never mind. His speech is worth a thousand pounds a word.'

'He didn't have to give an opinion as to cause of death,' Slider pointed out. That would be the job of the forensic pathologist – in this case Freddie Cameron, who was on his way.

He took one last look round the garden, noting how remarkably un-overlooked it was. The fence was too high for anyone to see over, and the neighbouring gardens had mature trees and tall shrubs which would block the view of the patio from upstairs windows. He could only see one window from here, belonging to the house in the next street and catty-corner to this one. That would put it about eighty feet away. Of course, everyone wanted privacy in their garden. Nobody anticipated actually *wanting* witnesses.

Now he had to look at the body, which was always, even after all these years, a shock. The rituals surrounding death in every society came about for this very reason, that humans, the only animals with awareness of their own mortality, found dead bodies unsettling. It was only a momentary thing before professionalism took over; but it was right that it existed. For the good of a policeman's soul, he should never stop feeling that scalp-prickle at the first sight of the mortal remains of a life untimely extinguished.

Rhianne Morgan had been about five feet five or six. She had been pretty, neat-featured, full-lipped. He saw the livid red mark around the neck, but the face was a normal colour, even pale. The eyes were shut. Her fair hair, a shade below blonde in colour, was loose, shoulder-length, wavy. The dress was fitted at the bust with a short row of buttons from the neckline down to the sternum. The buttons were undone, showing the tops of round young breasts. She had a small tattoo on her left bicep, the circle-and-cross female gender symbol and underneath it, in script, the words Just Be.

'Just be what?' Slider said.

'Hippy-dippy stuff. If you have to ask the question, you won't understand the answer,' Atherton said.

The short nails were painted pink, and she was wearing several cheap silver rings. The feet were bare, and the toenails were painted to match.

'What's in the tumbler?' Slider said. There was about an inch of dark liquid in the bottom. 'Looks like Coke.' He sniffed it. 'Maybe with something in it? We'll get that analysed.'

'So she was just lounging there, reading magazines,' Atherton said, inspecting them. '*Elle, Prima.* A couple of months old.'

'They're expensive,' said Slider. 'Maybe she couldn't afford them new.'

'Ah, but this *Vogue* is the current number.' He turned it over, and read the label stuck on the back. '"Wendell Dental Surgery. Do not remove." She nicked it, the little minx.'

Slider felt sad. This child – eighteen was still a child to him – had had nothing to do on a nice day in August but sit alone and leaf through fashion magazines full of clothes she couldn't afford and a glamour beyond her even if she could. Why wasn't she out with friends? Or doing a summer job where she'd meet people and have new experiences? Well, all her experiences were over now. *Just be?* Now she only *had been.*

'Scissors?' Atherton queried.

'No sign of blood on 'em,' Slider said. 'But bag 'em anyway. Maybe she was threatened with them.'

'No sign of a struggle,' Atherton said. 'If it weren't for that ligature mark . . .'

'Maybe she was wearing something tight round her neck – a scarf or something,' Fathom offered.

'It wouldn't leave a mark like that,' Slider said.

'And anyway, who took it off?' Atherton added. He looked around. 'Did he come in through the garden or did she let him in to the house? Renker said there's no sign of a break-in.'

'We'd better go and talk to the father,' Slider said. 'Find out how much got tidied up before Renker arrived.'

*   *   *

David Morgan was in his sitting room, the one at the front of
the house with the bay window. It had the feeling of a room not
often used. As with so many old houses nowadays, the back room
and kitchen had had their walls knocked out to make one large
room across the back where everything happened. The kitchen
area at one end looked new-ish and expensive-ish, while at the
other was a huge wall-mounted TV, an enormous shabby sofa,
a coffee table, cupboards and, spread around, all the clutter of
everyday living, things in use, things put down and never tidied
away. Between the two ends a pine table with six chairs around
it stood in as dining room, opposite the open French windows
onto the patio. There was a crumby plate and sticky knife on it,
along with a used mug, a nail file, a heap of what looked like
junk mail, a battered paperback entitled *Only For You*, open and
face down, and several local freebie newspapers that did not seem
to have been opened.

Messy it might be, but to the expert eye it was the normal
chaos of home life, no sign, again, of a struggle or unlawful entry.

By contrast the sitting room was tidy and clean. The mantel-
piece had been removed, and a gas fire had been installed around
hip-height – a glass-fronted box containing an arrangement of
pebbles. The walls were painted pale grey, the floor was laminate
grey oak, there was a modern three-piece suite in dark grey tweed
with contrasting scatter cushions in black and white, and a glass
coffee table. The television in one corner was much smaller than
the one in the kitchen, on a glass and chrome stand. The overhead
light was a modern chandelier of bare Edison globes. There were
no pictures or photographs on the walls, and the only other
furniture was a glass and chrome display cabinet filled with little
crystal animals. It was the most sterile room Slider remembered
entering. He could imagine young Rhianne coming in here in a
strop when she needed a door to slam but not anyone entering
the room for purposes of pleasure. So much grey, so much glass.
And what was with the flaming pebbles? What kind of sense did
that make?

Morgan was sitting on the sofa facing the unlit fire, and a mug
of tea stood untouched before him on the coffee table. A
uniformed PC, Jilly Lawrence, was keeping him company, or
standing guard over him, depending on your perspective. He

looked pale and strained, and his aftershave was competing in the small room with his sweat of distress. He was of medium height and medium build, with fair hair cut in a sharp style. His suit was as stylish as a high street chain could make it, his tie was silk, pale blue with a pattern of pale pink elephants – a little act of defiance against corporate diktats, or evidence of a sense of humour? – and his shoes were shiny and fashionably pointed. His features were pleasant, just this side of handsome. His skin was lightly tanned and smooth. Altogether, he looked like a man putting his best foot forward on a limited budget, a man to whom appearance was important. Slider guessed he would be in some public-facing job where he had to look good.

'Mr Morgan?' Slider introduced himself and Atherton. They settled in the two matching chairs, and Atherton took the notes. 'You're Rhianne's father?'

'Rhi*anne*,' Morgan corrected, putting the emphasis on the second syllable. 'Stepfather.'

'I'm very sorry for your loss. Please tell me about how you found her.'

'Well, I came home around four thirty. I called out, but she didn't answer.'

'You expected her to be home?'

'She might have been. School's out at the moment, and I didn't know of any plans she had.'

'Go on.'

'Well, I went through into the kitchen, and I saw the French windows were open. So I went across, and then I saw her, on the floor, crumpled up.'

'Did you move her?'

'Of course I did!' he said wildly. 'I didn't know what had happened. I ran to her, turned her over. Tried to rouse her. I shook her and called to her, and when she didn't wake up, I rang for the ambulance and started CPR on her. When they came, they took over, but—' His voice trailed off. He looked down at his hands. 'They said it was no good. They said she was already dead,' he went on, his voice low. He looked up. 'I wanted them to take her to the hospital. I begged them. I said there must be *something* you can do. But they said not. Then the lead paramedic said he had to call the police because it was a suspicious death.

Why?' He stared at Slider with wide, frantic eyes. 'Why is it suspicious? What were they saying?'

'Any death without an obvious cause is suspicious. And in this case—' He examined Morgan's expression carefully. 'You didn't notice the mark on her neck?'

'What? What mark? No. She has a mole. What's that got to do with it? What are you talking about?'

He was growing agitated again, and Slider left that for now. 'Never mind. When did you last see your daughter alive?' he asked instead.

'This morning,' Morgan said. 'She came down just as I was going to work.'

'What time was that?'

'Just before nine.' The routine questions calmed him down, and he answered easily. 'I don't have to get in until half past nine. We're open from nine, but Janine unlocks, and you hardly ever get people coming in that early.' Slider gave him an enquiring look and he said, 'I work for Buckfast's, the estate agents. I'm branch manager of the Acton office.'

That explained the smartness. 'And is four thirty your usual time for coming home?'

'Well,' he said. 'I work until six on weekdays, but I'm out and about a lot, looking at properties and seeing people, and I often pop in if I'm passing. Spruce up a bit. Have a cup of tea, check emails. I was looking at a house in Emlyn Road this afternoon, so I was just round the corner.'

'And is your wife usually at home?'

'No, she works. At Waitrose, ten till six. They're sending someone to fetch her, to tell her—' He glanced at Lawrence, who nodded confirmation.

'You didn't want to break it to her yourself?'

His mouth bowed in misery. 'I couldn't,' he said. 'She'll be . . . I couldn't be the one. She'll . . . It's better coming from someone official.' He shook his head. 'I can't believe this is happening. It's like some horrible dream. I can't believe just this morning we—' He stopped and rubbed his face with both hands, from the cheeks back towards the ears, as if he might reshape the actual fabric of himself. Then he looked sharply at Slider. 'Why are you here? I don't understand.'

'We have to investigate any sudden, unexpected death,' Slider said. Fathom appeared in the doorway and mouthed that Dr Cameron had arrived, and he nodded. 'We shall want you to make a formal statement,' he said. Morgan nodded miserably, staring at his hands again. 'By the way,' he went on, 'when you arrived home, did you let yourself in with a key?'

'Yes, of course.'

'And did everything seem normal? Did you notice anything out of place? Any signs of disturbance?'

'No. Nothing.'

'Did you notice whether the side gate was open or shut?'

'I opened it to let the ambulance men in,' he said, frowning in thought, 'so it must have been shut. But it doesn't lock. There was a bolt, but the screws worked loose in that storm we had in July, and it fell off. I haven't got round to replacing it yet. It's a tight fit; it stays shut if you push it to. I'd told them on the phone to come through the side gate to the back. They could have pushed it open themselves, but of course they wouldn't know that.' He met Slider's eyes, realization dawning. 'Are you saying someone . . . killed her? Someone came in and killed my daughter?'

'We're just asking questions at the moment,' Slider said gently. 'Has there been any trouble lately? Any threats to you or your family? Does anyone wish you ill? If there's anything at all, however small, you should let us know.'

Morgan shook his head. 'We're just a normal family. I don't understand anything about this.'

'So are we thinking someone wandered in from the street?' Atherton said. 'But how would they know the gate didn't lock? A burglar going from house to house, trying gates on the off chance?' He intercepted Slider's glance. 'That side gate is a nuisance. Otherwise it would have to be someone she let in, or someone with a key. Which would limit the pool of suspects usefully.'

'I can't think it would be someone wandering in by chance from the street,' Slider said. 'How would they know the gate didn't lock?'

'It might have blown open.'

'There isn't a breath of wind today.'

'The vibration of a passing skip lorry might do it.'

'Go and do something useful. Get the canvass started. Can't have our people standing around doing nothing.'

'OK. I doubt it will do us much good. These days, even when people are at a home, they're glued to a screen, not looking out of the window. Don't you miss the old days, when there was always a nosy neighbour twitching the net curtains?'

Freddie Cameron was exquisite as always, in a biscuit linen suit and cranberry bow-tie with dark blue spots. His hair, with a lot of silver in it now, was swept back, thick and glossy, and his shoes were what Morgan's only aspired to be.

'How are you, old bean?' he greeted Slider cheerfully. 'I haven't seen you in donkey's ages. How's the family?'

'All well. Teddy's going to start pre-school in September, very excited about it. And George will be going up to the juniors.'

'They grow up so quickly, don't they? And the other two?'

'Matthew's back-packing in Portugal with friends.'

'He's at . . . Exeter, is it?'

'Bath. History. Just starting second year. And Kate's got a job in Millet's, saving up for Oxford in October. She's the big surprise – PPE at St Hilda's. She wants to be a journalist.'

'Going over to the enemy, eh?' Freddie said with a wry smile. 'It seems only yesterday she was an eye-rolling Goth arguing for a nose stud.'

'I think she sees herself the new Kate Adie in a flak jacket talking to camera somewhere in the Middle East. Her mother just wants her to acquire a rich husband, two children, a Labrador and a Volvo.'

'The two may not be mutually exclusive,' said Freddie. 'And Joanna?'

'She's taken some time off while the kids are off school. Quite glad of a holiday – she's been doing a lot of Gilbert and Sullivan recently.'

'Always fun, G&S,' Freddie said, then cocked his head. 'Or not?'

'She's playing second violin, which she says is just oompah-oompah over and over again. She says it's like being hit on the head with a foam-rubber fish.'

'I have no idea what that feels like,' Freddie said solemnly.

'Me neither. But we're hoping to get away for a couple of weeks before school starts, take the kids to the seaside. If this case doesn't drag on. What's it looking like?'

'Strangulation, with a smooth ligature – something like a silk scarf, perhaps.'

'It doesn't look much like strangulation to me,' said Fathom, breathing over Slider's shoulder. 'I mean, she's quite pale.'

'You're thinking of the classic signs – cyanosis, congestion, petechiae?' said Freddie. 'You get those when strangling goes on for a long time, when sustained pressure on the jugular veins impairs the return of blood from the head to the heart,' Freddie explained kindly. 'However, sudden pressure on the carotid structures can cause parasympathetic impulses to travel down through the vagus nerve and produce a profound bradycardia.'

'I see,' said Fathom, untruthfully.

'Vagal inhibition.' Slider remembered reading it somewhere.

'We don't use that term any more,' Freddie said, 'but yes.' And seeing Fathom hadn't caught up, 'Essentially, the brain sends a signal to the heart and the heart stops. And it can happen too quickly for congestion to have been produced.'

'Oh,' said Fathom. 'How quick would that be?'

'You mean, how long must pressure be maintained to produce congestion? It's a matter for debate, but about thirty seconds in my opinion. I'd say this wee one suffered total cardiac arrest quite quickly. Usually the victim marks their own neck trying to prise away the ligature, but I see no sign of that. I've bagged the hands of course, in case there's any tissue under the nails, but it doesn't look like it. I'd say we're talking about fifteen to thirty seconds, and then collapse. She'd hardly have time to know what was happening. Anything else?'

'Time of death?' Slider asked.

'Warm and flexible. I'd say she's been dead between two and four hours.'

'Some time this afternoon, then. And when will you do the post?'

'Oh, straight away, as soon as I get back. There's no queue. August is always quiet.' He cocked his head at the sound of some activity at the front of the house, featuring a female voice, shrill with protest. 'Sounds as if the mother's arrived.'

Rita Morgan was short, tightly plump and, even in a plain knee-length navy skirt and corporate blouse, attractive. She had a full face of make-up and dark brown hair cut short and spiky, with some of the spikes cheekily tipped in brass blonde. Slider imagined her in normal circumstances as perky, lively, talkative and harmlessly flirtatious. She'd be a wow on the checkout at Waitrose, the sort who called old men 'my love', and other women 'darling' or 'pet'. Even now, with the evidence of strain in her face, she was holding it together remarkably well. She had seen the body, at her own insistence, had been told no, she couldn't touch it for the moment, and there had been no wailing, clutching or even tears. Slider guessed it hadn't really come home to her yet. His job was to keep her talking as long as possible until the realization came crashing over her like a tidal wave and swept her away.

Now the body was gone, he interviewed her in the kitchen, with DC 'Norma' Swilley, just arrived, to give her female support. Mrs Morgan sat at the table, hands folded on the top. Her eyes tracked in a detached way round the room as if wondering, just slightly, where she was, paused briefly on Swilley in tribute to her blonde glamour, and settled comfortably on Slider in the manner of one who knew how to talk to men all right.

She had started life as Rita Flanagan in a small house in East Acton, one of six siblings. She had married at eighteen, mostly, she said, to get away from home. 'Mum was a bit weird, and Dad drank a lot, and we were packed in like sardines. You couldn't breathe.'

Philip Edwards had been a lot older than her, thirty then, 'But I liked that. It made me feel safe. And he was a good husband, steady. He was a maintenance engineer down the British Rail depot at Old Oak. We got married at St Dunstan's and I fell for Ree straight away. Phil wanted to call her Rhiannon, which is a Welsh name – he was Welsh, you see – but I thought Rhianne was prettier, and he let me have my way. He always let me have my way.'

After that she got the hang of birth control. But when they decided to have another child, she lost it at five months. 'It was a boy, which was sad, because Phil would have liked a son, but I wasn't going to go through all that again, so we left it at the one.'

Edwards died tragically young – simply dropped dead at work one day. 'It was his heart. All that heavy work wore it out, apparently. I'm just glad he didn't suffer. But it was a shock to me. Rhianne was only eight, and I'd never been on my own. But I had his insurance, and luckily I wasn't on my own long. I met David.'

'And did Rhianne get on with him all right?'

'Oh yes,' she said easily. 'He's always been very good with her. Well, he had a daughter from his first marriage, Mia. And a son, Sam. She did secretarial and works in a solicitor's office. Sam's something in IT, works for Wellcome somewhere out in Cambridge. David's terribly proud of him, but I don't think he's anything very high up. We don't see a lot of them, because David was still married to Sharon when me and him met – though they were separated,' she added sharply, as though Slider had criticized. 'But you know what kids are like. They always think Mummy and Daddy are going to get back together, so the other woman is the Wicked Witch. And I don't think Sharon helped. She was very resentful, though I never gave her cause. Too much time on her hands, in my opinion. She'd never worked in her life – not like me, I've always had a little job. Well, you have to keep busy, don't you? She works now, but only on the information desk at the British Museum, which is more like charity work to my mind. I'm not sure she even gets paid.'

'Did you and David never want more children?' Slider asked, to steer her back closer to the subject.

'No, we both decided we'd done all that, now we wanted to enjoy ourselves. Well, as far as we can, with that Sharon bleeding him dry on the alimony. I wanted a nice house, nice things, you know? Go on nice holidays. Well, Ree was old enough not to need watching all the time. I can't understand people who fly off abroad with little tiny kiddies. So much work, you'd never enjoy yourself.'

'I suppose Rhianne's finished school now?'

'Yes, she's just done her A levels – Art, Geography and English. Waiting for the results. She wants to go to art school. She's got this Saturday job at the garden centre, had that since Easter. David said she ought to get a full-time summer job, learn what life is really about. He doesn't like to see her lazing around, only they're so tired at the end of term these days you don't like to push them—' She stopped abruptly. That was the moment when it hit her. Slider virtually saw the sea wall collapse. She dragged in a breath, her eyes stared in desperation at his face, her hands lifted, open, as if she was trying to grasp something. 'What's happening?' she said. 'I don't understand. Why would anyone want to hurt her? Who did this?'

Then came the long-delayed tears, in a choking, heaving flood. Slider left Swilley to it.

TWO
Buy Me and Stop One

Upstairs there were three bedrooms and a bathroom. The parents had the front room with the bay window, conventionally furnished, more grey, this time contrasted with yellow – yellow duvet cover, yellow velvet upholstery on the little tub chair and the dressing-table stool – with a white shag rug on either side of the bed, to save morning toes from the laminate flooring. The curtains were grey with a black-and-white geometrical pattern. The room was tidy, everything put away, but the décor – the colours and the attempt at sophistication – made it feel restless to Slider, as if trading up had not yielded the results Mrs Morgan had hoped for. Perhaps they never could.

The middle room was a combination home office and gym, with a desk and computer, a treadmill and a multi-gym training machine for arms, legs and chest that looked like the offspring of a praying mantis and a dentist's chair.

Rhianne's room was at the back. The wallpaper was pink with a small white daisy pattern – a child's choice, probably, dating from when they first moved in. The bed was a single, set against the wall, divan-style; there was a wardrobe with mirrored doors, and a dressing table/desk, above which the entire wall had been covered with a collage of pictures cut out of magazines, thumbtacked, Blu-Tacked or sometimes sellotaped up with no gaps.

'Ah, that explains the scissors,' Atherton said, with a hint of disappointment.

A lot of them were women's faces, glamorously made-up and with luscious hairstyles, staring wide-eyed and pouty-lipped at the camera – an aspiration of looks endlessly repeated. Others were film stars of both sexes, interspersed with male pop stars he vaguely recognized, cute dogs and cats, some postcard-sized reproductions of famous artworks – Munch's *The Scream* and Monet's poppies caught Slider's eye – and one or two arty landscape photos – one of birds rising from a misty lake at dawn, for instance, another of the sun seen setting through the columns of a ruined Greek temple.

She had put some care and effort into it, probably over a long period – some of the pictures were faded and curling at the edges. By contrast the rest of the room was wildly untidy, the bed unmade, the floor and every surface littered with discarded clothes, magazines, used tissues, dirty plates and cups, food wrappers. It was not untypical of the way a teenager chose to live, but it was more pointed when compared with the other bedroom and the sitting room. The kitchen fell in between, and he imagined Mrs Morgan conducting a running battle to make the whole house the way she liked it, while her captive barbarians despoiled as fast as she tidied. At some point, he thought, she had given up over Rhianne's bedroom. Forensics had told him the door had been closed when they first went up – perhaps that was Rita's last defence, to shut the door on the chaos within.

How much chaos had been within the girl herself was yet to be discovered.

In one of the drawers, mixed up with underwear, were several decorative scarves, the long, narrow type worn round the neck as a fashion accessory. Her laptop, which had been on the desk/ dressing table had been bagged and taken away, leaving a bare space in the drift of make-up tubes and bottles, tissues, used lumps of cotton wool, nail files and odd socks. There were several hairy hairbrushes of different sizes, and a jumble of grips and slides, some with sparkly ornaments attached, and five well-used scrunchies in different colours – black, neon green, neon orange, red and pale blue. Her mobile had gone with the laptop for the IT boys to examine, and SOC had removed a plastic bag they had found at the bottom of one drawer which contained a competently rolled doobie.

There had also been a box of six condoms with one missing. That made Slider even sadder than the spliff. She might have been tempted by someone to try a toke but had not yet got up the courage; but the six-pack looked like accustomedness. Sexual congress, he thought: the base-line biological imperative for the survival of the species and the whole tottering edifice of romantic love that was built on top of it, passion, yearning, turmoil and conflict. Thousands of years of art, literature and music, from Egyptian wall paintings, through *Romeo and Juliet*, to Taylor Swift. The Trojan Wars, the Catholic Church, the House of Lords, the Taj Mahal. The most enduring of human preoccupations throughout the ages was reduced for this teenager to a red cardboard box of foil-wrapped latex preventatives, with the intention of making the reproductive act *un*productive, and therefore nothing more significant than a pastime, like a harmless game of table tennis.

Atherton said, 'So she was doing it. But who with?'

A neat summing-up, Slider thought. He wished it wasn't.

Back at the factory, Jenrich, his other sergeant, was setting everything up with the help of LaSalle as Slider came in. She looked like a cruel warrior queen in one of those swords-and-sorcery sci-fi movies, lean and muscled, burning blue eyes, short spiky hair and cheekbones you could cut yourself on. She was a bit of an enigma, managing so far to keep her personal life completely private, which only increased speculation about her. Slider wondered if that was her intention.

'Stepfather?' she said on seeing him. 'Look no further.'

'Don't be so cynical,' he said.

'It's not cynical. It's always the nearest and dearest. Nearest, anyway.'

'Many thousands of people have step-parents and don't get murdered,' he reminded her. 'And he seems a nice, inoffensive chap. Though I don't think inoffensive was the look he was going for.'

'What, then?' she asked.

'Oh, I think he was going for sharp, dynamic and successful,' Atherton said, coming in behind Slider. 'On a limited budget.'

Slider turned. 'Anything on the canvass?'

'Nothing so far. It being August, a lot of people are away. And a lot of people were out – at work, presumably. And the patio's not overlooked.'

'Except by that one window.'

'Yes, we worked out which house that was, but there was no one in. There's a lot of houses we'll have to go back to later – including the neighbours on either side.'

'If they're not in now, they will have been out this afternoon,' Jenrich said. 'Which means they won't have seen anything.'

'Yes, helpful of you to point that out, but we have to go through the motions,' Atherton said coldly.

Slider's phone was ringing, and he went into his office to answer it. 'Is someone going to get me tea?' he called over his shoulder.

It was Cameron. 'Still there, old thing?'

'Apparently,' said Slider. 'What have you got for me?'

'Pretty straightforward. Cardiac arrest, caused by excessive stimulation of the carotid sinus and adjacent baroreceptors. In simple terms, pressure on the baroreceptors causes a reflex re-action which reduces the heart rate. Too much pressure slows it to the point where it stops.'

'And that was caused by the ligature?'

'Just so. The application was powerful enough to produce the effect in a very short time, especially as the victim had a pre-existing heart condition. An atrial septal defect, probably congenital.'

'Did she? The mother didn't mention that.'

'She might not have known. It's a very small hole, and it's often the case that they're not diagnosed until adulthood – some-times not even then if the person has a sedentary lifestyle. They might feel lethargic, or breathless on exertion, but not attribute it to anything in particular.'

'She didn't look the sporty type.'

'But a sudden, violent shock like this would be enough to cause arrest.'

'And what would happen then?'

'Immediate collapse and death.'

'So the perpetrator started to strangle her and she fell down dead?'

'In essence. There was, for the record, no sign of sexual penetration, no semen in the vagina, no bruising or other wounds. No skin or blood cells under the nails. She didn't have time to defend herself.'

'But he might have intended to commit a rape, and got scared off when his victim up and died on him?'

'That's not for me to determine. The intention might have been only to kill, or only to subdue or frighten short of actual death. There might have been no intention to commit a sexual act. On the other hand, if there was, you do also have to consider that the strangling might have been consensual. Some people like it, so I'm told. And she was not a virgin.'

'Oh.'

'You know I like to complicate your life,' Freddie said cheerfully. 'Appearances are that she was sexually active, and also that she smoked cigarettes. She had ingested alcohol within two hours of death – vodka mixed with cola if I'm any judge.'

Slider remembered the tumbler and bendy straw. 'We've sent the remains of the drink off for analysis. But there's no suspicion of poison? Or a date-rape drug?'

'Nothing in the pathology to suggest either.'

'They found cannabis in her room.'

'Do you want me to send off samples to toxicology? I suspect she might have used cocaine from time to time, but the pathology is inconclusive. Not a heavy user, at any rate.'

'Grateful for small mercies,' Slider grumbled.

It was nice to get home and find his wife there, waiting for him. With the erratic schedules they both followed – Joanna was a freelance orchestral violinist – it had never been a given in their lives. His first wife, Irene, hadn't worked and had generally been waiting for him, but that had not always been a pleasure. Suffering a chronic discontent with her life in general and him in particular, she had seemed to regard his coming home late as a deliberate ploy to vex her, rather than a feature of the Job. Joanna was always just glad to see him.

'Hungry?' she said when they had finished kissing. 'When did you last eat?'

'I had a sandwich at lunchtime,' he remembered, with an effort. It seemed like a week ago.

'There's cold chicken and salad, but I've got some of those baby new potatoes that'll only take ten minutes.'

'Why do they call them "baby"?' he complained. 'Baby sprouts and baby carrots – it's ridiculous.'

'It is, but you're tired. You always get semantic when you're tired,' she said.

Conjured by the word 'chicken', the Siameses were suddenly with them, winding sinuously round Slider's ankles. 'Atherton asked if we'd keep them a bit longer,' Slider remembered.

'I don't mind,' she said. 'But you'll have to be extra nice to Jumper. He's feeling outnumbered. Habeus pinched his basking spot by the French windows.'

'Where is he?'

'Sulking in the garden, I think.' She patted him kindly and shoved him gently in the same movement towards the stairs. 'Supper'll be ready by the time you've washed and changed.'

'Kids in bed?' he asked over his shoulder.

'I should hope so, at this time of night,' she said.

He changed out of his work suit, washed his face and hands, and looked in at the children. How much of his fathering had consisted of looking at the sleeping faces of his offspring? In fairness, Irene had had reason to complain, though having married a policeman, she should have expected it. She was settled now with a well-regulated replacement husband, so she was happy at last.

He really hoped they could get away for a holiday this month. People usually took time off from committing crimes in August. Come September they'd be up to their elbows in felony again. If only this Morgan case didn't drag on . . .

Supper was waiting for him on the kitchen table when he went down. He'd never much cared for salad, but the chicken was tasty, and she'd put butter and chopped parsley on the potatoes. 'And there's half a bottle of Beaujolais left from Sunday if you'd like a glass?'

'Will you have one? I don't like to drink alone.'

She sat down across the table while he ate, and he told her about the new case.

'So are you saying either someone wandered in via the back gate at random from the street – is that likely?'

'Completely at random is very unlikely, though not impossible. But someone could have been scoping the area, looking for a suitable victim. "Random" in that case means it needn't have been her in particular – just that the circumstances were right.'

'Or it was someone she knew, and let in.'

'Which seems more likely. Or someone she didn't know but

had a reason to let in. "Come to read your meter, love." Or, "We've had a report of a gas leak." Even fairly sensible adults can fall for that, and she was just a kid.'

'But if it was someone she knew, presumably that would be easier for you.'

'Much. In that case, you can usually expect someone to talk, sooner or later.' He forked a potato and put it into his mouth.

She watched him chewing, evaluating his frown of thought. 'Is this going to interfere with our holiday?' she asked when he had swallowed.

'I don't know. I hope not.'

'You don't like the look of it,' she translated.

'So far we've no evidence,' he said. 'Nothing to go on at all. But it's early days. Neighbours might have seen something, or at least heard something. If it was someone she knew, she's probably spoken to friends about him. If it was a stranger . . . well, there are no street cameras, of course, but someone will have seen something.'

She was about to say, *what about the stepfather?* but desisted, watching him tiredly eating. It was lazy thinking, and something he would particularly hate. He had told her that his boss, Porson, had once said, 'It's always the first person you suspect. Except when it isn't.' Anyway, if it was that, it would emerge in time. She didn't want to spoil his supper.

'Well, if I have to, I can take the kids on my own and you can join us when you can,' she said. 'It's not the end of the world. But you never know, it might resolve itself quickly. Boyfriend, for instance, larking about. Scared to death over what happened. He'll come forward in the end.'

'That's my Pollyanna,' Slider said. 'What have you been doing today?'

'Finger-painted with the kids. Walked to the park. Did some practice. I had to shut Tig and Vash in the spare room – they howl so dreadfully when I play. It reminds me of a Tommy Beecham story. They had a live horse on stage in an opera he was conducting – I forget which one – and when it dropped a pile he said to the orchestra, "Unfortunate, gentlemen – but what a critic!"'

As he ate, the Siameses were couched on top of the kitchen

dresser, observing in case of chicken-and-floor-related mishaps, and now Jumper, the striped cat, suddenly appeared from nowhere, stalking delicately in from the scullery and the cat flap into the garden. Slider bent and stroked along the cat's back and it arched to his hand. 'You smell of outdoors,' he told him. 'You're slow off the mark. I've eaten all the chicken.' 'He's had plenty of scraps,' Joanna said. 'They all have. Quite a menagerie we're acquiring. What do we do with them all when we go on holiday?' 'Atherton can bloody well reciprocate,' said Slider.

Detective Superintendent Porson was back from a long weekend off. Nicholls, one of the uniform sergeants, who always seemed to know everything, said he'd been to stay with his daughter Moira, who had recently moved from Swindon to Bath. He seemed preoccupied when Slider went in to report to him. He listened in silence, and when Slider stopped he said, 'All right. Let me know when you've made some progress,' in a way that was clearly a dismissal.

Back in the CID room, there was a savoury smell on the air. Someone had been out to Dave's coffee stall for refs. 'Yours is on your desk, guv,' McLaren articulated round a sausage half-baguette. Onions. Brown sauce. Slider's highly tuned olfactory apparatus knew all.

LaSalle looked up from his screen. 'Strangulation with a silk scarf?'

'I've still got money on the stepfather,' Jenrich said. 'I bet she was an annoying little toad, winding him up all the time. Teenage girls can be worse than nettle rash. He probably just lost it. Maybe she was wearing the scarf, he grabbed it, next thing she drops down dead and he's forced to cover his arse.'

'Why wouldn't he just cop to it, if it was an accident?' Gascoyne objected.

'Duh! Because he's the *step*father! Who's going to believe him?' Jenrich said with impeccable circular logic.

LaSalle, who had been waiting patiently, raised his voice. 'No, but you know whose thing that is?' he addressed the room in general. 'You know who's come out recently after doing seven years for ag rape?'

'Surprise me,' Atherton said.

Lœssop, who had worked with LaSalle for years, caught on. 'You don't mean Handy Andy?'

'Handy Andy Denton,' LaSalle affirmed. 'And Wendell's his area. He grew up in Bassein Park Road. Went to Wendell Park Primary.' LaSalle was a local boy: his historical information was often valuable. 'He was doing a ten-stretch for ag rape at the Scrubs, but I heard on the street he was out on licence.'

'Worth considering,' Slider said. 'Let's have a look at his record. And anyone else on the sex offenders register who might be tasty.' He remembered his cooling sandwich. 'Did anyone make me tea?'

'On your desk, guv,' McLaren said.

Andrew Steven Denton, forty-five, came from a respectable working-class family and had no reason to go to the bad. His father worked for London Transport, and since it was practically a family firm, he could have got Andy in somewhere, and would have been glad to. But Andy liked to go his own way about things. His father said in an interview that his mother had spoiled him because he was an only child – his older brother Simon had died in infancy, so she had cherished and worried over him all the more.

He was a bright boy, did well at school, went on to train as a carpenter, and went to work for GSF, the well-known shopfitters and exhibition stand builders. A good, steady, well-paid job.

He'd been in a bit of minor trouble as a juvenile – shoplifting, graffitiing, scratching cars, fighting – but had always got off with a caution. The view seemed to be that he was a high-spirited boy showing off to his peers and would settle down once he had some proper work to do. And he did disappear from police radar for a time.

When he showed up again, it was aged twenty-six, accused of assault by the woman he was seeing then, Victoria Mary Ames, who said he had hit her, attempted to strangle her and then raped her at her flat in Ethelden Road. Downstairs neighbours had said they had heard a violent argument, screaming and furniture being knocked over, and had called the police. They claimed that the couple often quarrelled and fought. Ames had choke marks on her throat and a black eye, Denton had scratches on his face and hands, a bleeding lip and a clump of hair torn out. Both tested positive for alcohol and cocaine.

Ames claimed he had raped her, Denton claimed that it was consensual and that, further, Ames 'liked it rough'. Both were taken to the police station and statements were taken, but after a couple of hours Ames withdrew the charge and said she just wanted to go home. Denton was given a warning, and no further action was taken.

Further information from that time on the file was that Denton had been changing jobs at frequent intervals. A trained shopfitter never needed to be out of work, but he didn't seem to be settling to anything, left employ after a few weeks or took on short-term exhibition work. He also didn't seem to have a settled home but stayed in cheap rentals or lodged with the women he was seeing. Both his parents were dead, having died of natural causes within weeks of each other, not long before the assault incident.

There was a further gap in the record when, apparently, he did not come to official notice, and then came the Marly Potillo incident.

Slider shouted for more tea and carried on reading.

Marly Potillo was an attractive mixed-race woman of twenty. After a troubled youth of petty crime and minor drug use, she was trying to straighten out her life and had got a job stacking shelves at the Tesco Express in Uxbridge Road. Denton, then thirty-six, was living in a room at the top of a house on the corner of Stronsa Road and it was his nearest store. He met her when he went in to buy cigarettes.

They started seeing each other. Potillo said he charmed her with his nice manners and flattery. Men in her experience were not like that. He wooed her, taking her out, buying her little presents, making her 'feel like a queen'.

But the sex, after the first couple of times, grew increasingly rough. She put up with it, because he didn't really hurt her much, and at other times he was an agreeable boyfriend. Then one night he put a scarf round her neck and strangled her until she passed out and raped her while she was unconscious. Afterwards, when he had gone home, she went to the police.

Denton claimed that there was no rape, that it was consensual, that she had not been unconscious, that they had been doing it like that for some time. Potillo enjoyed the pretend-strangulation. It was just a sex game. She had begged him to do it – himself, he'd have preferred it plain and simple. He had come across well when interviewed, and the police were not inclined to take it further. It looked like a couple's quarrel, with the woman weaponizing the sex to get the upper hand. There was no physical way to determine it was rape: it was her word against his. They did not take her seriously.

Potillo, however, had not backed down, and insisted she had been raped. A local journalist had got hold of the story and made a fuss. The police turned up the Ames incident and started to wonder. The story went viral, with Denton characterized as a dangerous serial rapist who groomed his victims first. Then two other women came forward with a similar story. Denton was charged, it went to trial, and he got ten years.

'Yes, I remember it,' Porson said, when Slider went to him with the story. 'I never liked him. Clever bastard. Mouthy. Too full of himself.'

'The Potillo incident didn't ring any bells for me,' Slider said.

'It wouldn't. It wasn't us. She was living in a council flat in Larch Avenue – that's across the border. It was Acton's case. But I remember reading about it – local press were all over it. It was one of those awkward jobs where it's just he-says-she-says, but then a women's lobby group started making a big fuss about the canteen-culture police not believing women. Then the other females started turning up, and that cooked his goose. He went down for a big stretch – national press were on it by then and the judge made an example of him.' He turned and looked out of the window, jingling the change in his pocket. 'So, he's out, is he?'

'Came out in March on licence,' Slider said.

'Just enough time to get itchy feet. He's worth having a look at.' He turned back. 'Find out who his probation officer is, whether he's been giving attitude. That's often the first sign the worm is for turning. Any other leads?'

'Nothing to go on yet. But we've barely started. Forensic's searching the streets around. We've got to interview her parents, her friends, find out who she was seeing, where she was going. Then there's her laptop and phone.'

'It's all right, I'm not nagging. Just asking. But Mr Carpenter will like the Denton angle. It'll keep him happy while we get on with our job. He looks like the obvious suspect.'

That was better, Slider thought as he went away, than the stepfather being the obvious suspect.

'Why was he called Handy Andy?' Swilley asked.

'Have you seen how fast those shopfitters work?' Lœssop said. 'Juggling six tools, whizz bang thank you ma'am?'

'Nah, it's just basic assonance,' Atherton said.

'You see, this is why people don't like you,' Jenrich said. 'You always have to be clever.'

'When did "clever" become a pejorative term?' Atherton said, uninsulted.

'Mr Porson said Denton was a clever bastard,' Slider remembered.

'He *was* a clever bastard,' LaSalle asserted.

'Lawdy, Miz Scarlet, now I'm a serial rapist?'

'Presumably, he used a silk scarf so it wouldn't leave a mark,' Fathom said, still reading through the records. 'So how come it left a mark on Rhianne Morgan?'

'Because she died before it could fade,' Atherton said. 'Once the heart stops beating, the blood can't disperse.'

'We know Rhianne owned a silk scarf,' Fathom said. 'There was one in her drawer. Maybe she had more than one.'

'Silk-ish,' said Jenrich.

'If we find one in Handy Andy's gaffe, that's good evidence,' LaSalle urged. 'I mean, why would a bloke own a silk scarf?'

'If it was the actual murder weapon,' Swilley pointed out, 'it would have skin cells on it. DNA.'

'Unless he'd washed it,' LaSalle said. He looked at Slider. 'Guv, we ought to have a word with him, do a search of his pit before he's had time to get rid of the evidence.'

'We have, as yet, no evidence against him, other than his record,' Slider said. 'We wouldn't get a warrant. The search would have to be with his permission.'

'If he refuses, that's against him,' LaSalle said eagerly. 'We ought to get after him quick, shake him up. He is the obvious suspect.'

'The stepfather is still the obvious suspect,' Jenrich objected. 'We don't know what history there was of aggravation between them. And he's the only one we know was there, on the spot. What was he doing, back home in the middle of the day? Being the one to discover the body – classic ploy.'

'Of course we have to look into the family history,' Slider said. 'So far we know next to nothing about Rhianne. But,' he turned to LaSalle, 'you and Lœssop can look into Denton. Tactfully,' he added, as they surged to their feet.

'He's on parole, guv,' Lœssop said. 'The first hint of a violation and he's going back – he knows that. If he's innocent, he'll co-operate all right. And if he doesn't . . . well, that's suspicious, right there.'

Mrs Morgan Mark 1, now Sharon Lessiter, was only too pleased to be taken away from her information-imparting to talk to the police, though it caused consternation to her fellow sybils since, this being August, the desk was besieged by tourists.

'Got to do your civic duty, haven't you?' she said as she slid out. 'That poor kid!'

Jenrich suggested they get a cup of coffee in one of the museum's catering spaces, but Mrs Lessiter objected. 'They'll all be jam-packed. There's a café across the road in Museum Street. That'll be better.'

Sharon Lessiter was soberly dressed in a navy skirt and light blue short-sleeved shirt, full make-up and very short hair, almost in a boy's cut, toffee-brown but grey speckled. She looked in her well-maintained forties, and there was no attempt, Jenrich noted, to look less than her years. Her manner was brisk and no-nonsense, like an experienced teacher. Perhaps dealing with confused tourists three days a week had developed the mode.

'Working three days is enough,' she said. 'It gives me a bit of walking-around money and gets me out of the house, but by Thursday night I've had enough. People are so unbelievably stupid. Our maps and guides are brilliant, but they come up clutching an open floor plan and *still* ask you where the toilets are.'

When they were seated with coffee, Jenrich asked how Sharon had heard about Rhianne.

'Oh, from a woman I know who shops in Waitrose. Rita was working on the customer service desk when the police came, so she sort of hung around and overheard enough. She knows my connection and texted me straight away, so I was probably one of the first to know. And then it was on my news feed later, of course. So, who d'you think did it? Have you got a suspect?' Abruptly she straightened her face and added, 'It's a terrible thing, obviously. Poor kid,' but it sounded perfunctory. You had to say that sort of thing or be thought Not a Nice Person.

'We're just gathering background information at the moment,' Jenrich said. 'Tell me about you and David Morgan.' A current wife would most likely be constrained by loyalty not to tell the unvarnished truth, but an ex-wife, probably with a grievance . . .

'Oh, we married too young,' she said promptly. 'He was twenty-two, I was only twenty, and then I got pregnant straight off. It was too hard. It put too much strain on our relationship. But then, he could have done that all by himself.' She looked at Jenrich expectantly for the prompt.

'How was that, then?' Jenrich asked obediently.

'What d'you think? Basically, he couldn't keep it in his pants. And I knew. Of course I did. All those pathetic excuses. "Something came up at work." I think we know exactly what "came up" at work! Playing squash with the regional manager. Someone's birthday drinks – got to go, love, I'll try not to be too late.'

'He was having affairs?'

'If you want to call it that. They weren't serious. Opportunistic, I call it. He's out and about, no one knows exactly where he is, he's got the keys to houses where no one's home, and women keep giving him the come-on. I sometimes think of all those posh houses he sold and wonder what the owners would think if they knew how many strange people were having sex on their beds.' She gave a mirthless laugh.

'Did you ever confront him with it?'

'Not until Rita. Well, he was earning good money, and I had two kids to bring up. I wasn't going to rock the boat. But he crossed the line with her.'

'She said you were already separated when she met him.'

'Ha! Well, she would say that, wouldn't she? Couldn't face the guilt of breaking up a marriage.'

'So you weren't separated?'

Her eyes slid away. 'We were and we weren't. I'd got sick of his shenanigans and one day when he came home stinking of her perfume, I threw him out. He went to a Travelodge. Makes me laugh when I think of him, with all his swank, living in one of those, out of a suitcase. But I probably would have taken him back, so it's not what I'd call separated.'

'When you say he crossed the line with Rita . .?'

'Like I said, he came home stinking of her, with some lame excuse, when I'd seen him with her, in his car, going off somewhere. And when I faced him with it, he admitted it, said it was different, she was special, all the usual old pony. So I threw him out – see how special it feels without your home comforts! He was never one for roughing it, David. I thought he'd come back when he wanted his laundry done. But she had her hooks into him by then.'

'It must have been hard for you.'

She shrugged. 'Well, it was and it wasn't. I mean, the kids missed him, it was hard explaining to them, but otherwise . . . I got the house and decent alimony, and who needs a man messing up the place? She thought it was love, silly cow! I could have told her, it was sex, pure and simple. After two kids, I was done with all that. But of course, *he* never stops wanting it. And he'll be cheating on her just like he did on me. You married?'

'You think he's still having affairs?'

'Conferring the great gift of himself on some half-baked female, you mean? They think the earth revolves around their dick. Ooh look, I've got a penis, I'm a god! There's this blonde tart in his office, Janine, looks at him with goo-goo eyes – I bet he's in there. I went in one time when I had to tell him something, and soon as I said who I was, she blushed scarlet. As if I cared where he's parking it these days!'

For a woman who hadn't been sorry to see him go, Jenrich thought, she did a nice line in bitterness. 'So you've had a rough relationship with Rita? You don't like her?'

'I don't give two hoots about her, one way or the other. Except that she's sucked him dry, financially. Why d'you think I've had to get a job? One of the things he promised me when we got divorced was that I'd never have to work. One of the many things. "You'll never want for anything, you and the kids." But when I wanted something for Mia or Sam, it was, "Money's tight. Have to think about that one." Only when Princess Rhianne wants a new diamond tiara, money's not so tight then, is it?'

'What do you think about Rhianne?'

She shrugged. 'I never really had that much to do with her. She was an OK kid when she was little. David was keen for Mia and Sam to be friends with her, but they were older than her, so they weren't interested. And Rita didn't want to give David an excuse to be coming round to our house all the time, so it wasn't encouraged. Then she hit the teens – Rhianne, I mean – and apparently she got moody and difficult. They've had a lot of trouble with her. David gets mad as hell with her. Then of course Rita sticks up for her and she and David have a row.' She sounded pleased about it. '*And* she runs him ragged over money – Rita does. Serves him right.'

'Did he ever hit her?' Jenrich slipped the question in casually, looking at her notes rather than at Sharon.

She answered easily. 'Rita? I wouldn't be surprised. She'd annoy the hell out of me – all that chirpy chatter, like a bloody budgie.'

'No, I meant Rhianne.'

'Not that I know of,' Sharon said, then stopped abruptly, and her eyes opened wide. 'Oh, is that what you're thinking? Interesting! No, I can't believe he'd . . .'

She thought about it, shaking her head slowly. 'David? No, I can't believe it – not deliberately. But he *has* got a temper. Him and I had some flaming rows – not that he ever lifted a hand to me. But that was then. Now, say if he was pushed too far, I suppose he might snap. He's quite senior at Buckfast's, but there's a lot of call on his cash, with my alimony and Rita wanting this, that and the other all the time, and then the kid drooping about and giving him attitude. He might just lose it and wallop her. But he'd never mean to really hurt her, no. I can't believe that.'

She looked at Jenrich like a dog eyeing the biscuit tin. Did she really hope her ex had slugged his stepdaughter and killed her? No, not really, Jenrich thought. She was gleeful at the thought of him being in trouble, and like most people was eager for a bit of excitement in her life, bit of *scand*, but she didn't really think he had gone that far. But if she knew Rhianne had been strangled, would that make a difference? Sharon believed he wouldn't hit, not hard enough to kill; but to choke someone who had maddened him to the end of his tether? That might be a different matter.

Jenrich would have liked to put it to her, but she couldn't of course. That information was not yet in the public domain.

THREE
Sulky, With a Whinge on Top

Rita Morgan had aged ten years overnight. In jogging pants and a T-shirt, and with no make-up on, she looked pale and exhausted. Slider and Swilley sat in the kitchen with her. The French windows were open, and from the garden came a breath of air, unwelcomely warm, like the warmth of a seat on the bus someone else has just vacated. With it came the sound of a robin competing with someone in the distance drilling. There was always building noise in London, except on Sundays when it was motor-mowers and leaf-blowers.

'Tell me about Rhianne,' Slider invited.

She thought for a bit before embarking. 'I was too young to have a baby, really. I couldn't cope at all. Phil was wonderful, though. He'd come home from a day's work, and the baby would be crying and nothing done in the house. And he'd pick her up and tell me to go and have a lay-down, or turn the telly on, and he'd do everything. She always stopped crying for him. He'd change her and everything, and then we had this baby-sling thing, and he'd put her in that, and carry her about while he made dinner and cleared up.' She shook her head in wonder. 'I never thought then about how tired he must have been. But he never once said a harsh word to me.'

'Weren't your family able to help?' Slider asked.

'Mum and Dad were no use to man nor beast. And the others were too young. I was next to eldest. Bernie – Bernadette – she was the eldest. But she'd met this Australian barman and went back with him, so she was gone. The others have all scattered to the four winds,' she added reflectively. 'Mum and Dad are dead now. Colm – he was the youngest – he got hit by a train on a level crossing when he was sixteen. Fidelma went to the Sisters in Ireland.'

'The sisters?' Swilley queried.

'She became a nun,' Rita clarified. 'And Maureen and Anne-Marie went the other direction from Bernie, to Boston.' She sighed. 'I suppose I'll have to let them all know. I don't know how I'll tell them.'

Slider didn't want her going down that path. He flicked a look at Swilley, and she said, 'But you managed all right, you and Phil.'

'I got myself sorted out after a bit, and we were all right. And once Rhianne started walking she was a little cherub. Always smiling, always so loving. She adored her daddy. She'd never go to sleep until he'd come home from work and tuck her in. Of course, money was tight. Everything we had was second-hand, clothes, furniture, everything. Even Ree's toys came from the charity shop. That's why I got myself a part-time job, once Ree was in infant school. That's how I went to Waitrose, because they were brilliant – they let you do ten till two if you had kiddies you had to take to school and pick up. And I've been with them ever since. They don't pay much, but you can do the hours you want, and we're all friends there, like a big family. But we were happy enough, Phil and me. He was so good at thinking of things to do that didn't cost anything. We'd do little outings on the bus. Go to the museums. Walk along the canal and feed the ducks. Like, if it was a nice day, I'd make sandwiches, and we'd go down Wormholt Park, and Ree would play on the swings, and we'd sit on the grass and have a picnic. Stuff like that.' Her eyes were distant, and not entirely happy.

'It must have been a terrible shock for Rhianne when her dad died,' Swilley offered.

'Oh, she was in bits,' said Rita. 'She couldn't understand. She'd keep saying when is Daddy coming back? And I'd say, he died, Ree, don't you remember? And she'd say I know, but when's he coming back?' She met Swilley's eyes. 'Kids!'

'How did you meet David?' Slider asked.

'I bumped into him. I mean literally. I was just coming out of work, and he was walking past, and we collided. And we sort of looked at each other and that was it. He said could he take me for a drink to say sorry, and I said I had to get back for Rhianne, but neither of us wanted to leave it at that. So he walked with me to the bus stop, and then he sort of slapped his forehead

and said what was I thinking, I've got my car parked up round
the corner, why don't I drive you home? So he did. And—' She
stopped.

'Yes?' Slider encouraged.

She didn't look at him; she looked at Swilley. 'When we got
to my place, we . . . well, we had a kiss and cuddle in the car.
I know I'd only just met him,' she added defensively, 'but it felt
so easy and natural with him. It was like I'd known him for
years. And he felt the same. So that was the start of it. I told
him I'd promised to take Rhianne to see *Frozen* the next day,
and he asked if he could come with us. He told me about how
he was fixed, living in a Travelodge, and missing his kids so
much. I was a bit nervous, you know, introducing Ree to him so
soon, but he was great with her, and they got on straight away.
I think she was glad to have a father figure in her life again.
Anyway, it was no life for a man, living in a hotel, so he started
to come round for a meal, and I did some of his washing, and
then he was staying over, and eventually there didn't seem to be
any sense in him stopping on in the hotel, so he moved in.'

'And then you got married,' Swilley prompted.

'Soon as his divorce was through.' She gave Swilley a shrewd
look. 'You're thinking I was too trusting. You're thinking I was
lucky, that it could have gone the other way. But it wasn't like
that. We were always going to get married. I never had any
doubts. We were a family practically from the first day. David
wanted it as much as I did. And he's been a great husband and
a great dad to Rhianne. Even though—' She stopped and shut
her lips tight.

'Even though?' Slider prompted. But she shook her head. He
had to find another way in. 'What about school? Did she do all
right?'

'She did OK,' she said defensively. 'She was always about
middle of her class. She got three A levels. Well,' she added,
'she's not got the results yet, but she's predicted to get three
grade Cs. David says her grades aren't good enough for art school
– it's so competitive.' Now it burst out of her, as if against her
will. 'He says she should have worked harder, because she's not
stupid, but she's left it too late. And even if she gets into art
school, what will she do afterwards? He wants to get her a start

at Buckfast's. Work for an RICS qualification on a sandwich course. He says it's a steady career. But it's not what she wants, and I say you've got to follow your star, only he's put her off so much she won't even apply. She just sits there all day. I've tried talking to her, but I just get attitude. David says if she really cared, she'd do something about it, not sit about sulking. They have terrible rows.' She heard herself and broke off. 'It's only because he cares so much. And she's a good girl, really. But they can easily get discouraged at that age.'

'Does she often wear a scarf?' Slider asked, using the present tense, since Rita had.

She looked mildly puzzled. 'What, on her head? Like the Queen?'

Swilley took it. 'No, like a fashion accessory – round her neck.' She made a vague, wavy gesture to indicate casualness.

'Oh, I know,' Rita said, thinking. 'Well, she has done some-times, lately, I suppose. She has her own ideas about fashion. I don't always agree with it, but she obviously thinks about her appearance, which is a good thing, really, isn't it?'

'Was she wearing a scarf yesterday?'

'I'm not sure. I don't remember. She does have a pink one, and she likes to match. She—' Then her eyes widened as she remembered what she had mercifully forgotten for some minutes. 'Oh my God!' she gasped. Swilley reached out an automatic hand, and she grasped it and held on. 'It's not happening! Tell me it's not happening!'

She didn't cry, but she gulped and clung. Then she stopped, sat up rigidly, stared at Slider and said, 'Who did this?' Demanded, as if he knew, as if he had been wickedly keeping it from her.

'I don't know,' Slider said. 'But we will find out.' And he got up quietly and went out, leaving her to Swilley.

LaSalle and Lœssop leaned against the counter of the customer service desk at D&K while the girl called for Andy over the Tannoy. 'Andy D to the customer service desk, please. Andy D to customer service.'

The DIY and home improvement retailing company was known for its public service ethic, giving jobs to prisoners on licence and retired people and starts to troubled youngsters coming out of care. It was named after its founders, Derek and Keith, who had said in an interview celebrating D&K's tenth anniversary that people had taken a chance on them when they were starting out, so they wanted to return the favour. Of course, it did mean their wages bill was kept very low, but you'd have to be a nasty old cynic to believe that was why they did it.

This D&K was in Acton Vale, part of a mini industrial estate, clustering round a shared giant parking area along with a Wickes, a Barney's garden centre, a World of Leather, a pet supplies superstore called Pets 4 Us and a soft furnishing store called CurtainRail. Lœssop, who had an enquiring mind, passed the time while they waited in speculating aloud why retailers thought shunting two words together with a capital in the middle made them more appealing, while the customer service girl stared at him with her mouth at half mast. If she could remember that expression, she could re-use it when she next saw a man grow a second head.

Andy Denton arrived wearing a friendly smile and a brown warehouse coat with the D&K logo on the breast pocket. He was not tall – about five feet seven – but compactly well-built, fair skinned, blue-eyed, with messy-cut, dirty-blonde hair just brushing his collar. He was good-looking when he smiled – LaSalle noticed the way the girl looked at him – but the smile disappeared down a rabbit hole when he saw them, and he said, 'Oh my good Gawd,' and led them aside, saying in an urgent undertone, 'Are you trying to lose me my job? Could you *look* any more like the filth? You might as well stick a frickin' cherry light on your head.'

'We just want a little chat with you, Andy mate, no biggie,' Lœssop said. 'Want to step outside?'

'Yeah, that wouldn't look suspicious at all, would it?' Denton grumped. 'Come and stand over here, and try and look as if you want to buy power tools.' There was a shelf just inside the door on which various catalogues were displayed in rigid folders for customer use, trustfully fastened through the folder spine with chains. Denton opened one and they pretended to be looking at it. 'So, what am I supposed to have done this time?'

'Just making general enquiries,' LaSalle said.

'In my arse. Is this about the girl who was killed in Acacia Avenue?'

'Now, how would you happen to know about that?' Lœssop asked invitingly.

Denton rolled his eyes. 'Please! Little thing called the internet, guys. Welcome to the twenty-first century. Also it's front page of the local freebie rag. What I don't understand is why you have to come bothering me every time someone commits a crime anywhere in the western hemisphere.'

'Western hemisphere?' Lœssop said. 'They were right about you – you are a clever bastard, I bet that made you popular inside. Cons love a bloke with plenty to say for himself.'

A shadow passed behind Denton's eyes. Sex offenders lived a perilous life in prison. 'I spent a lot of time in the gym,' he said tersely. He pointed at his biceps. 'These ain't rolled-up socks. Can we get on with it? I have to get back to work. You people always say you want us to make a fresh start, then you do everything you can to sabotage it. What do you want? I don't know anything about this Acacia Avenue business. My manager's going to start asking questions any minute. You know they watch us on CCTV all the time? Give you a fresh start, oh yes, but don't trust you as far as they can spit.'

'Yes, this job of yours,' Lœssop said. 'I suppose you were working yesterday?'

'Monday and Tuesday are my days off,' Denton said, and added impatiently, 'Are you going to make something out of that? Saturday and Sunday are the busy days, so most of us work weekends and have our days off in the week when it's quieter. You can ask the manager if you don't believe me.'

'You're very defensive for an innocent man,' Lœssop said.

Denton sighed. 'Look,' he said, 'I know how this game is played. You're trying to rile me up so I'll say something stupid. But that's not going to happen, because there's nothing stupid to say. It wasn't me, all right? I don't know anything about it. I've done seven years for a crime I didn't commit, finally the parole board was satisfied I was safe to be let out, thank you very much for nothing, and I sure as hell don't want to go back in. I just want to settle down and live a quiet life, and I will do if you people will just leave me alone.'

Lœssop gave him a long look, because you never let a suspect think you were buying it, even when you were.

Denton stood up to the long look without flinching. 'Can I go now?' he asked.

'In a minute,' Lœssop said. 'Where were you yesterday?'

'At home,' he said. 'My day off. I just knocked around. That's what I like to do when I'm not at work. I read a bit. Watched telly a bit. Fixed a dripping tap. Cut my toenails. A full, rich day.'

'At home, all day, all alone?' LaSalle queried.

'I didn't say that. Jen was there – my partner.'

'That's Jenda Squires?' LaSalle said. 'The woman you live with?'

'That's right. Chosen residence passed by the parole board, in case you're wondering.'

'We know. And she was with you all day, all the time?'

'Yep.'

'Neither of you left the house at any time?'

'We were in all day. In the evening we went out for a couple of pints down the Vic.'

'The Princess Victoria? In Uxbridge Road?'

'Yeah. We went out about eight-ish, back around half past ten.'

'Will anyone there remember you?'

'How the hell would I know?' he said. 'But they've probably got cameras. And Jen was with me. Except when she went to the ladies'. She might have taken five minutes to pee and wash her hands. Not long enough for me to get to Acacia Avenue and back. Are we done?'

'For now,' LaSalle said. 'You won't mind if we check with Ms Squires, of course?'

'Of course not. It'll be a laugh – especially if you call her "Ms Squires".'

'And you won't mind if we search your house?' He slipped it in casually as if it was matter-of-course, but Denton still noticed.

'Yes, I do mind. I don't give you permission. Let's be clear about that. You may not search my house.'

'I'd have thought, if you're innocent, you wouldn't have minded,' LaSalle said encouragingly.

'I am innocent, and I do mind. I don't trust any of you people. I did seven years in the Scrubs for nothing because I thought you lot could tell reality from fiction, silly me. Seven years of my life I lost – and in case you think life inside is a picnic, I can tell you it bloody well isn't. Try thinking how that feels, being stitched up by those lying bloody bitches and their feminazi lawyer for the sin of not being a woman. Seven years trying to keep my head above water and hoping I won't get my nuts cut off in the showers by some tattooed maniac with a sharpened toothbrush. Well, I survived – just – and I'm out, and now I want to be left alone like any other law-abiding citizen. I don't want you rifling through my drawers, and I don't want Jen upset.' He cocked his head at them. 'I know how it works, remember. If you had the slightest evidence against me, you'd get a warrant. This is a fishing expedition. You're targeting me because I've got a record. You're just going through the motions, marking time until payday. Well, I'm not playing.' He turned away, waving derisive fingers to them. 'Bye bye! Nice talking to you. Don't hurry back.'

He walked off, and they went out from the cloistral gloom of the DIY temple to the dry, hot-tarmac-smelling day. The sun glanced blindingly off car windscreens. The eco-trees insisted on by the council when the place was built drooped, dusty and thirsty.

'I wish he hadn't mentioned the Vic,' LaSalle said, licking his lips.

Lœssop was brooding. 'If he read about it yesterday, he knows he doesn't need an alibi for the evening. He was just yanking our chain.'

'That's why he was smiling,' LaSalle said. 'We can check the days-off business over the phone. Don't want to draw too much attention to him, in case he *is* going straight. But we'd better go and see this Squires female, before he has a chance to set her up.'

Lœssop shook his head. 'If he did it, he'll already have set her up. And if he didn't, he doesn't need to – she'll only have to tell the truth.'

LaSalle stared at him. 'You think too much. You're turning into Atherton.'

'I *think*,' Lœssop went on deliberately, 'we'd better check the Princess Vic alibi first, while we're out this way.'

'But he doesn't *need* an alibi for . . . Oh!'

'Can't ask questions without buying a drink, can you?'

'Got it,' LaSalle confirmed.

'And they do a nice pint of Landlord there.'

David Morgan, in chinos, open-necked shirt and moccasin slippers, was not mal soigné: he had shaved and combed his hair, but perhaps his grooming routine was too well-entrenched to disintegrate in one day. But he did have that blank, inwardly preoccupied, staring-at-the-wall look you saw in animals that were in pain.

'Did Rhianne have a boyfriend?' Slider asked.

He answered automatically, like one too tired to put any emotion into it, one way or the other. 'Not that I know of. Not anyone in particular. There was one boy who used to come round, when she was revising for her mocks. They used to revise together. Kenton. What was his other name? Williams? No, Willans. Kenton Willans.' Blankly, he watched Slider write it down. 'They seemed close. I don't know that he was a boyfriend, exactly. It's different from when we were at school. I went to a comp, but the boys hung with the boys and the girls with girls, and everyone had crushes on someone. Now they all mix together – just pals. Doesn't seem to matter that they're opposite sexes.'

'So she doesn't go out with this Kenton? On dates?'

He shook his head. 'They seem to go out in mixed groups, or she goes out with other girls. They'll meet up and go off somewhere together, clubbing, or a party, or whatever. It seems to be how they do things these days. The girls are more serious about exams and jobs and everything than when I was at school – they don't have time for romantic stuff. She hasn't mentioned any boy in particular, anyway. And Kenton hasn't been round since . . . well, several weeks. Rita would know better than me, but she's never mentioned to me that Rhianne had a boyfriend – and I think she would.'

'When Rhianne and Kenton were revising, where did they do it? In the kitchen? In here?' They were talking, as before, in the frozen zone of the sitting room.

'In her room,' Morgan answered.

'In her bedroom? Did you or your wife go in there while they were revising?'

'No. We've always given her the privacy of her room. It's important that they know they're trusted.'

'Was she ever alone in the house with him? When you and your wife were out?'

'Well, there must have been times when we were both at work. But what's that got to do with anything?'

'The forensic evidence, you see,' Slider said, watching his face, 'is that she was sexually active.'

'Sexually active?' It was a shock all right. But what sort of a shock? 'What the hell does that mean?'

'That she'd been having sex with someone.'

He stared at Slider, unseeingly, but not blankly now. He was thinking furiously. 'I don't know what to say,' he said at last. 'You can't be with them every minute of every day, can you? But she never seemed particularly interested in boys. I mean, when they've got a crush on someone, they can't help talking about them, can they? When Mia – my daughter from my first marriage – had a crush, it was Will this and Will that and Will says, all the time. She brought him in to every conversation. And we knew all about him. He came to the house. She crocheted him a cover for his mobile for his birthday. But Rhianne – never.'

'Would she perhaps be wary of talking to you about a boyfriend?'

'I don't see why. I've never tried to stop her going out or seeing her friends. I always believed that if you give trust, it's rewarded. I wouldn't have objected if she'd had a boyfriend, but she's never seemed particularly interested.'

'What was your relationship like with her?'

'It was all right. It was fine. When I first married Rita, she was very fond of me. Held my hand when we were out in the street. Always kissed me goodnight. Sat on my lap when I read her a story. That sort of thing.'

'But more recently,' Slider said. 'Have there been rows?'

'Well, you know what teenagers are like. It can't always be sweetness and light. We've had the usual difficulties, refusing to do chores, not picking up after herself, arguing about every last damned thing. Attitude. Slammed doors. You know the sort of thing. But nothing unusual. Nothing everyone doesn't go through.'

'You had disagreements about her going to college?'

'The art thing? That's completely unrealistic,' Morgan said, with a hint of heat for the first time. 'There are hundreds of kids trying to get in, thousands, and only a few places. And even if they do get in, there's no guarantee of a job afterwards, let alone a career. I was doing what a father ought to do, get a bit of reality into her thinking, guide her towards an area where she could make an actual living, but I got no thanks for it, just the sulks and the silent treatment. She sits there all day—' He stopped abruptly, and a sick expression crossed his face as he remembered who Slider was and why they were having this conversation. 'You said—' He stopped and started again. 'When you say she was sexually active, what does that mean? The forensic evidence? Just that she . . . wasn't a virgin? You know that can happen with doing sport, exercise, anything energetic enough. Girls these days—'

'It was more than that,' Slider said. 'There was a box of condoms in her bedroom.'

'Rhianne was a good girl!' Morgan cried. 'You talk as if it was her fault this happened. You're victim-blaming! She had a good home here, and loving parents.'

'I'm sure she did.'

'But she's . . . How could this happen?' He rubbed at his face, trying to rub away the knowledge. You always came back to disbelief. However much you read the papers or watched the news, you never expected the unthinkable to happen to you.

Slider waited for a respectful moment, then said, 'Can you account for your movements yesterday? You said you left home just before nine.'

'I went to work. I was at work. Why are you asking me?'

'It's just routine,' Slider said soothingly.

But he was angry. 'What are you suggesting? That I had something to do with it?'

'Not at all.'

'I've been a father to her for nearly ten years. I've done every-thing a father does. She's like my own daughter to me. If you're suggesting that I would ever—'

'I'm not suggesting anything, Mr Morgan.'

'Then why are you asking me for an alibi?'

'It's not a matter of an alibi. As a matter of routine, we ask everyone their whereabouts, so that we can have a complete picture of the situation, where everyone was, who they were with, what they might have seen or known about.' Morgan was still looking angry and rebellious. 'It's nothing to be concerned about, but I do need to know where you were yesterday.' Time for a teensy bit of pressure. 'If you'd be more comfortable talking to someone else down at the station . . .'

'I was at work,' he said in a sort of bark. Then he relaxed slightly, with a sigh of resignation. 'I was in the office all morning. In the afternoon I had two valuations to do, one at half past two and one at half past three.'

'The addresses?'

'One was in Bedford Park. Blenheim Road. House called Oakhurst. The other was in Emlyn Road. That's just round the corner.'

'How long does a valuation take?'

'Half to three quarters of an hour, depending on how much there is to see. Blenheim Road's a six-bed detached, so it took me a bit longer. I was running a bit late for Emlyn Road. I finished there about twenty-five past four, and since it was just round the corner I thought I'd pop in at home for a cup of tea.'

'The house owners didn't offer you tea?'

'I had a cup at Blenheim Road, as a matter of fact. Wasn't offered one in Emlyn Road. But by then, if you want the truth, I needed to pee, which was another reason to pop in at home. I don't like to ask to use the punters' facilities. I don't think it's appropriate.'

'How much were the valuations in the end?'

'I haven't worked them out yet. Bedford Park will be around three million. Emlyn Road probably one point six, one point eight. Why do you ask?'

It was a question thrown in to see if it unsettled him, but he answered smoothly enough. 'What time did you leave the office?'

'Shortly after two. Janine will tell you.'

'And you were intending to go back there?'

'Of course. I work until six usually, or six thirty if I've got a lot on.'

'And did you speak to anyone in the office on the telephone during the afternoon?'

'I rang in some time after four to see if there were any messages. There weren't.'

'Did you ring anyone else?'

'No.' He was defensive again. 'Are you done with the third degree now?'

'Thank you for your co-operation,' Slider said placatingly. 'You understand that we have to ask questions, however unsettling they may be.'

'Well, I hope you're asking questions outside this house. And getting some answers. Because while you're wasting time grilling me, the murderer's getting away.'

'I assure you, all our resources are being put into this matter. We will leave no stone unturned.'

'You'd better not,' said Morgan, with all his executive might. 'Because I want answers, and I'm damned well going to get them, or heads will roll.'

'Sounds like a solid alibi,' Atherton said. 'If Doc Cameron says she was killed some time between two thirty and four thirty, there's no way he could have done it.'

'I'm always glad when someone has a solid alibi. Means we don't have to keep digging around them.'

'Yes, but the process of elimination is only useful when you've got options,' said Atherton. 'If it's not A or B, it must be C. We've got no alphabet at all.'

'Early days,' said Slider. 'Whatever Morgan says, we know she must have had a boyfriend. Or boyfriends. Sex was being had with someone.'

'And with the unknown heart defect,' Atherton said thoughtfully, 'a bit of innocent larking about could easily turn sour.'

'The strangling might not have been intended to cause death,' said Slider. 'But to leave a mark like that, it was more than horseplay.'

'Unless—' Atherton said. He stopped, and Slider had to stop too, to look at him.

'Unless?'

'Morgan admits he was there at four thirty – four twenty-five, even. Still within the window.'

'The paramedics got there at ten to five. The 999 call was logged at four forty-three. He would have to have been exceptionally bold and level-headed to kill her at four twenty-five and call it in less than twenty minutes later. It's unlikely.'

'But not impossible. What was he doing in those twenty minutes?'

'CPR, he says.'

'It's a pity the paras weren't able to tell how recently she'd died.'

'Well, we are where we are.'

Atherton resumed walking. 'A man accustomed to carrying on extra-marital affairs and covering his tracks might well be cool-headed and resourceful in an emergency.'

'You're reaching a bit, aren't you?'

'I refer you to my previous comment on the alphabet.'

FOUR

All Cats are Grey

Most of Gayford Road was typical Victorian terraced housing, the sort of tiny, solid dwellings that were originally built for the working men of the industrial age. It was hard to remember that London had once been the biggest industrial city in Europe and that the skies had been darkened by the smoke from a hundred thousand factory stacks. Now the air was clear and these same doll's houses could only be afforded by white collar workers – and even then you'd need *two* good salaries. Lœssop had heard the guv expounding the subject many times. To LaSalle he only said, 'All gentrified up. Wonder what these go for?'

'Three-quart's a mill, easy,' LaSalle said laconically.

But near the Askew Road end, a small factory or workshop that had survived into the eighties had been pulled down and a bland, meagre three-storey block of flats had been erected by the local council. It was in one of these that Jenda Squires lived, moved and had her being. The block was showing its age now. No one would be gentrifying these in a hundred years' time, Lœssop thought. They'd never stand up that long. You had to hand it to the Victorians. They knew how to stick bricks together.

Jenda Squires was taller than Handy Andy, and thin, very thin. They must have looked comical together. She was in her late twenties, very pale of skin. Her head was shaved up the sides, and across the top, front to back, was a thick runner of hair dyed black with the tips touched in crimson. She had a small ring in her left nostril, and a tattoo of thorns around the base of her neck. She stared at them dully and in silence when she opened the door, and her eyes skipped over LaSalle, who was skinny and ginger, to light on Lœssop with his lustrous dark eyes, longish curly hair and Cap'n Jack Sparrow facial hair. LaSalle had worked

with Lœssop a long time and was used to it. It could be handy
in some circs to be invisible. They both showed their warrant
cards, and he said, 'Just want a word – can we come in, love?'
and because she didn't really see him, she nodded and stepped
back, holding the door open.

Inside, the flat smelled strongly of cigarettes and faintly but
insistently of cannabis and cooking fat. It consisted of one
bedroom, living room, galley kitchen and bathroom. The largest
room, the living room, was twelve by ten, and with 1980s low
ceilings the flat felt as small as it really was. They could see into
each of the rooms as they walked down the short, narrow passage.
It was sparsely furnished with the cheapest flatpack items but
was unexpectedly tidy. LaSalle wondered if it indicated habits
learned inside by Denton.

Jenda led them to the living room, which had the magnolia
walls and laminate flooring of heartless development. A two-seater
sofa in worn purple velvet with a coffee table in front of it faced
a giant television. A low two-shelf cupboard with a glass front
occupied a corner and contained a stack of miscellaneous papers
– bills, receipts and so on – and some worn-looking paperback
books. The window overlooked the tiny communal garden: a square
of threadbare lawn on which lay abandoned a toddler's tricycle
missing the front wheel. Shangri-bloody-la, LaSalle thought.

Squires stopped and turned to face them, not inviting them to
sit. 'What's it about?' she asked. 'Has something happened to
Andy?'

'No, it's nothing like that,' LaSalle said. 'Just a routine enquiry.
How long have you lived here?'

'Three years,' she said. 'Why?'

'And how do you know Andy?'

'I knew him before he went up.'

'Before he went to prison?'

'Yeah.'

'Were you his girlfriend?'

'Sort of. Why?'

'What do you mean, sort of?'

'Him and me brother were mates. We went out a few times.'

Lœssop took over. 'But you were close enough to him to invite
him to live with you when he came out.'

'Jordan fixed it up.'

'Jordan?'

'Me brother.'

'You're Jenda and he's Jordan?' Lœssop couldn't help himself. It sounded socially ambitious.

'Yeah. Why?' She thought for a moment and said, 'We're twins.' With this revelation she became suddenly expansive. 'Andy rung him from inside. He had to get an approved place to live, else he couldn't get parole. Jord couldn't do it himself, cos he's got a record, but I'm clean.'

'You weren't worried, then, about living with Andy, after what he'd done?'

'He never done nothing. Jordan told me all about it – them women just told lies about him because they were jealous.'

'Right,' said Lœssop.

'So, about yesterday,' LaSalle said. 'Were you at your job?'

She goggled for a moment. You could almost hear the chuntering machinery, like when Captain Kirk's computer intoned, *Working*. 'I'm on Disability,' she said. 'I got a bad back.' And, in case they hadn't got the point, 'I can't do a job. I got men'al 'elf as well. I'm under the doctor for bad nerves.'

'How long you been on Disability?' LaSalle asked.

'Dunno. About five years maybe. I was on Jobseekers before that, but Disability pays better.'

Lœssop couldn't help himself. 'Have you ever had a job?'

She gave him the stink eye. 'Dr Chakrabati signs me off. You can ask him if you don't believe me.'

He got back to the point. 'So where were you, then? Yesterday?'

'In here,' she said. 'I was home all day.'

'Doing what?'

'Nothing. It's Andy's day off. We just sat around and stuff.'

'Did you go out at any point?' Lœssop asked persuasively. 'Maybe to get cigarettes or something? Buy milk? Just popped out for a little while for a walk in the fresh air?'

She didn't do irony. 'We've got milk,' she said. 'Andy don't have it in his tea, so we don't use much.'

'So when you popped out, where did you go?'

She struggled with the form of the question but at last said, 'I never. I told you. I never went out.'

'So you were at home all day? And where was Andy?'

'At home. With me. Why you asking?'

'But you weren't in the same room together all the time?' Lœssop suggested.

'We was in here,' she said, sounding a bit puzzled. 'Where else would we be?'

'I mean, if Andy had popped out, you wouldn't necessarily have known.'

'Course I would. In this flat? I'd hear him.' Good point, Lœssop thought. 'Anyway, he never. We was in all day. Then we went down the Vic in the evening. So what's going on?'

'Nothing at all. We're just checking up,' LaSalle said.

'Well, I wish you'd give it a rest,' she said with all the ferocity she could muster – of the order of a peck from an ailing budgerigar. 'Checking on him all the time when he's not done nothing, it's not fair. He's just trying to get on with his life.'

Porson had been up to Hammersmith to deal with the Big Bosses. And the press officer: Arlene Summers, a tall, fit blonde Australian who had good contacts at the BBC and was loved by the camera, having excellent teeth and cheekbones and not much nose to cast an annoying shadow. At present, the press officer's job was to *re*press.

Porson was sitting on the edge of Swilley's desk, which was the tidiest, with a cup of tea. He liked his tea in a proper cup. There were two custard creams in the saucer. 'So basically, we say nothing,' he said.

'Arlene Summers puts the "mm" into schtumm,' Atherton said.

Porson didn't hear him. 'If anyone asks questions, we prevasticate. But don't raise suspicions. Say something, without saying anything. Got it? Not that it's not all over the internet already, but we can't do anything about that. We have to keep the Home Office happy, and they have to keep the politicians happy. So until we've got something to go on, officially it's an unexplained death. Least said soonest mentioned.'

'Yes, sir,' Slider answered for them all.

'Right, what are we following up?'

LaSalle told about the interviews with Andy Denton and Jenda Squires. 'We checked with Dr Chakrabati, and he confirms he's signed her off work with a bad back and depression. So it looks like Denton's got an alibi. I don't think she's bright enough to have made it all up, anyway.'

'He could have coached her,' Jenrich pointed out.

'Yeah, but he didn't have much time, and she's really dumb.'

'Dumb birds can be taught to talk. Ask a parrot.'

'I think she's too dumb to hold a story together. Even when we tried confusing her she didn't fall apart.'

'Denton still claims he was innocent of the Potillo rape, and the others,' Lœssop said.

'Well, here's a wild thought,' said Atherton. 'Maybe he *is* innocent. It's been known to happen.'

'He claimed from the beginning he didn't do it,' LaSalle remembered.

'You're forgetting,' Slider said, 'that the parole board won't issue a licence if you insist you didn't do it. You have to own up and show you've learned your lesson.'

'True,' said Atherton, 'but you'd have to be a very strong character not to think in the end that it was worth saying "I dunnit" if it gets you out.'

'Might be worth following up, finding out what he said to the board, and then asking him why he said it,' Slider mused.

'He's a sort of likeable bloke,' LaSalle said, as if it was an annoying trait. 'And we checked with the management at D&K. It's true what he said about having to work weekends and getting weekdays off. He's always had Mondays and Tuesdays since he's worked there. And his line manager says he's a good employee, always punctual, works hard and got a good way with the customers.'

Porson intervened. 'The fact is we haven't got anything on him apart from his record.'

'It's quite some record,' Jenrich said.

'Give a dog a bad time and hang him,' said Porson. 'It's not enough. You happy with the alibi?'

Happy wasn't the right word for LaSalle, who exchanged a look with Lœssop and said, 'It'd be hard to break it.'

'Then put Denton aside for the moment,' Porson said. 'What else are you looking at?'

'The door to door, of course,' Slider said. 'Nothing so far, but we'll plug on. The neighbours in the attached house are on holiday, coming back on Friday apparently, so we can talk to them then.'

'If they're on holiday, they won't have seen anything,' Porson pointed out.

'No, but they might have some background information. I'm afraid at the moment we have no other way to go, just looking into the victim's life, finding out who she knew, who she was seeing, what she was doing. If it was someone she knew, which seems the most likely, we'll get a better idea when we get her laptop and phone back. If it was a stranger who walked in off the street—'

'We're up a gum tree,' Porson interjected glumly. 'Without a paddle.'

Slider nodded. 'No CCTV cameras in the road. There might be a doorbell cam or two, but most of the houses have hedges shielding them from the street, so they're unlikely to have caught anything. Once we get a suspect – if we get a suspect – we can look at cameras further afield: there's one on the park gates and one on the school, various shops in the main road and of course bus cameras, all useful for recording comings and goings into the immediate area, if not the street itself. But until we know who we're looking for . . .'

'What about the stepfather?' Porson asked.

'We've got no reason to think he had anything to do with it.'

'You never have a reason until you get one,' Porson said.

'Of course, we will check his alibi,' Slider said. 'We'll interview any relatives we can scrape up, see if there was ever any concern about him. And we'll talk to her friends. Then there's this possible boyfriend Kenton Willans, though he seems to have faded out of the picture. My feeling is that she was seeing someone we don't know about yet, who was influencing her. There's the sexual activity, and the cannabis. She had some sort of secret life going on.'

'Show me the teenager that hasn't,' Porson grunted. He stood up. 'Well, keep buggering on. We've got a day or two of grace before the spit hits the spam.'

* * *

There was overtime for a small team who were to revisit some of the houses where no one had been in during the day. The rest Slider sent home. 'There's nothing more you can do today.'

Atherton lingered by Slider's desk as he tried to clear up a few things. Slider looked up. 'Did you want something?'

'No,' said Atherton. Then, 'Have you got any plans for tonight?' he asked casually.

Too casually. 'No. Have you?'

'I'm meeting Stephanie later. I think I'm going to do it. Tonight.'

'I thought you did it every night.'

'Not that. Well, yes, that. But I meant . . . you know.'

'It was *you-know* I was talking about.'

Atherton manned up. 'Tonight's the night I'm going to ask her to marry me.'

'Oh. Well, good luck,' Slider said, a bit at a loss.

'You think I need luck?' Atherton said, with slight irritation. 'Thing is, can you keep—'

'The cats another night? Yes. I've said they can stay as long as you like.' Atherton had a tiny terraced house in West Hampstead while Stephanie had a much grander split-level flat in Castletown Road. Until and unless they merged their households, the cats' requirements meant much travelling back and forth.

At that moment Slider's phone rang. It was the duty sergeant downstairs. 'There's a woman here asking to see you, a Mrs Alison Forster. Says she's the sister of David Morgan. Mean anything?'

Swilley had discovered the existence of a sister only that afternoon and had been intending to seek an interview when she came in tomorrow. If the woman was now offering herself, it was an opportunity not to be missed. Certainly, you couldn't send her away and then bother her the next day.

'I'll see her,' Slider said. 'Can you put her in the soft room? I'll be there in five minutes.'

'Put who in the soft room?' Atherton asked as he put the phone down.

'David Morgan's sister. Want to come? Or are you dashing off?'

'I'll come,' Atherton said. 'I'm not meeting Stephanie until later. She's got post-op rounds until eight.'

Slider hoped he was imagining that Atherton sounded happy about the distraction.

'I'll just have to ring Joanna and tell her I'll be late,' he said.

The soft room was part of the interview suite for minors and non-suspects – people you didn't want to intimidate. Atherton opined that it was still torture, just a subtler kind: hotel bedroom décor, right down to the bland flower prints on the wall. Mrs Forster was waiting there with PC Coutinho for company. Slider introduced himself and Atherton and said, 'It's good of you to come and see us. Can I offer you tea or coffee?'

She accepted coffee and Coutinho went to arrange it, while Alison Forster inspected Slider and Atherton with intelligent, noticing eyes. She was a couple of years older than her brother, but there was a strong resemblance of features which meant she was an attractive woman; and there was a firmness in her face that Slider felt his lacked – though to be fair, most people would lose a bit of firmness in his circumstances. She was smartly dressed in a skirt suit, her hair cut short in a choppy bob, the same colour as David's and without any grey, her face carefully made-up to look as if she wasn't wearing any. Something in business, he thought, or a middle-management-level civil servant.

He thanked her again for coming.

'I thought you would probably want to talk to me, and as I was in the neighbourhood, I thought I'd save you the trouble,' she said.

'Why did you think we would want to talk to you?' Slider asked.

'David was the one who found Rhianne. And he's her step-father. I know how your minds work. You'll be thinking he may have had something to do with it.' Slider continued to look at her steadily, receptively, and obligingly she filled in the silence. 'Look, I know Rhianne wasn't a blood relative, but she was my sort of step-niece by marriage, and I cared about her. I'm reading on the internet it was suicide – is that true?'

'Haven't you spoken to your brother?'

'He's not answering his phone, and I couldn't get anything out of Rita. But I read one account that there was bad blood between David and Rhianne and that drove her to it, and I *know* that's not true, so I want to set the record straight.'

'In what way?'

'Well, David's not the easiest person to understand. It'd be easy if you didn't know him to assume certain things. But I'm his sister. There's no one who knows him better than me, and I can tell you he would never have hurt that girl. Never. It's inconceivable.'

Slider nodded. She'd come to do some special pleading, and the fact that she'd gone to the trouble of volunteering rather than waiting to be contacted suggested a certain defensiveness. Or it could just be deep sibling affection – being older than Morgan, she might feel extra protective of him. Well, either way, it was grist to the mill. 'Tell me about him, then. Are there just the two of you?' he asked, to get her started.

'That's right. I'm the eldest. Our father wanted a son, so he was disappointed when I arrived. Then they had to wait another four and a half years for David. They didn't think they'd be able to have another after me. So you can imagine how thrilled they were about him. But I don't want you to think, just because he was so precious, that he had an easy childhood.'

Coutinho brought her the cup of coffee and retreated out of her eyeline.

'Why not?' Slider prompted.

'Dad was fiercely ambitious for him, and never cut him any slack. He had to be the best at everything, no excuses, and if he slipped below Dad's standards . . . well! Dad loved him, don't get me wrong, but he wasn't the sort of man to show it. All stick and no carrot. And David, poor lamb, wasn't exactly the sharpest knife in the box. I'm afraid I got the brains of the family. He got the looks.' She paused fractionally as if she usually got a compliment at that point, but Slider was too slow, and she went on. 'However hard he tried – and he really did try, poor lamb – he could never quite get the top grades. He was always disappointing our father. And our mother, for some reason, got it into her head that David was delicate, and she spoiled him and tried to wrap him up in cotton wool. She called him her medical miracle. She kept saying he had to take care of himself, and of course, as a little kid, naturally he milked it.

Any little bump or scratch, he was on her knee and being given biscuits. Then Dad would come in and haul him out and call him a sissy. Between the two of them, they destroyed his self-esteem.'

'What about you?' Slider asked.

'What do you mean?'

'You seem to be a very confident person. Didn't they destroy yours as well?'

'Benign neglect. I wasn't the favourite,' she said shortly. There was some resentment there, Slider thought, and waited in receptive silence for her to elaborate. Most people can't resist a silence, especially when they're talking about themselves. She went on. It didn't matter what I did. I was only the girl, so there was no pressure on me. And I can tell you I was far from spoiled. I had to help around the house, run errands and so on. David was always let off chores because he had to have peace and quiet to study. Dad wanted him to be a lawyer or a doctor. Nothing less would do. He was so disappointed when David didn't make the grade he went into a decline.'

'Really?' Slider interjected.

'Well, not really, of course. It was cancer from smoking all his life, but that's what David believed. He blamed himself for letting Dad down. Being an estate agent wasn't good enough.'

'I see,' Slider said, making time.

She frowned. 'Do you? Because what I'm trying to tell you is that he had a lot of childhood troubles to compensate for. And since he was quite good-looking, the way he compensated was by being popular with the girls. He was never going to be looked up to by our father, but girls were all over him, and it was a way to feel better about himself. Being chased after was the one thing that gave him confidence. Of course he shouldn't have carried it over into his marriage. You couldn't expect Sharon to understand that he needed other women's attention psychologically – and I'm not saying she should have. She was his wife, and she shouldn't have had to put up with his nonsense. And she didn't. But I'm his sister, so I *can* understand.'

'And do you think this has some bearing on what happened to Rhianne?' asked Atherton, who was never as patient as Slider when it came to hearing out life stories.

She looked distracted. 'That's what I'm trying to tell you. Because inevitably you're going to find out about his womanizing, and I don't want you to think that, because of that, he's a bad man. He's a very kind and loving person, when he gets the chance. I like Rita. I always felt she was good for him. She's very practical, she has her feet on the ground, she's just what he needs.'

'What about Rhianne? What was his relationship like with her?'

'Oh, he was brilliant with her. You see, it was a bad divorce, and Sharon was very hard. She didn't want him to see the children at all, put difficulties in his way, tried to turn them against him, and he loved those kids. He was devastated when he was kept away from them. So he treated Rhianne like his own. And of course, she was wild for him at first, like every girl. He was catnip to all females, if you know what I mean.'

Slider could feel Atherton beside him not smiling. Out of Mrs Forster's sight, he could see Coutinho looking at Atherton and smirking slightly, because he was just such another ball of wool to the feline paw. It was said he could drive women into a tizzy just by standing quietly in an adjacent room.

'What do you mean when you say she was wild for him "at first"?' he asked.

Alison Forster looked put out. She evidently had not meant to say that. 'Well, she did become a stroppy little madam later on, but that was nothing to do with anything David did. She just hit the terrible teens. He's always done his best with her, but you know what they're like when they get to that age. All the eye-rolling and flouncing. Getting into a strop, bursting into tears, shouting "you're not my real father" and storming off and slamming the bedroom door. It happens in the best of families. And Rhianne was a prime example. Honestly, sometimes I could have strangled the kid myself, she was so—' She broke off as she heard herself and blushed scarlet. 'I didn't mean that,' she said hastily. 'It's just a figure of speech.'

'Of course,' Slider said soothingly. 'But David does have a temper, doesn't he? There'd be shouting on both sides.'

'Well, anyone would lose their temper – teenage girls are infuriating when they get like that. He'd done everything for that girl – *everything* – but just lately she's gone from stroppy to sullen and secretive, and that's even more annoying. Wouldn't do anything to help herself. Just sat around the house all day, sulking. David tried reasoning with her – I mean, she has to earn a living, she can't stay at home for the rest of her life – but she just gave him the silent treatment, the shrug, the "whatever". But get it out of your minds that he would ever hurt her. We fought like cat and dog when we were kids and there was shouting and breaking each other's toys, but he never hit me, however much I provoked him. He would never lift a hand to a woman or a child. He's just not like that.'

'Did Rhianne have a boyfriend?' Atherton asked

'They don't go in for that sort of thing these days, girls. They don't see the point of boys. They'd sooner hang about with their girlfriends.'

'Would you necessarily know? I mean, how often did you see them?'

'Peter and I went over there for Sunday lunch about once a month. And I talked on the phone with David in between times. I knew what was going on, all right.'

'Did Rhianne confide in you?'

She hesitated. 'Not recently. They're under a lot of pressure with exams these days, kids. She's had mocks and then the real A levels. And she's hit this moody phase.'

'Did she ever?'

'Well, she's only my step-niece. But there was a time, when she started to get interested in clothes and make-up and so on, and I showed her how to do her face and what to wear, because, let's face it, Rita's sweet, but she hasn't much idea. She was quite fond of me then. So of course, she'd tell me what she'd been up to and so on. And I can tell you, when she talked about David, she always called him "Dad", in the same sort of voice she used to call Rita "Mum". So you see?'

'Interesting,' Slider said, as he and Atherton trod down the stairs together.

'At least,' said Atherton. 'She thinks he did it.'

'Is *that* what you got?'

'Maybe not as definite as that. She came to convince us he

simply wasn't capable of doing it because deep down she's afraid that he was. Pre-loading his account.'

'I'm not sure she's an impartial witness,' Slider said. 'She's carrying a lot of childhood baggage. Only child for five years, then along comes baby brother who takes all the attention and gets all the love.'

'What were they thinking? People ought to get extensive training before they're allowed to breed,' Atherton said. 'Anyone would hate the intruder in those circumstances.'

'Hate him but also love him,' Slider said. 'Five is just the age to be fascinated by a new baby. And it's amazing how early maternal instincts kick in. George wants to wrestle with the cat, but Teddy wants to put him in a doll's pram and push him about. Do you really know what you're getting yourself into,' he tacked off, 'asking Stephanie to marry you?'

'Hold the phone, Central. I'm proposing marriage, not patriarchy. Speaking of which,' he went on, looking at his watch, 'I've got to dash.'

'You must be starving,' Joanna said when he got home.

'I think I've gone through hungry and out the other side. Anyway, it's too late for a meal.'

'But you ought to eat something. I could open a tin of soup.'

'Heinz tomato?'

'Is there another sort?'

It was infinitely comforting, sitting at the kitchen table, spooning up the familiar brew, with Joanna sitting opposite, listening intelligently while he parsed his day.

'Wow,' she said to Alison Forster's testimony.

'She called him "poor lamb" at least twice,' Slider remembered.

'Deflection pity,' said Joanna.

'But what she said about girls not wanting boyfriends?' he probed. 'Is that true?'

'Well,' Joanna said, 'it probably only applies to middle-class girls, but judging by my nieces, she's spot on. They think boys are stupid and sex is yucky, and they don't want to get married, and they *definitely* don't want to have babies. OMG!' She made a teenager's face. 'My sister Rachel's two – I don't think they've ever had sex, and they're in their twenties now. They went out in mixed groups when they were younger, but the boys were only honorary girls. Now they only go out with their "mates", who are all female.'

'If they don't like – call it dating for want of a better word – what *do* they like?'

Joanna shrugged. 'Chat, and bantz, and sending each other photographs of absolutely everything. Appearance is important to them – clothes and make-up and looking sharp. And getting good exams so they can get a well-paid job so they can buy nice things. You have a teenage daughter yourself – you ought to know.'

'She used to talk about boys and getting married one day. Not so much recently,' he remembered, 'since she started getting serious about her exams.'

'There you are, then,' Joanna said. 'And it may be that she had a more traditional attitude before that, because from my observances, Irene is a more old-fashioned kind of woman – wouldn't you say?' She had to be careful not to sound critical of Bill's first wife, because she wasn't *that* sort of girl. 'A stay-at-home wife and homemaker?'

'That's fair, I suppose,' Slider said.

Irene had re-married, and Ernie Newman was extremely well-off and could keep her in the style to which she would have liked to have become accustomed from the start, with new clothes, meals out, expensive holidays and endless refurbishment of the detached house in a nice neighbourhood Slider had never been able to afford for her. She had gone from her parents' home straight to his, had never lived alone or supported herself, and his long and irregular hours and far-from-generous salary had put too much of a strain on her and their relationship. He was glad she was happy now, as he was.

'So our poor Teddy is doomed to eternal spinsterhood?' he said. 'And what will become of the human race?'

'Extinction,' she said. 'It's the inevitable trend of civilization. Why would a woman want to give birth once she knows what's involved, and if she has the choice? And in civilized societies, she gets the choice. We're all doomed, honey.'

'But you're a woman—'

'Last time I checked.'

'And you've had two children.'

She smiled. 'It's you. I just can't resist you, Bill Slider. Take me to bed!'

'When I've finished my soup,' he said loftily. 'Don't rush me, woman.'

'Sorry, lord.'

FIVE
God Is Walking His Porpoise Out

S ince he'd missed the children's bedtime two nights running, Joanna got them down to share breakfast time with him, everyone in their jimmy-jams except him.

Habeus was on the breakfast table, plodding slowly, nails slipping, towards the bit of lettuce George was holding out for him. He was in an enquiring mood. 'Dad, do tortoises eat scrambled egg?'

Joanna answered for him. 'No, they're herbivores. No meat, no eggs.'

'You have to think what they would come across in the wild,' Slider said. 'That means grass, flowers and leaves. Very occasionally a fallen blackberry.'

'We gave him grapes at school. He loves them.'

'What people love and what's good for them are not always the same thing,' Joanna said.

'Like cakes and sweets?'

'Exactly. You can look up what tortoises eat online.'

George nodded, forking in egg. 'Dad,' he said, swallowing convulsively, 'in the olden days, when you were a boy, did they have computers?'

'Not when I was your age,' Slider said, spreading marmalade on his post-ovum slice of toast.

'Why?'

'Because nobody had invented them.'

'So, but, then, how did you do things?'

'Do what things?'

'Everything. Stuff you do on computers?'

'We looked things up in books. Wrote things down on pieces of paper. Worked them out in our heads,' Slider said.

To be fair, it was getting vanishingly hard to remember what it was like without computers and the internet. Having to go into a travel agent to book a holiday, for instance, and sitting there while they listened to a telephone ringing engaged for half an hour at a time. It crossed his mind to mention blue police phone boxes, but George was too young to reference *Doctor Who*.

Teddy was watching him across the table, and when he looked at her, her face lit in a smile of flatteringly unalloyed delight. 'Daddy,' she said, 'I can buss my teef myself.'

'Clever girl,' he said.

'I do have one, two, four, seven teef.'

'No three, five or six in your world?'

'Sometimes,' she said sternly, 'I do say four, seven and then *no more*. Like a doggie,' she added helpfully.

Slider's brain reeled slightly. 'O-kay.'

'Dad,' George said, 'when they didn't have computers, how did they invent computers, if they didn't have one? To invent on?'

Slider stood up. 'You know who's really good at answering questions?' he said. 'Your grandad. I've got to go to work now.'

'Is Grandad your dad like you're my dad?' George pursued, unwilling to let him go.

Joanna stood too, to kiss him goodbye. 'Extinction of the species not looking so bad now, eh?'

There didn't seem to be much work going on in Buckfast's, though that was perhaps understandable given the absence of the boss and the compelling nature of the office goss. It was typical of estate agent's offices, with eight desks in two rows of four facing the street, each with its computer screen, keyboard and a telephone, while along the back wall was a bank of filing cabinets and a door, presumably to the staff room and WC. Three of the desks looked unused; a fourth, at the back, was presumably David Morgan's, given that it was larger and slightly more mahogan-y, and had a plastic parlour palm in a pot standing behind it for ambience. Three people were gathered round the second desk on the left, a young woman sitting and a young man and an older woman standing, and the girl at the front desk on that side had swivelled her chair round to face them. They were so engrossed in their conversation they didn't notice Gascoyne come in.

Eventually the man looked up, nudged the front-desk girl, and she swivelled back, blushed slightly and said, 'Can I help you?' The other three plunged back into their conversation, keeping their voices low. People didn't always immediately clock Gascoyne for the filth, with his pleasant, fair face and unworryingly average good looks. To someone in the know, his eyes would give him away as Job – the considering police eyes that registered everything. There was nothing you could do about that. They all had them. His wife, Karen, said he even looked at her like that sometimes – though she rather liked it. 'I'm kinky that way,' she said. But she had been in the Job too, before they married – a PC. However, the average civilian didn't notice, and the staff were not noticing him like anything, either as a policeman or even as a potential customer. He half wished he actually *was* looking for a house so he could walk out in protest at being ignored.

They stopped talking to each other, however, when he introduced himself to front-desk girl – who turned out to be the Janine that Morgan had mentioned – and started earwigging shamelessly.

Janine's face took on a suitable cast, and she said, 'Oh, it's terrible! What a terrible thing to happen. That poor girl.'

She seemed in her early twenties, with long, dead straight fawn hair hanging around a carefully made-up face, cheekbones blushered in, eyes smudged around to make them look bigger, as recommended by all the beauty pages. Her nail and lipstick colour matched. An 'A' for effort, Gascoyne thought, and wondered who it was all for.

'They're saying on social media that she just dropped dead suddenly, and no one knows why. Only, I wonder why the police are involved, if it was, like, just medical?'

'We have to investigate all unexplained deaths,' Gascoyne said. 'Have you spoken to David Morgan since Tuesday?'

'No, and I'm glad in a way. I wouldn't know what to say. Poor David,' she went on, blushing under the blusher, and giving Gascoyne a hint as to who she hoped would notice her one day: *My God, but you're lovely!* – though she wasn't wearing glasses to be snatched off, and her hair was already loose. 'You never think it's going to happen to someone you know, do you? Just think,' she confided, wide-eyed, 'if he'd got home a bit sooner, he might have been able to save her, like called an ambulance or something. Like, there was one blog that said that maybe she'd eaten something, like poison or something, or something she was allergic to, and he could have, like, used an EpiPen and brought her back. He must feel terrible.'

How did this stuff get about? Gascoyne wondered. No matter what the official statement said, it seemed to seep out like effluent from a leaky septic tank. 'Don't believe everything you read on the internet,' he said.

Janine was evidently willing to believe anything at all, as long as it alleviated the boredom of her daily round. He let her chunter on for a bit to put her at ease, while the other three moved to their desks and at least pretended to do a bit of work. Then he asked her about Tuesday.

The eyes went big again. 'Ooh, whyever're you asking that?'

'Don't worry, it's normal routine,' he said. 'We like to know where everyone was so that we can get a fuller picture. Now, you were first in, I understand?'

'I'm always first in. I have the keys, you see. I have to unlock at nine o'clock, so I always get in about five minutes before.' He took her through her routine – she liked being asked: it was attention, it was fame of a sort – before bringing her round to David Morgan.

'He was at his desk all morning, doing stuff,' she said.

'What stuff?'

'Oh, the usual. Office stuff. And he had a lot of phone calls – but he always does. Then in the afternoon he had houses to visit.'

'What time did he leave?'

'I don't know exactly.' She thought. 'One o'clock I went over to Waitrose for sandwiches for everybody. He had his at his desk, and I made coffee, about two, just before. He had a cup before he left, so I suppose it would be about ten past. He rung about a quarter past four to see if there was any messages, and I said there wasn't. And of course, he never came back, because of what happened.' She goggled at the thought.

'When did you find out what had happened?'

'Well, he rang again, it would be about five o'clock, to say he wouldn't be back in, there'd been an accident at home. I said,

"Is everyone all right?" and he said, "Not really," and then he rang off. I suppose he didn't want to talk about it.'

No shit, Sherlock, Gascoyne thought.

'And that night my sister rang me to say it was all over the internet. She knew David was my boss, you see, so she knew the name. I tried ringing him, but he wasn't picking up.'

'Why did you ring him?'

'Oh!' She seemed at a loss to explain. 'Well, to see if he was all right, I s'pose. He's ever so nice, David is. Everybody likes him.'

'Does he talk about his family much?'

'Oh no. Well, he wouldn't do that. He's the boss. He doesn't talk about private stuff. But you know how some bosses make you feel like dirt, and others make you feel like they really value what you do?'

'And he's that sort?'

'Yeah. He's nice. He's quite strict. If he wants something done, you have to do it, and he can blow you up if you do something stupid. But he's very fair. And he always says please and thank you.'

Gascoyne saw some nods of agreement from the others at their desks, who weren't listening, of course. 'What were the two houses he went to see?' he asked.

'You want the addresses? They'd be on the system. I know one was in Emlyn Road, and one was in Bedford Park somewhere.'

'Didn't you arrange the visits?'

'No, he did that himself. Everybody makes their own appointments, mostly. I'm more office reception and that. Printing out sets of details and mailing them and that sort of thing.'

'So when people are out of the office, what happens if you have to get in touch with them, if you don't know where they are?'

She looked puzzled by the question. 'Well, they've got mobiles, haven't they? But, anyway, it doesn't happen. There's nothing urgent that can't wait until they get back.'

'Can you find those two properties for me?'

She seemed pleased, again, to be asked, and made a show of efficiency, sitting up straight, rattling keys and scrolling with insouciance. 'It'll be in his online diary. Let's see . . . Emlyn Road. It must be this one. I'll print it out for you. And Bedford Park. I don't know the road name, but there's only one, so that must be it. It's really nice. That'll go for a lot.'

'Do you get a commission?' he asked.

'*I* don't,' she said. She didn't say, *I'm just the office junior*, but her look was eloquent.

Andy Denton's parole officer had no complaints about him but gave them the name of his community support liaison during his period of licence, who was the assistant priest at St Aidan's Church.

'I'd have thought a period of *licence* is the last thing Denton needed,' said Atherton when Slider mentioned this.

'You know what I mean. He's also a member of the prison chaplaincy and worked with Denton inside.'

'Worked with or worked on?'

'You're very picky this morning. Both, possibly. Anyway, we might get a better insight into Denton's current state of mind from this Rev Richardson.'

'If he's his sponsor on the outside, he's bound to say he's a changed man.'

'Well, we don't have anything on Denton, so why not? If it weren't for the silk scarf motif, we wouldn't even be looking at him.'

'The Silk Scarf Murderer. Move over Agatha Christie.'

'To be fair, he hasn't murdered anyone that we know of.'

'Not for want of trying. Now who's being picky?'

The heat wave was still holding: the streets baking, the sky a dusty neutral colour between grey and mauve, no breeze to move the air or shape clouds. London felt lethargic. But it was August-empty, which helped a bit. Traffic was light, pedestrians were fewer, and the magnificent plane trees that lined the streets of Shepherd's Bush sucked up a lot of the pollution. Slider silently thanked the Victorian planners who'd had the civic spirit to plant trees that would come to full magnificence a hundred-plus years into their future. 'But we've got HS2,' he said aloud.

'How's that?' said Atherton, who was driving.

'Every age has its monument. The Crystal Palace. The

Wembley Exhibition. The Millennium Dome. Ours is HS2. A sort of truncated, residual organ. Like a shrivelled appendix.'

'Are you trying to depress me?'

'I was just thinking about what we'll leave behind.'

'We have the London Eye. Decus et Utilis, as it doesn't say on pound coins. Decorative and useful. You can't do better than that. This is it. Thank God for residents' parking bays.'

'Especially when the residents are out,' Slider said.

St Aidan's had a vicarage, but the assistant priest shared a house with the curate – a raw 1990s box of pale yellow brick in the take-it-or-leave-it style of modernist architecture. Two beds, one bath, no soul. Inside was as raw as outside, and smelled a bit like a school, of shoes, books and pine cleaner. Richardson greeted them with a wide smile that didn't touch his eyes, and an unnecessarily vigorous handshake. He was tall, taller than Atherton, which made the ceilings seem even lower. He looked very buff, with muscular arms and legs and a lean, tanned face, with the kind of visible muscles in his cheeks and jaw that suggested he lifted weights with his teeth. He had a large chin, straight nose and broad forehead: combined with pale blue eyes and blonde hair he looked like an advertisement for eugenics.

He was wearing a gleaming white T-shirt, the sleeves too short to cope with the bulge of his biceps. He had a dolphin tattooed on the left one, and when he moved and the muscles flexed, it appeared to leap. Was there anyone left in the world who didn't have a tattoo? Slider wondered sorrowfully. He dreaded discovering Matthew or Kate had one, because he was afraid he wouldn't be able to stop himself objecting, provoking terrible offspring-wrath. Richardson's dolphin was wearing a halo and smiling roguishly, and he grappled for a moment with what it could mean. The fish was a symbol of Christianity, but a dolphin? Or was it just because everyone felt goodwill towards them? *Love me, I'm a dolphin-lover.*

Apart from the T-shirt, Richardson wore only flip-flops and khaki shorts, for which he apologized. 'Too hot for trousers, unless you have to. I spend all too much time dressed up, so I like to take a break when I can. I hope you don't mind? I can put the dog collar on if it makes you more comfortable.'

Unlike most Englishmen, he had the legs for shorts, brown and well-muscled. 'Not at all, Mr Richardson,' Slider said. 'Kevin,' he corrected. 'They call me the Rev Kev, of course. Come through, we'll talk in the kitchen, if you don't mind. The sitting room's full of pamphlets and hymn books. We're getting them re-covered. The hymn books, not the pamphlets. And folding chairs that need repairing. There's nowhere else to store them, so we get lumbered with them.'

He strode ahead of them, giving them a view of his muscular buttocks at work under the tight cotton like a well-matched pair of plough horses. Slider reflected that if you were going to minister to cons, you wouldn't want to be a weedy, pasty, speccy specimen. On the other hand, you probably wouldn't want to provoke homoerotic fantasies. He hoped the Rev Kev never went to the Scrubs in Lycra sportswear.

In the kitchen he invited them to sit at the table and offered them coffee. Slider spotted the economy-size jar of own-label instant standing beside the kettle and declined politely. Richardson sat down opposite them, pulling the chair well out with a muscular flick and sitting on it, legs well spread, in a manner that suggested he'd been *this close* to twirling it round and sitting on it backwards.

'So, you want to talk about Andy Denton?' he said.

'Yes, I understand that you had a lot to do with him while he was serving his sentence. You're the Anglican chaplain at the Scrubs?'

'I'm on the chaplaincy team,' Richardson corrected. 'I do two days a week there. The rest of the time I'm here. But my parish outreach work includes mentoring the recently released. The HMPPS chaplaincy works with and alongside prisoners during their time in custody to bring hope, a sense of identity and belonging, and to help the individual to address issues such as forgiveness within a context of celebrating faith and belief. But as an individual looks towards release, we also help them to prepare practically, mentally and spiritually. We assist in identifying potential positive community links, and once they're outside, we do all we can to help them lead law-abiding and positive lives.'

The speech had the hallmarks of being lifted complete from

a document written by a civil servant. Slider guessed that if he went online and Googled HM Prison and Probationary Services Chaplaincy, he would somewhere find those very words, gleaming inspirationally under a Government logo. Richardson spoke the speech trippingly off the tongue – but then, learning rigmarole off by heart was a skill an ordained man had to acquire, so it was no wonder he had it off pat.

'I didn't know prison chaplains could be part time,' Atherton said.

'The management level are full time, of course,' Richardson said. 'But down at the coal face, they're having difficulty in recruiting, plus so many of the experienced chaplains are retiring they've had to accept part-timers. Frankly, I think it's better not to spend all your time inside. You keep a better sense of perspective when you have work in other areas as well. It's too easy to "go native" if you only ever speak to prisoners.'

'I'm sure you're right,' Slider said. 'So, tell me about Denton. How did he strike you?'

He thought about it. 'He'd never done time before. It took him a while to adjust to being inside. I think it was a terrible shock to him. You sometimes find the more intelligent they are, the harder it is to adjust. Some of them never do. They just keep beating their head against a brick wall. But Andy used his intelligence. He thought it through, realized you can't beat the system, that it's there to help you, if you work with it. He settled down, made the best of his situation, tried to bring something positive away from the experience.'

'Such as?' Atherton asked.

'Most importantly he helped out with the literacy outreach. I don't know if you knew, but over fifty per cent of prisoners are functionally illiterate, which means about the same proportion have had little to no education, have no qualifications, and struggle to get any kind of job outside. It's one of the prime causes of re-offending. Learning to read is the biggest step they can take towards rehabilitation. Andy joined the programme to teach his fellow inmates to read. He was amazingly patient and had a very good success rate. He also helped with the prison library. And towards the end of his sentence he took an active part in my Faith to Faith sessions and my Thriving in

Custody workshops, sharing his experience and mentoring other inmates.'

'So, a model prisoner,' Slider suggested.

Richardson gave him a sharp look, as though he suspected irony, but seemed reassured and said, 'Towards the end, yes. I was able to give him a very good report to the parole board. I think I was material in getting him his licence. I was happy to agree to sponsor him on the outside. And he's repaid my confidence. He's got a decent job and he's doing very well.'

'You're not worried about him living in sin, then?' Atherton asked.

Richardson gave him a kindly smile, but his eyes were hard. 'We don't use words like that any more. We don't talk about sin. The concept is unhelpful.'

'Really?'

'It smacks too much of top-down authoritarianism. And it has wholly negative connotations. We prefer to emphasize the positive. We talk about forgiveness and redemption.'

'But isn't religion *about* authority? Doesn't the word "religion" mean "a system of rules"?'

The kindly smile intensified. 'I'm afraid that's the sort of old-fashioned thinking that has turned people away from the Church. We aim to be *in*clusive, not *ex*clusive. To welcome, not to condemn. Everyone comes to Christ in their own way, and it's our job to facilitate their individual journey – a journey that will be different and unique for every person.'

Slider felt they were getting off the point. 'What was Denton's attitude to his offences? I presume you must have talked about them during your pastoral interviews.'

'Yes, of course, and we did make enormous progress. He insisted that his sexual activities with Marly Potillo had been consensual. But he came to understand in the end that it is not within God's plan to inflict hurt or harm on another human being, even if they say they consent. And that consenting to inflicted pain is never an act of agency or free will: it is a symptom of a soul so damaged they cannot give informed consent, any more than a child can. Oh, he was very clear at the end that what he had done was wrong, and that he must never do it again.'

'So he confessed to his crimes? He admitted he was guilty?'

Richardson looked lofty. 'It depends what you mean by guilty.'

'When he was interviewed by some of my team yesterday, he insisted that he was innocent, that he had served time for a crime he didn't commit. And his partner told us that he also told her he was innocent and that the women in the Potillo case were lying.'

Richardson now looked uncomfortable for the first time. There was a little beading of moisture on his upper lip – though in fairness it was warm and airless in the kitchen, and he was sitting in a bar of sunshine coming in through the window. 'That was his position when I first met him,' he said. 'He said that Ms Potillo had been got hold of by an activist lawyer and talked into making the charges. That she had never objected to the – er – nature of their sexual relationship – had in fact initiated it. He insisted that it was not rape. And he said that he had never even met the other women, that they had been "bought and paid for", in his words, by the lawyer to advance her career.'

'You say that was his position at first. Did he subsequently change it?'

'As I said, he came to understand that abuse can never be consented to. He saw that what he had done with Ms Potillo was wrong.'

'And the other women?'

Richardson met Slider's eyes unwillingly, but his look was hard. You didn't survive being a sky pilot in Wormwood Scrubs by showing any chink in your armour. 'He still insisted he didn't know them. He said he had no recollection of ever meeting them.'

'Are you still mentoring him?'

'I'm not his probation officer, you understand – that's Keith Chapman. I liaise with Keith as a matter of course, and he's very satisfied with Andy's rehabilitation. I see Andy about once a month on a voluntary basis, and I encourage him to keep in touch, and of course I let him know I am always there for him if he has any doubts or needs help of any sort, or even just someone to talk to.'

'Does he come to church?'

'He came once. But it's not compulsory, you know. Everyone has their own pathway to God. We're there to help, but we don't impose conventional churchgoing if it doesn't sit right with them.'

'I understand. So, in your opinion, is Denton genuinely reformed? Is he to be trusted?'

'I trust him. He's turned his life around in a very satisfactory way. Of course, you can't say of anyone that they won't ever stumble, but I believe Andy is now equipped with the tools he needs to help himself, and to keep himself on the right path.'

On the way out, Slider said, 'Do you mind my asking – about the tattoo?'

Richardson gave an indulgent smile. 'It's pretty much obligatory to have at least one, if you're working inside. And everyone loves dolphins. It's another way, you see.'

'Another way?'

'To God. A path. A bridge. In our business you have to make use of what's to hand.'

Outside, Slider said, 'So a dolphin is a bridge.'

'A humpback bridge,' Atherton said.

'No, that'd be a whale. I hope you haven't got any tattoos.'

'Just one. I have "Wendy" tattooed on my manhood.'

'Wendy?'

'That's how it appears in standby mode. Fully unfurled it reads, "Welcome to London. Have a nice day."'

Having had a chat with the other three in the office, Gascoyne left and was walking down to where he'd parked the car when he heard pattering footsteps behind him and a voice calling, 'Hello? Excuse me?'

He turned and saw the older woman hurrying towards him in the sort of semi-crouching totter necessitated by four-inch chopstick heels and uneven pavements. He stopped and looked enquiring.

'It's about David,' she said breathlessly, and in a low voice. 'I didn't like to say anything in front of the others.' She glanced behind as if they might be creeping up on her. 'I told them I was popping out to Boots.'

'Would you like to walk and talk, then?' he invited.

She looked grateful for the understanding. He had already taken her name down as Patricia Urquart. She seemed in her late forties or perhaps well-preserved fifties, carefully made-up, with a firm figure in a dark green skirt suit and short-cut grey hair.

She fell in beside him. He modified his stride to fit hers, and to give her more time. 'What about David, then?' he asked.

'Well,' she said, 'I don't want to make trouble for him. I really like him, and he's a good boss. I don't want you to think I've got any reason to think he's ever done anything, well, wrong.'

'Of course not,' he said soothingly.

'Only I *do* know he was having an affair with one of my colleagues, despite being married. They both were – married, I mean. She's left now. Melissa Wright her name is. She left about six months ago. But they were carrying on for quite some time. I walked in on them in the rest room one time. I'd left for home at the end of the day, but I remembered I'd left my cardigan behind and went back, and there they were in a clinch, and his hand was inside her blouse. Well, she collared me the next day and told me they were having an affair and begged me not to tell anyone. I said it was none of my business, and anyway, the only time we met each other's partners was at the Christmas party, and I was hardly likely to tell her husband then, or David's wife. She told me they were in love, her and David, and that he was going to leave his wife, and they were both going to get divorces and get married, and I thought, well, there's one born every minute. Because they never do leave their wives, do they? They just say stuff like that to get what they want. I thought she was a mug, but like I said, it was none of my business. I'm not one to spread gossip, and anyway, who's interested? So I never told anyone. And then she left. I don't know if they're still carrying on. She went to Hamilton's, the King Street branch, I think, and I haven't heard from her since.'

'I see,' he said. 'And why do you think this has something to do with—?'

'Oh! No, I didn't mean that. I only mentioned that because, well, everyone's saying he's such a nice person, and he *is*, except that nobody's perfect, are they? And you have to take into account that he was cheating on his wife, so he's not a hundred per cent honest, is he? But what I really wanted to tell you was that a few weeks ago, he came into the office in the morning with scratches on his face, and a red mark next to his eye, like the beginnings of a bruise, as if somebody'd hit him. Well, naturally, I said, "What happened to you?" and he said he'd been teasing the cat and it scratched him. He laughed about it and said it served him right. But they didn't look like cat scratches to me. I *have* a cat, so I know. Cat scratches are sort of thinner. And a cat doesn't give you a black eye, does it?' She stopped, slightly breathless, and looked into his face for a reaction.

'When was this?' Gascoyne asked.

'I couldn't tell you exactly, but it was a few weeks ago. Three or four, maybe. I was right to tell you, wasn't I? Because I'm not trying to make trouble. I'm not saying he's done anything wrong, but there's that poor girl to think about, his stepdaughter, and in a case like that it's your duty to tell if you know something, isn't it?'

'Have you ever seen or heard anything to suggest that he was abusing her?' he asked.

She looked shocked, but underneath, he thought he detected a kind of excited pleasure. 'Oh no! Never! But he doesn't talk about his home life at all – which is a bit odd when you think about it, really, because we all do. You know, you come in in the morning and you say what you did last night or at the weekend while you're making the coffee – it's just normal chitchat. But he never says a word. I only knew she was his stepdaughter and not his actual daughter because—' She stopped herself and blushed painfully.

'Yes?' he asked, fixing her with a kind but official eye.

'Well,' she said, writhing a little, 'I looked him up online one time. After I found out about him and Melissa.'

'Why would you do that?'

'I wanted to know,' she said, reaching for indignation now. 'He was having an affair, and I wanted to see who he was hurting. I never said anything to anyone, so I wasn't doing any harm. Which is more than you can say for him.' The words seemed to burst out of her now. 'She got promoted to senior sales negotiator when it should have been me, and you can't tell me he didn't have something to do with it!'

Hamilton's in King Street, Hammersmith, was a rung further up the social ladder from Buckfast's, the houses advertised in its windows bigger and more expensive and sprinkled with aspirational country properties. And inside the office was more spacious, the fittings better quality. Melissa Wright was late thirties, slim and smart, with a smooth curve of shiny custard-coloured hair, a gold bracelet on her brown wrist, gold stud earrings and a gold necklace, a fine gold chain with a pendant that he thought was a Sanskrit symbol. Altogether a class act. A certain tension came into her posture, a wariness to her eyes, when Gascoyne announced himself but, to be fair, most people went in for a bit of instant self-examination when unexpectedly sought out by the police. *Be thou as chaste as ice, as pure as snow, thou shalt not escape calumny,* as they said on Sundays.

When she found out what he wanted to talk about, she took him into the staff room, where there was a sofa, table and chairs, coffee-making equipment and a near-jungle of potted plants. 'I read about his daughter on social media,' she said, sitting down opposite him at the table. 'They say she got stung by a bee and had an allergic reaction, her throat swelled up and she choked to death. It's awful. I can't imagine what he must be feeling.'

'You haven't talked to him about it?'

'Well, no, I wouldn't want to intrude. And I don't work there any more – as you can see.' She gave a tight, nervous smile, to acknowledge it was a foolish thing to say.

'But you weren't just an employee at Buckfast's, were you?' Gascoyne said. 'You and David Morgan were a bit more than colleagues.'

'What do you mean?' she said cautiously.

Not going to commit herself, Gascoyne thought. 'You and he were having an affair,' he said neutrally, as though it was no biggie.

'Who told you that?' She sounded indignant.

'Someone saw you.'

'Patsy Urquart, I bet,' she said witheringly. 'Look, you can't rely on anything she says. She's a bitter woman – fancies David herself and gets mad jealous if anyone else so much as talks to him. I think there'd been something between them, a long time ago, some totally trivial thing, but she'd blown it up out of all proportion. A drunken fumble during the Christmas party or something, and she could never get over it. She was always prickly at work. Ask anyone. If she had any sense, she'd have left, instead of making a fool of herself, embarrassing him by fawning over him. But I suppose she couldn't bear the idea of not seeing him every day. You could feel sorry for her, if she wasn't such a cow,' she concluded.

'So she didn't walk in on you and David in a passionate clinch in the staff room?'

Her blush gave her away. 'Is that what she said?'

'Are you saying it's not true?'

She looked down, tracing one of the coffee-mug rings on the table with a forefinger. She was going to regret that later.

'Look,' he said kindly, 'I'm not here to make moral judgements, but you must tell me the truth. Lying to the police is a criminal offence.'

She looked up, with a hint of spirit. 'I don't see what it's got to do with – you know – his daughter's – you know—'

'Let me worry about that. Just answer the question. Did you have an affair with David Morgan?'

'Yes, all right, I did,' she said petulantly. '*We* did. For about eighteen months. But I haven't seen him or spoken to him since I left Buckfast's.'

'What happened?'

Her blush intensified. 'The usual story. He said he was going to leave his wife.'

'You're married too?' Gascoyne suggested.

She nodded. 'We were both going to leave our partners. But you know how it goes. He says he's going to tell his wife about us, get the ball rolling, but something always comes up. Some reason why he couldn't do it right this minute.' This sounded convincingly sour. He gave a little shake of the head expressing sympathy, and she seemed to warm to him. 'In the end I realized it was never going to happen, and I was wasting my time. So I broke it off and got a new job. And that's that.'

'So he talked to you about his daughter?'

'Yeah, sometimes.'

'He was fond of her?'

'I suppose so. She was only his stepdaughter, you know, his wife's kid from her first marriage. He had two of his own from *his* first marriage. He talked about them, too.'

'His relationship with Rhianne – was it a bit stormy sometimes?'

She shrugged. 'No more than anyone else's. Everyone moans about their teenagers, don't they? Have you got kids?'

'Have you?' he countered.

'No, thanks,' she said emphatically. 'Never wanted them. It's one of the things David and I got straight right at the beginning. He's not one of those men that leaves his family and starts up a new one with some baby-mama. There's nothing worse than some sad old guy pushing a pram, pretending to be young again, changing nappies when he's got silver hair and a bad back.' She shuddered. 'I mean, he's fifty now – does he want to be running about the park kicking a football with a ten-year-old when he's sixty?' She stopped, looked at him. 'This thing about Rhianne – I'm really sorry, you know. It must be hell for them both.'

'What has David said about it?' he tried, very casually.

She drew a breath to answer and let it out. 'I told you, I haven't spoken to him. I should think I'm the last person he'd want to talk about it to.'

'Oh, I wouldn't say that,' Gascoyne said and gave her a reassuring smile.

SIX

Je Ne Regrette Rhianne

'I'm not convinced it's as over as she's saying it is,' said Gascoyne. 'She kept talking about him in the present tense. But she left Buckfast's six months ago and says she hasn't spoken to him since.'

'But if she is still carrying on with him, what's that got to do with the case?' Jenrich asked.

'I don't know,' said Gascoyne. 'Maybe nothing. But maybe she knows more about what was going on than she lets on.'

'What about this story about the scratches?' Swilley asked. 'The Morgans don't have a cat. Are you saying Morgan and Rhianne had fights?'

'We probably ought to take Patricia Urquart with a pinch of salt,' Gascoyne said. 'There seemed to be a bit of resentment there, and she may just be making trouble. On the other hand—'

'Why would she deliberately make trouble for David if she's in love with him?' Swilley finished for him.

'Aren't you forgetting Congreve?' Atherton said. 'Heaven has no rage like love to hatred turned, nor hell a fury like a woman scorned.'

'Who's Congreve?' Fathom asked. 'Wait, is he that bloke on the sex offenders reg that snatched that girl on Old Oak Common?'

'No, that was Congleton,' McLaren said. 'He's still inside, anyway. There was a Congreve who was a con man, took deposits for conservatories and replacement windows and never done the work, but he moved to Birmingham when he come out. And he was never a nonce.'

'Shut up, you two,' Jenrich said impatiently. 'Forget Congreve. Look, it doesn't matter whether Urquart's in love with Morgan or not – we need to find out whether there's any truth in her story about the scratches. Obviously she's hinting there was a history of abuse.'

'We had better ask Rita if there were scratches,' Slider said. 'Just to clear up the point.'

Fathom said, 'Maybe she found out about the mistress and went for him.'

'Why ask her and not him?' said Jenrich.

'Because if there was abuse, he's not likely to tell us the truth,' said Slider.

Gascoyne spoke. 'Sir, given that we have to consider that he *might* have killed her—'

'Remember, we have nothing against him, so we must tread lightly,' Slider said.

'Yes, sir, but what worries me is the ligature. If it was a manual throttling, it could be spur of the moment, loss of temper after being seriously provoked. But the use of a ligature looks more deliberate.'

'I take your point,' Slider said. 'However, it could still be loss of temper – if, for instance, she was wearing the scarf – say it was hanging round her neck and he grabbed it in the heat of the moment. Remember, it was not a prolonged choking. Cardiac arrest happened very quickly. And further to that,' he went on, 'it needn't have been a man at all. We shouldn't rule out the possibility that a woman could have done it.'

'So who d'you think did it?' Fathom asked.

'No thinking. We haven't got enough evidence for thinking,' Slider said.

'That'll be a relief to you, Jezza,' Swilley said.

'How did you get on with Denton's holy roller?' Jenrich asked.

'He gave our boy a glowing report,' Atherton answered for him. 'So given that he has an alibi and there's nothing to link him with Rhianne, he's off the hook.'

'Until and unless,' Jenrich said darkly.

It wasn't until some time later, when Atherton was passing his door, that Slider thought to call him in and ask him how the proposal the previous evening had gone.

'I didn't do it,' Atherton admitted. 'The occasion didn't seem to be quite right.'

'What does that mean?'

'Well, she was tired, and it wasn't a very romantic setting. I want to do it right.'

'This isn't America. You don't need to go all rose petals and candles and down on one knee. It's a perfectly straightforward question.'

'All right, I lost my nerve,' Atherton admitted. 'All the way over there I was thinking out what I'd do if she said no. I ran through so many scenarios I couldn't face it in the end. I'll do it next time.'

Slider thought that if it was so hard to put the question, maybe it wasn't the right question, but it wasn't his business to say so. He hadn't had any doubts about wanting to marry Joanna, from the first moment he met her. But Atherton had never been married, so it was probably a much longer leap for him. Living alone became a hard habit to break.

'So you don't want the cats back yet?'

'I'll take them if it's a nuisance.'

'I told you, we're happy to have them for as long as you like. Or until we go on holiday, anyway. Until and unless.'

Swilley came to the door. 'Rita Morgan's given Rhianne's best friend as "probably" Victoria Venner. She seemed a bit vague about it,' she added sternly. 'I know the names of all my Ashley's friends, and which one's the current bestie.'

'Your Ashley's only seven,' Slider said. 'She can't very well see her friends without your input. I think it's different when they get to be seventeen and eighteen.'

'I suppose so. Anyway, I've got the address.'

'We have to start somewhere. Go see her, take Atherton with you. Lucky it's school holidays,' he added. 'It would be hell having to interview them at school.'

The Venners lived in an old house, but no expense had been spared inside to disguise the fact. Walls ripped out, glass-roofed extension, hardwood floors, minimalist Swedish furniture, computer-controlled lighting. 'They've shui-ed the feng right out of it,' Atherton murmured admiringly as they were conducted through to the back and the inevitable full-width kitchen-living room, varied this time with the sort of sliding patio doors that opened the whole back of the room and allowed the outside to flow inside. Or perhaps vice versa. Visible on the patio was expensive hardwood furniture, a brick-built pizza oven and one of those Mexican chimney outdoor heaters. Year-round al fresco living.

Mrs Venner, who had opened the door to them, had been as thoroughly modernized as the house. Bone thin, youthful clothing, full make-up. Vertiginous Jimmy Choo strappy sandals – in the house! On a weekday! Short buttercup-yellow skirt and crisp white sleeveless blouse, the bare arms and legs as browned as a nicely roasted chicken but with much less meat on them. Thin gold bangles and a number of diamond rings. Swedish-blonde hair pulled tightly back from the face into a bun, perhaps the better to demonstrate its entire lack of lines. She'd had so much Botox she'd have to drop a cup to express surprise.

By contrast her daughter Victoria was old-school, a snubbily pretty face with a spot or two on the chin, untidy long off-blonde hair, cropped cotton jeans and a baggy T-shirt, slightly grubby bare feet. She was normally upholstered for a teen, not fat by any means, but against her picked-carcase mother she looked chubby. She was pale, and her eyes were puffy, with the tell-tale marks under them that suggested much weeping over the past couple of days. When Atherton and Swilley came in, she had been sitting on the huge leather sofa, one leg tucked under her, listlessly noodling on her mobile. She looked up in alarm, and immediately a fingernail crept into her mouth. Atherton noticed they were all bitten right down. He also noticed the quick head jerk of annoyance from her mother – she couldn't really frown, of course. 'Nails, Victoria,' she snapped.

It was clear from the beginning that Mrs Venner was going to be the one doing the talking. Victoria, hunched defensively, watched her with big eyes over the constantly chewed fingers in a way that suggested this was the normal course of events. Plainly, Mrs V was a dissatisfied woman. She rocked on her heels, walked about the room, abjured Victoria to sit up properly and *stop biting your nails!* while the narrative flowed from behind a face as incapable of expressing emotion as a kabuki mask. It was unnerving.

'I never wanted Victoria to get involved with Rhianne Morgan. I always thought her an unwholesome influence. The mother's

Irish, you know, and who her father was, well, heaven only knows! She's certainly clawing her way up the social ladder, Rita Morgan is, because David's clearly a cut above her, but I suppose there's nothing much he can do about his stepdaughter when there's bad blood to start with. And bad blood will always out.'

'Mum,' Victoria murmured in shocked protest.

'Don't interrupt, Victoria. It was all right when they were younger, I suppose, but once they reach late teens you have to keep a constant eye on them. Everything you do now, Victoria, I've told you again and again, will affect your future. I haven't worked and slaved all these years to give you everything, just so you can throw it all away. What we've spent on this girl you wouldn't believe! Piano lessons, horse-riding, skiing, Mandarin, yoga. Foreign travel to broaden the mind. Her own tennis coach. Elocution lessons. Fencing, for suppleness and deportment. But you've got to do the work, Victoria, no one can do it for you. You've got to put in the effort.'

'I do, Mum.' Tears were welling again.

'You say that, but as soon as my eye is off you, you slack off. We'll see, when the A level results come in. I don't think there was nearly enough revision going on. You thought because you did all right in the mocks you could rest on your laurels. And I'm not just talking about academic work, either. Even if your grades are good, you know that's not all there is to getting into a really *good* college. Everyone who applies is going to have the grades. You have to *present* well as well. *Stop biting your nails!* Heaven knows I've done everything I can to help you. I've told you again and again. You *know* what to do. But do you do it? Diet and exercise, diet and exercise. What do you weigh now?'

'Mu-um!'

'And grooming. Do you think it's *easy* to look like me? Do you think I like having to watch what I eat *every single day*? Oh yes, I could give up, let myself go – nothing easier! I could slouch on a sofa all day eating snacks! But I don't. Because I have a duty to you, and to your father.' She swung round on Atherton and Swilley. '*That's* why I didn't want her seeing Rhianne. The rubbish that girl put into her body! Victoria knows fizzy drinks and Pringles and chocolate bars are forbidden, but

Rhianne led her astray. You only had to look at her – she was *fat!*' It was the ultimate horror.

'She wasn't fat any more, Mum. She was really thin,' Victoria pleaded. 'You don't know. You've not seen her.'

'It wasn't just her weight,' Mrs Venner went on regardless. 'Her attitude was appalling.'

'Mum!'

'Everything you *don't* need to copy, Victoria. That girl was a car crash.'

'I haven't seen her in ages, Mum.' Victoria looked sulky. 'She—' She broke off and gnawed another nail.

'I think we'd better have a word with Victoria on her own, if you don't mind,' Atherton said.

'I do mind,' Mrs Venner said sharply. 'She's *my* daughter. Anything you want to say to her you can say in front of me.'

'How old are you, Victoria?' Swilley asked.

'Eighteen.'

'Then you're an adult. Would you like to show me the garden?' The girl still threw her mother a nervous glance, but Atherton deflected Mrs Venner by saying, 'I would like to have a talk to you on your own, as well,' and Swilley escaped through the missing wall with the daughter.

'Your mum's a bit of a glamazon, isn't she?' Swilley said confidingly, girl-to-girl.

To her surprise, Victoria looked worshipful. 'She's *wonderful!*' she said. 'When we go shopping together, no one believes she's my mother – she doesn't look old enough. At school things, she makes everyone else's mum look frumpy, she's so fabulous. *And* she runs her own business – Nicole Firman Interiors. That's her maiden name. She's a successful businesswoman in her own right.'

The last sentence had the sound of something the girl was repeating, a badge of honour – or a justification. Swilley thought Mrs Venner seemed like a nightmare. In her view, a person only got one mother, so it had better be a motherly one. 'It sounds like a lot to live up to,' she said.

Victoria threw her a quick look and seemed to hunch into herself. 'I'm always letting her down. I *do* try, but it's so hard.

I'm such a disappointment to her. No matter what I do, I can't seem to get my weight down.' She blushed, making her spots stand out. 'I starve myself,' she said in a low voice, 'and then I get so hungry I just grab anything, and before I know it . . . I ate a whole packet of biscuits on Monday,' she added in miserable confession. 'Mum says I've got no self-control, and I suppose she's right. She says I always try to take shortcuts because I'm lazy, instead of putting the work in. Like starving myself is a shortcut, instead of proper diet and exercise. But I've *tried* that, and it doesn't work!' she went on in a muted wail. 'No matter what I do I just keep getting fatter!'

'I don't think you're fat at all,' Swilley said, matter-of-factly.

The look Victoria gave her said, *nice try, but you just don't understand.* 'And she wants me to do law, so I can get a high-paying job and marry a posh, rich barrister,' she went on, evidently getting it all out now she'd started.

'Don't you like the idea?'

'I want to be an analytical chemist and work for a big pharmaceutical company, discover new drugs for treating disease and do something that will help other people.'

'That sounds like a decent ambition,' said Swilley.

'Mum says the pay is terrible and I'd just be a glorified lab assistant washing out test tubes, with acid burns on my fingers.' She bit her lip. 'I said once that if I worked in a lab, it wouldn't matter *what* I looked like and she went spare,' she confessed. 'She said it was just my laziness again and not wanting to put the work in.'

'Is that why she didn't like Rhianne?' Swilley said, feeling she had got her going nicely. 'Did she think she was lazy?'

'She says she was a bad influence on me because she ate rubbish. She thinks Rhianne's mum let her do whatever she wanted. Once when I went home after seeing her, Mum could smell cigarettes on me, and she went *extra*.'

'Do you smoke?'

'No, I think it's stupid, but Rhianne did. We used to—' She stopped.

'Yes? You can tell me.'

'We'd have these sessions, drinking vodka and her smoking and talking about stuff. Sex and stuff.'

'Was Rhianne having sex with someone?'

'She said she was. She said she'd done it a lot. I don't know if it was true.'

'You think she was making it up?' Victoria shrugged. 'Exaggerating?'

'I dunno.' She looked down and said almost inaudibly, 'I've never done it. But she . . . She seemed to know a lot about it. She said she'd done it with a lot of boys.'

'With Kenton Willans, for instance?'

She looked up. 'How d'you know about him?'

'He was mentioned. Tell me about him.'

From Victoria's jumbled sentences, she gathered that Kenton was That Boy: every school had one, the impossibly gorgeous, fabulously popular boy that every boy wanted to be and every girl wanted to go out with. The one who gathered round him the circle of the cool kids. The one whose attention was the ultimate prize. A girl Kenton approved of had it made.

'How come Kenton picked her?' Swilley asked.

'They were both doing Geography, and they used to revise together. He used to go round to her house, and she said they did it in her bedroom when her mum and dad were out.' She looked troubled. 'Maybe that's why—'

'Why what?'

'Oh, nothing.'

'You think that's why he chose Rhianne, because she let him?' Swilley said bluntly.

'I don't know. He seemed to be really into her. Until—'

'Yes?'

'I think they might've broken up, after the end-of-school dance.' An indignation broke out of her. 'We wanted to call it the prom. But Mr Underhill wouldn't let us. Our head teacher. He said it was an Americanism.'

'Kenton and Rhianne went to the prom together?' Swilley asked.

'Yeah. And she looked fabulous – like I said to Mum, she'd got really thin, and she had this great dress and everything. But she was like a wild thing that night, and I don't think Kenton liked it.'

'What do you mean, like a wild thing?'

'Oh, you know – really hyper. Like super manic, dancing and laughing and acting up. I was afraid one of the teachers would say something – we're not supposed to have alcohol there and I think she must've had something. She was so crazy. And I could see Kenton looked a bit off it, you know? Well, she wasn't paying him a lot of attention. She danced with a *lot* of boys. But I didn't see how it ended. Well, I was . . . There was this boy I like a bit . . .'

She blushed, and Swilley said, 'I understand. You had other things on your mind.'

'Yeah, so I didn't see what happened between her and Kenton, but I think they must've broken up, because I texted her afterwards, and she said she was fed up with boys our age, she was into older men.'

'When did you last see her?'

'At the prom.'

'Not since then? That's four weeks ago.'

'Well, we're not in school now. And Mum's made me help out with her business, and I'm s'posed to be going to college open days and stuff. I texted Ree a few times, but she never answered.'

'That didn't worry you?'

She shrugged. 'People don't always answer.'

Swilley remembered a recent report that half of young people between eighteen and thirty-four said they had never answered their phone, and only rarely answered texts. She supposed you had to actually stand in front of them and flap your hands to get a response.

'But you did get a reply after the prom?'

'Not right away, but days later. I'd messaged was she all right and were she and Kenton OK and she just sent back something about how schoolboys were dumb, older men were more exciting, and that's the last I heard. But she's posted on Instagram since then about a new bloke she was seeing.'

'Do you know who?'

She frowned and shook her head. 'She never said a name, but she said he was really fit, and smart, and sophisticated, and she was really into him. Ellie and Emma – we used to hang out, the four of us – they reckon she was getting stuff from him. Like, you know, drugs. Don't tell my mum!'

'No, this is between us.' The girl bit her lip, staring worriedly at nothing. Swilley looked down compassionately. 'You can't get Rhianne into trouble now, you know,' she said.

'I know.' Tears welled again. 'See, Rhianne, she was different from us. She was the only one of us who smoked. And she drank the most of all of us. And did sex . . .'

'Just Kenton, or other boys as well?'

'She said there were others. And—' She stopped.

'Anything you can tell us that may help us find out what happened . . .' Swilley urged.

She looked up. 'I think she did cocaine sometimes. See, she said I should try it because it helped you lose weight. And she used to be – not fat, but you know, like me – and she'd really lost a lot lately. And she said to me she bet that was how my mum kept so thin.' This called for the most worried expression of all. 'Cocaine chic, she called it. All those models in the magazines, they're all like skeletons, and she said that's how they did it. But she'd no right to say that about my mum. Mum would never do that!' she averred in stout defence. 'That'd be a shortcut, and she doesn't do shortcuts. She puts the work in.'

Swilley left a beat of respect for the wonderful Mrs Venner, then said, 'Are you sure Rhianne didn't mention the new man's name?'

'No, definitely not.'

'Do you know where she met him?' Shake of the head. 'His house? Her house?'

'I don't know. All I know is she posted pictures on Insta of places he'd taken her and said, like, about how boys our age never knew how to treat a woman. You had to have an older man for that.'

They were on their third circuit now. Out of the corner of her eye, Swilley could see Mrs Venner looking towards them from inside the house, as if longing to intervene. Poor Victoria would get a grilling when they'd gone, and what were the odds she'd find herself spilling everything she'd said? Her ma was a force of nature. Better get the last question in before she erupted from the house.

'How did Rhianne get on with her dad?'

Victoria looked blank. 'OK, I suppose. She never talked about him, really. We all thought he was cool, actually,' she added confidingly. 'I mean, most people's dads are, well, *dads*, if you know what I mean. Just old and boring. But Mr Morgan's ever so good-looking, and smart, and kind of . . . twinkly. He acts like he's still alive, not half-dead and droning on about mortgages and the stock market and all that *dad* stuff.'

'Did she ever mention having rows with him?'

She shrugged. 'Only like all of us. It's what parents do, isn't it – try and stop you doing things.'

Her face said she had suddenly thought of something. She'd better not take up pro poker playing as a career, Swilley thought. 'Yes?' she said.

'I just remembered,' Victoria said, blushing again. 'It was years ago, though.'

'You never know what's important. Tell me.'

'Well, she said she'd found out her dad was having an affair. She'd seen him going by in the car with another woman. She was blonde.'

'Could have been a client?' Swilley suggested.

'No, she said this woman was leaning over and laughing and she kissed him while he was driving. She said it was obvious what was going on. And when she asked her dad, he said she'd imagined it and got really angry with her.'

'Did she say anything to her mother about it?'

'No, she said she didn't want to hurt her, so she kept it secret.' She looked awkward. 'Should I have said anything?'

'God, no! It wasn't for you to get involved.'

She looked relieved. 'Ellie and Emma thought it was super cool to have a dad that was fit enough to have an affair. They think he's hot. But I think . . . well, what if the woman was married as well? What would her family feel? My mum's blonde.'

'So am I,' Swilley pointed out comfortingly.

Atherton, meanwhile, had got the other side of the story.

'That girl was completely out of control. Alcohol and cigarettes. Her mother seemed to let her run wild. And boys. She already had a reputation. There's so much more temptation for them now. That's why upbringing is all the more important. I've told Victoria, she's much too young for physical relations. That sort of thing

can wait – and it *must* wait, until after the important things are
in place. But you can't imagine Rita Morgan having that sort of
conversation with Rhianne, when she played the field herself.
And with a married man. It's no wonder Rhianne was a mess.
And—' She drew a breath. 'I didn't want to discuss it in front
of Victoria, but I'm pretty sure she was into drugs.'

'What makes you think that?'

'Victoria came home one evening after being round at
Rhianne's house, and I'm sure I could smell pot on her clothes
and hair.' She looked at him keenly. 'I'm reading on the internet
that Rhianne's death was caused by a drugs overdose. Is that
true?'

'I can't discuss that with you.'

'Well, it can't have been natural causes, or you wouldn't be
investigating. And what natural causes could there be, anyway,
with a girl that age? I don't believe everything I read online, of
course,' she said piously, 'but there's a lot of buzz that it was
cocaine, that she got hold of some stuff that was stronger than
usual. There's so much—'

Atherton interrupted. 'Did you ever speak to the Morgans
about Rhianne's bad behaviour?'

'We've never really been on those terms. I only knew them
as the parents of Victoria's friend. We don't move in the same
circles, so I'd only see them at school events, and then only at
a distance.'

'Still, given you were so concerned about it . . .'

Her eyes slid away. 'I did once drop a hint to Rita at a parents'
evening, but she didn't seem to catch on. Not very bright, you
know.'

'What about Mr Morgan?'

'He doesn't go to school things much – too busy working, I
suppose. And the girl was only his stepdaughter, so I suppose
he left the bringing-up to the mother, which is a pity. He ought
to have stepped in.'

Atherton guessed she had been less concerned at the time than
she was now, when an attitude could safely be struck. Criticizing
someone's child to their face was very likely to provoke an ugly
scene.

Mrs Venner went on quickly to skate away from the point.

'I'm just glad that Victoria didn't seem to be seeing Rhianne at the end. I hope she's learned a lesson. There are other girls much more worthy of being her friend – nice girls, like Emma Bachelor, girls who set the right example. I want my daughter to do well in life – is that a crime? I want her to marry the right sort of man, a man with a good career, like her father, a man who can give her the good things in life – a nice house, a car, clothes, travel, good schools for her children. It's what any mother would want for her daughter.'

The 1950s called – they want their attitudes back, Atherton thought.

'Well, she won't get those things by hanging around with rackety girls like Rhianne Morgan,' Mrs Venner went on, her voice contemptuous, though her face remained as smooth as a Prozacked Buddha. 'That one will be lucky to marry at all, never mind a nice man.'

'Indeed, you're right,' Atherton said, and Mrs Venner looked as disconcerted as it was possible for her to.

'I didn't mean . . . You know what I mean.'

'So, this older man Rhianne was seeing,' Atherton said as he and Swilley drove back. 'Could it have been Denton?'

'Could have been anybody,' Swilley said. 'If he even existed. Sounds as if Rhianne was boasting, bigging herself up. All that about boys being silly and liking older men, that's classic teen talk. Doesn't mean she was acting on it.'

'Do girls do that?'

She gave him a *duh!* look. 'The one thing you know about teenagers is they'd give their eye teeth to be ten years older than they are.' She shrugged. 'Then as soon as they hit thirty, they'd give anything to be ten years younger.'

'Not easy being female, is it?' Atherton said.

'Are you ragging me?'

'Just a little bit. I've just had a horrible thought – the older man couldn't have been Morgan, could it? Could a girl get a crush on her stepfather?'

Swilley didn't immediately answer, giving the question proper consideration, which threw Atherton. 'Yes, it's possible,' she said. 'Girls do get crushes on mature men, even uncles sometimes.

She was just the right age, and Morgan's attractive enough. Victoria said they all thought he was cool. But supposedly Rhianne was having sex with this man and doing cocaine with him. That's a whole different picture.'

'Though you said that could be an empty boast,' said Atherton. 'I wonder if she was conflating two things: an ordinary boyfriend – albeit one who was on the naughty side and provided the occasional wrap and spliff – and a mini crushette on her stepdad, who was the "older man" of her fantasies.'

Swilley grunted. 'Sounds plausible, but you're just making up stories, and we can't ask her, so we'll never know.'

'Unless she kept a diary.'

'SOC didn't find one in the house.'

'Or discussed it with one of her friends.'

'Or posted something on social media.' She pondered for a moment. 'One thing, though – it's a mistake to assume that when a teenage girl talks about an older man she necessarily means someone in their thirties or forties. When you're seventeen, someone of twenty-one or twenty-two seems to be in a whole different world of experience – especially if he's got a job and a car. He looks like a god to a sixth-former.'

'OK. Noted,' said Atherton. He sighed. 'The trouble with having to dibble around in these girls' lives is you just can't tell if they're making stuff up or keeping things back for what seem like perfectly good reasons to them. With adults you can generally tell, or at least you can work out why they're not telling you everything, but being a teenager is a sort of insanity. The passions, the fears, the cliques, the fashions. Wanting desperately to fit in. The boiling hot shames: prepared to dice and eat your own liver rather than admit something that wouldn't make the slightest sense to an adult.'

Swilley gave him an amused look. 'Yeah. All that – and it's twice as bad for girls as for boys.'

'You say that, but you have no idea. I *was* a boy, and I can tell you it was walking barefoot over hot coals most of the time. Barefoot and naked.'

'Yeah, poor you. Ginger Rogers had to do it backwards in high heels.'

* * *

McLaren stuck his head round the door. 'The neighbours are back, guv.'

'I thought that was tomorrow,' said Slider.

He shrugged. 'They rung up, anyway – wanted to know if anyone was going to interview them. Sounded up for it.'

'Oh.'

'Yeah, *that* sort.' He hesitated. 'D'you want me to go round? I was just going home.'

'Got something on?'

'Me and Nat were going out f'ra meal with friends. Italian.'

Slider gathered somehow it was the meal that was Italian rather than the friends. 'It's all right, I'll do it. You enjoy yourself. You're going to have a hard time on Saturday.'

'What? Oh, yeah, I'd forgotten that. Thanks, guv. I'll get off, then.' The head was withdrawn swiftly before Slider could change his mind. The anti-war march on Saturday was pulling in officers from all over London and indeed the country, and all Slider's firm had been requisitioned. Policing these big protests was hard and exhausting, and another burden on London's police service – they never happened on the same scale in other cities – along with major crime, terrorism and the protection of MPs and Royals. It was what you got for being a global capital.

The Eversaints were elderly, well-dressed, well-spoken and indignant. They didn't exactly say so, but Slider gathered that having a murder happen next door brought down the tone of the neighbourhood and, not incidentally, the property values.

'I'm very sorry for them, of course,' said Mrs Eversaint, 'but I'm not entirely surprised that girl came to an unfortunate end.' She had an odd facial tic, as if she were chewing a raspberry seed between her front teeth.

'What did she do to earn your disapproval?' Slider asked.

Mr Eversaint answered. He was smart and silver-haired in a beige linen suit, pale blue shirt and darker blue tie. Slider could imagine he had once been told that wearing blue brought out the colour of his eyes. He was very, not to say unnaturally, tanned, like Cary Grant in a 1950s early-Technicolor film. 'She flaunted herself. Sunbathing in the garden, practically in the nude. My wife was forced to mention it to Mrs Morgan.'

'You can't see the patio from your windows, can you?'

'You can from further down the garden,' he said, giving himself away. Perhaps realizing this, he went on, 'And she didn't confine herself to the patio. She took the sunbed out on the lawn as often as not, in full sight of all the houses along this side. Strutting about the garden in a bikini so brief, well, it was hardly there at all.'

'I see. Was she always alone on these occasions?'

Mrs Eversaint answered, with a minatory look at her husband. 'We weren't constantly watching, you know. We have other things to do than monitor next door's teenager.' She chewed the pip more vigorously.

'Quite. How well do you know the Morgans?'

'Not well,' she said quickly. 'Just as neighbours. I've never been inside the house.'

'They aren't our sort of people,' said Mr Eversaint. 'But we *heard* them often enough. That's the problem with a semi-detached. Your neighbours are "too much with you, late and soon".' He gave a nod and kindly smile to emphasize that this was a literary quotation with which Mr Plod might not be familiar.

'Wordsworth,' Slider said, glad to disappoint. 'What do you mean, you heard them?'

'The rows,' Mrs Eversaint said. 'Terrible shouting and screaming arguments. Slammed doors. Things thrown about.'

'Arguments about what?'

'We're halls-adjoining,' Mr Eversaint said, a touch loftily. 'So we can't hear the actual words, only the tenor of the exchange. Which was heated, not to say violent.'

'Can you give me an example of that?'

Mrs Eversaint seemed only to have been waiting for the invitation. 'A few weeks ago. In July. I gather the girl had come home late from some party or other. Slammed taxi doors out at the front, raised voices. I imagine she was drunk. Then inside the house, the shouting, the angry argument. *Then,*' she reached a triumphant climax, 'they took it outside, into the garden. When I heard them, I went to the window.'

'It was beyond acceptable,' Mr Eversaint put in. 'It was after midnight.'

'The girl stormed down the garden and Mr Morgan went after

her. I didn't see the mother. I suppose she was watching from the patio, because we'd heard her voice inside. She has a very shrill voice when she's quarrelling.'

'Could you hear what the row was about?' Slider asked.

'We gathered the girl was being told off for coming home late – and possibly for other things – and she was objecting to being reprimanded,' said Mr Eversaint.

'I heard her shout, "You're not my real dad, you can't tell me what to do,"' his wife added. 'She's Mrs Morgan's child by a previous marriage.'

'Which could account for many of the problems,' Mr Eversaint added.

'We couldn't hear everything that was being said, but she was screaming at him, and he was shouting at her, and then we saw him grab her and shake her violently.'

'Grabbed her where?' Slider asked.

'By the shoulders. And she seemed to be trying to fight him off. And then Mrs Morgan intervened, and they all went inside. We didn't hear any more until someone ran upstairs a few minutes later and slammed a bedroom door. The girl, probably. She's not light on her feet, and neither of the parents usually run up the stairs.'

'And this was a few weeks ago?'

'That's right,' said Mr Eversaint. 'But it's not unusual to hear raised voices in there. They are not considerate neighbours. The girl, playing pop music loudly in her room and in the garden. We've had to speak to them several times about that. There are ear buds these days. No need to annoy other people with your ghastly noise.'

SEVEN
Beau of Burning Gold

Friday was overcast, still very warm, but with just a hint of air movement. When Slider left for work, he found his father in the front garden, weeding.

'You don't need to do that,' Slider protested.

Mr Slider straightened. 'Someone's got to,' he said with a faint smile. 'Got to keep it tidy. What would the neighbours think?'

Slider shuddered. 'I had a bellyful of neighbours thinking yesterday. Not mine – the victim's.'

'Getting anywhere with that?'

'No.'

'Ah well. Early days.'

'It's all very well for you to be serene and philosophical,' Slider grumbled.

'That's because I have complete faith in you.'

Slider looked at the sky. 'I think it's brewing up to rain.'

Mr Slider looked, snuffed the air. 'Nah. Clouds are too high. It won't rain today.'

Slider grinned. 'Says the old countryman-weather-sage-guru. Is it the way the spiders are spinning their webs or the height the geese are flying?'

'It was on the wireless this morning,' Mr Slider deadpanned. 'S'called a weather forecast.'

Slider went on his way, refreshed by the exchange.

The Morgans seemed to have sunk into apathy, and the tragedy had separated them rather than brought them together. Rita in the kitchen and David in the sitting room stared at the walls, beyond weeping, beyond talking, past even dread and horror, like people held in a sinister waiting room for so long they had almost forgotten what procedure they were waiting for.

It was easier, in a way, to talk to them in this state, than in the volatile early stages when their reaction could not be calculated.

Slider tackled David Morgan first. His automatic grooming system had faltered at last, and although he seemed clean and his hair was brushed, he was unshaven and dressed in trousers and a T-shirt and with bedroom slippers on his feet. He looked at Slider with the empty eyes of a victim who had passed beyond hope.

'I want to talk to you about a time a few weeks back when you went into the office with scratches on your face.'

It took him a moment to engage speech mode. 'Who told you that?' he asked dully.

'Do you remember the incident?'

'Incident? It wasn't an incident.'

'You said you'd been teasing the cat, but you don't have a cat.'

'Who told you that?' he asked again, as if the accusation annoyed him. 'Office gossip,' he added dismissively.

'Did you go into work one day with scratches on your face?'

'Barely,' he objected. 'Clacking women. They'll make a mountain out of any mole hill.'

'How did you get the scratches?'

'Like I said, I was teasing a cat. Serves me right.'

'What cat?'

'I don't know. There are lots of cats wandering about. They come over the fence from other people's gardens.'

'What colour was it?'

He hesitated just too long. 'Black. Black and white.' Slider looked at him in silence for a long time. Normally Morgan would have felt obliged to add something more and make things worse, but he was weighted with the inertia of tragedy and only sighed as if nothing mattered. Slider looked at Atherton, for him to ask the next question.

'Would you like to comment on an allegation that you had a violent quarrel with Rhianne out in the garden very late one night, a few weeks ago?'

Morgan looked at him with slow resentment. 'I know who told you that. Those busybodies next door. They came round the next day to complain – after hanging out of the window so as not to miss a word.'

'So you remember the incident?'

'There you go with the "incident" again! What are you trying to cook up?'

'What actually happened?' Atherton insisted.

'Rhianne came home very late, well after the time we expected her. Her mother was naturally anxious. When I told her off for upsetting her mother, she got angry. You know what teenagers are like. They can't accept criticism. She ran out into the garden, I followed, there was a bit of an altercation, Rita said shush, you'll disturb the neighbours, and we all went inside and up to bed.' He sighed again. 'That's all there was to it.'

'So the witnesses were wrong when they said the argument got physical?'

He grew just a little animated. 'You're calling them witnesses? Nosy neighbours earwigging on a private conversation, two old windbags with empty lives drawing inflated conclusions from something that's none of their damned business? *Witnesses?*'

'Quite understandable if you lost your temper with Rhianne,' Atherton said. 'You'd been anxious about her, worried for her safety, and relief often turns fear to anger.'

A look of pain crossed his face. 'You'd take their word over mine? I would never hurt my daughter,' he said. 'Never. You've no right to suggest it.'

Slider sat opposite Rita at the kitchen table, making it one-to-one, cosy confessional style, Atherton away behind her, out of her sight line. 'I just want to talk to you about a night a few weeks ago, when Rhianne came home very late. The night of the prom, wasn't it?'

'End-of-year dance,' she corrected without emphasis. 'They didn't like calling it a prom, for some reason.'

'But that's what it was?'

She didn't answer immediately. She was looking at a memory. 'We didn't have them when I was at school, but it's lovely for the girls to get all dressed up. Like being proper grown-ups for the first time. And the boys in dinner jackets. I took Ree out to buy her a dress for it. I was afraid she'd pick something . . .

well, inappropriate. But we both saw the same thing at the same time. We agreed on it straight away. Like it was just waiting for her – her dream dress. Fuchsia taffeta, very plain, no frills. A sweetheart neckline and just narrow straps. Really tasteful. It was expensive, but it was worth it. It was perfect. And I took her to the hairdressers for an updo and a manicure. She looked gorgeous. Like an angel,' she concluded sorrowfully.

'It was Kenton who took her, was it?'

'He didn't call for her. They met the boys there. She and Emma and Ellie went together in an Uber. But Kenton was her date for the night, as far as I understood. He's a nice boy.'

'And did he bring her home?'

'She came home in an Uber, but I didn't see if there was anyone with her. It was very late. The dance ended at eleven and she should have been home at half past at the latest. We said no going anywhere afterwards. Half eleven's quite late enough for a girl that age. And she knows to call if there's any reason – like she can't get a cab or anything. David would always go and collect her, no matter where. But we didn't hear a thing, and when I tried ringing, her phone was turned off, and it was going on one o'clock when she finally turned up. David was furious, for my sake really. He said how dare you frighten your mother like that, and then it all kicked off. She said we couldn't treat her like a child any more, and David said as long as you live in this house you'll obey the rules and she said you're not my real dad, you can't tell me what to do, and that's really hurtful, because he's always seen himself as her dad. I could see how it hurt him. Anyway, she ran out into the garden, and he followed her and there was some shouting, and next door slammed their window shut, which they do when they disapprove of something, and I went after them and made them come inside. And it was all over by then. Ree ran up to her room, and that was that.'

'Did you find out why she was so late? Where she'd been?'

'I asked her the next day, but she was still angry and sort of sulking, and she wouldn't tell me. She said a bunch of them had gone somewhere afterwards and I wasn't to make a fuss. She . . .'

'Yes?'

'She said—' This obviously hurt. Rita gulped. 'She said if we treated her like a prisoner, she'd leave home.' She met his eyes. 'I was afraid she just might try it if she was upset enough, and she could never have coped on her own. How could she even afford rent? She'd get into trouble, get into the wrong company, and then—' She stopped again, and looked away from him, back into the blankness of loss. 'Well,' she concluded, but that didn't seem to go anywhere.

Slider waited a moment, then said, 'Out in the garden – there was some kind of . . . tussle, or fight, between her and David?'

She looked at him again, more sharply this time. 'It was nothing,' she said. 'Why are you bringing that up?'

'He went to work with scratches on his face the next day.'

She rubbed her eyes wearily. 'I didn't think they showed. I put some concealer on them for him. I thought it covered them up all right.'

'Someone at work noticed. Tell me what happened.' She didn't answer, frowning in thought. He pushed her, but gently. 'David was shaking her violently, in anger, and she defended herself, tried to push him away?'

'What? No! It wasn't like that.'

Slider waited again. She didn't want to say. 'You must tell me exactly what happened.'

'Why? It's got nothing to do with anything.'

'If you don't tell me, I'm bound to think the worst.'

'What's the worst? My daughter's dead. There's nothing worse than that. She had a heart defect, and I didn't know. I'm her mother and I didn't know. All these years . . . I looked it up. She might have dropped down dead at any time. If we'd known, we could have done something about it. Now it's too late.'

'But you want us to find out exactly what happened to her? And everything is part of it, even if it doesn't seem important to you.' She continued to frown. 'The row in the garden,' he reminded her. 'If the explanation is innocent, there's no reason not to tell me.'

'Innocent?' she said and looked at him again. 'I don't know what you're trying to suggest, but if you think David would ever . . .' She paused, and then it came out in a rush, as though squeezed out of her. 'She went for him. She was drunk, I think, and angry, and she went for him with her nails, went for his eyes. He grabbed her wrists to stop her, and she struggled, and one of her fists hit him in the eye, but he wouldn't let go. I ran out to stop them, and she sort of sagged, and then he let her go, and we all went in. She'd started crying, and she ran up to bed and locked her door. And that was all there was to it. We didn't even realize she'd left any marks until the next day, and I saw the scratches and a bruise. We thought he'd get a black eye, but it never came to anything more.'

'It's all plausible,' Slider said, 'and their stories match. We've no reason to think it was anything different.'

'No,' said Porson. He pulled thoughtfully on his lower lip. 'We've been lucky so far that there's no national media interest in it.'

'Just the chatter on the internet.'

'Can't stop that. Anyway, it's all over the place. That works to our advantage. Multiple theories – nothing sticks. Divide and conquer. Consensuality's what we've got to fear.'

'If it wasn't for the ligature mark, it could have been natural causes,' Slider said.

'And it could still be Morgan,' Porson said, giving him a sharp look. 'I know you don't like it, but in the heat of a row – and teenagers are the devil. Even my Moira went through one of those phases when, bloody hell, I could have strangled her she was such a contrary little madam – he just grabs the ends of the scarf and pulls, just to shut her up. And bingo, the dicky ticker kicks in.'

That wasn't easy to say, Slider reflected, particularly with a finger and thumb pulling your lip out into a sugar scoop.

'But if it wasn't intentional, why wouldn't he admit it?' Slider said in frustration. 'Maybe not at first, but by now, on mature reflection – if he's not a bad man and he did care for her.'

'Did he?' Porson put the question.

'His wife and his sister both say he did.'

'Well, they would, wouldn't they. Maybe there's something else going on – something they don't know about.' He let his lip go and sniffed to indicate a change of subject. 'What else are you looking at?'

'Other sex offenders in the area,' Slider said. 'LaSalle and

Lœssop are checking up on half a dozen who might conceivably be in the frame. And there are other schoolfriends to talk to, see if we can get any more on this older man that she said she was seeing. We're still waiting for the IT report. I'd put money on it that she'll have posted something about him somewhere.'

'If he exists,' said Porson. 'And unless there was some reason she had to keep it secret.'

Slider winced. 'I wish you hadn't said that.'

Porson shrugged. 'And now there's this march tomorrow. They've stuck me in Silver Command. A tribune to my long experience as a copper, no doubt.' His eyebrows did ironic things. He was not popular with the top brass. 'What have they left you with?'

'Just a PCSO to man the phones.'

'Well, you can't be expected to do much with that.'

'I can review all the evidence. And Saturday's a good day to do interviews, when people aren't at work. And teenagers are still in bed.'

Porson sighed. 'I've got a feeling this one's going to run into the sand. Unless it *was* the stepfather, in which case he'll crack eventually and cough up an idunnit.'

Joanna was surprised to get a telephone call from Stephanie.

'Are you busy today? Could I come over and see you?'

'You know Bill's not here? He's gone in to work.'

'And Jim's policing the march somewhere on Westminster Bridge. That was rather the point – I wanted to talk to *you*.'

'Well, be my guest. What time?'

'I've got rounds this morning but nothing else. About two-ish?'

'OK. See you then.' Joanna rang off, intrigued. Atherton had been going out with Stephanie for – what? – sixteen, eighteen months now, and they'd spent quite a bit of time together as a foursome, but she'd never had any intimate exchanges with her. She liked her but couldn't say she really knew her on a deep level. Perhaps Stephanie thought it was time she did.

She arrived just after two. It was like a visit from Grace Kelly. She was tall, for a start, and Princess Kate slim, and was wearing nude heels and a very beautiful beige silk draped dress that had clearly come from the sort of shop Joanna would not have dared to enter for fear of being chased out with a broom. Her mouse-blonde hair, whose delicate highlights were probably natural, was done up in a French pleat, and her make-up was subtle and immaculate, even after a morning at work. Joanna, barefoot in jeans and a T-shirt on which she was fairly sure someone had spilled something that morning, felt instantly short, fat and dishevelled.

'You look terrific,' she said, and Stephanie looked surprised for an instant – which was one of the reasons she liked her.

'Thanks,' she said, hesitated a blink and then didn't say 'so do you' – another of the reasons. It would be so easy to reach for the obvious response and devalue the compliment. 'Do you want me to take my shoes off?' she went on to ask, as people did these days. Or perhaps having clocked Joanna's naked plates.

'Only if it makes you feel better – there's nothing in this house you could possibly damage.'

'I will then – they're killing me,' Stephanie said, heel-and-toed them off and shoved them aside as if they hadn't cost several hundred quid *a shoe*. She appeared to listen. 'Are you alone?'

'For a bit. George has gone with Granddad to the garden centre, and Zoe's downstairs with Granny Lydia making jam tarts. I've got an hour or so to myself.'

'You called her Zoe,' Stephanie noticed. 'You always call her Teddy.'

'It's George's nickname for her. I'm trying to train myself out of it. Things are going to get complicated at pre-school if she has two names. Did you want to go out to lunch, then?'

'Oh, no, thanks.' She grinned. 'I'd have to put my shoes back on.'

'I can make you a sandwich. Or there's some lentil soup Bill's dad made.'

'I don't want to put you to any trouble.'

'A girl has to eat. I was just going to make myself a cheese sandwich.'

'That would be heaven. I love cheese sandwiches.' She followed Joanna into the kitchen and watched as she made them. 'You grate the cheese,' she observed.

'The taste is on the edge. The more edges, the more taste. Also, you should always butter the bread. Butter is the flavour-vector.

I have a friend in America who uses mayonnaise instead. Big mistake. Huge.'

Stephanie smiled. 'You take sandwich-making seriously. I like that. Always do everything to the best of your ability. Otherwise, what's the point of doing it at all?'

'I agree with you in principle. But when there are children in the house, you sometimes have to cut corners just to get things done. Never mind the quality, feel the width. Shall we go out in the garden?'

It was warm, overcast, but the threatened rain had gone elsewhere, probably looking for a garden fete or a wedding to pee on. They sat at the table on the terrace. A blackbird was on the lawn, running and listening for worms, which must all have gone too far down in the dry spell. 'I keep meaning to buy an apple to chop up for them,' Joanna said, pinching off a bit of crust and throwing it. 'So, not that it isn't a pleasure to see you, but it's rather unexpected.'

Stephanie looked away for a moment. 'You see,' she said diffidently, 'I don't really have any girlfriends. And no sisters. Only child. So, no one I can really talk to.'

'If you mean *talk to* talk to, I wouldn't confide in my sisters. In the same way that I wouldn't use steel wool as a loofah.'

'I never really had friends at school, either. Too gawky, too serious. Good at lessons, bad at games. Fatal combination. I suppose you had lots of schoolfriends.'

'Are you kidding me? I played the violin. Though I have the last laugh, because there are musician chums I can talk to if the urge comes over me. And there's always Bill. He's a great listener.'

'Ah,' said Stephanie, significantly.

'This is about Jim, is it?'

'You've known him a long time. You probably know him better than me.'

'I doubt it,' Joanna said dryly. 'What's the problem?'

'Not a problem, exactly. Last night, he asked me to marry him.' She observed Joanna's reaction. 'You didn't know? I got the impression he'd told Bill he was going to. I assumed Bill would have told you.'

'Maybe he told him in confidence. Bill's terribly honourable. So, what did you say?'

'I said I had to think about it.'

'Ouch! Poor Jim.'

'Really?'

'I don't think he's ever proposed to anyone before. It must have taken a lot of screwing to the sticking-point for him.'

'Oh dear. I was afraid of that. The last thing I want to do is hurt him.'

'You don't want to marry him?'

She looked unhappy. 'I can't see the point.'

The Willans family lived in one of those tall Victorian houses with the semi-basement, originally the kitchen quarters but these days usually made into a separate flat. Inside, the house was home-like and welcoming, the edges worn comfortably soft, a faint smell of bacon left on the air from breakfast, and a slim marmalade cat who ran straight to Slider, tail erect, as though he knew him. Mrs Willans, who opened the door to him, had a lived-in face and a smile that started with the eyes. Slider liked her immediately.

'Oh, that poor, poor girl!' she said with feeling. 'I can't bear to think what her parents must be going through. Of course, we'll do anything we can to help.'

She led him along the passage – original Victorian patterned tiles, he noticed – to the kitchen at the back, where the door was open onto the garden, and a married daughter was tending to a chubby baby of about nine months, who was exercising her gums on a toast crust. They both smiled at Slider before they even knew who he was – whatever Mrs Willans had, it was being passed down the generations.

'This is Megan, and baby Poppy – they're staying with us while Megan's husband's away for his work. He's an engineer,' she added proudly. 'He's working on a bridge in Kenya. Kenton's not come down yet,' she went on. 'I'll go up and fetch him. He's very tired, poor boy, what with exams and . . . everything.' She nodded to convey that 'everything' included Rhianne's unexpected death.

Slider was not so sure about Mr Willans, who came in from the garden at that moment and scowled at the words. He was tall and bony like a superannuated horse, with small, hot blue eyes, a cheese-cutter nose, a disapproving mouth and a chin like a piece of pumice.

'Is he still in bed? Go and get him up at once, the lazy brat!'

'He needs his rest,' Mrs Willans protested gently. 'He's had a hard year, with his A levels. He worked very hard revising for them.'

'I should bloody well hope he did!' Mr Willans barked. 'It's *his* future that depends on them, nobody else's. Though I dare say you'd have done the revising *for* him if you could have! You do everything else for him.'

Mrs Willans gave Slider the sort of smile people give third parties when their partner is embarrassing them and disappeared.

'I used to get up at five o'clock every morning to do a paper round before school,' Mr Willans was saying. 'Nobody ever said *I* needed *my* rest. It's beyond me that you're supposed to treat him with kid gloves just because he's done a few routine exams. A levels these days are nowhere near as hard as when I did them. She seems to think he's some kind of hero for doing what he's supposed to do in his own selfish interests. It's not as if he's just ended world hunger or cured all known diseases. *And* I cleaned my own shoes!'

This last was evidently so frequently revisited a complaint it was like a smelly old family dog that had to be taken out for a walk at regular intervals but was otherwise ignored. The daughter, pottering peaceably, asked Slider if he'd like a cup of tea, while the baby gave him a ravishing smile and offered him the soggy end of her toast with such bountiful generosity it seemed that if anyone was going to end world hunger, it would be her.

Kenton came into the room wearing a T-shirt, trackie bottoms and the sticky look of someone who'd just woken up. He glared sulkily at his father and said without preamble, 'I wasn't in bed. I was reading.'

Mrs Willans hurried in after him. 'I expect you'd like to talk to Kenton alone,' she said to Slider with an air of throwing herself on a grenade. 'Why don't you go into the sitting room, where you can be private. Kenton, you lead the way for Mr . . . Inspector . . .'

Slider was used to people not knowing how to address him or

refer to him. He smiled reassuringly to her and followed the boy back along the passage and into a comfortably shabby room. Here Kenton stopped dead and turned to face Slider, though without meeting his eyes. Slider could see at once why he was That Boy. Even dishevelled, he was an Adonis, tall enough and nicely built, with the golden hair, the smouldering blue eyes, the cheekbones, the Grecian nose and the exquisitely carved, brooding mouth all present and correct. Interestingly, there was a distinct resemblance to his father, though his mother's input of genes had evidently softened the Easter Island granite façade into a more accessible beauty.

In the continued absence of eye contact, Slider had to open the batting. 'Your dad's a bit of a handful,' he suggested, inviting complicity.

Kenton wasn't complissing. He jammed both hands in his pockets and flung himself down on the sofa, slouched far back, spread-legged and chin down. Slider recognized the ploy. He was now supposed to loom over the boy and berate him, conferring on him the coveted status of victim. And all a victim had to do was endure, not actually say anything or contribute to the process.

Slider looked round, saw an upright chair by the door, fetched it over and sat facing Kenton and much more on his level. 'I expect your mum told you that you had to talk to me about Rhianne,' he said. 'This is a serious business, you know.'

'I know she's *dead*,' Kenton jerked out. 'I'm not *stupid!*'

It was said unnecessarily rudely, the attitude either of the insecure or of the over-secure. Given what looked like a hard-boiled father and soft-boiled mother, Slider thought it could actually, oddly, be both – which was a hard combination to develop through. And still he hadn't looked at Slider once.

'Let's lose the attitude, shall we,' Slider said firmly. 'You're over eighteen, you're not a child any more, you're an adult. Your parents aren't going to do this for you. So either you can answer my questions here, or you can come down to the station and sit in an interview room and we can do it that way.' The flicker of blue was a brief glance that said as clearly as words *you can't do that. Not to me.* Entitled youth. Slider went on, 'You should know that you're already in the police computer as a person of interest. That goes away if your answers are satisfactory. If I have to arrest you for refusing to co-operate, that stays on your record. So don't put a stain on your whole life, just because you want people to think you're James Dean.'

'Who's James Dean?' he asked contemptuously, but a degree less rudely.

'Bad-boy actor. Something like Johnny Depp,' he translated, 'only he died age twenty-four.'

He looked up at last. 'How?'

'Crashed his car driving too fast, because he was trying to look cool. How cool do you think he looked being dragged out of a mashed car with most of his bones snapped like toothpicks?' Kenton opened his mouth to answer, and Slider cashed in. 'Take your hands out of your pockets and sit up properly.' The boy was surprised into obeying. 'Now, tell me about Rhianne.'

Kenton chewed his lip. 'Is it true she got mixed up with a cult?'

'Who told you that?'

'I read it online. Some sort of religious sex cult. Like, with this charismatic leader. They groomed her. And she got too far in and, like, did away with herself.'

'There's no truth in any of that,' Slider said, a little wonderingly.

'Then, how—?'

Slider wasn't going there. He guessed he was going to have to ask specific questions to get answers and went with, 'How long did you go out with her?'

'Dunno. A few months,' Kenton said, compensating for the fact that he was having to answer by muttering as close to incomprehensibly as possible.

'When did you last see her?'

'Weeks ago. A month at least. We weren't still seeing each other.'

'Who ended it – her or you?'

'Her. But I would have anyway.'

'Why?'

He didn't want to answer that, and Slider's instincts pricked. His Slidey sense.

'Why?' he said again.

He said, after a pause, 'She was getting weird.'

'Weird in what way?' Slider insisted.

But Kenton only shrugged and began picking at a fingernail to avoid the moment.

Joanna didn't want to ask it, but she couldn't think of any other way to put it. 'But do you love him?'

Stephanie made a moue that acknowledged the yukkiness of the question and the deep water they were getting into. 'Well, yes, of course,' she said. 'Whatever "love" is.' Joanna had no idea if she was quoting or not. 'Why did you marry Bill?' Stephanie went on quickly.

'So as to be with him all the time – or as nearly all the time as possible.'

'But I can already see Jim as often as I want to.'

'Really? You a surgeon and him a policeman?'

'OK, there are times when our schedules get in the way. But they would anyway. And there are some logistics to work out—'

'But that's it, you see. At the end of the day, *we* both come home to the same place. We know we'll see each other.'

'I don't mind the working out,' Stephanie said. 'It's part of the fun.'

'But it's a waste of time when you could be together. All that travelling back and forth to each other's houses—'

Atherton's cats had found them. Vash jumped straight on to Joanna's lap with loud and pointed remarks about people going out into the garden without telling other people they were going, while Tig stood back and eyed the table with the unmistakeable air of judging the distance for a jump. Joanna had to put one arm round Vash and make a grab for Tig with the other. 'They both love cheese,' she apologized to Stephanie. 'It's their favourite thing. I'm afraid lust overcomes their good manners.'

'That's another thing, you see,' Stephanie said. 'Who would move in with who? His place is tiny, and I've got the two upper floors. There's no garden for the cats.'

'You could both sell, put your money together and buy somewhere that suited you both. That's what civilized people do. Jim's property's worth a decent bit now – you could buy somewhere bigger and fancier between you.'

'A bigger place would mean moving further out. I don't want to move further out.'

'There are some big places in Kensington.'

'But I like being able to walk to work.'

'It sounds to me as though you're trying to find reasons to turn him down,' Joanna said as delicately as possible. Stephanie looked stricken. 'Do you want to break up with him?'

'God, *no!*' she said with encouraging immediacy. 'But why can't we just go on as we are?'

'Time's wingèd chariot?' Joanna suggested. 'Don't you want to have children?'

'*God*, no!' A different emphasis this time.

'Does he know that?'

'We've never discussed it either way.' She looked thoughtful. 'Do you think, if I said I didn't want to get married, that he'd break it off?'

Joanna hesitated. 'I think he'd be devastated. He behaves like a lounge lizard at times, but he's surprisingly sensitive underneath. And, as I said, he's never proposed to anyone before.' They were silent for a while. Vash had curled up in Joanna's lap and was purring like an oil-fired generator. Tig had spotted Habeus taking a walk along the terrace and sauntered off to see if he could torment him. 'I never had any doubts about marrying Bill,' she said after a bit, in case it helped. 'We're two halves of the same thing – it didn't make any sense not to. And there came a time when children seemed to be the obvious next step.'

'And you don't regret having them?'

'Of course not!'

'No, obviously you'd say that – but your career? Haven't you had to choose between them and it?'

'I was never a high-flyer like you. Just a jobbing musician. Yes, there have been times when I've had to turn work down. But we're lucky having Bill's dad living in the granny flat, always ready to help.' She examined Stephanie's face. 'There's always help, you know, especially if you've got money.'

'Nannies?' Stephanie made an amused face. 'Do you really think I could trust Jim in the same house as a nubile nanny?'

Joanna knew she was joking. 'Choose a fat, spotty one,' she said with a grin. 'Look, I can't make up your mind for you. I can only say that at the end of a long day, with all the usual problems and frustrations, and the things – yes – that you have to give up, to know I can curl up in the same bed with my darling husband is the ultimate bliss. It's worth the whole entry price.'

'Mmm,' said Stephanie. 'Don't you ever long to get away by yourself?'

'I escape into music. Bill escapes into his job. The problem isn't never getting away from each other; it's getting enough time together. And you have your job. When you're doing it, doesn't it occupy your whole mind?'

'Oh yes. When I'm operating, the whole world is that one small open square in the surgical drapes.'

'Yes, it's like that when I'm playing. The dots are all there is. You couldn't drag my attention away with a five-pound lump hammer.'

'But then there's—'

At that moment they were interrupted by the arrival of Zoe running out from the house, followed by Lydia. 'Mummy, Mummy, I did made dam tarts,' she said ecstatically. 'They're for Daddy for tea.'

'Damn tarts is probably about right,' Joanna said. 'So where are they?'

'In the kitchen.' Zoe took in the presence of a visitor and became instantly silent and observant.

Joanna performed the introductions. 'Is your kitchen a war zone?' she asked Lydia.

'We tidied up,' Lydia said serenely. She was a very peaceful person to have around – nothing seemed to ruffle her. 'Quite a lot of the jam ended up in the tarts, really.'

Joanna examined her daughter's sticky condition. 'How did you get it in your hair? Don't go near Aunty Stephanie with those jammy hands.'

'Is she staying for tea?' Zoe asked, still staring. It was not, Joanna understood, rudeness, but wonder.

Luckily, Stephanie realized that too. 'Will there be enough jam tarts if I do?'

Zoe thought about it. 'No,' she said at last. 'They're for Daddy.'

Stephanie smiled and stood up. 'Then I'd better go.'

'But I spect there will be *one*,' Zoe amended, realizing the glorious visitor was about to escape. 'We did make a *lot*. Free and seven and some more.'

'But I really have to go. I have paperwork to finish,' Stephanie said. She was addressing Joanna, but Zoe took it to herself.

'My daddy does do paperwork,' she confided. 'But my mummy does do dots instead. You've got no shoes on. Your hair is pretty.'

Joanna saw Stephanie out, unsure whether she'd helped at all, or whether a preserve-bespattered toddler was the straw that would break the camel's back.

EIGHT
Cocaine Overture

Kenton didn't want to tell the story, and it took a lot of coaxing and oblique threats to get it out of him. He was used to being Old Man Kangaroo, very truly run after, and the story didn't play to his credit.

It had been exciting at first, being involved with Rhianne, because she was willing, actively wanted to have sex with him. Despite his looks and popularity, other girls would not go all the way. It was, Slider understood, the zeitgeist. Having a boyfriend was all about being seen with him at the right places, and the photos you could post about it. *X and me at Nando's, X and me at the Hard Rock Café, X and me having a laugh on Red-Nose Day.* Both of you looking handsome, perfectly presented, fun, enviable. There were no glamorous photographs to be extracted from 'doing it'. And there was a line to be drawn for the boy, too, because there were girls who would 'do it' who you nevertheless wouldn't want to admit to going out with. Rhianne, pretty and suitably middle class, had managed to combine sexual availability with respectability – at least at first.

But she had been getting weird, said Kenton, and he'd already started thinking he would have to break up with her.

'Weird in what way?'

'Well . . .'

It had been exciting at first when she suggested they watched porn together, but he had begun to get uneasy. It *was* kind of . . . not nice, really. Embarrassing, when you got over the first thrill. And then there was . . .

More coaxing was needed, and a bland assurance from Slider that he wasn't going to get into trouble, before he would admit the drugs. They had smoked the odd spliff together, and he didn't mind that – everyone did that – but she'd started talking about taking cocaine. He didn't want to go down that path, especially not with A levels coming up. But there were times when they were out together when she'd go to the ladies' and come back in a different mood, really hyper, and he'd suspected belatedly she'd been doing lines. Though she could be a lot of fun when she was *up*, she could also be really annoying. And then she'd get depressed when it wore off, very dark. He didn't like to think that what he'd supposed was her naturally wild, free character and avid readiness for sex might have been fuelled by the idiot dust.

'I thought,' he said, dragging the unwilling confession out of a deep well inside him, 'that she was mad about me, but then it turned out it was just the chaille, and I could have been anyone, and it . . . killed it. I didn't feel the same about her.'

Hurt pride, Slider thought. He'd found out that, contrary to what he'd been told for years by admiring handmaidens, he was not so much irresistible as available.

'I'd not really been seeing much of her anyway, since exams started,' he went on. 'I mean, we don't have to be in the school except when we've got an exam, unless we want to use the library or the computer room to study or whatever. And everybody's too wired to, like, socialize much.'

Exams had started mid-May and went on to the end of June, and in that time he'd only seen her a few times alone, and a few more in groups. 'So I don't really know what she was up to, or anything.'

Slider got the impression it was really pretty much over, and that Kenton was as much relieved as anything. He thought she might have been seeing someone else by then, anyway. Everything got messy during exam time – your whole future life was being decided and you couldn't concentrate on anything apart from those papers.

'But you still took her to the end-of-year dance,' Slider said. The don't-call-it-a-prom had taken place on the Saturday a week after the end of term, the 6th of July.

'Yeah, well, it'd been arranged a long time and she'd bought the dress and everything. I couldn't let her down.' There was decency in him yet, Slider thought. 'I'd not been in school since the week before, and I'd not spoken to her, so I gave her a ring to check if she still wanted to go with me, and she said yes. She said, "Don't you dare bail on me now," or something like that. I said of course I wouldn't, and she said OK then. We chatted a bit and it was OK, nice, and I half thought we might go on seeing each other. I thought maybe she'd just been weird cos of exams. I mean, everybody gets fraught around A levels. But then—' He stopped and reddened. 'She—'

'Yes?'

He looked away, now clasping his hands between his knees, his posture very different from the beginning. 'At the dance. She was acting mad, laughing and flirting with everyone, and sort of looking at me sideways as if she was doing it to annoy me and wanted to see me react. And then . . .'

'Go on.'

He didn't want to. 'She went off with somebody else,' he admitted at last. 'She said she was going to the loo, but she didn't come back, and I was worried, so I went looking for her. And I saw her leaving the hall with . . . with another guy. Arms round each other and giggling like maniacs.' Indignation overcame the shame of being ditched. 'I'd rented the tux and paid for the tickets and everything! And she just walked out with . . . someone else.'

'Who was it?'

'I don't know,' he muttered, sinking his chin into his chest again.

'I think you do,' Slider said.

'She was always going on about older guys being more cool, as if . . . as if—'

'Was it one of the teachers?' Slider guessed.

Kenton didn't answer immediately, plainly calculating whether to say it was, or whether that would involve him in further complications. 'No, it was just some . . . I didn't know who he was.' He was reddening again.

'This was a school dance. I don't think there would have been random strangers there. I think you do know who he is, but for some reason you don't want to tell me.'

No answer, just averted eyes and red cheeks. In his discomfort he looked younger than his years, no strutting love-god but a confused child needing someone to tell him what to do. Slider let him squirm under scrutiny for a bit and then said quietly,

'You're missing the bigger picture here, Kenton. Rhianne Morgan is dead. It's possible someone killed her.'

His eyes flew up, stunned and questioning. 'I thought—'

'You're *not* thinking; that's the whole point. This is about a lot more than your fractured love life.'

'But I'm sure he didn't do anything,' he said with appalled earnestness.

'That's not for you to say. If you get in the way of our investigation, you could be charged with perverting the course of justice. You can go to prison for that.' Kenton's lips trembled. 'Come on,' Slider appealed to the decent boy inside. 'She was a schoolmate and your girlfriend. You have to help her, now she can't help herself.'

'You don't understand,' he said, close to tears. 'I *can't* tell you. It's . . . he's—'

'Someone you know very well? A mate? You don't want to drop him in it? But he may not have done anything wrong. We need to know everything about Rhianne's last days. This person might have vital information.' Kenton was silent, thinking, cheeks red. That was the bummer about that fair, transparent complexion. 'Don't hang this out. You will tell me eventually, so just get it over with.'

Now he looked up, defiant and afraid. 'It's my brother. But you can't tell him I told you. He'd kill me. And you mustn't tell Mum and Dad. They . . . they've got enough to worry about, with Grandma not being well, and tuition fees and everything.'

The law said that an eighteen-year-old was an adult, but the world, seen through their eyes, could be at once enormous and terrifying, and laughably parochial. But still terrifying.

'I didn't know you had a brother,' Slider said mildly.

The Willans family was well spread in ages, owing to the periodical absences abroad of Mr Willans, who was a structural engineer like his son-in-law and had been employed in his salad days on big overseas projects like dams and bridges and power stations. The children represented periods back in England between contracts. Slider wondered whether his irritation stemmed from being cooped up at home after the wide open spaces of his youth. And controlling large and diverse workforces would have made him a disciplinarian and impatient of being disobeyed.

Married Megan was the eldest, at twenty-eight. There was another sister, Lauren, who was twenty-four and working as a party planner in New Orleans. Then came Corey, who was twenty-two, and was reading for a master's in electronic and electrical engineering at Brunel.

'Corey's Dad's favourite,' Kenton said with a touch of resentment. 'He wanted me to go in for engineering as well, but I'm not into that stuff. I want to do psychology. Dad says that's not worth paying uni fees for. He says if I *must* do it, I should take out a student loan, because I'll never earn enough with a psychology degree to have to pay it back. But Mum wants me to come out debt-free, like Corey and Megan did. Lauren didn't go to uni. She never really wanted to do anything in particular, but Dad never got on her case like he does on mine.'

No wonder there was tension between the parents, Slider thought. And to cap it all, the Golden Boy didn't even clean his own shoes!

Slider could see that Kenton believed that if Corey got into trouble over Rhianne, *he* would end up getting blamed for (a) having brought the undesirable connection into the family in the first place and (b) snitching on Corey to the police.

'How come Corey was at the dance?' Slider asked. 'Wasn't it for students only?'

'Oh, they let older brothers and sisters come, if they went to the school as well,' said Kenton. 'Mrs Price-Emmet – she's the deputy head – she thinks it makes it more sophisticated and better for the girls. And she thinks older siblings keep us from getting rowdy.'

'And why do you think Corey went off with Rhianne?'

'Just to bum me out,' Kenton said sulkily. 'He's always making fun of me. Calls me Pretty-boy. Says I don't want to do engineering cos I'm afraid of getting my hands dirty. Stuff like that. He gave me a Barbie doll for Christmas one time.' It burst out of him, in a hot flash. 'He pretended afterwards that he'd meant it for Lauren and put the wrong label on, but I saw him grinning at me and making, you know, gestures. He meant it all right.'

'Did you say anything to him about Rhianne?'

He looked away and shrugged. 'What's the point?' Then he added, tellingly, 'He's bigger than me. He was always thumping me when we were kids. Giving me Chinese burns and stuff. He's just a big bully!' Another hot burst. Then he recollected himself. 'I was going to break up with her anyway, so it's sucks to him.'

Slider remembered what Swilley had said about a twenty-two-year-old seeming like the epitome of sophistication to a seventeen-year-old girl. Could this have been the 'older man' Rhianne had boasted about?

'I think I had better have a talk with Corey,' he said and saw a look of satisfaction cross Kenton's face, closely followed by apprehension. *Yay, he's gonna get in trubb-ul!* Followed by, *No-oo, he's gonna thump me!* Family loyalty had deleted for him the idea that Corey might have been the one to hurt the girl.

Slider didn't have far to go to find Corey: he was living in the separate basement flat of the family house. It was another cause of resentment to Kenton, who intimated that Corey paid no rent for all that privacy and luxury, and that his tuition fees for his master's were also being covered, while Dad was making the biggest fuss about Kenton getting 'a free ride' at university, and thought it was funny to calculate at the supper table how much he was costing them in food and lodgings.

Corey Willans – stick a comma in that and he already sounded like an engineering firm, Slider thought – was at home, and despite its being considerably later than when he started his interview with Kenton, Slider could see when he answered the door that he had been in bed and quite possibly asleep when the doorbell rang.

The flat, accessed by the separate door down in the area, was dark and had the frowsty smell of a student pit. The door opened straight into what would have been the kitchen in the original house and was now a kitchen-living room, going all the way front to back, where a barred window high in the wall looked onto the retaining wall of the garden. The access to the garden was only from the floor above: Victorian servants weren't supposed to go out there. There was a closed door to the right of the room, which from experience Slider guessed would give onto the stairs to the upper floor, and to the left two half-open doors gave a glimpse of a tiny bedroom and tinier bathroom. It was a typical boy-flat, everything in shades of grey and navy, cluttered with unwashed clothes and unwashed dishes, smelling of trainers, cigarettes and, Slider thought, a faint whiff of cannabis. Corey stared at him stupidly until he showed his warrant card and introduced himself, upon which the eyes widened slightly and did a sideways flick that told Slider he was briefly wondering whether anything incriminating had been left in view.

'I'd like to talk to you about Rhianne Morgan,' he said.

Corey stared a moment, then said, 'I don't know who that is.' Slider mentally rubbed his hands. Along with the Eye-flick of Guilt, the Stupid Denial gave him something to work with. 'Can I come in?' he said and stood not upon the order of his entering but entered at once.

Corey followed him in, trying to work up some indignation. 'Oy! I never said . . . Look, you can't just—' he began.

He wasn't really dressed for a Grand Remonstrance, though, Slider thought, in a crumpled T-shirt printed with an image of a gorilla dressed as a US soldier and a pair of what might have been either boxers or swimming trunks in jolly Caribbean colours, with long hairy legs and bare feet at one end and a matted mop of hair and stubbly chin the other. In the looks lottery Corey had lost out to his younger brother, very much resembling his father, without the softening influence of his mother. The wedge of nose and grim mouth had come down to him without mitigation and gave him a commanding but not attractive face; while his hair was a nondescript colour and texture, far from the silky gold locks Kenton only had to shake to get attention.

His tone was somewhere between resentment and unease as he faced Slider and said, 'What's all this about? I haven't done anything.'

Slider looked down at the bare legs and saw the left knee start to jiggle. 'You were seen leaving the school dance last month with Rhianne Morgan, so it's no use pretending you didn't know her. Now, are you going to make this easy for yourself, or hard? We can talk here, or down at the station.'

He looked blank for a moment, thinking, then said, 'Look, can I get some clothes on? I feel a bit of a dork talking to you in my shreddies.' In what was obviously a completely unconscious gesture, he scratched under his balls, which had the effect of rearranging matters with unfortunate results.

Slider winced. 'You're showing brain, son. Go and put some pants on.'

Corey disappeared into the bedroom, and Slider had a quick look around. Among the dirty dishes on the kitchen table was a mess of unopened junk mail and what looked like some bills and official letters. On the sofa was a scatter of text books and notes, and on the coffee table in front of it a laptop and an overflowing ashtray. Next to that was a four-by-four-inch square of polished slate, the sort of thing you could buy in National Trust shops for a coaster. Why were the books not on the table? An image came to his mind, of Corey slouched comfortably on the sofa last night, feet up on the table, watching something on the laptop, joint between fingers and thumb, ashtray to hand. But a coaster? The coffee table was made of wood, certainly – a solid pine thing, obviously old and a bit battered, which he had no difficulty in imagining being bequeathed from the house upstairs – but was there anything about Corey to suggest he would worry about leaving a ring on it? Had the piece of slate some other purpose? You certainly wouldn't want to sniff anything off the table top for fear of getting a splinter up your nose. Slider crouched to get as close to the slate as possible without touching it and tilted his head this way and that to get the light on it at different angles. Yes, there was a faint dusting of something there.

A slight sound made him look up. Corey had come out of the bedroom, dressed in cotton trousers, a different T-shirt and trainers, and was staring at him in alarm. And as Slider rose to his feet, the lad bolted. He was right next to the front door, and Slider was at the other end of the room with furniture to negotiate, so he was out of the front door before Slider could reach him. What with the start, slamming the front door between them to slow pursuit, and mounting the steps out of the area three at a time, with his long legs, youth and panic, Corey was out of sight by the time Slider reached street level, and he could only run to the corner to see if there was any sign of him, which there wasn't.

*   *   *

Porson, back from Westminster, said wearily, 'The father's kicking up a pavlova about you interviewing his son without his permission. Wants to make an official complaint.'

'He's twenty-two,' Slider pointed out.

'Oh, I told him he'd got no grounds, but that sort don't take no for an answer. Says you upset his younger son as well, with "aggressive interview techniques".' He made hooked finger inverted commas in the air.

'Eighteen,' said Slider. 'And since Daddy wasn't in the room—'

'Don't sweat it. We'll talk him down. This Corey – he's a suspect now?'

'He knew the girl, and he had it away on his tiny toes. I'd like a warrant to search his flat before he comes back. And before his parents decide to go and tidy it up.'

'Yerss. If they don't have a spare key, my arse is an apricot,' Porson said. 'You've got a list of friends and family?'

'As far as it goes,' Slider said. 'The mother was trying to be helpful, but she doesn't really know who his friends are.'

'She's co-operating?'

'She's convinced of his entire innocence, so our talking to him holds no fears for her. It's interesting that the father's reaction is different.'

'I wouldn't read too much into that. He's the sort who'd sue you for pulling him out of a septic tank. So the younger boy – he's clear now?'

'He said he was at home on Tuesday afternoon and the mother confirms it. Of course, since he was up in his bedroom with the door shut, he could probably have sneaked out without her noticing, but I don't get the feeling he's who we're looking for.'

'Despite her cheating on him with his brother?'

'I think he was more relieved to be done with her than anything. No brooding, thwarted love there. His resentment of his brother predates Rhianne. And postdates it. No, I think Corey's more interesting.'

Porson sighed. 'Well, we've got the call out to all areas, and the photo circulating, but with everyone and his dog policing the march, he could get a long way before anyone spots him. You've got someone on the flat?'

'Yes. He might come home, of course – he didn't take anything

with him, clothes and so on. It'll say something about him if he
does. Meanwhile, if we can get the warrant, we'll toss his pad
– I'm pretty sure we'll find some charlie in there, which'll give
us something to hold him on – and start talking to people at
Brunel, see what we can find out about him.' Slider sighed too.
'I should have been more on my guard.'

'Don't beat yourself up,' Porson said. He grinned. 'Leave that
to Mr Carpenter – he'll do it better.' As Slider reached the door,
he said, 'Any juice in sweating the kid brother some more? It
was his girlfriend – he might have taken an interest.'

'Maybe. There's a lot of resentment there.'

'On the other hand, families can start pulling together if they
feel threatened from outside. I leave it to your judgement.'

The old man was making an unusual amount of sense this
afternoon, Slider thought.

'You don't want to stir up a hermit's nest,' Porson concluded.

'Right,' said Slider. He was a suppository of wisdom, all right.

'I can't believe I've got you at home for a whole Sunday,' Joanna
marvelled.

'Not much I can do until we nab Corey,' said Slider.
'Unfortunately, he left his mobile in the bedroom, or we could
track him that way.'

'What sort of a young person doesn't keep their phone on
them at all times?' Joanna said in shocked tones. 'He sounds a
desperate character.'

The beef was in the oven and filling the kitchen with a glorious
smell. Joanna was preparing vegetables, and Slider was whisking
the batter for the Yorkshires. From the drawing room, where
Lydia was playing some daft board game with the children, came
the lifting sounds of Teddy giggling and George saying 'It's not
fair! You're not doing it right!' Mr Slider was strolling in the
garden accompanied by Vash and Tig, who adored going for
walks, and Habeus and Jumper were sharing the latter's bed by
the French windows, having finally come to an accommodation.
All was well with the world.

'Do you think he could have done it?' Joanna asked.

'He's made himself interesting by legging it. Certainly he's
physically capable – he's twice Kenton's size. And looks as

though he's got a temper. According to Kenton, he's thumped him a lot. Apparently he used to torment him by suggesting he was – er – fond of musicals.'

'Too graceful? Light on his feet?'

'Doesn't follow the football, as it were.'

'And is he?'

'Who can say? He claims to have had a full-frontal relationship with Rhianne, anyway.'

Joanna chopped a carrot. 'Talking of people not being gay,' she said and told him about Stephanie's visit.

'Ought you to be telling me this?' Slider said, uncomfortably.

'She didn't say it was in confidence. In fact, she implied she believes you tell me everything, and vice versa.'

'I don't want to get involved with Atherton's personal life. I have to work with the man.'

'But he's your *friend*,' Joanna objected.

He was amused. 'I don't think you understand how friendship works for men.'

'Oh, I understand. You spend four hours in a pub with your best mate, talking, and still don't know his dog died.'

'But he'd still know I cared,' Slider said.

'A hand on the arm can be quite continental, but football is a man's best friend.'

'*A hand on the arm?* How demonstrative do you think I am? How did you leave it with Stephanie, anyway?'

'I thought you didn't want to know. I told her she should say yes.'

'What? You can't go round telling people to get married!' he said, aghast.

'Why not? Everyone should get married.'

'When people ask your advice, they don't actually want you to give any,' he told her firmly.

'She didn't ask my advice – she just wanted to confide. But I wasn't going to miss an opportunity to promote my favourite institution. You can stop beating that batter now.'

'Oh, now you're going to tell me how to make Yorkshire pudding?'

'You're so cute when you're laying down the law I was thinking of coming over there.'

'Put down the sharp knife first.'

They were interrupted by George's disapproving voice from the door. 'You're always kissing!'

Joanna looked at him over Slider's shoulder. 'Don't you ever knock?'

'Knock what?'

'Never mind. Did you want something?'

'I want to play Monopoly, but Teddy's too little. She doesn't do it properly. And Granny Lydia says two isn't enough.'

'We'll play a game of Monotony after lunch,' Joanna promised.

'It's Monopoly.'

'That's what I said. Go and see if you can help Granny Lydia lay the table.'

He looked suspicious. 'Are you going to kiss Daddy again?'

'I might. Any objections?'

'Kissing's yukky.'

'That's why I'm doing it, so you don't have to. You can thank me later. Now scoot.'

When he'd gone, Slider said, 'You'll give him a complex, telling him to scoot.'

'Children need hardships to overcome. It strengthens the character,' she said. 'Now, where was I?'

'If we didn't have lunch to get, I'd strengthen your character right now,' he said admiringly.

Gascoyne was not needed on Monday for the search for Corey Willans, so got on with his own to-do list. Next up was checking David Morgan's alibi for Tuesday afternoon. He went first to Blenheim Road, where the detached Edwardian houses were suitably palatial. There was residents' parking, which usually made things easier for policemen on a weekday, but so many people were working from home these days he had to go right to the end of the road to find a space and walk back. It was a wide, tree-lined street, though the trees were drooping from the recent lack of rain, their leaves yellowing already. Autumn was evidently going to come early this year. There was no For Sale sign outside the house, but they were often forbidden in this sort of area, or if not forbidden, frowned upon by the neighbours.

He was prepared to find no one in, but the door was opened by a tall, slim woman in her early forties, in dark grey cigarette pants and a garnet-red short-sleeved blouse. She was fair-skinned with classical features, a cloud of red-gold curls and bright blue eyes. Gascoyne presented his warrant card with a smile, and she examined it and his face with calm, intelligent eyes. She had private school and old money in every line of her body, and confidence was bred into her sort from childhood upwards. Naturally enough, most of Gascoyne's working life was spent among the guilty or the guilty-related, provoking fear, suspicion, hostility and not infrequently violence just by turning up. But to the likes of this woman, the police were there to protect and serve: they were no threat to peace of mind. She invited him in as a matter of course.

He followed her into the drawing room. The house was immaculate, smelling of furniture polish and lilies – there was a vase of them on the hall table – and full of the sort of furniture you inherited, Persian carpets and proper paintings on the walls. Everything glowed from the hand of a diligent and professional cleaner. The ceilings were high, the atmosphere was serene, there was no clutter anywhere. It was so swank, he thought, he could spoil it just by sitting down.

She invited him to sit. Her name was Diana Russell, and she was a Diana to the fingertips. 'It's lucky you came today,' she said. 'I only work from home on Mondays and Fridays.'

Gascoyne asked what her work was.

'I work at the Treasury,' she said. No surprise there, he thought. 'The part that deals with manpower and recruitment for the whole civil service. Used to be a separate department, but it was transferred to the Treasury in the early eighties. One of the cost-cutting programmes. So, what did you want to talk to me about?'

'It's peripheral to an ongoing investigation,' he said, his vocabulary getting an upgrade by contagion. 'I understand your house is on the market with the Buckfast's agency.'

She smiled apologetically. 'I'm afraid your information is out of date. It *was* on the market, but that was quite some time ago. Almost two years, I think, without checking.'

'It's not up for sale now?'

'No. You see, we were thinking of moving to the country, once

the children were off our hands, but first there were problems
with the chain for the house we'd found, and the vendors withdrew it, and then Clive – my husband – was offered a promotion
which would have made the commute unviable, so we decided
to stay put and took this house off the market.' She gave him a
look of puzzled enquiry. 'What *can* this be about?'

'We're looking into the recent actions of the manager of
Buckfast's local office, a David Morgan. Do you know him?'

'David Morgan,' she mused. 'I think that was the name of the
person I dealt with when we were thinking of selling. Dark-haired
man – rather good-looking?'

'That's the one. Have you seen him recently?'

'Well, no. I'd have no reason to. I didn't know him socially.
He came here to the house, I think, three or four times during
the process, to take details, take photographs, update us and so
on. He seemed a very pleasant man, certainly seemed very professional about his job. They produced a handsome brochure of the
house. We felt rather bad about withdrawing it after all that work.
But of course, that's priced into the fee. They certainly would
have made enough if we *had* sold. What has this person done?
Something fraudulent? I would never have taken him for a
criminal.'

'Oh, it's nothing like that. His daughter was found dead in
unexplained circumstances—'

'How dreadful! The poor man. You surely don't suspect—'

'We have to establish the whereabouts of everyone in cases
like this. It's purely routine.'

She wasn't buying it. 'But why did you think I might have
seen him? Why did you think this house was for sale again?'
Her eyes narrowed. 'What has he told you? Has he said something
about me?'

'Obviously a mistake has been made,' Gascoyne said, getting
up, with his most soothing smile. 'A mix-up of paperwork at the
agency. I'm sorry to have troubled you, Mrs Russell—'

'It's Lady Diana, actually,' she said, rising too, with a sort of
stately implacability, like a factory chimney demolition film in
reverse. 'And I really think I should speak to your senior officer.
The borough commander, isn't it?'

'There's really no need,' Gascoyne said, working his favourite-nephew vibe to the hilt, while inwardly cursing Morgan for picking this particular unwitting shill. 'I assure you there is nothing to worry about. This was a routine enquiry and obviously based on some out-of-date information. Please don't concern yourself about it for a moment.'

He extracted himself without further comment from her, but he had the feeling that, rather than dismissing the whole incident from her mind, she was keeping her powder dry for a more worthy target.

The IT man, Jason Adebayo, would never be mistaken for a nerd. He was appallingly handsome, with a sculpted bod, shining gold-hazel eyes like a wild cat, and his pale-brown hair, with highlights, was done in witty blown-out dreads, like Sideshow Bob's cooler younger brother. He looked as though he ought to be stalking through one of those movie adverts for high-end male fragrances. Jenrich told him he could have been a model and earned a seven-figure salary. He gave her one of his straight-to-camera smiles and said he *did* earn a seven-figure salary – it was just that two of the figures came after the decimal point.

'Sorry it's taken so long,' he said, reporting to Slider, 'but we're absolutely snowed under, what with this march and Special Branch investigating the protest leaders. Hammersmith did say yours was only unexplained death, not murder, so it wasn't top priority.'

'They said that, did they?'

'So I'm told,' he said with a bright smile. 'Anyway, there's nothing immediately alerting to tell you about. The usual teenage chat back and forth with friends who check out from the list. Lots of stuff posted on Instagram. She used Hinge a bit, but just to chat – they call it flirting – without any apparent intention of meeting in person. They do that a lot nowadays,' he added informatively. 'We've checked the latest contacts there and there's nothing suspicious about them. I've listed them with their online data if you want to chase them up. List of all phone contacts in and out for you to follow up if you need to. Phone data shows she answered a WhatsApp at 2.26 on the Tuesday, but there's no activity of any sort after that, on the phone or online.'

'Right,' said Slider.

'I've copied all the Insta photos and videos for the last three months onto a firestick for you, but content going back further is available if you want it,' said Adebayo. 'Nothing noteworthy in online searches. Shopping sites, celebrity news, a lot of fashion sites – nothing sinister. She used to play Candy Crush and 2048 a lot but seems to have dropped them in the last eight weeks.' He grinned. 'Maybe A levels took priority? Anyway, I'll leave all this with you. If there's anything more I can do, let me know. Still unexplained death, is it? I haven't seen any more about it in the media, and the online chatter has lost interest. I expect you're glad about that.'

'It never helps,' Slider acknowledged

So she was alive at 2.26, Slider mused, and David Morgan found her dead at 4.30. That was pretty much as Freddie Cameron had said. She hadn't been surfing the web when her caller arrived. She'd been on the lounger in the garden leafing through magazines at some point. Waiting for him to arrive? Or had she not known, when the doorbell rang, who it was? Or had he known about the unlockable gate and come in that way? Surely not a random stranger, or there would have been some evidence of a struggle. Surely she knew him. She'd let him in or led him from the garden into the kitchen. She'd let him in, with a spliff and condoms in her bedside drawer upstairs – but whatever she was expecting, it was not that her defective heart was about to conk out on her.

Gascoyne went straight from Bedford Park to the Emlyn Road address and was not surprised to find no For Sale board there either. An elderly couple, the Lewises, received him at the front door with deep suspicion, not allayed in the slightest by his warrant card. 'No offence, young man, but things like this are easy enough to forge,' said Mr Lewis, handing it back with an air of wanting to wipe his hand down his trousers.

'Only you hear things all the time,' said Mrs Lewis from behind him, peering over his shoulder.

'If you would like to telephone the police station, they will confirm who I am,' said Gascoyne.

'We haven't got the number,' she said with minor triumph.

'You could look it up,' he suggested.

'We haven't got a telephone directory,' said Mr Lewis.
'Anyway, what's this about?'

'We're very busy,' Mrs Lewis said. 'Getting ready for our son
to visit. He'll be here any moment. He's a lawyer. A criminal
lawyer.'

From the faintly annoyed look that crossed Mr Lewis's face,
Gascoyne guessed this was pure invention. He wondered why
she hadn't said he was a heavyweight boxer. Or an FBI agent.

'It's really nothing to worry about,' Gascoyne said, in soothing
mode again. 'It's about your house being for sale with Buckfast's,
the estate agents.'

'It's not,' she said with sharp triumph. 'It's not for sale at all.
I don't know where you get your information from—'

'We *bought* it from Buckfast's,' Mr Lewis said, with careful
clarity, as if dealing with the intellectually confused. 'Bought,
not sold. A year ago.'

'More than a year,' she corrected. 'It was April last year we
moved in.' She didn't say, *so there*! But it was implied. 'And I
think it's disgraceful that you come round here harassing decent,
law-abiding people instead of chasing criminals! A car was broken
into on Wendell Road just last week, and what have you done
about it? Nothing! You hardly feel safe in your bed any more.'

'You should do your house-hunting on your own time,' Mr
Lewis said, tacking off across the wind. 'Remember it's people
like us that pay your wages. I think I should complain to your
superintendent about this. Wasting police time,' he added, from
some memory of legal jargon.

'And not even in uniform,' Mrs Lewis complained. 'How do
we know you're really the police? I think I should ring 999,
Douglas.'

In a last attempt to get off the rocks, Gascoyne brought up a
photograph of David Morgan on his phone. 'Do you recognize
this man?'

Mr Lewis peered at it, but Mrs Lewis said immediately and
without looking, 'Who's that, one of your accomplices?'

'No, I don't know him,' said Mr Lewis. 'Never seen him before
in my life. Who is he? He looks like an actor.'

'Is he that one in the advert for Gold Blend?' Mrs Lewis asked.
'We don't watch the adverts. We prefer BBC. Are you an actor?

I think I've seen you in something. Were you in *Casualty* last week? One of the ambulance drivers.'

'No, Mavis, he says he's a policeman,' Mr Lewis said in the same extra-clear tone, whose origin Gascoyne now understood. 'He wants to buy our house. But it's not for sale, young man, so please go away.'

It was as much a relief to Gascoyne as to them when they closed the door firmly on him and prevented any further conversation.

NINE
The Science of the Lambs

Atherton was in late, with the morning off in lieu of the overtime on Saturday. Slider caught him up on the Corey Willans situation, and what Jason Adebayo had reported. 'Oh, joy,' he said. 'Now we have to trawl through this tiresome girl's tedious teenage twitterings for clues. Memes, jokes, GIFs and bantz. Why didn't I listen to my mother and join the Fire Brigade?'

'What are you so grouchy about?' Slider said.

'My love life is up on bricks,' said Atherton. 'She turned me down.'

'She did?' Slider refrained from saying *that's not what Joanna told me*.

'Not exactly. She said she had to think about it. Which is worse.'

'How is it worse?'

'It's the pity refusal. Softening the blow. Breaking it gently. "Stand up all those boys whose mothers are alive. You can sit down, Jones."'

Slider shook his head. 'You're such a drama queen. She's not a gooey-eyed teenager. She's a grown woman with an independent life. Of *course* she'll need to think about it.'

'A "yes in principle, details to follow" would have been acceptable.' Atherton sighed. 'I'd better take my cats back.'

'No, don't do that,' said Slider. 'They've settled in, and the children love having them. I'll keep them until Stephanie gives you an answer. Don't want you begging me to take them back again so you can have a post-acceptance honeymoon weekend.'

'If you insist. So we're after the big brother now, are we?'

'He who ups and runs away, we must track another day,' Slider misquoted. 'You'd better get over to Brunel and talk to people about him, interview his tutors, get the lay of the land.'

'That used to be my sobriquet – the Lay of the Land,' Atherton said, turning away.

'Your modesty will be your downfall, you know,' Slider said in valediction.

Gascoyne was almost apologetic as he explained that David Morgan's alibi had been blown out of the water. 'He lied to us,' he concluded. 'And I was feeling sorry for the bastard.'

'Not just lied,' Slider said. 'It wasn't a slip of the tongue or a heat of the moment panic. This was a thought out, here's one I prepared earlier, false alibi. Which means he's got something he's anxious to hide. Damnit.'

'But what about Corey Willans?'

Wasn't it always the way, Slider thought. You wait ages for a suspect, then two come along at once. 'Obviously we have to find him too. But Morgan has to be favourite.' He drummed his fingers on the desk a moment, thinking how best to proceed. 'Bring him in,' he concluded.

'Arrest him, guv?'

'Try not to. Only if he won't come voluntarily. And take Swilley with you to talk to the wife. She may have something interesting to say once she thinks he's a suspect.'

David Morgan had gone to work.

'I didn't want him to,' said Rita. 'It's too soon. But he said he couldn't sit around doing nothing – it was driving him crazy. He needed to take his mind off. Mine's never off. I'd like to go to work myself, but I'm just too tired.' She looked up at Swilley hopelessly. 'Funny, isn't it? I keep falling asleep all the time, but I'm still so tired I can hardly get my legs moving.'

'It's a natural reaction,' Swilley said kindly.

'Is it?' she said.

Swilley threw a look at Gascoyne and jerked her head towards the door. 'Why don't I make you a cup of tea?' she said to Rita.

'I'll leave you to it, then,' Gascoyne said obediently. He wasn't sorry to have to beard Morgan at work – he was less likely to make a fuss there, in front of work colleagues.

*   *   *

The atmosphere was taut inside Buckfast's, with everyone at their desks clattering on their keyboards and so deliberately *not* looking at David, at his desk at the back of the room, it was like a form of abuse. He looked as though he had lost a stone and gained a decade, but he was properly groomed and dressed for work, though it was not clear if he was actually doing any. He was staring at his computer screen, but his hands weren't moving, and his gaze was blank. Gascoyne doubted he was actually seeing anything in front of him.

He walked down between the desks with all the heads turning like owls. David didn't look up until he was actually in front of him, and then it was as if he didn't recognize him. Gascoyne leaned in a little and spoke quietly, not to be overheard. 'Would you mind coming down to the station with me, sir? My governor would like to have a word with you.'

'What about?' It seemed an automatic reaction rather than a real question.

'Just something that's come up. Would you mind coming now? I've got the car outside.'

Morgan looked past him down the office and Gascoyne practically heard the heads snapping back. The subtext of *you don't want to talk about private stuff in front of this lot* was working. 'All right,' he said.

Morgan led the way out without looking to the left or right, and when Gascoyne turned to close the street door behind them, everyone had already swivelled into gossip position. *That'll be splattered all over social media by teatime*, Gascoyne thought. Like the results of forgetting to put the lid on before turning on the Magimix. Things had been so much easier when people had to ring the local paper and talk to someone.

Rita sat at the kitchen table and watched Swilley moving about making the tea. Gradually her dazed state lightened until she was able to take an interest – the effect, Swilley knew, of having someone else take responsibility for a little while.

'How do you know where to find things?' Rita asked at last.

'It's not my first rodeo,' Swilley said, pouring from the kettle onto teabags in mugs.

Rita digested this. 'You mean . . . I suppose you often have to make tea for . . . for upset people? It must be a terrible job, yours.'

'It has its moments,' Swilley said. 'Milk and sugar?'

'Just milk, ta. Got to watch my figure.'

'I won't ask about biscuits, then.' Swilley tried a small smile. Rita didn't respond. Her mind was working again. 'Why do you want to speak to David?' she asked.

'Oh, just something that's come up, something that wants clarifying.' Swilley put the mugs down and sat opposite Rita. 'I hope that's all right. I guessed you'd like it strong.'

'Clarifying about what?' Rita persisted

'About his whereabouts on Tuesday.'

Tuesday? The day Ree . . . died? He was at work. You know that.'

'Well, not the whole time. He left the office for a time in the afternoon.'

Rita stared as intently at Swilley as a dog trying to work out self-assembly instructions. 'You're not trying to pin something on him, are you?' she said at last. 'You're not suspecting him of something?'

'We're just trying to collect all the facts,' Swilley said. 'And we have to check everything. We checked that *you* were at work that day.'

'Me? But I'm her mother. You checked up on *me*?'

'You wouldn't want us *not* to check everything, would you? You wouldn't want us *not* to be thorough, when it's your daughter?'

'No, I see you'd have to be thorough. But David?' Rita was no mug, now her engine was running. 'I s'pose you always have to think like that, when it's a stepfather. But it wasn't like that. David loved her like his own. He would never, never . . . OK, he's got a temper, but he would never deliberately hurt anyone.'

'He's never, in a moment of anger, gone too far? Even though he regretted it later?'

Rita's mouth hardened. 'I'm not even going to answer anything that stupid.'

'I notice, for instance, that you have a bruise on your forehead.'

Rita's hand rose automatically to touch it. 'I banged my head on the cupboard door.' She stared at Swilley. 'It was that cupboard up there, where you just got the teabags out of. I was trying to reach the new packet of salt at the back, and I knocked the teabag tin over, and it fell on the floor. I bent down to pick it up, and as I stood up I banged my head on the open door. You don't believe me? Ask David—' She stopped abruptly.

Swilley sipped tea, creating the silence for her to fall into.

Rita went on. 'I've got so clumsy, since Rhianne died. I keep dropping things and bumping into things. I'm so *tired*. And forgetful. I go into a room and can't remember what I went in for. I went to make myself a sandwich for lunch and forgot to butter the bread. Then I couldn't find the cheese. I'd taken it out of the fridge and put it down somewhere. I found it on top of the microwave. And *then* I went to call up the stairs to Rhianne to see if she wanted anything.' She looked at Swilley hopelessly. 'When does it end? I don't want to go on feeling like this. But then, I don't want to get to where it's ordinary that she died. To where it doesn't matter any more.'

'You never get to there,' Swilley said, in spite of herself.

'No, I s'pose not.' She returned doggedly to the point. 'What do you want to talk to David about?'

Time to inject a little doubt. 'He wasn't where he said he was on Tuesday afternoon.'

Swilley witnessed Rita's little shock, but she quickly rallied. 'He'd have gone out for work, something to do with work, that's all. I'm telling you, he would never have harmed a hair of her head. He's a *good* man.'

Swilley nodded non-committally. It was classic Stockholm Syndrome, of course, where the abused continue to protect the abuser against their own interests. The caged bird that won't escape even when you leave the cage door open.

Brunel University, just outside Uxbridge, was a jumble of modern edifices, including an unusually large number of residential build-ings – most London colleges were non-campus, making accom-modation one of the biggest problems. It meant that there were always lots of people about. Even in August there were interna-tional summer schools, so the place was still humming. On a good day there were sixteen-thousand-odd students, over fourteen hundred academic staff and over fifty administrative staff milling about. It was going to be near impossible to track any one person's movements, Atherton realized.

At the main reception building he learned that with the regular students down, many of the academic staff were on holiday. He was directed eventually to the Bannerman Centre, which contained the main student centre and the library, to meet the senior PGR programmes administrator – PGR, he learned, stood for Post-graduate Research. Mrs Broomfield was a woman in her early fifties with a wild mass of curly dark hair, heavy-lidded brown eyes and lots of teeth, who reminded Atherton of Lleanor Bron in her heyday. She met him in the Bannerman foyer area, a bleak space of strip lighting, dreary industrial-grade carpet and light-oak-veneer woodwork, like a modern hospital, and led him to another area, similar but with one or two of those meagre bucket armchairs you get in airport lounges, in which you can neither lounge nor sit upright, which send a subliminal message to the sitter to get up and go and do something more useful.

'You understand,' she said, when Atherton explained his visit, 'that PGR students aren't like undergraduates. They spend their time researching, reading and writing under their own steam, and come and go as they like. We don't have routine contact with them, like tutorials and seminars. We're here to help and advise rather than supervise.'

Shown a photo of Corey, she recollected seeing him around once or twice. She understood he was bright and likely to get a good grade, but she had no other knowledge of him. The programmes administrator with nominal oversight of him, Bob Bachelor, was on holiday and would not be back until September. When Corey was on campus, she said, he was most likely to be found either in the Hamilton Centre, where the shops, bars, restaurants and function rooms were, or here in Bannerman, which housed the library, computer rooms, research commons and PDC.

'Professional Development Centre,' she translated for Atherton. 'Reference books, information and advice on possible future applications of one's degree.'

'Like a careers office,' Atherton said.

'Something like that.'

At his request, she gave him a quick tour of the facilities, which proved to be a series of enormous rooms in the same modernist style, with acres of carpet, plenty of computers, thousands of books and no security cameras. In the PDC there was an information desk that was always manned with at least two people, but otherwise it was a haven of peace and anonymity.

David Morgan had come out of his dark reverie on the way to the station, and when Slider came into the interview room with Jenrich, he met them with an alert and grim look. 'What's all this about?' he asked. 'Am I under arrest for something?'

'Not at all,' Slider said. 'You're helping us with our enquiries. You're free to leave at any time.'

He stood up. 'In that case, I'm going.'

'But I wouldn't, if I were you,' Slider said. 'Investigation has thrown up some disturbing anomalies in your account of yourself, which I really think you want to clear up.'

'And if I don't?'

'Mr Morgan, you want to help us find out what happened to your daughter, don't you? Because if you don't, the question arises, why?'

'Is that a threat?'

'An observation. Please sit down and answer some questions. I'd much sooner you did it voluntarily.'

He digested that and sat down. 'It sounds like a threat to me.'

'What can I have to threaten you with?' Slider said. 'I'm sure there's some simple explanation.'

'For what?'

Slider let Jenrich take it. She opened the file she had brought in with her and fixed Morgan with her chilliest gaze. 'You told us that on Tuesday afternoon you visited two houses in the course of your normal duties, two houses that were for sale with the Buckfast agency.'

A tremor of the mouth was all that gave him away. Otherwise his control was rigid. 'What about it?'

Jenrich went on. 'The householders of both houses have said that you did not visit them on that day.'

'We don't always see the owners on these visits,' he said. 'They may have been out at work. They often are. They leave the keys with us so we can show prospective buyers round in their absence.'

It was a good effort. It sounded firm and natural. The professional enlightening a layman about the intricacies of his craft.

Jenrich shook her head. 'They were there, all right. But you weren't. In fact, Mr Morgan, neither house is actually up for sale.'

He had no answer for that. He was thrown back on bluster. 'What are you trying to say?'

'I'm not trying to say it; I'm saying it,' Jenrich said. 'You were not where you said you were. You gave us an alibi which is false from start to finish.'

'Why would I need an alibi if I haven't done anything?'

'Exactly my question, Mr Morgan. Where were you on Tuesday afternoon, and what were you doing?'

'I refuse to answer that. You've no right to ask me.'

Slider took it back. 'Mr Morgan, I don't think you realize how serious this is. Lying to the police is an offence in itself, and in the case of a sudden, unexplained death, it becomes a real problem for you.'

Morgan closed his lips tight and turned his head away.

'You see,' Slider went on, 'if it was the case that you lost your temper – and we all know how annoying teenagers can be – and really didn't mean to hurt her . . . A momentary loss of control that you bitterly regret . . . That's one thing. That could go down as manslaughter.'

He left a pause, but Morgan didn't speak. Slider hardened his tone. 'On the other hand, what we have here looks like a deliberate attempt to deceive, a false alibi concocted in advance, which suggests intent. And intent means a different and much graver crime. Intent means murder. This is your chance to clear things up, tell us the truth, put your side of the story. I can't emphasize enough how important that is.'

No answer.

'It's a time-limited offer, Mr Morgan. Take the opportunity now, before you dig yourself into an even deeper hole.'

Morgan unsealed his lips, but only to say, 'I'm not talking to you. Leave me alone. I haven't done anything.' He folded his arms across his chest and stared at the wall.

Slider stood up, and Jenrich with him. 'I'm going to leave you alone for a while to think about things.'

'I want to go home,' Morgan said.

'If you try to leave, I will have to arrest you,' Slider said.

That shocked Morgan, who opened his mouth and closed it again, and stared at Slider with concern as well as anger. It was hearing it said aloud, Slider thought. He must have known that was what the threat was all along, but the reality hadn't hit home. 'I'll be back,' Slider said, 'and I hope to find you in a more co-operative mood.'

Outside, Jenrich said, 'He's guilty, boss. I can smell it. How stupid is he, to put up an alibi that's so easy to break?'

'The trouble will be to prove anything,' Slider said. 'He found the body, but he was at home, where he had every right to be. He admits he moved the body, but for nominally a good reason. Unless we can trace his movements and prove he went home earlier than he said he did . . . And even then, it doesn't prove he killed her. Unless he breaks and confesses, all we've got against him is the false alibi.'

'There'll be something,' Jenrich said grimly. 'There's always something.'

That was determination, not confidence. 'There isn't always.'

'Then we'll break him,' she said.

'You think he might fall down the stairs on the way to the cells? Or accidentally brutally beat himself up with a telephone directory?'

'The cells aren't down any stairs,' Jenrich said. 'And there aren't any telephone directories any more. It's all online.'

'When did life become so complicated?' Slider mourned.

It took a lot of talking for Atherton to get the mobile number of Corey's programmes administrator out of the Brunel records department. The woman in charge kept citing the Data Protection Act, at first resentfully then anxiously, to refuse to reveal anything so intimate. *I'll get into trouble*, she didn't say. *I am trouble*, Atherton didn't reply. There was a wss-wss-wss confabulation between her and her boss of the sort where they kept watching Atherton with hostility as they whispered. Eventually a query was directed higher up by internal telephone and permission came down, and the number was grudgingly yielded.

Bob Bachelor, when he answered Atherton's call, was somewhere out of doors and windy, with a dog barking in the background. 'Lake District,' he shouted. 'We come every year for the walking. Walla Crag to Ashness Bridge today. Sophie, *sit*! Wait a minute till I get out of the wind – I can hardly hear you.'

There was a good deal of rustling and banging and the submarine echo-sounder noise of the wind hitting the phone's mic, and then a relative calm, some muted conversation and finally Bachelor's voice coming over clearly, with a background puttering of rain on leaves 'Just got under a tree. It's raining cats and dogs here. Now, start again. You're who?'

Atherton introduced himself again and outlined the problem.

'Good God, why should I have any idea where he is? I don't socialize with my students. I get enough of them inside the college. Besides, he's postgrad. They're autonomous adults.'

'I appreciate that, but I thought you might know who his closest friends are, from having seen him with them around the campus. I know how observant you academics are.'

Bachelor accepted the flattery uncritically. 'It's not a matter of observing; I simply don't see him except for one-on-one supervisory meetings, and then the talk is academic. However,' he went on at the last minute as Atherton drew breath to end the call, 'he is working on a mechatronics project with another postgrad, Nick Runcorn. They spend a lot of time in the lab together, so he'd probably know more about him and who his friends are. But you'll probably find he's holed up with a girlfriend,' he added.

'He has a girlfriend?'

'Bound to have. They're all at it like knives. I would be, in their place. Last moments of freedom before reality clicks in and it's job, mortgage, wife and kids until they put you in a box.'

Cheerful fellow, Atherton thought, as he rang off. *I'd definitely turn to him for tender sympathy and advice.*

In a stroke of luck Nicholas Runcorn, whose phone number Bachelor was able to furnish from his mobile's contacts file, turned out to be on campus working and agreed to meet Atherton in a café in the Hamilton Centre. He came in looking grumpy, with a small rucksack over his shoulder, wearing cargo pants and a black T-shirt printed with the image of a floppy disk saying, 'I am your father' to a USB drive that was crying, 'Noooo!' Nerd humour, Atherton thought. He was tall and skinny and awkward-looking, with one of those bodies that seemed to be made entirely of knees. He had short-cut red hair, a pale, freckled face and features that, while by no means grotesque, looked slightly misshapen, as though he was a nice-looking boy who'd been left too near a radiator before he was properly set.

'This is not really convenient, you know,' he opened, when he had identified Atherton. 'I was in the middle of something. You can get a lot done in vacation when it's quiet.'

'It is lunchtime,' Atherton suggested. The smell of toasted cheese was in the air.

'I don't bother with lunch,' Runcorn said loftily.

'Well, I appreciate your time. I'll try not to keep you long,' Atherton said. 'You're lucky not to need a vacation job,' he added as Runcorn folded ungracefully onto a chair, like a giraffe getting down to drink at a water hole.

'I do have one, as a matter of fact,' he said resentfully. 'I work evenings in a bar, so I can keep my days free for this.' He dumped the rucksack beside his chair as if it was 'this'. Atherton supposed he had his notes in it. 'So, what do you want to know about Corey?'

'He's a friend of yours?' Atherton asked.

A snort. 'Hardly! We're working together on a project, that's all. Outside of that, I have nothing to do with him.'

'You don't like him?'

His eyes slid away. 'We have different interests.'

Atherton had the feeling that was not what he had been going to say. 'What are his interests that you don't share?'

'We're different people,' Runcorn stonewalled stubbornly.

Atherton leaned forward. 'Come on, help me out here. You obviously don't like the guy. I need to get a handle on him. What's wrong with him?'

'I don't like the people he hangs out with,' Runcorn said at last, reluctantly.

'And who are they?'

He frowned, licked his lips – which, though thin, were a curi-
ously deep pink, as though he'd been sucking a raspberry lolly
– and said, 'The rowdy lot. Loud and rough. There's always some
on every campus. Overgrown undergrads. You know the sort I
mean.' Atherton continued to look enquiring, and Runcorn went
on, trying to sound grown-up and responsible. 'Look, I don't
want to grass on somebody, and it's none of my business if he
wants to waste his time drinking and taking drugs. He can make
fun of me all he likes – it's water off a duck's back. We'll see
who's still laughing when I get a distinction and a top job, and
he barely scrapes through and ends up servicing my car.'

'In what way does he make fun of you?'

He shrugged. 'Oh, calling me nerd and geek and so on. As if
I care.'

'Is that all?'

Now he blushed. 'And saying I've never had a girlfriend –
which is *not* true, by the way. I just happen to treat women
with respect, as equals. What's wrong with that? And if I'd
sooner have a proper relationship than meaningless hook-ups,
does that make me some kind of a freak? What he did to Shan
Halligan was virtually date-rape. Getting her to take drugs and
then forcing himself on her. I tried to get her to report him. I
said it was her duty. I said, people who do that sort of thing
will do it again unless they're stopped, but she just wouldn't.
She's so . . . *nice*. Unworldly. Well, that's what makes it worse,
of course. I'd have reported him myself, but she begged me not
to, and . . . well . . .'

'Shan Halligan,' Atherton said, making a note of the name. 'Who
is she?'

'One of the postgrads. She's doing a master's on dense suspen-
sions rheology. I see her around.'

'Is she his girlfriend?'

He snorted again. 'He's not the sort to have girlfriends.
One-night stand is more his style. He doesn't care about any of
them – treats them like dirt. I tried to get her to see that, but she
still has a thing for him and won't listen. I can't understand it.
Why do girls always fall for the bad guys?'

He stared at Atherton moodily, and Atherton divined that Shan
Halligan was at the bottom of the antipathy, preferring the

unworthy Corey Willans to a decent chap like Runcorn who would worship at her feet.

'Women are funny like that,' he said, sympathetic man-to-man. 'Do you think she would know where Willans might be hiding?'

He looked alarmed. 'You don't think he's with her, do you? Surely even she wouldn't harbour a . . . what is it he's done, again?'

'We don't know that he's done anything. We think he might be a witness, and we really want to get hold of him and find out what he knows. So if you can help us find him – give me the names of people he hangs out with . . .'

He thought about it. 'It wouldn't come back on me, would it? I mean, you wouldn't tell him I'd told you? Because he's a big bloke, and scrappy, and I'm not . . . well, I'm, not the physical type. And I've got a ton of work for my master's – I can't afford to take time off sick if he came and beat me up.'

'Just give me names and addresses,' Atherton said soothingly. 'I won't bring your name into it.'

'And you won't get Shan into trouble? You'd think doing engineering she'd be tougher, but she's really . . . I mean, she's no match for him.'

'She won't get into trouble,' said Atherton.

Not through him, anyway. *The Assyrian came down like the wolf on the fold,* he thought. Corey Willans, ruthless predator: nerds and romantic girls were all lambs to him.

Slider went up to the canteen for a late lunch. Porson was there, sitting at a table in lonely splendour as befitted his bossness, and waved to him to join him, so Slider carried his cottage pie, peas and carrots but *no gravy* across and sat down.

Porson had opted for the braised beef and colcannon. He poked at it moodily and said, 'Looks like bubble and squeak to me. Why've they changed the name?'

'It's Irish, so I suppose they think it sounds sexier.'

'But they stopped calling stew Irish stew because it was supposed to be cultural appropriation or something. What's that about?'

'Beats me,' Slider said.

Porson sighed. 'I can't keep up with all this stuff, what you're supposed to say and not supposed to say.'

'You were at Hammersmith this morning?' Slider guessed. It never did anything for Porson's mood.

'Good news is they're not focused on the Morgan case, now that social media has lost interest.'

A new story had grabbed the yellow jersey over the weekend, about a schoolteacher romancing a pupil. The teacher was female and the pupil a boy, which was a nice twist to start with, but a chat site had gone one better and suggested the boy was actually a transitioning girl, and a frenzy had taken over.

'Luckily the mainstream press hasn't picked up on it,' Slider said, referring to their own case.

'Nothing to pick,' Porson said, but not as if it pleased him. 'We've not exactly got a prefola of clues, have we? How're you getting on with Morgan?'

'He's refusing to talk. On the other hand, he's not asking to go home any more. Seems to be gripped by apathy. He hasn't even asked for a solicitor.'

'Hmph. That's a bit of a two-edged wossname. "No solicitor" can bite you in the arse further down the line. Still, if he's happy where he is, so be it. We'll keep him a bit longer. Give him time to think. If it was an accident, he might realize it's better to cop to it now than be forced into it when it's Hobson's chance.'

'That was my thinking.'

They ate in silence for a few moments, then Porson said, 'What about the other suspect?'

'He's getting more interesting. The search of his flat has turned up a wrap of cocaine, a bag of marijuana and some unlabelled pills we have to get analysed. Also his laptop screen wasn't password-protected, so they were able to look at his browsing history. Quite a lot of porn our boy was viewing.'

'Oh?'

'Not the very bad stuff, I'm glad to say, but unhealthy in terms of quantity if not quality.'

'Any more trouble from the parents?'

'The father was shouting on the phone earlier on, until I told him about the drugs. Then he went quiet. I didn't mention the porn – keeping that in reserve in case he starts up again.'

'So you think he's tasty for it – the lad?'

Slider hesitated. 'I still think Morgan is the more likely suspect. On the other hand,' he went on, 'there's this "older man" she said she was seeing. That could be Corey Willans.'

'It could be any bloody one,' Porson said irritably. 'You've got two suspects already. Then there's the younger brother – what's his name? Kenton. He could have sneaked out without his mum knowing. And who knows who else she was seeing? Uncle Tom Cobley and all. This case is a mess.'

'Atherton's looking into Corey's background. Maybe something will firm up there.'

'Maybe butters no parsnips,' Porson retorted.

'Or Morgan might confess.'

'So might Dunnit Duncan. You just better make sure all your ducks are on the same page before you charge anyone.' He took another forkful of food, and then sighed. 'I'm thinking of chucking it in.'

Slider was startled. 'Sir?'

'This is between you and me. Strictly sub jaundicy. I've not floated it with anyone yet. But you know my daughter's moved down to Bath. She's suggested I take early retirement and go down there too. Settle near her.'

Slider read his face in the silence that followed. The Old Man had been devoted to his wife, and since she died it must have been desperately lonely for him. His only other family was Moira, his daughter. Slider had met her once. She was a nice, sensible woman, very fond of her dad, and not at all prone to mangling language.

'We'd all miss you, sir,' Slider said. He meant it – not only on a personal level, but because anyone they got in Porson's place was likely to be in the modern style, a thrusting young go-getter on the lines of Mr Carpenter, the borough commander, a *Guardian*-reading graduate eager for promotion at any cost. Porson protected them as far as possible against the shit-shower from on high, but a new man would be all pro-shit. Under Old King Log the frogs did all right. Young King Stork would pick them off one by one.

'Well, nothing's decided yet,' Porson said, snapping out of it. 'It might come to nothing, so don't say anything to anyone. I just thought you deserved a heads up.'

'Appreciate it, sir.'

Porson grinned suddenly. 'Give you a chance to make sure your paperwork's all up to date. New broom coming in would go through everything with a five-tooth comb.'

'Blessed are the pure in heart, sir,' Slider said stoutly.

Porson's grin widened. 'For you can see right through 'em.'

TEN
Ice Cold, With Malice

Shan Halligan was at her holiday job, working in a branch of Zara in the Westfields Centre. A fellow worker pointed her out, with a look of interest and blatant curiosity, but when Atherton introduced himself, Shan looked only alarmed.

She was a plump girl with the prettiness of youth that fades with maturity, that of firm flesh, clear skin and shiny hair. Her hair was fawn, long and straight, and she was dressed in exaggeratedly fashionable clothes – perhaps a requirement of the job – with a low-cut and off-the-shoulder top revealing her full bust, a tight micro-skirt and heavy black lace-up ankle boots with clunky heels that seemed to anchor her to the floor and suggested if she was pushed, she would simply right herself like a Wobbly Man.

She inspected Atherton's warrant card and looked up in moist-eyed fear. 'How do I know this is genuine?'

'You can ring the station and ask about me. They'll confirm who I am.'

She was very cautious, would not take the number from him, but Googled the station, and stood at a distance from him to ring it. She held a conversation with someone at the other end, watching him over her shoulder, and he heard her ask for a description of him as well. Finally she came back and said, 'It seems to be all right. But can we talk outside? I don't want people here listening.'

So they passed out onto the teeming pseudo-street of the shopping mall and found an unoccupied bench at a little distance. There were lots of people around, but all busy with their own concerns, and between their indifference and the echoey background noise, of clacking feet, conversation and piped music, they were as private as if they were alone.

Shan Halligan was still wary. 'What do you want to know about Corey?' she asked. 'Is he in trouble?'

'We need to talk to him, and we can't find him. I hoped you'd know where he was, as you're his girlfriend.'

'Who told you that?'

'Nick Runcorn said you were.'

'Oh, Nick! You don't want to listen to him. He's sort of stuck on me, and he gets stupidly jealous if anyone else even talks to me. As if I'd ever go out with him!' She rolled her eyes.

'But you *were* going out with Corey Willans?'

'Was. At one time. Not any more.' She was a girl who seemed to have an excess of moisture in her, which had to come out Her skin looked damp, her eyes were watery, even her hair looked like some kind of water-borne growth. Now as she denied Corey her eyes flooded.

'You chucked him?' Atherton suggested considerately.

'He chucked me,' she admitted, and wiped her nose on the back of her hand. 'He's such a *dick*! He won't even speak to me when we pass each other at college. He pretends he doesn't see me. I mean, who *does* that? After we've been, you know . . .'

'Intimate?'

She turned her head away slightly and shrugged.

'I was told there was an incident between you, when he forced himself on you. Tantamount to date-rape, I was told.'

Her head swung back. 'Bloody Nick again, I suppose? I wish I'd never told him, but I was upset at the time. I just had to tell someone, and I thought *he*'d understand. But he just went on about dobbing Corey in and how it was my duty to other women.'

'Tell me what happened, between you and Corey.'

'I don't want to,' she muttered, staring down, eyes moistening again.

'It's important, or I wouldn't ask you. He forced you to take drugs?'

'He didn't *force* me. He had some charlie and he wanted me to do it with him, but I don't do drugs – I think it's stupid. I said no, and he didn't try and make me.'

She wasn't telling him everything. Obviously she wanted to but needed coaxing. 'Did he have something else as well?' he tried. 'Maybe some E?'

She avoided his eyes. 'He had some dope. Hash, you know.

He said to try it. He said don't be boring.' That was obviously a telling point – what girl didn't want to be thought cool by the man she admired? 'He said you can't say you don't like it if you've never tried it. And it's not illegal or anything.' She looked at him at that point, for emphasis.

'Actually, it is,' Atherton said. 'But go on.'

'Well, I didn't know,' she said anxiously. 'He said it wasn't, or I wouldn't have tried it. It made me feel very sick – I hated it. I felt sort of sick and woozy. But then after a bit it must've worn off because I felt all right.'

'And then you had sex with him. Did he make you?' Atherton asked.

She shook her head and muttered something, looking down.

'What did he do? You can tell me. Was it something you didn't like?'

She looked up, damply. 'He wanted to tie me up. Tie my hands to the bedhead. I didn't want to. I was scared. But he said don't be lame; it's only a game. He said it wouldn't be a proper knot; I could pull free at any time. I . . . I didn't want to be uncool and spoil the mood. So I said OK.'

'What did he use to tie you?'

'A couple of scarves – like, he said they wouldn't leave marks. And then—'

'You had sex.'

She shrugged. 'S'pose so,' she muttered. 'But then—'

'Go on.'

'I wanted to get up, but I couldn't free my hands. It *was* a knot. And I got scared and told him to untie me.' Her cheeks flamed, and her eyes filled. 'And then I saw his mate, Reece, in the doorway. I don't know how long he'd been there.'

'You didn't know he was in the house?'

'It was Reece's flat. Like, the three of us had been for a drink before, but when we got back, Corey and me went into the bedroom and Reece stayed in the living room. He was s'posed to be watching telly. It was never meant to be . . . nobody said anything about—'

'A threesome?'

She nodded. 'Corey said Reece wanted to do it too. And then I got really scared and started struggling. I couldn't pull my

hands free, and Corey just laughed, and I started screaming. Then
he got scared and untied me and told me to shush, the neighbours'd
hear. I was upset and crying and everything. I said I wanted to
go home, and he called me an Uber while I got dressed and I
went home and that was that. After that he never rang me again,
and when I saw him at college he pretended not to see me. I
mean, that's so cold. How could anyone be like that? As if
nothing'd happened. It's like he hated me for what *he*'d done to
me. He's, like, inhuman!'

'Why didn't you report him?' Atherton asked.

'Who to? The police? It wasn't as if . . . I couldn't say I didn't
do it of my own accord, could I? And . . .' A pause and gulp. 'I
was embarrassed to talk about it.'

'You talked about it to Nick.'

'He doesn't count. I couldn't talk about it to an official person,
a stranger. It'd be humiliating. And I didn't want to get him into
trouble.'

'Really?'

'He's . . . I thought he . . .' A tear escaped and she wiped it
off her cheek with a finger and swiped her nose over the back
of her hand again. 'I told Nick, and he was all like, you've got
to go to the police, and they'll send him to jail, and I didn't want
that. I just wanted to forget it, really.' She lapsed into silence,
staring at her thoughts, and Atherton gave her a moment. Then
she looked up and said, 'Has he done it again, to someone else,
like Nick said? Is he in trouble?'

'We need to talk to him, that's all. We think he has some
information we need. Can you think of anyone he might be holed
up with?'

She hesitated. Obviously it was as Nick had said – she was
still stuck on Corey. 'I don't want to get him into trouble.'

'He dumped you,' Atherton reminded her. 'You said what a
dick he is.'

'Yeah,' she said, on a long exhale. 'He's probably dossing
with Reece. They're best mates. They're always going round
together. Reece Gibbons.'

'Can you give me his address and phone number?' Atherton
asked.

*   *   *

Atherton went back to the station from Westfields to report progress and walked into the cloud of gloom always generated by Borough Commander Carpenter – the fly in the sandwich, the wasp at the picnic of policing. He was in Slider's office, looming over him, with Porson at his heel. Atherton knew the guv didn't like to be loomed over. Carpenter must have commanded him to sit down, or he wouldn't have put himself at that disadvantage. Atherton did a nifty, not to say balletic, reverse from the doorway between the CID room and Slider's, and listened out of sight. In the CID room heads were down in ostentatious diligence.

'Remind me again why you're spending so much time on this?' Carpenter was saying.

'A young woman is dead, sir,' Slider said stonily.

'For all we know, from natural causes,' Carpenter said.

'With a ligature mark round her neck?'

'Did she die from being strangled?'

'Indirectly.'

'Indirectly! Or not at all. Was she raped? Interfered with in any way? No,' he answered his own question. 'For all you know, she was fooling around, trying on the scarf to see how it looked, pulled it too tight herself.'

Slider didn't roll his eyes. 'But then who took the scarf off?'

'Probably the father, and he forgot to mention it. In the emotion of the moment. Have you arrested him?'

'No, sir.'

'No, sir,' Carpenter mocked. 'Because you haven't got enough evidence against him. Or any evidence at all, when it comes right down to it. Is this a good use of taxpayers' money, persecuting a grieving parent whose child turned out to have a fatal heart weakness, unbeknownst to anyone?'

He actually said 'unbeknownst', Atherton marvelled.

'You have to think of the optics, Slider. And the optics are not good.'

'Optics are not my concern—' Slider began.

'Well, they bloody well ought to be! And they're certainly mine. We serve the public, and the public deserve to know that we are allocating scarce police resources in the optimum possible way. I'm not having this run on and on, the way some of your cases have, when your only suspect is a bereaved father and you've no reason to suspect him of anything.'

'He lied about his whereabouts,' Slider said, 'not only to us, but beforehand, to his office colleagues, which suggests an alibi set up beforehand for a purpose. That makes it intent.'

'Intent to do what?' Carpenter asked impatiently.

'That's what we have to find out,' said Slider.

'We can't do nothing, Mike,' Porson intervened. 'What if it turns out Morgan was an abuser, and we hadn't checked where he was that day? How would that look? The optics'd stink.'

'Have you got any evidence he was an abuser?'

'That's what we've got to find out,' said Porson doggedly.

There was a silence, then Carpenter said, 'All right, you can have a few days more. But handle him carefully. Everything by the book. I don't want another complaint of wrongful arrest and an expensive settlement, or an even more expensive court case. You know how litigious people are these days. And our lords and masters like nothing better than sticking it to the police.'

Silence fell, and Atherton went to the other door and looked out, to see the backs of Carpenter and Porson retreating down the corridor, with Porson talking urgently and in a low voice as he bobbed like a working tug beside Carpenter's luxury liner at full steam ahead.

'She's coming in after work to make a statement,' Atherton concluded. 'Morgan's still not talking?'

'He's sunk into a lethargy again,' Slider said. He drummed his fingers on the edge of his desk in thought.

'If he's not asking to go home, that's handy for us, isn't it?' Atherton said. 'We don't have to arrest him.'

'A night in the cells might make him think better about co-operating,' Slider said. 'But there's the "optics" to think about, if he *is* innocent.'

'Nobody's entirely innocent. He's probably glad to get away from his wife for a bit. Did Swilley get anything out of her?'

'She's still sticking by him, though she's sporting an interesting bruise on the forehead. Said she hit it on a cupboard door, but Swilley doesn't believe it.'

'If he's been knocking her about, she must be having doubts

about him and Rhianne by now. Maybe she should come in and visit him.'

Conversations between husband and wife when they didn't know they were being listened to could be revealing.

'Hmm. But if she persuades him to come home with her—'

'Then we arrest him for the alibi. Gives us a bit of time, anyway.'

'We don't have much. You heard what Mr Carpenter said.'

'How did you know I was listening?'

'Saw you duck out of the doorway. Who do you think you are, The Shadow?'

'Huh?'

'You've never heard of The Shadow? Comic book detective? He made himself invisible by hypnotising people so they couldn't see him.'

'I love it! I want to be him!'

'He hid behind a secret identity as Lamont Cranston, a globe-trotting millionaire playboy.'

'But that's me! From now on, call me Lamont.'

'You need to get out less. And hadn't you better go and find this Reece Whatsit bloke and see if he's got Corey stashed in his pad?'

'Javohl, mein commandant.' Atherton saluted and turned away.

'Go get 'em, Lamont,' Slider said.

Reece Gibbons's flat was in an ugly 1970s block in Acton Town. It probably hadn't been much to look at when it was new, but now shabbiness and neglect were adding to its disfavour. Atherton had taken Funky Lœssop with him as cover, because he didn't look like a policeman, let alone a detective. The instinct was proved good when the door to Gibbons's flat was opened by a bleary Corey Willans, whose momentary lack of wariness was enough for Lœssop to insert himself into the doorway before Corey spotted Atherton, said, 'Oh bollocks!' and tried to close it.

Atherton put his shoulder behind Lœssop, and they entered as one, as Corey backed so fast down the passage he lost balance and sat down hard on the floor. They stopped to allow him to get up, rather than help him and risk a cry of assault. He was looking frowsy, his hair a mess, his chin unshaven, his eyes gummy – though he was wearing a clean pair of trackie bots and an oversized T-shirt with the Motorhead warpig logo, presumably borrowed from his mate. The flat smelled of stale living, feet, takeaways, cigarettes and marijuana.

On his feet again, Corey backed before them. 'Look, this is not my flat,' he said. 'It's Reece's. He's going to be well pissed off if he hears the po-po have been in.'

'He's not here, then?' Atherton asked.

'He's at work.'

He had nowhere further to back except into the living room, which was in semi-gloom with crooked curtains drawn across the window. A battered sofa faced the television, which was showing a movie: Jason Statham was in a disused warehouse, fighting off six villains who, fortunately, had not worked out the benefits of combined assault and took turns to attack him individually and get a fist in the face or a fire extinguisher in the bread basket.

Between sofa and telly was a coffee table covered with lager cans, fast food litter and ashtrays, on one of which a joint was smouldering and about to go out.

Lœssop looked at it and grinned. 'Well, take a goosey at that,' he said.

'It's not mine!' Corey protested at once. 'I told you, this is not my flat. Everything in here is Reece's.'

'And he's smoking weed remotely, is he?' Atherton said. 'Zoom doping – that's a new one on me.'

Corey looked both arrogant and sulky. 'What d'you want, anyway? You can't come busting in here like that. It's a free country.'

'We can when we have a warrant for your arrest,' Atherton said.

'Yeah, man, you're busted,' Lœssop translated for the hard of thinking. 'Possession of charlie and weed, which we found in your gaff.'

Corey swallowed, but his arrogance intensified. 'They're not mine. My parents have got a key to my flat. It hangs on a hook in the hall with all the others.'

'You surely can't be claiming that your parents have planted drugs in your flat?' Atherton asked.

'Well, Kenton could've taken the key any time, gone down there to party.'

'Your little brother Kenton? You want to stick it on him?' Atherton said with wide contempt. 'I suppose he was smoking that spliff as well. Hiding under the sofa, is he? Corey Willans, you are under arrest for the possession of Class A drugs. You do not need to say anything . . .'

He continued with the caution and only when he had completed it did Corey's façade crack, and he turned in one surprising moment from spit-in-your-eye arrogant twenty-something to cringing six-year-old jam-stealer. 'Don't tell my dad,' he begged. 'He'll kill me. Please don't tell my dad.'

Atherton almost felt sorry for him. He offered him a counter irritant. 'We also want to talk to you about your possible involvement in the death of Rhianne Morgan.'

His eyes widened. 'Dude. That's some next-level shit,' he breathed.

'It is,' Atherton agreed. 'It really is.'

On the screen, Mr Statham sent the last villain flying head-crunchingly into a wall to slide down it into unconsciousness. Hero six, villains nil.

Rita Morgan had put on a smart jersey dress and high heels to come to the police station, almost as if she was going to a wedding, but she looked worn to a thread and exhausted. Still, she managed to look around the soft room with curiosity and faint disapproval, as though she might stalk across and run a finger along the top of the picture frames. She glanced at Slider, but it was Swilley she addressed. Their cup of tea moment earlier that day had created a connection. 'I don't understand why I'm here. And why have you arrested my husband?' she said with a gallant attempt at attitude.

'We haven't arrested him,' Swilley said, but added, 'Yet. He's helping us with our enquiries. But, frankly, he's not being very helpful. He's refusing to talk to us. And we hoped you might be able to change his mind.'

'I've no influence on him,' Rita said at once.

'I'm sure that's not the case,' Swilley replied swiftly. 'Even if it's not direct, a wife modifies her husband's behaviour. That's why marriage is so important.'

She seemed slightly flattered by this assessment, but said, though less certainly, 'He won't change his mind about something just because I say so. He's very stubborn. If you disagree with him, it just makes him more determined. Rhianne's the same way – tell her she can't do something—' She broke off.

'It must have been hard for you,' Swilley went on sympathetically, 'two stubborn people in one house. I bet they were locking horns all the time – and you in the middle trying to calm things down.'

'I know what you're trying to do,' Rita said. 'Trying to turn me against him. Well, it won't work.'

'Of course not,' Swilley said, 'That's the last thing. I want you to help him. You always help him, don't you? Like that time they had the screaming row out in the garden, and you were the one to shut them up and get them indoors, so the neighbours wouldn't complain.'

'They did anyway – nosy articles,' she said bitterly. 'I reckon they stand there with a tumbler pressed to the wall, listening to every word we say. Nothing better to do. But it wasn't a screaming row,' she rallied. 'Just a bit of an argument. Raised voices, that was all. And I told you before, it was Ree went for her dad – he was just holding her off. He didn't hurt her.'

'I understand. But there were a lot of rows between them, weren't there – two headstrong, stubborn people with opposite views?'

'David's not headstrong. He's an adult; he's entitled to have views. And Ree's just a girl, starting out, finding out what she thinks about things. You have to go through it. Kids challenge their parents all the time – that's how they learn. My dad was always lamping my brother—' She broke off again. She stared at Swilley, then Slider, then Swilley again. 'Don't you trick me into saying things, then count it against me! David never hit Rhianne. He loved her. And she loved him. *I* was the one gave her a tap now and then, just a little tap on the hand when she was being unreasonable, just to get her attention, never to hurt her. But David, never. He wouldn't.'

'All the more reason, then, for you to help us by helping him. Make him talk to us. Because if he goes on with this silent treatment, we'll have to arrest him, and then things get very serious.'

'Arrest him for what?' she asked, the shrillness of her voice saying she *knew* what. Oh yes, she knew all right.

Swilley didn't answer directly. She looked at Rita steadily for a moment, and then said, 'I've been looking into Rhianne's medical history.'

Slider saw Rita's scalp shift backwards, tightening her eyes. 'You done what?' she said harshly.

'Presented at A&E aged ten with cuts and abrasion and a broken rib—'

'She fell off her bike!' Rita cried. 'David bought that for her – she loved it. Kids always fall off their bikes when they're learning. And it wasn't a broken rib; it was just cracked.'

'You remember the incident very clearly.'

'I'm her mother! Of course I remember it! And it wasn't an "incident" as you call it. She was trying to copy the boys in the street, riding her bike up on the kerb and down again at full speed, and she got in a tangle and came off. Cracked her rib against the kerb edge, scraped her knees and an elbow on the pavement. She was late learning to ride a bike because Phil and I couldn't afford to buy her one. She never had one till I married David. She'd always wanted one. She was so excited when she got it for Christmas.'

'And then there was a broken arm when she was fourteen,' Swilley went on impassively.

'She'd climbed up a tree, just to annoy her dad, because he'd said not to. I told you, telling her "no" just made her more stubborn. The more he told her to come down, the higher she climbed, and then a branch broke and down she came – which was just what he'd warned her about. We were having a picnic in Richmond Park, and we had to cut it short and get her to A&E. We'd been having a lovely day out and it was all spoiled.'

'What about the incident just two years ago, where she presented with a dislocated shoulder?'

'She fell down the stairs!' Rita cried.

'And a possible fractured cheekbone.'

'It wasn't fractured. They ruled that out. It was just a bruise.' She stared at Swilley's silence. 'You think he *hit* her? She fell down the stairs, I tell you! All right, she was drunk. She'd come home later than she was allowed, and she was clearly drunk, and

David gave her hell – shouting at her, I mean, nothing else,' she amended hastily, 'and she tried to run off up the stairs and slipped, or staggered, or something, and fell. Her arm got caught between the banisters – that's what dislocated it – and she must've hit her face on one of the stairs.' She rose to her feet, impelled by anger. 'I'm sick of this! You make all these allegations. Kids hurt themselves all the time, doesn't mean anyone's mistreating them. They fall off their bikes! They fall over! Do you stick every dad in a cell every time a kid turns up with a grazed knee or a cut lip?'

'Every kid doesn't end up dead,' Swilley said.

Rita blanched but kept fighting. She turned to Slider now. 'I've seen how this works. Some kids are more accident-prone than others, but some social worker gets a bee in her bonnet and starts writing down every little normal cut and bruise and suddenly the parents are abusers! Good, decent people get their kids taken away and their lives ruined and get called criminals and have to go into hiding from the press, and there's nothing there! Nothing! You give a dog a bad name and hang him!' She was panting with rage and distress now. 'Three times we had to take Ree to A&E. Three times in ten years!'

Swilley spoke in a tone of calm reasonableness. 'Not every blow leads to a hospital visit. In these cases the abuser generally knows how to hit without leaving a mark.'

'Don't you call him that! Don't you call him an abuser!'

'Mrs Morgan,' Slider said, 'your husband was unaccounted for at the very time your daughter died, and he won't tell us where he was. More than that, he made up a false alibi, and he made it up beforehand. Not afterwards in a moment of panic, but *before* the time of her death.'

She sat down, the energy drained out of her. 'What are you saying?'

'That possibly he had a reason to want her out of the way. That possibly there was a history of abuse, and maybe she was threatening to blow the whistle on him. He made an excuse to leave work, went home, knowing she'd be there—'

'No!' she cried out in a voice of unbearable pain. 'He would never!'

'Then talk to him,' Slider said. 'Make him understand he has to tell us what went on that day. I can't conceal from you that it's looking bad for him. Make him see he has to tell his side of the story if there's to be any mitigation.'

'You've made up your minds he did it,' she said bitterly. 'You wouldn't talk about "mitigation" if you hadn't. You want to pin this on him – him who loved her like his own.'

'Talk some sense into him.' Swilley took over. 'Please. You said he was stubborn, but this is the wrong time and the wrong place for it. Just talk to him.'

'She's good,' Swilley said, as they watched through the window of the pokey. 'Look at her! You'd think she really believes he's innocent.'

'Maybe she *does* really believe he's innocent,' Gascoyne said.

'They always know. Deep down, they always know,' Swilley said. 'How could you not? I'll never understand a woman who prioritizes her husband over her kid.'

'Maybe he *is* innocent,' Gascoyne persisted, worriedly.

'Shush!' Jenrich said. 'I want to hear.'

'Please,' Rita was saying. 'Just tell them where you were, and all this will go away.'

Morgan didn't look at her. His face was set and grim. 'Don't be so naïve,' he said. 'It won't go away. Once they decide you're guilty, they don't let go. They get you one way or the other. Go home, Rita. Distance yourself. Save something from the wreck.'

'How can you *talk* like that?' she cried. 'I don't want to distance myself. I want you to come home with me. I've lost Ree – I can't lose you as well. For God's sake, David, just tell them the truth! They can't prove you did it if you didn't.'

He shook his head. 'You believe that, you'll believe anything.'

'David, please! I can't go on like this!' She was crying now.

But he went on shaking his head, staring at nothing, shoulders slumped.

'He's not going to crack yet,' Swilley said. 'But he will.'

'Well, I don't believe it,' Atherton said. 'My money's on Corey Willans. He's a ripe little bastard. He'd rob a blind beggar for the fun of it.'

'You can't get over Morgan's false alibi,' Swilley said. 'That makes it intent.'

'You can't really believe he set up an alibi so he could go home and murder his stepdaughter in cold blood. In broad daylight?'

'Maybe he didn't intend to kill her, just give her a good shaking,' LaSalle said.

'Then he wouldn't need the elaborate alibi,' said Atherton. 'Anyway, why would he kill her, then go away for a couple of hours and come back?'

'He was waiting for someone else to find her, Swilley said impatiently. 'He expected to get the shocked phone call. When it didn't come, he couldn't stand the waiting, his nerve broke and he went home to "find" her himself.' She did the inverted commas on the air.

'But that's not typical abuser pattern,' Gascoyne said. 'When they do kill, it's usually in the course of their usual abuse – they go too far, not actually meaning to kill. Or meaning to, but in the heat of the moment. They don't plan it.'

'But if she was threatening to blow the whistle on him . . .' Swilley began.

'That's pure speculation on your part,' said Atherton. 'You've got nothing to go on.'

'She told her friend she'd seen him with another woman and braced him with it.'

'That's not the same as abuse.'

'It's an added cause.'

'Whereas Corey Willans has a history of violence towards women—'

'That's an over-statement.'

'—and he's a drug user, so he's out of his gourd half the time. It's much more likely to be him.'

'I agree he's the more likely suspect,' Gascoyne said cautiously.

'He's certainly got some questions to answer,' Slider said.

'Which I shall happily put to him as soon as he's been processed.'

'Speaking of processing,' Porson said from the doorway, startling them all, 'I think we have to arrest Morgan, now we've got these old injuries in the basket as well. It might just shock him enough to cough. And get him a brief, whether he wants one or not. Can't go any further with this voluntary shit. It'll come back to bite us.'

'Yes, sir,' said Slider.

Porson eyed him. 'You look like you've woken up at your own autopsy. What's the problem?'

'I don't like it. His attitude smells all wrong to me.'

'Drama.' Porson dismissed it. 'He's watching himself playing the dying swan. Take away his audience and he'll be like a fish out of school. Who's his solicitor?'

'I doubt if he's got one on tap,' Slider said. 'He's never been in trouble before.'

'But he's an estate agent,' Swilley pointed out. 'He probably knows lots.'

'Not criminal briefs.'

'Meanwhile,' Atherton said, 'I've got a toerag festering nicely, waiting to be grilled.'

'Grilled toerag?' Slider murmured, pained.

Porson looked disapproving. 'I don't like this business of running two suspects at once. How sure are you about him?'

'I'd put my money on him,' Atherton said.

ELEVEN

Some Days You're the Dog, Other Days You're the Bone

Corey used his permitted phone call to contact his mate Reece. Why he thought Reece uniquely qualified to deal with all the ramifications of arrest was not clear – perhaps he simply felt he owed him an explanation – but Reece evidently had less confidence in his own grasp of the situation and phoned Corey's parents. As a result, Willans senior had come flying full steam to the station almost before the handset was cold. In his righteous rage he looked about seven feet tall and hewn out of pure sarsen. If he'd time travelled back five thousand years, they'd have had him on the rollers and on the way to Salisbury Plain before you could say flint knife.

Slider sent Jenrich to deal with him. She was pure steel and used stone to sharpen herself on.

'I demand to see my son! You've no right to lock him up without informing me!'

'The procedures and rights of arrest are clearly defined by legislation. You'll find them all laid out on the Metropolitan Police website. And he's an adult.'

'He's still my boy, and I want to see him.'

'Later it might be possible. At the moment, you can't.' Her eyes were burning blue and implacable.

His nostrils flared. 'This is outrageous! I'll speak to my MP! I'll take this all the way to the Home Secretary! I'm a taxpayer; I pay your wages. You can't keep me from seeing my own child.'

'Who is an adult,' Jenrich said again, with the patience of the unassailably right. 'Procedures were followed to the letter, Mr Willans. There's nothing for you to object to here.'

'We'll see about that! If anything the slightest bit improper has happened, you'll answer for it. All of you. Has he got a solicitor?'

'Not yet.'

'Ha! You're denying him his rights!' Willans said with premature triumph.

'Not at all. He'll have one as soon as he asks for one.'

'From some pool of local failures, no doubt. Tell him I'm sending him someone. My son is going to have the best. I'm not having him represented by some junior hack with no experience and no prospects. Tell him not to answer any questions until he has the proper support.'

'He has been told he doesn't have to answer questions without a solicitor present,' she said.

'You had better be sure everyone concerned knows that. If I hear anyone's been bullying my boy or putting pressure on him, heads will roll.' The nostrils got another workout. 'And, by the way, I don't like your attitude, young lady. You haven't heard the last of this!'

'I bet I have,' she said softly to his retreating back.

Corey Willans had left his C-Dog attitude at the door and was coping with the unfamiliar and therefore intimidating circumstances by sealing his lips tight and saying only yes and no, if possible without moving them. Processing was long and complex, to protect the arrestee and to prevent legal challenges further down the line, but it had the bonus effect, from the police point of view, of taking a lot of the piss and vinegar out of the stroppy offender. On the other hand, the nervous offender could be lulled by the sheer length and breadth of the bureaucracy. When Corey had been passed as fit by the doctor, settled in his cell and offered food and drink, he was asked if he wanted a solicitor to be present and finally unclamped his lips, something of his confidence restored.

'I don't know any solicitors,' he said. His father's message was relayed to him, and he sharpened and said, 'I definitely don't want someone of Dad's.'

'You can have someone from the pool, if you prefer,' the officer on duty, PC Detton, told him and explained the system.

'I'll have that,' Corey said. 'If Dad sends someone, they'll be on his side, not mine. And they'll report everything back to him.'

'Just as you please,' Detton said.

'And if he comes here – Dad – I don't want to see him.'

Slider telephoned Joanna to say he'd be late. 'We can't interview him until the brief gets here, so I'm stuck. Say goodnight to the children for me.'

'George will be disappointed. He made you something.'

'How nice. When I was a boy it was always an ashtray.'

'What century are you in? I'm sworn not to tell you what it is, but as a hint, it's something you use to keep your place when you're reading a book.'

'Is it a bookmark?'

'Drat, you guessed. Not my fault you're so clever.'

'Well, a bookmark is useful.'

'If you're reading a large atlas. It was a big square of card to start with and I tried to persuade him it needed to be cut down, but there wouldn't have been room for the drawings. He's done a hammer, a saw, a spanner and what I think is meant to be a screwdriver. He says dads like tools and making things.'

'He does know *I'm* his father, doesn't he?'

'My secret is blown. I cavorted with a handyman before he was born. Don't let on you know what it is before you see it, will you?'

'Come come. I may not be a master cabinet-maker, but I am *that* much of a father.'

The solicitor at the head of the duty list was Michael Friendly, in his late twenties with a whippy figure, thick wavy fair hair and a wide mouth that seemed best suited to a big soppy grin. He could have doubled as a Golden Retriever. There was nothing intrinsically wrong with resembling a dog, but most lawyers would probably rather it was a Doberman or a Rottweiler. Possibly hampered by his surname, he didn't seem like prosecution-counsel material; his suit was off the peg and well worn, so he probably wasn't making big bucks either. But once Corey had quizzed him to make sure he had no connections to Willans père, he was content with him. With Friendly on his side of the table, he even regained some of his cockiness.

Atherton went for the direct approach. 'Did you provide drugs to Rhianne Morgan?'

'I don't know who that is,' Corey said sublimely.

'Oh, really? Strange, then, that you've got the same tattoos.' He pushed two photographs across the desk, the first taken of Rhianne's body and the other taken when Corey stripped down in custody. Corey's was of the circle-and-arrow male gender symbol, and underneath, in curly script, Live Free or Die. 'Same design, same size, same position on the body, same script, same ink. His 'n' hers matching tatts, eh? Very cute.'

He looked sulky. 'That was her idea. I thought it was stupid.'

'Live free or die? Seriously?'

'She wanted me to have "Wild and Free", but I said that was too fuckin' Glasto. I'm not a hippy; I'm a metalhead. And "Just Be"? What's that about? I thought Goths were supposed to be cool.'

He seemed not to have realized he'd admitted knowing her.

'Was she a Goth?' Atherton asked, to keep it going.

Corey shrugged. 'Who knows? That was one weird chick, I tell you that. But she was rizz, or I wouldn't have touched it. Wish I hadn't, now,' he concluded gloomily. Then he recollected himself. 'Not that I did. I barely knew her – just met her the once. She was Kent's girlfriend. You should ask him.'

'Oh, we did. He was quite upset that you stole her from him.'

Conceit won over caution. 'He should have fought for her. He's such a fuckin' wet end; no wonder she preferred me. I mean, strap on a pair, bro!'

'Excuse me, what has this got to do with the arrest for possession of drugs?' Friendly interrupted.

'Rhianne Morgan was anecdotally known to take drugs. She had drugs in her bedroom. I want to establish whether Corey was the one to supply them—'

'I don't sell drugs,' Corey said indignantly.

'—with or without payment.'

'No, man,' he said. 'I told you, that gear in my flat wasn't mine. Someone planted it.'

'It has your fingerprints all over it,' Slider said impassively. 'Cocaine and marijuana. Also some pills, which turned out to be Ecstasy. With your prints on the packaging.'

Friendly gave Corey a look. 'I should co-operate if I were you. First offence, probably just a suspended.'

'We may be able to make the whole thing go away,' Slider said, 'if you tell us the truth about Rhianne.'

Corey looked at him warily. 'What about Rhianne?'

'She told her girlfriends that she was seeing an older man. We think she took drugs with him.'

'Not me,' he said promptly. 'Musta been some other guy.'

'But you were seeing her?'

As he hesitated, Atherton took over. 'You were seen leaving the school dance with her, arms wrapped round each other. And she didn't get home until very late.'

Corey glanced at Friendly, then said cautiously, 'What d'you want to know?'

'Was that the first time you went with her?'

'Nah. I'd been seeing her a while.'

'While she was still seeing Kenton?' He shrugged. 'How did it start?'

He roused himself. 'She came on to me, not vice versa. I'd seen her once or twice at the house with Kent, but even then she was giving me the eye, you know? Then one day she turned up at my flat. She said she'd come looking for Kenton only he wasn't in. No one was in, she said, and could she use my loo. Well, I said, sure. I let her in.'

'When was this?'

'Beginning of May. See, I knew she wasn't really looking for Kent, because he was at school doing one of his A level papers, and she must've known his schedule, right, if they were going out together?'

'So what do you think she was doing there?'

'Well, she wanted to have sex with me. It was obvious.'

'Was it?'

He grinned. 'Yeah. She wouldn't be the first. And she was all done up like a dog's dinner, sexy clothes, make-up and everything. And you should see the looks she was giving me! She was hot to trot.'

'So you obliged her?'

He shrugged. 'Why not? It's what it's there for, right?'

'Even though she was your brother's girlfriend?'

'Hey, he didn't own her. Women are free agents, right? And if it didn't bother her, why should it bother me?'

'And you went on seeing her?'

'Why not?'

'You got matching tattoos. That's a couply thing.'

'It was her idea. It seemed like a laugh at the time. We were stoned, and you do stupid things when you're high.'

'Did Kenton know about the tattoos?'

'Dude, he never knew anything, till the school prom night. She was doing both of us!' He grinned.

'Did you just do weed with her, or charlie as well?'

'Yeah, that as well. Mostly weed but sometimes white, when I'd got any, and vodka. She was up for everything. But I tell you, she was one troubled babe.' He stopped.

'You might as well go on,' Atherton said.

'Well, sometimes she'd be all crazy laughing, then suddenly she's all dark and moody and won't talk. Then she gets really down and starts crying, and she's all clingy and saying, "You do love me, don't you?"' He shrugged. 'Well, I said "Course I love you, babe." You've got to, haven't you, when they get like that? But it was never about love, man, it was about having a good time. They can't change the rules halfway through the game.'

'I think I'm getting a pretty clear picture now,' Atherton said. 'What else?'

'I tell you, she was one weird chick. She wanted to call me "Daddy". She wanted me to, like, tell her off and stuff. Punish her like a dad. While we were doing it. That's too bent for me. I like fun stuff, not that dark shit.'

'We seem to be getting away from the subject,' Friendly said. 'I can't allow any fishing expeditions.'

'Mr Willans is voluntarily helping us with an enquiry,' Atherton said.

'Yeah, man, anything to get me outta here.'

'What other fun stuff did you do with Rhianne?'

'Well, like, it was her idea to watch porn together. And then she wanted to try stuff we'd seen.'

'What sort of stuff?'

'Bondage stuff.'

'You like that sort of thing, don't you?'

Another shrug. 'I can take it or leave it.'

'You seem to like it. You've done it with other girls.'

'Chicks expect it. They want variety. You can't do plain vanilla all the time.'

'Shan Halligan didn't seem to be expecting it. You carried out a sexual assault on her involving bondage, didn't you?'

'This is new to me,' Friendly said sharply. 'Is my client accused of that assault?'

'Would you like him to be?'

Corey looked alarmed. 'She said she wouldn't call me on that.'

'She said that to you?'

'No, she told Nick Runcorn she didn't want to make a complaint. So that means she liked it.'

'That's not what she told me. She said she screamed for it to stop.'

'Well, it did stop. Nobody forced her.'

'And, for your information, she doesn't need to make the complaint herself. A prosecution can be brought without her participation.'

'Prosecution? Look, she came on to me. She was gagging for it. And then afterwards she's all weepy and oh-what-have-I-done. I thought an engineering student would be more together – you know, cool, like Rosie the Riveter. They shouldn't let girls on engineering courses if they can't take the heat.'

'I think we have to call a halt to this line of questioning,' Friendly said. 'What exactly are you accusing my client of?'

'Possession of Class A drugs,' Slider said. 'We haven't charged him yet. If he chooses voluntarily to help us with another investigation, we may manage to forget to do so.'

Corey chipped in. He was unsettled now, his eyes flitting, his left knee – the well-known Knee of Shame – jiggling. 'If it's about Rhianne snuffing it, I don't know anything about that. She took an overdose or something.'

'Where did you hear that?'

'I read it on social media. Look, she was a wild chick, she came on to me in the beginning, and all that stuff was her idea – the tatts, the bondage. All I did was what any guy would do—'

'Take advantage of her?' Atherton put in smoothly.

He flushed. 'No! We did a little harmless weed together. She never got really loaded when she was with me. And we had some sex – consensual sex.'

'Where were you on Tuesday?' Slider asked.

Corey looked confused by the change of line. 'Last Tuesday? I dunno.'

'Have a think,' Slider suggested. Corey frowned. 'Were you at college?'

'It's vacation, man.'

'Other grad students go in to use the facilities. Or do you have a vacation job?'

'I don't need one. Dad gives me an allowance.' He looked vaguely guilty as he heard the words on the air.

'So that you can concentrate on your studies?' Slider suggested.

Corey looked sulky and shrugged.

'For the tape, please.'

'He gives me an allowance. He doesn't ask me what I'm doing every fuckin' minute.'

'So you were at home on Tuesday?'

'I don't remember. I s'pose so.'

'Nothing much to do. A bit bored. So you went round to see Rhianne.'

'I wasn't seeing her any more.'

'Why not?'

He didn't want to say it. 'She dropped me.'

'*She* dropped *you*?'

'Yeah.' Reluctantly he continued. 'She was seeing someone else. She said he was an older guy.'

Atherton took over. 'You were the older guy when she dropped Kenton – older and cooler. Now someone else was cooler than you. That must have stung!'

'I didn't care about her anyway,' he said angrily. 'There's girls everywhere, all begging for it. I don't go short.'

'So there you were, at home and bored, nothing to do, and angry with Rhianne because she dumped you—'

'I never said dumped!'

'So you decided to go round to her house and make her have sex with you, to prove you could still get her. Only, to your shock and horror, almost before you'd begun, she dropped down dead.'

'That's not what happened!' he cried.

'You were scared, so you ran away. You didn't know what else to do.'

'I wasn't scared! I mean, I wasn't there!'

'Why did you run away when I called at your flat?'

'I don't know. I thought you'd seen the dope on the table.'

'I had. I was going to invite you to come to the station with me.'

'So I was right, then.' He seemed confused.

'You run away. That's your modus operandi.'

'My what?'

'That's what you do.'

'I dunno what you're talking about,' Corey said pleadingly. 'Look, everybody does dope. There's nothing to it. It's a victimless crime. And charlie? MPs do it! They get it couriered to the House of Commons by the shed load! Are you gonna arrest all of *them*?' He turned to Friendly. 'I bet you know a load of lawyers that do coke. Judges, even. Yeah, I bet you do. All those rich blokes in their fancy flats at their fancy parties. Don't tell me they're not doing lines in their marble fuckin' bathrooms! They keep a special gold straw in their pocket to toot up with!' Indignation had made him eloquent. He turned back to Atherton. 'But no, you turn a blind eye to them. It's just the little guys you go after! Guys like me with no money and no friends in high places. You call that justice?'

'No, I call it the law,' Atherton said. 'Where were you on Tuesday?'

'I *don't remember.*'

'Well, you'd better try.'

'And I'm going to call a halt now,' Friendly said. 'I think this has gone far enough.'

'I want to go home,' Corey cried.

'Do you?' Slider asked, raising an eyebrow.

Corey got it. His father would be there. He seemed to shrink. 'If my dad comes, I don't want to see him,' he said again.

Outside, Atherton spoke to Friendly. 'Without an alibi, he's in trouble.'

'You don't have any direct evidence against him, I presume? Or you'd have arrested him for that, instead of the drugs.'

'There's plenty of circumstantial,' Atherton said. 'He's admitted the relationship, the drugs, the bondage sex. And there's the assault on Shan Halligan to show a pattern of behaviour.'

'Not enough, and you know it,' Friendly said. 'But I'll talk to him again, try to get him to remember where he was. You scared him so much he couldn't think straight.'

'I think he's more scared of his father than of anyone here.'

Friendly shrugged. 'Once you've got his alibi, it will all be settled.'

'You'd think so, wouldn't you?' said Atherton pleasantly.

'You look tired,' Joanna said. 'Was it bad?' Slider made a helpless gesture with his hand. 'I don't suppose you've eaten?'

'I'm not really hungry.'

'You don't think you are, but you have to fuel the engine. How about some cheese and crackers?'

He smiled wearily. 'I could probably manage that.'

'Go and sit down and I'll bring it. Put some music on. Shoo the magic beast.'

'I thought it was soothe the savage breast?'

'I know what I said.'

As soon as he sat, Vash and Tig appeared, materializing from under the sofa, and climbed onto him, purring like engines. Vash settled on his lap, and Tig arranged himself along the back of the sofa across Slider's neck like a furry bean bag. Jumper was in his basket and raised his head for a moment to look, before deciding it wasn't worth disturbing himself for. Between the Scarlatti sonatas and the comforting heat of the cats, he was almost asleep when Joanna came in with the supper tray.

'You were right,' he said, rousing himself.

'I'm always right. Has the beast run away?'

'It's retreated.'

She had buttered the crackers and laid a slice of cheese on each so he didn't even need to wield a knife, just convey the food to his mouth. He was just about capable of that. And there was a glass of malt whisky, too. 'Tullibardine,' she informed him.

'You are the perfect woman. Will you marry me?'

'Sorry, I'm spoken for.' She sat beside him, and they listened in silence for a while.

'Kids OK?' he asked once, between mouthfuls.

'I think George is getting another cold. He was coughing a lot. Teddy's fine. She'll start getting them when she goes to pre-school. Dirty little beasts, children are.'

'It all helps to build immunity,' he said.

When he put the empty plate away from him, she said, 'What was it, in particular?'

'Dirty little beasts,' he said. 'Dirty big beasts.'

'This – Corey, was that his name? – he's a dirty beast?'

Slider pondered, sipping the whisky. 'I was thinking about what we were talking about the other day. Girls not wanting to date or get married. And when you talk to boys like Corey, you can see why.'

'Not a boy, if he's a postgrad student.'

'But he's still a boy. They don't seem to grow up in the way we had to. And sex has become so complicated and . . . unpleasant it's no wonder the girls don't want anything to do with it.' She waited. 'They watch pornography. They get their ideas from there. They think that's how it's done. They think it's normal. Bondage. Choking. And worse.'

She thought she knew what bothered him. 'I'm sure Kate and Matthew don't.'

'But I don't know, do I? They might. Other kids might introduce them to it, egg them on. It's not something they're going to come and tell me about. Or admit if I ask. And what sort of world will George and Teddy grow up into? Will they ever be able to have normal relationships?'

'Look, it's not like that everywhere. Thousands of normal young men and women get married every year. You get depressed because you don't see them. You always work at the fuzzy end of the lollipop.'

'Corey Willans is not exactly from a deprived home in a sink neighbourhood.' He took another sip. 'He talks about women as if they're a commodity.'

She hitched closer and put her hand on his arm. 'You didn't have the upbringing of him. He's not your responsibility.'

'She was from a decent home, too – Rhianne. Nice semi-detached in a road with trees. Respectable parents. Enough money. Good school. And she did drugs and watched porn. Had sex with

multiple partners. She thought that was normal behaviour. And
she's ended up dead.'

'It was for her parents to look after her. *You* can't save
everyone.'

'Sometimes it seems I can't save anyone.'

She was silent a moment. Then she said, 'Does it ever occur
to you you're in the wrong job? You care too much.'

'How much is too much?' There was a pause. 'Mr Porson said
he's thinking of retiring.'

'He's not that old, is he?'

'You can take a reduced pension from fifty-five. His daughter's
moved down to Bath and wants him to go and live near her. And,
of course, he could always get another job if he didn't want to
be idle.'

'Security guard in Morrisons? Night watchman?'

He turned to her. 'Night watchman? What century are you
in?'

'Cheese sandwich, flask of tea, large torch, *Daily Mail* folded
in the pocket. I've seen them on films.'

'Ealing comedies, maybe.'

'That's better. That was nearly a smile.'

'Nothing to smile about over Porson leaving. Can you imagine
what we'd get in his place?'

She considered. 'Maybe he won't go.'

'That's all you've got?'

'It's the best answer to everything. Don't trouble trouble till
trouble troubles you.'

'You sound like my mother.'

'Another smidge of Tully?'

'If you'll join me.'

While she went for the whisky, he thought how lucky he was.
And imagined Porson shuffling about his empty house getting
his sad-bachelor supper – which was even sadder when you were
a widower.

Very lucky.

The morning was fine again, the sky milky with fair-weather
clouds, the pale gold early sun pleasant but promising heat later
when it got up to speed. There came a point, Slider discovered

as he drove in, when you almost found yourself hoping the weather would change. The English soul could only stand so much favour from the gods of meteorology: you kept waiting for the other shoe to drop. The longer it took, the more likely it was to end in cataracts and hurricanoes.

On his way in from the yard he was stopped by Nutty Nicholls, the custody sergeant, a dark and handsome Scot with a soft accent steeped in the peaty mists of the Western Isles. 'Morgan wants to talk, Bill,' he said.

'Oh. Good. How is he?'

'Suffering. He hardly touched his breakfast. You don't look so very good yourself this fine day. Did you have a bad night?'

Slider shrugged. 'You know how it is.'

'You should never take your work home with you. And music is the great healer, you know. When I'm tense, I sing, and Mary plays the piano.'

'I played Scarlatti last night,' Slider said. When he saw Nutty's eyebrows go up, he added quickly, 'On a CD, I mean. Has Morgan asked for a solicitor?'

'No. He's sunk in a sort of lethargy. You know how it takes them sometimes.'

'I'll make sure he has one. If he's going to confess, we'd better have it all by the book. As soon as the brief arrives, let me know and I'll come down.'

'Right you are, Bill, I will do that. And you have time for a cup of tea.'

'Is Mr Porson in?'

'He arrived just now.'

David Morgan still refused to ask for a solicitor and got Padmavati Singh from the pool, an impossibly slim, impossibly beautiful young Indian woman with hair like a yard of midnight water and the brisk, cool manner of the fiercely ambitious. Morgan paid her no attention at all, and to judge by Ms Singh's air of controlled irritation after their private séance, he had not co-operated with her much.

Preliminaries over, and with Swilley beside him, Slider began with, 'You wanted to talk to me?'

'I want it over with,' Morgan said. His voice was leaden, his face dragged down to the bow of misery that was his mouth. 'My life is over, anyway.'

Slider didn't want to deny it. 'Then you have no reason to hold anything back.' Morgan didn't speak, staring at nothing, his hands locked together on the table top. 'Your wife is suffering, Mr Morgan. There may be no hope for you, but at least you can give her a little peace.'

'Peace?' he queried, as though it were a ludicrous suggestion.

'The peace of knowing what happened to her daughter. She deserves that, at least.'

'Rhianne was my daughter too,' Morgan said. 'I loved that girl. You have no idea. She was so sweet, when I first married Rita. Her little face used to light up when I came home from work. She'd run to me and jump up in my arms. And when we all went out together, she'd hold my hand and skip along beside me and chatter away. She was so pretty and innocent and . . . open.' His voice had lightened while he remembered, but it grew heavy again as he went on, 'I don't remember Mia being like that with me. She was always her mother's daughter. I suppose I worked such long hours I never saw enough of her. I was a rotten father, really. Three children and I've failed them all. And Rhianne – her most of all.'

'When did that early relationship change?' Slider asked unemphatically, slipping the question in so as not to disrupt the flow.

He seemed to think about it. '*She* changed. I wonder . . . Was there some outside influence? Or was it just her own character coming through? We were too alike, I think. Sometimes I forgot that she wasn't mine by birth because we *were* so alike. People who didn't know would say she looked like me, but that's just because we were both fair and Rita was dark. But still . . .'

'In what way were you alike, apart from colouring?'

He looked up for a moment, but not as if he really saw Slider. He went on as though speaking his thoughts. 'She was always a determined little girl, knew what she wanted and was determined to have it. Like when I bought her the bike. She wouldn't let me help her ride it; she had to do it all herself. And if she couldn't have what she wanted, she'd cry. But it never lasted long. Minutes later she'd be all sunshine and chuckles again. But when she got a bit older, when she got into her teens, that part of her got harder. She wouldn't be guided; she wouldn't be told. She became stubborn and unreasonable. People say I'm stubborn. I know it's a fault I have. Things have to be done my way, and if people contradict me or work against me, I get frustrated and angry. But it's not a bad thing at work, when you're the boss and account-able for outcomes. People have to do what they're told, or there's chaos. And I'm always fair. People who work for me say that: I'm strict but fair. Only . . .' He drew a sigh that seemed to come up from the floor under his feet. 'It's different at home, with your family. It's different with a growing girl, a teenager going through all the changes they do.'

'She wouldn't do as she was told,' Slider suggested quietly.

He looked up again, more sharply this time. 'I was responsible for her. I had to keep her safe, guide her, help her grow up into the right sort of person. That's what fathers do. That was my job. Have you got children? Teenage girls – they're the hardest. There's so much to worry about, so many dangers out there that they simply don't understand. You worry *all* the time, and when they won't *listen* to you, when they *defy* you, and you're just trying to keep them safe . . .' His hands had clenched into fists.

'You got angry.'

'How could I help it? She's so innocent – she thinks she knows it all, but she doesn't. She doesn't see the dangers out there.' He didn't seem to realize he had slipped into the present tense. 'But as soon as you tell her not to do something, she's hell bent on doing it. Opposition just makes her more determined. She won't listen to reason. Then its temper and tears and "you don't under-stand" and "I'm doing it anyway". She shouts at me, and then I shout back. I can't help it; I get so *frustrated* with her. Like that damn stupid tattoo. When she said she wanted one I explained to her, I said it will give people the wrong impression of you. And when you're older it will look terrible. And you could get an infection; you can get hepatitis from those needles and that's a life-changing disease. But she did it anyway. You can't be with them twenty-four hours a day.'

'I bet there was a row about that.'

'The biggest. And days of sulks and glowerings. I didn't want it to be like that with her. I wanted us to be on good terms. I wanted my little girl back, who used to sit on my lap while I told her a story. It's like someone came in and stole my little girl and replaced her with a demon.'

'A demon?'

'How can you be a good father to someone so alien? I do my best, I really try. She doesn't understand that her whole life depends on getting the fundamentals right. She thinks she can do as she pleases and there'll be no consequences. She *won't* understand that you don't get a second chance; you can't fritter away your school years and make a mess of yourself and then get a reset. Life is not a video game. But she won't listen. It's like a madness.'

'It must have been very hard for you,' Slider said. 'I can see how angry it made you. It's no wonder that you lost your temper sometimes. You just wanted the best for her, good A levels and a good job, and then she starts that nonsense about going to art school.'

His reddened eyes glared. 'I told her, there's hundreds – thousands – of people coming out of art school every year and just a handful of jobs. It's like not getting on with your life because you think you're going to win the lottery.'

Slider nodded sympathetically. 'And when you came home that day and found her lounging in the garden reading fashion magazines, it must have been the last straw. You just snapped – and who could blame you?'

Morgan blinked. 'What?' he said.

'You said you wanted to talk to me,' Slider said gently. 'You wanted to tell me everything.'

'Yes,' he said, looking bewildered. 'Everything.'

'Right. Well, go ahead. Don't lose momentum now. This is the hard part, but I promise you you'll feel better when you've got it all out. Just tell me everything. I'm listening.'

'Tell you . . . everything?' Morgan said. He stared at Slider, then looked at Swilley and then at the solicitor. It was the look of a man who's woken up from a nightmare, to find that the nightmare is still going on in broad daylight.

TWELVE
L'après Midi D'un Phone

'It is the hard part,' Morgan said slowly. 'And I suppose Rita has to know.'

It wasn't the reaction Slider had expected. 'I think that's inevitable,' he said, with irony.

'She'll never forgive me. My life will be over.' He sighed again. 'Well, it's over already. How does anyone get over this? To lose your child. And then to lose Rita too.'

Swilley stirred at this. Slider glanced and saw her frown. She was always impatient with self-pity. 'It's a bit late to be thinking like that,' she said. 'You should be considering what she must be going through. At least have the decency to tell the truth now and give her a bit of closure.'

'But I never wanted her to find out,' he pleaded. 'What she never knew couldn't hurt her.'

'You'd prefer her to spend her whole life wondering who killed her child,' Swilley said, 'than to find out it was you? Well, I suppose you would think like that,' she concluded coldly.

'But I didn't kill her!' Morgan cried. 'How could you think it? I'm not a murderer. I'd never have harmed a hair of her head.'

Slider and Swilley exchanged a glance. 'You said you wanted to tell me everything,' Slider said. 'Are you rowing back on that now?'

'About where I was that day,' Morgan said, a little wildly. 'About what I was doing. I would never have told otherwise. It's not my secret to tell, not entirely. But I have to now. I can't have you thinking I killed Rhianne. Only . . . there's going to be hell to pay.' He raked his fingers through his hair at the thought.

Slider had a bad feeling about this.

'What were you doing that day?' he asked.

'I was with someone. A woman,' said Morgan.

* * *

It couldn't be said that Corey looked any worse for a night in custody, but he'd looked pretty rough anyway. The clean T-shirt he'd been provided with – plain grey – was at least an improvement.

'I understand you've remembered where you were on Tuesday,' Atherton said, after the preliminaries.

'Yeah. I was at home,' Corey said. 'In the flat.'

'Alone?' Atherton asked.

'Well, yes, but—'

'You may need a little more than that. Can anyone confirm you were there?'

'I was just gonna tell you. Dude, give me a break!'

'Get on with it. And don't call me "dude".'

'Fine, fine, don't get stressy. I woke up late and just bummed about for a bit, and smoked a little weed, and then – get this – I ordered a Domino's!' He looked at Atherton with eager joy. 'Thin and crispy with extra pepperoni. D'you get it?'

'Yes. You think they'll have a record of the order and the delivery.'

'You're quick, man. And, well, I read online that Rhianne, she died in the afternoon, right?'

'I can't comment on that.'

'Well, it musta been about two fifteen that I ordered it, and it came about two thirty, so that lets me out, right? The delivery guy will remember me.'

'What makes you think so?'

He gave a grin, half sheepish, half cocky. 'I had the spliff in my hand when I opened the door. I offered him a drag.'

'You understand that we will check this,' Atherton said sternly. 'And if it turns out that you're lying—'

'Why would I do that? I want to get out of here.'

'Very well. What did you do next?'

Corey's crest fell. 'Isn't that enough? It proves I was at home. I've got a witness.' Atherton maintained silence. 'Well,' Corey went on, more subdued. 'I ate the pizza, I suppose.'

'You suppose?'

'Well, I was stoned, man. What can I say?'

'I'm afraid that's not good enough. You need an alibi for the whole afternoon. Did anyone visit you? Did you go out anywhere?'

He shook his head, thinking. 'No, I stayed in. It was just me on my—' A smirk came over his face. 'I remember now. What I was doing.'

'What?'

'I don't want to say.'

'I think the time for reticence is long past.'

'No, I mean, I know how I can prove I was at home. All afternoon. But it's, like, personal.'

Friendly intervened. 'It's in your interests to speak up now, if you really can prove where you were.'

'No, but it's kinda dopey. You do stupid things when you're loaded,' said Corey. He looked from one to the other, suddenly seeming younger than his age. His sheepish look had a gap in its teeth and a catapult in its back pocket. 'I was taking photos. On my phone. Of . . . myself.'

'Yes?' said Atherton.

'And, like, you know when you open a picture in the picture file, and click on "details", it tells you the time and date it was taken, but it also shows where. Shows it on a Google map, with a pin. Right down to the actual road.'

One of the wonders of modern life, Atherton thought. But how long does it take to take a picture? *We could still have him.* 'I'll pause the interview while the phone is fetched,' he said.

'Oh, man, do you have to see?'

'I'd love to take your unsubstantiated word for it,' Atherton said, 'but Mr Friendly will tell you that's not how the law works.' He raised an eyebrow. 'Why don't you want me to see the pictures?'

'I was photoing myself,' he said awkwardly. 'My – er – you know. My dick.'

'Ah,' said Atherton. 'And why was that?'

'I told you, I was fried, and I got a bit silly. Like, I remembered Reece told me he'd read somewhere that everyone's is the same length, within a couple of millimetres, and I didn't believe it. So I thought I'd photograph it against a tape measure and prove it. I was gonna send him the pic and bet him mine was longer than his. But I couldn't get the angle right just looking down, so I stood in front of the bedroom mirror. But you couldn't see the numbers on the tape, so I had to put it on zoom. It took a while to get it right.'

'I see. Where did you get the tape measure from?'

'It's one of those retractable steel ones. I borrowed it from upstairs ages ago and forgot to give it back. It was remembering I had it that made me think of the pics. And then—'

'Yes? Do go on,' Atherton said politely.

He looked at the recording equipment. 'Is this all going on the tape?'

'I'm afraid so. That also is the law.'

'But . . . I don't want my parents to hear all this.'

'At the moment, I see no reason they need to. Go on. What did you do next?'

'Well, I'd taken my pants off, see? For the pictures. And I had sounds on – Nine Inch Nails, *The Hand That Feeds* – and I was sort of dancing around and I started feeling good. So I took my top off as well and danced naked in front of the mirror. I thought I looked pretty good, so I took some more pics for my next girlfriend to enjoy. And then the Old Man started waking up.'

'Your father?'

He reddened. 'No, the lad. The one-eyed trouser snake. So I . . . I got a bit silly. I started hanging things on it, to see how much weight it would take.' He had the grace to look embarrassed.

'And you photographed that as well?' He nodded. 'So this was going on for quite some time?'

'Yeah. I dunno – maybe an hour. And then I got the munchies, so I went and heated up the rest of the pizza. I'd only eaten half. And I photographed that.'

'Why would you photograph a pizza?'

'Well, I decorated it, see. Rearranged the pepperoni slices to look like a . . .' He shrugged. 'You know.'

'I'm afraid I do. What then?'

'I ate it.'

'And after that?'

'After the pizza? I fell asleep on the sofa. It was about half past eight when I woke up. But I know she'd been found before that, because it was on social media, so that lets me out, right?' Despite his apparent goofiness, he had held on to the main point.

'I will pause the tape while the phone is sent for,' Atherton said wearily. The things you were expected to do for a public-sector salary, he thought.

Slider was naturally a cautious man, who believed in reason and balance, and tried to bring patience and compassion into the way he did his job. But his first instinct was to punch Morgan in the face for having wasted all their time over something so trivial, and for having prioritized keeping his extra-marital jiggy secret over finding out who killed his daughter.

His second thought was that maybe it wasn't true, that it was a new smoke screen. Perhaps Morgan was more cunning than he appeared and, sensing the hunter's footsteps getting closer, he was throwing out another false trail. Slider therefore had better proceed cautiously and postpone the pleasure of whacking him about until later.

'What woman would this be?' he asked.

'A woman I'm . . . having an affair with. But she's married and I don't want to get her into trouble. If her husband finds out . . . Can this be kept between ourselves?'

To her credit, Padmavati Singh was looking ashamed of her client.

'I can't promise anything,' Slider said. 'What is this woman's name?'

'Melissa,' he said reluctantly. 'She works at Hamilton's in King Street.'

'Melissa Wright?' Slider said. 'Who used to be one of your employees at Buckfast's?'

He looked stunned. 'How did you know that? How do you know about her?'

'You weren't as discreet as you thought you were. One of her co-workers at Buckfast's told us you'd been having an affair, and we interviewed her.'

'Oh my God! You talked to her? You didn't go to her home? If Mark finds out – her husband—'

'We interviewed her at work,' Slider said coldly. 'And she told us that you and she had broken up when she left Buckfast's. That it was over between you.'

He shrugged awkwardly. 'We did break up. But then we got

back together. It was her I was with all afternoon. Well, for a couple of hours, anyway. Mel had to go around four fifteen, something at work she couldn't get out of. So I went home, to take a quick shower before I went back to the office. And found Rhianne. Dead.'

Swilley wasn't going to let him retreat into sympathy country. 'You realize that we are going to check all this?'

'I know,' he said resignedly. 'It has to be. But it's the truth. We were at the Commodore Hotel, in Glenthorne Road. I went straight there from the office, got there about ten past two, and she joined me there around two fifteen. And, as I said, we left together around four fifteen.'

'That's a lot of subterfuge for just two hours,' Swilley said.

'Usually we have longer, but she had this work thing. But just to be with her . . . We'd missed each other. It was worth it to us. Until this happened. Now, I can't imagine ever feeling anything again.'

'Why didn't you shower at the hotel?' Swilley pursued.

'Obviously you've never been to the Commodore. It's not exactly luxurious. The shower's over the bath, which has brown water stains and a plastic curtain with missing loops, and the towel is so thin you could read the paper through it. I preferred to go home and shower. I'd forgotten that Rhianne was at home until I was pulling up outside. But I'd still have showered. It was a hot day, and I was wearing a suit, and I'm in a public-facing job, so I had to.'

'If the Commodore is so down-market, why do you go there?' Swilley asked.

'You can't find smart hotels these days that let you take a room for a few hours,' he said. 'It's all international chains with everything online and digital. The Commodore takes cash and no questions asked. It's clean,' he added, as if in exculpation. 'Just a bit shabby.'

'How romantic,' Swilley said.

Slider took it over. 'If they're cash-in-hand and non-digital, how will it prove you were there?'

'It's where we usually go. They know us. And we sign the register – that'll be there.' He looked uncomfortable. 'We sign as Mr and Mrs Smith.'

'Very traditional. Perhaps there might be several Smith couples there?'

'But it will be in our handwriting. And if you show them a photo, they'll recognize us.'

Slider glanced at his file and said, 'You rang the office at around four fifteen that day.'

'Yes?'

'To check that your story was still holding, I suppose – that there'd been no cover-blowing enquiries about you?'

'Just to check if there were any messages,' he said, looking annoyed. 'If I'm out and there's something that needs a visit it makes sense to go on to it and not waste time going back to the office.'

'I see. And where were you when you made that call?'

'Still at the Commodore. I did a quick ring in while Mel was in the bathroom.'

'Get on to the mobile phone company,' Slider said to Swilley as they walked back to the CID room. 'Check the location of the phone when that call was made. And I suppose we must send someone to the Commodore and someone to talk to Melissa Wright.'

'She could be covering for him,' Swilley said. 'Even if the phone call was made from the Commodore, doesn't mean he was the one making it.'

'You really want it to be him, don't you?' Slider said.

'I don't like him. He's a user. And like too many users, he sees *himself* as the victim. Don't you still think it was him?'

'I'll wait for the facts before I make up my mind. But much as I want to kick his tail from here to the green, I don't think he'd be making this up – it's too easy to check.'

'His previous alibi was easy to check,' Swilley pointed out.

'True. But he knows now that we'll do it. OK, let's get on with it. Knock down those sand castles so we can start again from scratch. I'll send McLaren to the Commodore, in case they're sticky.'

'From what he said I bet everything there's sticky. And I'll do Melissa Wright,' Swilley said grimly. 'It'll be a pleasure to puncture her bubble.'

'Not *too* much pleasure,' Slider warned.

'Oh, I'll leave enough to bury.'

LaSalle had to wait at the Domino's for the delivery driver to come back in from a job, but the deliveries were all local and it was only fifteen minutes. The manager of the shop had checked the record and provided the driver's name. The pizza had been ordered at two sixteen and was delivered at two thirty-one, by Mohammed Ghani, a regular gig worker.

He puttered up on his moped, with smelly exhaust and the L-plate stuck to the box on the back. LaSalle automatically clocked enough infractions to detain Mr Ghani if he didn't co-operate. He was a small man, muffled in thin puffy waterproof pants and jacket – possibly to keep him clean since there was no rain forecast – and a red crash helmet with a crack across it. When he pulled it off on LaSalle's instructions, he turned out to be very young-looking and apprehensive, probably not more than twenty, with a face weathered nut brown and moist dark victim's eyes. Probably an illegal, LaSalle thought.

'You're not in trouble,' he told him. 'Understand me? You – are – not – in – trouble.' Getting no reaction, he added, 'You speak English?'

'English, yes. Some speak. Read not so good.'

'Where are you from?'

'Aldine House, Aldine Street, Flat 10,' he said, as one chanting a memorized incantation.

LaSalle suppressed a smile. 'Before that. What country?'

'Afghanistan, sir.'

Poor bugger, LaSalle thought. 'Last week, Tuesday, you made a delivery. Basement Flat, Priory Gardens.'

'Please?'

LaSalle called up a map on his phone and showed it to the man. He nodded vaguely. 'Customer was a tall young man, scruffy.'

'Please?'

'Untidy. This is him. You remember him?'

He showed Mr Ghani the mugshot of Corey, and he stared at it blankly. How many pizzas did he deliver a day? *And we probably all look the same to him*, he thought. 'He was smoking marijuana. Kush,' he translated.

Now the little man looked alarmed. He pushed the photo away in an automatic reaction. 'No see. Not know him. I go now – must work.'

LaSalle caught his arm. 'No trouble for you,' he said, giving him his most honest stare. 'You're OK. OK? Just tell me, you see this man? Last Tuesday? Priory Gardens?'

Warily, after a long stare into LaSalle's face, he nodded, then gestured towards the shop. 'Boss send me. Boss tell you.'

LaSalle smiled and patted his arm. 'Yeah. Good man. You're sure, now? You delivered a pizza to this man?'

'Thinacrispy. Extra hot.'

'Right. That's all I need to know. You OK – you can go now.'

He nodded uncertainly and turned towards the shop door, his nylon legs brushing together with a sound like an audience shushing a noisy sweet-eater.

'Hey,' LaSalle said. He turned back, enquiringly, anxious. 'If you don't read English, how do you find your way around?'

It took a repetition before he understood the question, then his face broke into a grin. 'Satnav!' he cheered, with a fist-pump.

The Commodore looked like any number of cheap London hotels, residing in one of those tall Victorian houses with the steps up to the front door under a portico and over a railed semi-basement that had seen better days. Paint was peeling off the pillars and the black-and-white diamond tiles in the step treads were cracked in several places. It had the name back-painted on the fanlight over the door.

McLaren pushed in through the front door to a smell of dusty carpet and, more reassuringly, furniture polish. The narrow hall had stairs straight ahead and to the right a reception desk partly carved out of one of the downstairs rooms: a high wooden affair bearing a large, black-bound ledger next to a chained biro, with pigeon holes and a key board on the wall behind. A man was leaning on the counter on his elbows reading a newspaper. He straightened and looked at McLaren warily. He was tall and thin and had a remarkably sculpted face: an eagle's beak of a nose, cheekbones that seemed to be about to burst through the skin, a jaw like a bladed weapon, and ears that stood out from his head like wings, but backward-swept as though by the wind of passage. With an Arab horse under him and a hawk on his arm, he'd have looked right at home in the desert. Though carrying no spare flesh, he gave the impression of ruthless strength. He looked as though he could knock down houses with his forehead.

'Police?' he said, before McLaren had opened his mouth. 'I'm legal. I have all my papers.' He had a London accent overlying something more exotic.

McLaren showed his warrant card. 'I'm not from immigration,' he said. 'I want to know about some people who might have stayed here last week. Name of Smith.'

'Very common English name,' he said unsmilingly.

McLaren brought up the picture of Morgan. 'Last Tuesday. He came on his own, just after two o'clock, and the woman joined him five minutes later. Very nice-looking blonde lady.' The man hesitated, and he added, 'There's no trouble in this for you, bloke. I just need to know if they were here.'

'Trouble for me if it gets about I'm talking about them. People come here for privacy. I'll lose my trade.'

McLaren leaned forward slightly. 'You'll lose more than your trade if you get arrested for running a house for immoral purposes. Just answer my questions and I'll go away. Otherwise . . .' He let it hang.

The man considered and looked at the picture again. 'Yeah, I know him. Used to be a regular. Then they stopped coming. Then started again. Same woman each time.'

'You're sure?'

'Yeah, I recognize him.'

'And they were here last Tuesday?'

He shrugged. 'I don't remember the date. You can look in the register.' He opened it and flicked back the pages, then turned it to face McLaren. 'Yeah, it was Tuesday all right. That's them. See the time?'

McLaren took a photo of the page. 'You got CCTV?' he asked.

'Down here? In the rooms?'

The man looked indignant. 'What do you think I am? It's not *that* sort of hotel.'

'Damage. Theft. Leaving without paying,' McLaren said patiently. 'You're entitled to protect yourself.'

'I take the money up front,' he said as if it was selbstver-
ständlich. 'People wouldn't come if they thought they were being
filmed.'

Joanna phoned. 'I had a call from Martin Hazlett – you know,
the fixer. He's asked me if I'll do a concert tonight.'
 'Tonight?' said Slider. 'That's a bit last minute.'
 'That's rather the point. Someone's had an accident, hurt her
wrist, possible fracture. Rehearsal at five, concert seven thirty, the
Buttered Bread and Russlan. Lots of scrubbing. It's in Bedford,
so I shouldn't be too late back. You don't mind, do you?'
 'Why on earth should I mind?'
 'Oh, you know. Lady friend leave de nest again, make Yellow
Bird very sad.'
 'What?'
 'It's a song. Yellow Bird up high in banana tree?'
 'I must have missed that one when I was a chorister at St
Paul's.'
 'The thing is, if I help Martin out, he says he'll owe me big
time, and that will be good for me when I go back to work in
September. He handles a lot of gigs.'
 'You do what you have to do.'
 'That sounds like yessing with faint noes.'
 'Sorry, I mean good for you. Go to it.'
 'Better. I'll drop the kids downstairs before I leave, and Dad
and Lydia said they'd do baths and bedtime if you're not back.'
 'I'll try to get home at a decent time tonight,' Slider said. 'I
was planning on it anyway, even before you said you wouldn't
be there.'
 'Sorry, haven't got time to feel guilty. I've got to go and look
out my glad rags and then do a bit of warming up. Haven't played
for days. Love you!' And she was gone.

Swilley was disinclined to tread softly on Melissa Wright anyway,
but then she went and gave her attitude.
 'Oh, really, this is too much!' she said with a toss of her corn-
fed barnet. 'I told the other policeman everything I knew. You
can't keep coming and interrupting me when I'm at work. Some
people have jobs to do, you know.'

'I'll talk to you here,' Swilley said, while everyone in the room stared open-mouthed and didn't even pretend not to be listening, 'or I'll talk to you down at the station, but you've been taking the bare piss and if I don't get some straight answers from you, I'll arrest you and we'll see if that gets your head straight.'

'I don't know what you're talking about,' she said indignantly, for public consumption, but then lowered her voice to hiss, 'Not here! In the back room! I have to work with these people, for God's sake!' Then, aloud again, 'Let's go somewhere more private and see if we can sort this out. I'm sure it's a case of mistaken identity.'

In the back room, she turned on Swilley, red-faced, but Swilley got in first. 'Mistaken identity? Is that the best you can do?' she said with a superior smile.

'I don't know what your problem is,' Melissa said angrily, 'but you've got no right—'

'Don't be stupid. Of course I've got the right. You lied to my colleague. You said you'd broken up with David Morgan—'

'It wasn't a lie! We did break up!'

'But then you got back together again.'

'What if I did?'

'You told my colleague you hadn't seen David or spoken to him since you left Buckfast's.'

Now she looked sulky. 'I didn't see why my private life was any of his business. In any case, I'm married, and if any of this got back to my husband—'

'Who you were prepared to leave when you thought David Morgan might marry you.'

'Oh, you're the morality police now as well, are you?'

'I'm not interested in the state of your conscience. I'm interested in where David Morgan was last Tuesday afternoon. He says he was with you. What do *you* say?'

'Look,' she said – the word that traditionally prefaced either a big fat lie or a desperate attempt at justification. She chewed her lip. 'Can you promise this won't get back to Mark – my husband?'

'I promise nothing, but at present I've no plans to speak to your husband.'

She sighed. 'All right, I was with David. All right? We *did* break up – that *wasn't* a lie. But then one day I bumped into him in King Street. Well, he pretended it was a coincidence, but I'm pretty sure he was hanging around hoping to see me. He said he wanted to talk, said let's go for a coffee. We talked, and it was . . .' Her expression softened. 'So good. Like old times. I'd missed him so much. And he said he'd missed me like hell, life was just grey without me—'

'Spare me the Mills and Boon,' Swilley said. 'What about last Tuesday?'

She looked sulky again. 'All right, I was getting to it. We met at this hotel near here, the Commodore, in Glenthorne Road.'

'Time?'

'Between two and half past.'

'You've been there before?'

She shrugged. 'It was one of our places. It was safe. The manager there . . . He's discreet.'

'What time did you leave?'

'Quarter past four. I had a viewing I had to get to, otherwise—'

'Yes, all right. Was David there the whole time?'

'Of course he was! What d'you think?'

'And if necessary, you would swear to that?' Swilley said, mostly to torment her.

Melissa looked alarmed. 'What, in court? I can't! Mark would have to find out. You promised—'

'I didn't, actually. But it may not come to that.' Swilley turned to go, but turned back to say, 'Just out of interest, you broke up because he wouldn't leave his wife, and then you got back together. What changed your mind? You didn't really think he was going to do it, did you?'

She got on her dignity. 'He put it to me in a different light,' she said. 'He said since we didn't want to have children together, why did we need to marry? We could see each other nearly whenever we wanted, and we didn't want to hurt our spouses, so wasn't this the best solution.'

'Very noble.'

She looked annoyed again. 'I don't expect *you* to understand, but David and I have a very deep connection, something that goes beyond the everyday, and it's too precious to throw away for mere convention.'

'Right,' said Swilley. 'It's something rare and fine that has nothing to do with bumping uglies.'

Melissa flushed. 'You've no right to speak to me like that.'

'Sorry,' said Swilley. 'I get it, I really do. You complete the living shit out of each other.'

Everyone was gathered round to look at Corey's pictures.

'My eyes! My eyes!' Jenrich screeched.

'I told you not to look,' said Lœssop.

'Now I've seen that, I can't ever *un*-see it.'

'What is it with men and their junk?' Swilley said, shaking her head.

'Junk? Do you mind?' said Atherton. 'You are belittling the most tender, selfless, almost *spiritual* love that exists only between—'

'Shut *up!*'

'Is it me,' McLaren began thoughtfully, head slightly on one side, 'or does it look like—?'

'Don't say it! I sweartogod, Maurice—!'

'The last chicken in the shop?' Lœssop said innocently. 'I was just thinking that.'

Atherton took charge. 'I think we're all rather missing the point—'

'Point! Hur, hur!' said Fathom.

'—which is the time and the location pin – please, Jezza, it's a digital pin, all right?'

'Digital! Hur, hur!'

'Is this a private party, or can anyone join in?' Slider said from the door, where he had just appeared with Detective Chief Superintendent Porson.

'Jocularity is the thief of time,' Porson added sternly. 'Nobody got anything to do?'

'It's Corey Willans's alibi, sir,' Atherton said, as everyone was suddenly sober and several tried to melt into the background. 'The pictures were taken at frequent intervals between two forty-five and four twenty, and all at the same location, in Priory Gardens. It doesn't give the house *number*, of course, but that hardly matters for our purposes. You can see enough of the background in several of the shots to identify his flat. We have the witness of the Domino's delivery driver that Corey came to the door at two thirty, and if Rhianne died between two thirty and four thirty, there's no possibility he could have got to Acacia Avenue and back between shots.'

Porson eyed him suspiciously through this exposition. 'You don't need to sound so pleased about it,' he said at the end, and turning to Slider: 'Do we let him go?'

'There's the question of the Class A drugs possession, sir—'

Porson shook his head. 'We haven't got time to fanny about with that. Give him a warning and get his dad to come and fetch him. That'll be punishment enough. What about Morgan?'

'Just waiting for Vodafone to come back on his mobile's location when he made the four fifteen call,' said Slider, 'but the other evidence checks out. It seems that he's covered. He's wasted a lot of police time.'

'Well, we can come back to that later if we want to. He's not likely to abscond, is he? Let him go, then. What else have you got?' He looked from Slider to Atherton and back. 'Like that, is it? Bloody Nora! Mr Carpenter'll do his pieces.'

'It wasn't *just* accidental death, sir,' Slider said desperately. 'Someone was there, and someone meant her harm.'

'We've still got her social media to go through,' Swilley offered.

Porson snorted. 'Reams and bloody acres of it, no doubt. And how many man hours will it take to sort out the wheat from the goats? If any. Well, I hope you can get *something* together in the next forty-eight hours or it might be noticed that it's not only Morgan who's been wasting police time. Get on with it!' he barked, turning away. 'Time and tide gather no moss! Slider – with me.'

Slider went to see Morgan in the cells to tell him he was free to go. Morgan didn't look either overjoyed or mightily relieved at the news.

'Just between us,' Slider began.

'Do I need the solicitor back?' Morgan interrupted.

'No. We have verified your alibi.'

'So you believe me at last, that I would never have hurt my daughter?'

'I don't believe you were directly responsible for her death, but you did hurt her. You said she changed from a loving little girl into a demon – your word.'

'I shouldn't have said demon. I didn't mean that.'

'But she did change. Do you associate that change with any particular incident?'

He shrugged. 'Just normal teenagerhood. They all go through difficult times.'

'So it didn't date from the time she discovered you were having affairs?'

He looked as though Slider had slapped his face. He swallowed a few times and moistened his lips before he could say, 'What?'

'She told her best friend she'd seen you with another woman. She faced you with it.'

His lips moved soundlessly, then he said, 'She was mistaken. I told her she'd imagined it.'

'In my experience, children are very clear about what they see and what they imagine. You telling her she was wrong wouldn't have changed her mind. And I gather that she'd become very moody lately?'

'That thing – that was years ago.'

'Withdrawn? Secretive? You didn't have any idea what she was thinking or even what she was doing much of the time.'

'You have to give them their privacy. They have their own lives to lead. Besides—'

'Does it occur to you that perhaps she knew about your extra-marital activities? That she's known all along, since she discovered the first one?'

He was silent a moment, then he said, 'You've no evidence of that. You're trying to say this was all my fault?'

'I've nothing more to say to you,' Slider said. 'You're free to go.'

Slider left him to go upstairs again. Someone had once said to him that wives always know. He didn't know if that was true or not. But Rhianne had evidently been a troubled child. And not everything in her apparently nice, middle-class suburban garden had been rosy.

* * *

When he got back to his office, most of the firm had gone home.
Atherton came lingering to his door and said, 'Would it be OK
for me to come over this evening? I'd like to see my kitties,
before they forget me entirely.'

'Joanna's out tonight,' Slider said absently.

'I know. She's working.' Slider looked up enquiringly. 'I overheard you on the phone earlier.'

'Oh. Well, you can come home with me from here if you like.
I'll be leaving in about ten minutes. I don't know what there'll
be to eat. We could order a takeaway.' He looked at his watch.
'The kids'll be in bed. I've missed them again.'

'Fix your mind on that lovely holiday you'll be taking soon,'
Atherton said soothingly. 'Sun, sea and sand.'

'In Burton Bradstock?'

'Two out of three ain't bad.'

THIRTEEN
Alibi of Bird Land

The house was quiet. Slider's father came out from the kitchen and met them in the hall. 'Ah, you're back. Hello, Jim.'

'Hello, Mr Slider.'

'It's George. I've told you.'

'Hello, George,' Atherton said obediently.

'Kids in bed?' Slider asked.

'Yes, and asleep. No dramas.'

'Thanks for stepping in, Dad. I don't know what we'd do without you.'

Mr Slider shrugged thanks away. 'Always a pleasure. I'll be off, then, if that's OK. Snooker's on tonight. The finals. Lydia and I like to watch it together.'

'Who are you rooting for?'

'Franklin. He has nice hands.'

Slider was often unsure whether his father was joking or not. 'Really?'

'You see a lot of their hands. All those close-ups of the shots.'

'But all hands look much the same, don't they?' said Atherton.

'Get on! They're as different as faces! I'd know Franklin's anywhere. Keeps 'em nice, too,' he added. And left.

Atherton stared at the space he had vacated and was just saying, 'Was he joking?' when the Siameses, woken from their latest doze by his voice, erupted into the hall. Sredni Vashtar was in the lead, scudding like a blown leaf, tail upright and rigid as an iron bar, making piercing remarks about heartless desertion. But Tiglath Pileser overtook him and ran straight up Atherton to his shoulder. When they were kittens he had often walked around his house with one perched on each shoulder like a short-sighted and gullible pirate, but they were too big and heavy to balance there easily now, and Tig had to screw in every available claw to maintain position.

Slider had experience of what that felt like. 'Ouch,' he said, by proxy.

'I don't care,' Atherton said. 'I've missed these guys.'

'You can have them back, you know.'

Atherton disengaged two of the more painful claws, picked up Vash and followed Slider into the kitchen with his arms full of heavily purring attachment. 'She hasn't given me an answer yet.'

'Oh. G&T?'

'Please. She's gone to a conference in Birmingham, back on Thursday, so I can't expect a decision before then. I'd take them back with me, but the disruption . . .'

'No problem. They can stay.'

'Thanks. Maybe this weekend I'll get an answer. One way or the other.'

Slider concentrated on pouring tonic and adding ice, then turned with a glass in each hand. 'Well, good luck.'

Atherton put the cats down and took one. 'How do I persuade her? Have you got any tips?'

'It's important to you – getting married?'

'Isn't it important to you?'

'Oh yes. It's everything. But you didn't use to think that way.'

'I want what you've got. I want a home. It *is* different, isn't it?'

'What? From living together? Yes.'

'How?'

Slider thought for a long time, sipping. The cats revolved about Atherton's ankles, gazing up adoringly. Jumper sidled in and circled Slider's, as if proving a point. 'I don't know,' he said at last. 'It just is.'

'The same woman every night for the rest of your life?' Atherton teased.

'God, yes!' Slider said, not at all ironically. 'I never envied you your tom-catting. I know it's supposed to be every red-blooded man's dream, but . . .' He didn't have the words. He didn't want to sound like a girlie movie. 'Family is everything,' he said in the end, lamely.

'Families can be hell,' Atherton suggested. Slider only shrugged. 'How do I persuade her?' he asked again.

'If it's meant to be, it'll happen,' Slider said.

'Gah! Don't go all new-agey on me!'

'Sorry. I didn't have anything else.' He opened the fridge. 'There's cheese. And eggs. And bread. Or I can ring for a takeaway?'

'I'll make omelettes, if you like. Takeaway might make you feel like a sad bachelor.'

'I love your omelettes.' He was still rummaging. 'There are some tomatoes, too.'

'You shouldn't keep tomatoes in the fridge.'

Slider turned, grinning. 'That's the sort of thing a sad bachelor would say.'

'With two cats? That makes me a spinster,' said Atherton.

On the corner of Askew Road and Uxbridge Road was a pub called The Askew. More or less catty-corner opposite was a little convenience store called Uxbridge News. They didn't go in for challenging names in these parts. In the background of the sign over the door was a ghost of the 7-Eleven name and colours, left over from 1997. They didn't go in for much repainting round here, either.

All McLaren knew about the shop was that it had recently been taken over from a Persian called Khatibi; and he only knew that because they had been called in once a few years back when Khatibi had been robbed and stabbed. It had been called Vale News in those days. Because this part of Uxbridge Road was called The Vale. He'd never had cause to go into it since then, and only noticed it on Tuesday morning because he was stopped by the traffic lights right outside it, just at the moment when he discovered he was out of cigarettes. The pack in his pocket was empty, though he could have sworn there had been two left in it last night. He suspected Natalie of taking his fags, not to smoke them herself but to throw them away – she was trying to get him to give up. It'd be like her to leave him to find an empty pack when he was out of her sight and couldn't grill her. She'd be thinking it would deter him, that he'd think, 'oh I can't be bothered to go and buy a new pack, maybe Nat's right, and I'll give it a try.'

But McLarens were made of sterner stuff. The McLarens were an ancient battling clan who had fought bravely at Culloden. He knew that because he had collected Clans of Scotland cards out of packets of Brodies Tea when he was a lad. He'd got the full set. They'd been big tea-drinkers in his house. The lights turned green, and he pulled just round the corner and parked. They didn't call them convenience stores for nothing.

He stopped dead, however, with his hand about to push the door open, not from a griping of conscience, but because he spotted Jenda Squires, Andy Denton's partner, inside the shop. The hair was a dead giveaway. She was not trying to buy anything, but behind the counter. He dodged back and out of sight behind the many posters that plastered the window. She had been list-lessly serving a customer with a newspaper and a packet of Murray Mints and hadn't been looking his way, so he reckoned he hadn't been seen. So, the little minx had got a job, had she? Despite being signed off on the sicker with bad nerves. Now, had she only just started it, having made a miracle recovery – which seemed unlikely – or had she been already working last week? The customer came out, throwing a glance at McLaren, and before the door closed he took a quick peek and saw an Asian geezer behind another counter at the back of the store, the counter that sold alcohol, bus passes and took Evri parcel drops. These shops worked on a shoe string, so the geezer was likely to be the proprietor. A word with him looked to be favourite.

A gaggle of noisy teenage girls pushed past him to enter the shop, and he went in with them, using their bodies as a human shield to get to the back of the shop without being seen. He was in little doubt that he looked like police, at least to those with experience of the species. The girls were pawing over magazines and chocolate, so when he reached it he was alone at the rear counter. He showed his warrant card to the Asian guy and said in a low voice, 'Are you the boss?'

'Yes,' the man said suspiciously. 'Is this about—?'

McLaren put a finger to his lips. 'I want to talk to you about your employee over there, but I don't want her to hear. You got a room at the back?'

An intelligent light came into his eyes. 'Wait one moment, while I get the wife. I cannot leave the counter unattended.'

He disappeared through the doorway at the back, which was obscured with a screen of vertical plastic strips which had once been gaily multicoloured and were now just frankly sad. Fortunately the girls were making a lot of noise and occupying Jenda's attention at the other counter. Finally a large woman pushed through the plastic, cast him a shy look and took up position behind the counter, while the proprietor beckoned McLaren through.

The back room was crammed with boxes of stock, barely leaving room for two shabby armchairs whose orange-and-brown tweed declared their 1970s vintage, and a tin tray sitting on a small, battered coffee table. On it was an electric kettle, attached by a long extension lead (trip hazard!) to an overloaded socket which was also powering a tiny fridge and an electric fan (fire hazard!). The tray also bore a couple of stained mugs, a tea caddy and a used spoon resting in its own small sticky pool (health hazard!).

McLaren took out his note pad.

The proprietor's name was Jarwar. He and his wife lived above the shop. They'd had a similar shop previously in Hayes but had moved to be nearer family.

'Right,' said McLaren. 'That young woman – Jenda Squires – how long has she worked for you?'

Jarwar thought. 'Five weeks. It will be six weeks, if she stays until Friday.'

'Why wouldn't she stay?'

'I think she is stealing from me.' He shrugged. 'So much stealing you accept. Chocolate bars. Cigarettes. They take for themselves. But when they start taking for other people – that you must put a stop to. They don't like to work,' he explained, 'so they get bored, and when they get bored, they steal. The young ones are the worst. No moral sense. I don't know what their parents are thinking. This one was older, so I thought she would be better, but I think she is stealing more each week. One day I will catch her, and then I must dismiss her. If she doesn't leave by herself. They get bored, they steal, then they leave.' He shrugged again. 'That is the pattern. Have you come to arrest her? What did you say her name was?'

'Jenda Squires. Didn't you know? How do you pay her without a name?'

'I pay cash,' he said. 'Don't need to learn their names. They don't stay long anyway.'

'Employing people that way is illegal,' McLaren couldn't help saying.

'So is stealing.'

'You could lose your alcohol licence.'

'It is in my wife's name,' he said simply.

McLaren didn't want to alienate him at this point. He got down to business. 'Was she working last Tuesday?'

Jarwar nodded. 'Monday to Thursday she comes, eight thirty until four thirty. I have another girl comes Friday, Saturday, Sunday.'

'So she was here, working for you, on Tuesday last week? You're quite sure?'

'Of course I'm sure.'

'Did she leave the shop at any time, for any reason?'

'Only for a lunch break, here in the back room. But my wife was in here with her. We don't leave them alone with the stock.' He gestured towards a corner where cartons of crisps towered nearly to the ceiling. 'There is another door to outside there. I am not so much a fool as to leave them alone in here, sir. They would clear the place.'

'Right,' said McLaren. Even he, no sunny optimist by nature, thought this was a bleak world view. But perhaps it was based on experience. Or did mistrust invite betrayal? Probably Jarwar couldn't afford the experiment to find out. 'Thank you. You've been very helpful. Please don't tell her you've spoken to me, or what you've told me. I don't want her to know that we're after her.'

'After her? For stealing?'

'Something more serious. You'll keep schtumm?'

'If you mean silent, yes, I will not tell her, if it helps you to catch her. But when you do, will you charge her with stealing from me as well?'

'I'll see what I can do,' said McLaren. He found one of his cards. 'If she looks like leaving, or changes her behaviour in any way – if she doesn't turn up to work, say – will you let me know?'

Jarwar took the card with a discontented look. 'You should

be quick. Five weeks is long. Next she will have a boyfriend come in and she will load him up with my cigarettes. Then she disappears. This is what they do. You be quick.'

McLaren nodded sympathetically. 'I'll see what I can do,' he said again. 'Can I leave by the back door so she doesn't see me?'

Porson smote his forehead. 'What is it about this case and alibis? And what about this doctor that signed her off?'

'Nothing against him,' Slider said.

'There is now. Blimey, if you can't even trust doctors any more . . . What do you want to do with this?'

Slider had already been thinking about it. 'We still don't have any evidence that Denton knew Rhianne. It's only because of his record we even looked at him.'

'Understood. So it's softly softly catchee mouthy little scrote?'

'I think I should go round myself and confront him. It may put a scare into him. Tuesday's one of his days off. He should be at home.'

Porson looked discontented. 'And that's it?'

'Well, we've got wasting police time to hold against him.'

'That's all you've got to hold against anyone,' Porson barked. 'Talk about bricks without straw! We haven't got much time, you know. It's about time you saw a light at the end of the tunnel!'

'With my luck, it'll be an oncoming train,' said Slider.

Denton opened the door himself, neatly dressed in chinos, moccasins and a short-sleeved shirt. He was clean-shaven and smelled fragrantly of aftershave and fabric softener.

'Going out somewhere?' Slider said.

Denton looked sharply at Slider, and at Atherton standing at his shoulder. 'Well, well. And what do I owe this honour to?' he said.

Slider presented his warrant and started to introduce himself, but Denton waved it away. 'I know who you are. The big man up at Shepherd's Bush nick. Slider of the Yard. What's this they call you? The terrier? Once you get hold of a rat, you won't let go? Or is it the Bulldog? Very British. We will fight 'em on the beaches and so on. Inspector Slider, feared by the bad, loved by

the good – what's that song? Hard but fair, that's what they say
on the street.'

'And what they say on the street about Handy Andy is that he
loves to talk,' Slider said pleasantly. He had no objection to
letting Denton run on. It was villains who wouldn't talk who
were the problem. All that 'no comment' bollocks. Once they'd
seen it on the telly, they copied it – thought it made them the
hard man. But he was very happy to be the inviting silence.
Nature abhors a vacuum, he thought. It also abhors power drill
chuck keys, but that was another matter.

Denton turned his attention to Atherton. 'And who's this long
drink of water?'

'Detective Sergeant Atherton,' Slider said.

'I've heard the name. So this is your boy, is it? You're short,
like me – don't you find tall blokes give you the willies?' He
settled himself against the door frame, folding his arms. 'Last
time it was the monkeys, now they've sent round the organ
grinder. Must be serious.'

'I'd like a word,' Slider said. 'Can we come in?'

'Nice try, but no, you can't.'

'I don't think you want to be discussing this on the doorstep,'
Slider suggested.

'I'm quite comfortable with it, ta. My neighbours can listen
to every word if they want. I've nothing to hide.'

'If you've nothing to hide,' Slider said, 'why can't we come
in?'

'Because it's my house,' Denton said, with a hint of acid. 'My
private space. It's a pleasant change for me to have one of those.
Ever heard of random cell checks? Well, I don't have to put up
with them any more. Seven years with no privacy – now I don't
have to have anyone tramping about my little dog kennel that I
don't want. And I don't want you. If I came to your house, would
you let me in? Didn't think so. So what do you want?'

'Is Jenda in?' Atherton asked.

'My bird is Miss Squires to you, thank you very much,' Denton
said. 'And no, she's not.'

'Just popped out for some cigarettes, has she?'

'Not that it's any business of yours, but yes, that's exactly
what she's done.'

'Getting them from Uxbridge News, on The Vale, I suppose?'
'I don't know where she's gone for them. She's a free agent.
She can go where she likes.'
'Well, that's where she's stealing them from, according to the
proprietor.'
'That's a slander. I'm surprised at you.'
Slider took over. 'She's working there, Andy.'
He grinned, but there was a fraction of a second of discon-
certedness before it. 'Someone's been doing their homework. So
she's got a job. So what?'
'She was working there last Tuesday, all day, when you said
she was at home with you. Your alibi's gone tits up.'
Denton only shrugged.
'So why did you lie to us?'
'Didn't want to get her into trouble. You obviously know she's
claiming benefit. Well, you can't live on that, am I right? So she
gets a little job for extra cash. Nothing wrong with that. But if
the nasty old DWP finds out, they'll cut her off. So I said she
was with me.'
'Nice twist,' Atherton said. 'You're her alibi instead of her
being yours?'
'I don't need an alibi,' Denton said promptly. 'I haven't done
anything.'
'Well, for a start, you've lied to us, wasted police time,' Slider
began.
'Oh, not that old chestnut,' Denton said with a weary look.
'The *police* are a waste of bloody time.'
'This is a serious business,' Slider said sternly. 'You have no
alibi for the time that Rhianne Morgan was murdered.'
'I've told you, I didn't know the girl. Never met her. All I
know about her is what I've read on social media. Where, by the
way, it says it was an allergic reaction, or maybe a drug overdose,
maybe suicide. Not murder.'
'You shouldn't believe everything you read on the internet,'
Atherton said. 'Where were you last Tuesday?'
'Here. At home. All day. My day off – I like to lounge about
and do nothing.'
'Alone.'
'As it happens.'

'Why did you say Jenda was with you?'

A little touch of anger. 'Because you wouldn't have believed me otherwise. Would you? No, didn't think so. If *you* said you were at home all day, OK, fine, but *I've* got to prove it. Your monkeys only came bothering me because I've done time. No other reason. I've done my stretch and that's supposed to wipe the slate clean, or hadn't you heard? I'm trying to turn over a new leaf, make a clean start, get my act together, however you want to put it. But that's not good enough for you lot, is it? Any time you get a crime on your books it's, let's go and hassle someone with a record, see if we can fit him up for it. Saves us having to think.' He swung the lamp of his indignation on Slider. 'Hard but fair, they call you. Well, this isn't very fair, is it? You pester and bully for no reason, when a man's trying to get on, get his head down and make a decent life for himself. Pester and bully until he gives up, he says, oh what's the point, I might as well do the crime if I'm going to get blamed for it anyway. So they come off the straight and narrow. I've seen it time and again. And then you say, I knew it – I knew all along he was bent! Talk about playing with loaded dice! Us poor bastards don't stand a chance, do we?'

Slider waited for him to stop. 'You make some good points,' he said. 'But the question remains, can you prove you were here at home on Tuesday last?'

'No, the question remains, can you prove I wasn't? Because you've got nothing else on me. If you had anything, you'd have brought it out before now.'

'So there's something on you to *be* had, is there?'

'Here we go! No, there isn't. I am an innocent man. I had nothing to do with that little girl's death. Never met her in my life. Understand? Got that through your thick copper heads yet?'

'Oh, I understand what you're saying, all right,' Slider said, with an emphasis on *saying*.

'Gor blimey, you're something else, you are!' Denton said sourly. 'I start to think you're enjoying this.'

'Nothing could be further from the truth,' Slider said.

Lœssop was waiting for them when they got back to the station. 'Guv,' he said, 'I was thinking – would it be worth checking at the garden centre where she worked? I mean, she did stick at it, when her mum and dad said she was bone idle and never got off her backside. So maybe there was a special reason why she liked to go in?'

'Special reason?' Slider queried vaguely, his mind on Denton. 'Well, usually at that age it's a romantic crush on someone, isn't it? Maybe she had a thing for one of the other employees. I remember when I was a Saturday lad at Wickes, there was this girl in the office . . .'

'Right, I'm with you,' Slider said, snapping back to the present. 'It's a thought. This older man she was supposed to be seeing . . .'

'Some horny-handed son of the soil?' Atherton said. 'Giving her smouldering glances as he thrusts his fingers into the potting compost? Very D.H. Lawrence.'

'Get a grip on yourself. It's an urban garden centre on an industrial complex,' Slider said. 'All the plants come pre-packed from a commercial nursery.'

'There's still an atmosphere of fecundity,' Atherton objected. 'That's why people visit them so often, even when they don't need anything.'

'My mum likes to visit her local garden centre, and she doesn't have a garden,' Lœssop said.

'There you are, then.'

'She likes it because they've got a nice caff. They do home-made cakes.'

There was no café at Barney's, and not much air of fecundity. There were trays of bedding plants, though the season was all but over, and rows of tired-looking perennials and pot-bound trees and shrubs. But the majority of the space was given over to dead stock: garden chemicals, tools, patio furniture, plastic flowers, cachepots and so on. Also, and for what reason the gods only knew, toys, children's books – and the inevitable packets of fudge.

I'll have the big bag of Weed'n'feed, a large Tomorite and . . . have we got enough fudge, Marjorie?

Better get another couple of packets, dear. We don't want to run out.

Lœssop asked to speak to the manager and was conducted to

his office at the back. The manager, whose name was Varley, was a very big man. Big in all dimensions. The biggest man you could get before you had two men. He had an air of calm confidence. Lœssop supposed that when you were as big as that, the only thing you had to worry about in life was the tendency of small objects to roll towards you. Or changing the orbits of minor planets.

'Oh yes, Rhianne. Poor kid! It was heart, wasn't it? Terrible when it gets them that young.'

'Where did you hear it was heart?' Lœssop asked.

'Her mum rang me up to say she wasn't going to be coming in on Saturday. Poor lady, she didn't need to do that. It was polite of her, but I already knew Rhianne was dead. My staff all do social media; they've been talking about it all week. Wild talk, for the most part, but you know what those websites are like. We'd got white slave gangs and weird sex cults and all sorts. I've clamped down on it whenever I've heard it. Natural causes, I told them. Though there's not much natural about a kid her age having a bad heart. What did you want to know?'

'How long had she been working here?'

'Well, she came, let's see, the weekend before Easter. Frankly, I didn't think she'd last. A lot of these youngsters, they don't seem to understand the concept of employment. They like to have a job, but they don't like to do any work. It's as if that's optional. Not all of them,' he corrected himself. 'I've got some cracking youngsters here. But Rhianne, she seemed indifferent when she first came, and I thought she'd come once or twice then drop out. But she seemed to buck up quite suddenly, and she turned into a reliable girl, one of my better ones.'

'Any reason you could see for her bucking up?'

'Nothing I could put my finger on. Maybe her parents gave her a talking-to. I don't know.'

'Did she have any special friends here, among the staff? Anyone in particular she hung around with?'

'Not that I noticed. Of course, she was working on the tills, and you don't get the opportunity to chat to anyone there. If anything,' he added thoughtfully, 'she was a bit of a loner. Not unfriendly, but happy with her own thoughts. You didn't see her having a group giggle with the other girls in the staff room.'

'Other girls? Are all your staff female?'

'Oh no. We're an equal opportunities employer,' he said with a smile.

'I was wondering, you see, if she had a crush on one of the male employees – that might account for her keenness to come to work.'

'Well, I did suspect she had a bit of a thing for me, but who could blame her? Fine figure of a man that I am – broken hearts strewn all over the place.' Lœssop opened his mouth to speak, and Varley lifted a hand. 'Little joke. Sorry. I suppose I shouldn't joke when the poor child is dead. No, I can't say I ever spotted her making sheep's eyes at anyone. We've a few Saturday boys, but they mostly work out the back, unloading and shifting the heavies for the customers – bags of compost and so on – so she wouldn't have seen a lot of them. My regular male staff are all a bit on the senior side, I'd have thought, to appeal to a lass of eighteen.'

'She did mention to friends that she was seeing an older man.'

'Sounds like me again. Sorry. No, I don't think I can help you there. What makes you think it was someone she met here?'

'We don't, especially, it's just that we have to look everywhere.'

Varley was trying to be helpful, thinking about it. 'I wonder if it could have been a customer, then? Someone who came in regularly?'

'I wouldn't have thought the average person went to a garden centre every week.'

'Not all our customers are private punters. We get commercial gardeners as well, and they come in regularly.'

It didn't seem very likely to Lœssop, but on the other hand there was Atherton's son-of-the-soil reference, and a well-set-up young man with a muscular frame, big boots and an outdoor tan could well be appealing. 'Do you have CCTV?' he asked.

'They keep it a month,' he told Slider when he got back, 'so we've got three Saturdays to look at. I'll start at her last Saturday and work back. There are two cameras covering the tills plus one on the customer help desk, though Varley said she was never on that, but I took it anyway, and one in the back that covers the

staff room door and the externals. So we'll see if she went in
and out with any of the male staff.'

'What about the other Saturday girls?'

'I've got their names and addresses, so we can interview them
if we get nothing from the tapes. But there was one of them, a
girl called Kim, who's working there full time in the holidays,
and I spoke to her. She wasn't much help. All she wanted to do
was ask me questions about how Rhianne really died. When I
did get her to concentrate, she said more or less what Varley
said, that Rhianne was OK but not especially chummy, and that
she didn't think she had a crush on anybody. So it looks as though
my idea was a crock.'

He looked so disappointed Slider said, 'There's still all the
CCTV footage to go through. You never know what might turn
up.'

And we've got nothing else to go on, he added internally.

FOURTEEN
Straight Is the Gait

Swilley was taking her turn at trawling through Rhianne's Instagram account. Her own daughter was, thank God, too young for that sort of thing yet, but she supposed she had it to come, unless the craze for snapping everything you did faded in the next few years, which didn't seem likely. But she had some experience from other cases, as more and more often police work involved searching these online records for clues. Sometimes they were blatant. A surprising number of people lived under the delusion that once they went online they were invisible and untouchable – which accounted, of course, for the bad online behaviour. But it was also a fact that most criminals were very, very stupid, and/or very, very conceited. They put stuff online either to boast about their deeds or believing they would never be caught. An intelligent criminal mastermind – what Atherton called a Moriarty, a reference Swilley pretended not to understand, to annoy him – was as likely to be found, as McLaren would put it, as tits on a bull.

And of course Rhianne Morgan was no genius. Like most girls of her age she posted selfies, pictures of places she had been, of outfits and items she had bought or would like to buy, meals she had eaten, fancy cocktails embellished with fruit, umbrellas, even sparklers. Things were described as 'lush' or 'gross', sometimes 'dope' or 'tight', occasionally 'sick', which was not always derogatory, or the ages-old 'cool', which went out and came back in regular phases but never seemed entirely to die. It was wearying stuff, but it had to be done, and by several people working separately, because it was fatally easy to drift into a coma-like state while scrolling and miss something.

Finally, she went to Slider. 'Boss, you know how when you stare at something for a long time, it becomes meaningless. Then when you sort of half close your eyes, you see a pattern?'

'Sleeping on police time again, constable?' Slider said.

She gave him the look mothers develop to suppress silliness.

'Seriously, boss. I think I'm seeing a pattern in Rhianne's postings.'

'That's good. Let me hear it,' Slider said gravely.

'Can I show you?'

He went with her to her desk. Some of the others drifted up behind in the hope of a breakthrough. 'You see, going back a few months, it was all pretty normal. Selfies with girlfriends – you know, when you jam your faces together and hold the camera over your head. Me and my bestie. Making faces at the camera. Admiring each other's hair and make-up and new clothes.' She scrolled as she talked. 'And there are selfies of her with Kenton . . . All very innocent . . . Except maybe this one.'

Rhianne was gurning at the camera in what Slider recognized as her room, and in the background Kenton could be seen sitting on the bed, which was strewn with books, with a foolscap note pad on his lap and a biro in hand. He was fully clad and looked completely absorbed in what he was reading. It was captioned 'Kent and me revising – in my bedroom!!! Oo er missus!!!!'

'Do people still say that?' Slider asked.

'Nineteen-seventies camperie never goes out of style,' Atherton offered, arriving just then. Slider gave him a look. 'It was recently a fad in schools, I understand,' he amended. 'Some currently fashionable comic said it on BuzzFeed and it caught on.'

'The joke tone and the number of exclamation marks are meant to take the reality out of it,' Swilley went on. 'We know that her and Kenton were having sex, but she doesn't really want anyone else to know. She doesn't mind if they guess, but she's not going to confirm it.'

'It's complicated, isn't it?' Slider said.

'Yes. I wouldn't want to be young again,' said Swilley. 'But look – this is what I meant by a pattern. There are selfies with Kenton and another boy I've identified as William Vigo, another schoolmate and apparently a platonic friend, but there are none with Corey.'

'Maybe Kenton looked at her Insta postings and she didn't want him to find out,' LaSalle suggested.

'Maybe. But after a certain date there are no selfies of her with anyone else, and then no selfies at all. In fact, she's posting pictures of places and food – lots of food! – without any people in them, except accidentally in the background.'

'She's being cautious?' Slider asked.

'That's what I think, boss. But why? Or rather, who taught her to be?'

'Natural caution?' Atherton suggested.

'In an eighteen-year-old?' Jenrich said caustically. 'Get real. They're creatures of impulse.'

'Disturbed children *do* conceal things,' Slider offered.

'But what is she disturbed about?' Swilley said.

'Corey,' said LaSalle. 'We know she was seeing him. And there's no pictures of him.'

'They're doing things that are not plain vanilla, as the lad himself says,' said Atherton.

'He was doing his brother's bird and didn't want him to know,' said LaSalle. 'He told her not to post his ugly mug.'

'Ye-es,' Swilley said reluctantly, 'but does Corey really strike you as the cautious kind? Would he have cared if Kenton found out? He liked to torment him, didn't he? Wouldn't he have wanted to brag?'

'He didn't care about being seen when he ran off with her at the school dance,' Slider said. 'And, no, he didn't strike me as having discretion deep in his DNA. He seemed to want to boast about his conquests.'

'Besides,' Jenrich added, 'taking photos with your phone is so automatic with that age group it probably wouldn't even register she was doing it. Let alone thinking about where it might end up.'

'And,' Swilley went on, 'she told *Corey* she was seeing an older man, so Corey couldn't have been him.'

'We've already postulated that there was someone else,' said Atherton, who didn't like Swilley being too clever.

'We didn't *pus*tulate,' she said, deliberately mispronouncing, 'that this older man would make her conceal his existence. He must have had some heavy influence to stop her posting him on Insta. That's like—'

'Keeping an elephant away from water,' Slider helped her out.

'Maybe she just made him up,' LaSalle said. 'You know, the fantasy perfect boyfriend. There's no pictures of him because he didn't exist.'

'*Somebody* was there last Tuesday,' Atherton said. 'It wasn't the Invisible Man – though it might as well have been for our purposes.'

'Settle down, Jim, we're not finished yet,' Swilley said. 'I've got an idea.'

McLaren drifted up with the remains of a Ginsters Steak and Onion Slice in his hand, reminding Slider it was past lunchtime. 'Idea? I had one once,' he said. 'Didn't like it.'

'Take that smelly thing away, Maurice,' Swilley snapped. 'Last time you dropped a dollop of something disgusting on my desk.'

He obliged efficiently by shoving the remainder into his mouth all at once. 'What's your idea, then?' he said indistinctly, spraying crumbs.

She hunched her shoulders protectively and scrolled some more. 'A lot of these postings are of meals she had with the mystery man. If we can identify the cafés from the pictures, they might remember her and have an idea who she was with.'

'They might have CCTV,' McLaren said approvingly after a heroic swallow.

'Good thinking,' Slider said. 'Get on with it, then. McLaren, you can help.'

Slider was looking over her shoulder at one of the postings she was talking about – a plate of food on a laminated table top – a basic café then – and nothing to be seen of her companion but, towards the top of the picture, a hand resting on the table. Obviously a man's hand. As he thought that, he checked himself and thought, yes, it *was* obviously male, you could tell that much at a glance. And he remembered his father saying hands are as different as faces. If they could only identify her companion, they could possibly use the image of the hand as proof.

'Not just for fingerprints,' he said aloud.

'Boss?'

'Never mind. That's for later. Carry on.'

He went up to the canteen for a quick lunch (macaroni cheese and salad), and when he came down there was an excited group around Lœssop's desk.

'Well, lookie here,' Atherton said as he entered.

'You've found a new suspect?' There was no harm in hoping.

'Quite the contrary, as the seasick man said when the steward asked him if he'd dined.'

'What?'

'We've found an old suspect.'

'I'm collating it,' Lœssop said, fingers busy. 'I'll get it all on one flash drive. But I've got it cued. Look. This is last Saturday – I mean,' he corrected himself, '*her* last Saturday.'

There was Rhianne at work, standing behind the checkout desk, in a dark green fleece top with the Barney's logo over the left breast, just finishing with a customer. As he walked away, the next customer came up to the till and put a basket down, and her face lit up. It gave Slider a pang. It was always hard to see video footage of someone you had only met dead, seeing them in the full of their life, all unaware it was soon to end. It was particularly hard to see them smiling. The customer, in a light blue T-shirt, had bent his head and covered his mouth to cough as he approached, so you could not see his face, but from the rear the stocky build and the mussed fair hair, slightly long at the back, looked familiar.

'Is this the best—?' Slider began, but Lœssop anticipated him. 'Wait! He gets caught by the door cam. But look at Rhianne.'

She was listening intently to something the customer was saying, then replying. She was animated and obviously engaged, though the expression was not exactly what Slider would have expected from a girl with a crush. It was hard to tell emotions from camera footage, even though the Barney's system was state-of-the-art, but there was less smiling going on than he'd have expected. Tension, he thought, or excitement rather than innocent joy.

The customer was keeping his head turned away from the camera, but there were enough glimpses of a part profile for Slider to be pretty sure who it was.

'It's not good enough for the CPS,' he said, 'but isn't that—?'

'Wait, guv, please,' Lœssop said. It was his show; he wanted to do his own reveal.

Rhianne scanned the items in the basket without looking at them, talking with and listening to the customer the whole time.

She seemed to be being very leisurely about the scanning – prolonging the contact, perhaps. She dealt with the payment – cash, Slider noted – and handed over the change.

'Watch this,' Lœssop said.

It was quickly done, you had to be watching, but as the customer took the change he caught Rhianne's fingers for a moment and squeezed them. Then he leaned forward slightly and obviously said something, because she registered what he had said, and then smiled and said – you could read the lips – *yes, OK*.

And she watched him walk away

'Now the door cam,' Lœssop said and worked the keys.

A new feed came up, showing the doors to Barney's from outside and slightly above. The automatic sliding doors opened, and the same customer came out. You could see by the build, the hair and the colour of the blue T-shirt – which had the Rolling Stones tongue logo on the front – that it was the same man. His head was bent, putting his change away in his pocket, but then he straightened up and raised his head in the moment before he turned away and out of sight, walking with that cocky upright strut of the confident but not very tall man.

Lœssop froze the image. 'Handy Andy,' he said triumphantly. There was a moment's silence out of respect for his endeavour and showmanship. 'He didn't know the camera was there. You see how he covered his face coming up to the checkout?'

'He should have guessed,' LaSalle said. 'There's always a camera on the door.'

'Too pleased with himself,' Jenrich said. 'Look how he's smiling. Tosser. He said he'd never seen her in his life.'

'Take a breath,' Slider said. 'This isn't proof of anything except that he's a cocky bloke who chats to checkout girls and flirts with them a bit.'

'That was more than a bit,' Jenrich said.

'It's perfectly possible – and I'm sorry to say this, but it's true – for someone with that sort of personality to shoot the breeze with a shop assistant and never really register them as a person at all. Same with barmaids and waitresses. It is possible, and he could argue this, that an incident like that passed out of his recollection the moment it was over. Even a perfectly nice person can exchange a few words while paying for something and not be able to recognize the assistant afterwards.'

'Yeah, guv,' Lœssop said, 'but you've not seen everything yet. Remember Denton works at D&K's, just across the lot from Barney's?'

'He's been in before?' Slider said.

'I've only got the last three Saturdays on tape, but he's there on all three. And this is a bloke, remember, who doesn't have a garden!'

'What's he buying?' Atherton asked.

'You can't always tell. But I've seen rat poison, one of those little watering cans for watering house plants, Baby Bio, greetings cards. A pack of paper napkins with robins on. Fudge.'

'Of course,' said Slider. There was always fudge. It was everywhere. It was like a secret alien invasion. One day all the cubes of fudge in all the tourist tat shops and National Trust shops and garden centres and airport duty frees would hatch and it would be too late. Goodbye dominant species status. 'Well, they're legitimate purchases,' he concluded.

'We never saw any house plants when we went in his gaff,' LaSalle pointed out.

'He might have thought of getting one,' Atherton said, purely for the sake of balance. 'Or he could be buying things for someone else. I'm just saying that's what he could claim,' he responded to LaSalle's expression. 'Suppose he was visiting some housebound old lady as part of his rehabilitation efforts?'

'Every week?' Lœssop said. 'And he can get all those things in other shops. Why Barney's?'

'Because he works just across the way. It's handy for Andy. He can pop in on his break, or after work.'

'I wonder if he only went in on Saturdays, or if he was there other days?' said Jenrich.

'We could find out,' said Lœssop.

'Let's see the other encounters,' Slider said.

In each case, Denton obscured his face with some casual gesture on his way up to the checkout. In each case he paid cash. And in each case, he engaged Rhianne in conversation. On the middle Saturday, the chat was quite extensive, perhaps because there was no other customer immediately to hand. And in each case, they got a good look at his face as he left the store. There was no doubt it was him.

'But I get the feeling,' Slider said when they'd watched the earliest of the three, 'that this wasn't the beginning of the connection. The way they seem to be talking – don't you think that's something that's been going on for a while?'

'Yes,' said Atherton, 'but that's speculation. Without tapes going further back we can't prove it. But it does explode the lie that he'd never seen her in his life. You might dismiss one chat with the checkout girl from your mind, but not a chat each week with the same one.'

'Still doesn't prove anything,' Porson said moodily, prowling up and down his cage – the strip of carpet between desk and window.

'I know,' Slider said.

'So what? That's what he'll say. Haven't you ever shot the shit with a pretty girl, he'll say.'

'I got a long lecture from him on the unfairness of targeting a man just because he has a record,' Slider said. 'If we ask him why he lied about knowing her, he'll say, because you'd never have believed it was an innocent encounter.'

'And we wouldn't have. He hit the nail for six there.' He stared unhappily at the window – not through it, because of the grime on the outside – and said, 'It's like nailing jelly to the wall, this case. I hate to say it, Bill, but everything he's said makes sense. If he was unlucky enough to have flirted a bit with a girl who later turns up dead, well, he's bound to tell a few porkies to keep us at harm's length. We have to take into consideration that he may actually be innocent.'

'I know,' Slider said again. 'And I know we have to get a lot more proof – direct proof – before we can move on him. But there are so many little things. He came out just before Easter and got the job at D&K's. Rhianne starts working at Barney's just about then. She starts talking about seeing an older man. He's gone three weeks running – and probably more than that – to shop in a garden centre when he doesn't have a garden.'

'Circumstantial.'

'And now she's posting pictures on Instagram of outings with the new boyfriend without ever showing his face. Why? When a girl's got a new boyfriend she wants pictorial proof of it to show her mates.'

'You think he's stopped her taking pictures of him?'

'Why would he do that, if he's got nothing to hide?'

'Or it could be a married man she's seeing,' Porson said. 'She's just the right age to fall for a married bloke.'

'Yes. I know.'

'But if it *was* Denton . . .' Porson considered. 'You think he was grooming her, do you?'

'I'm not in a position to think anything,' Slider said. 'All we *know* so far is that he chatted to her at the checkout.'

'One swallow doesn't make a meal.'

'On the other hand, there's no smoke without fire. And a leopard can't change its spots.'

Porson gave him an odd look but went on, 'Well, I'll try to get you more time. Won't be popular. You need to—' He stopped himself and resumed lamely. 'Get a move on. Time and . . . Just get a move on.'

'Yes, sir.'

'Don't let me down.'

'Have I ever?'

'No.'

'Well, I might this time,' Slider said and left, feeling guilty and hoping he hadn't put Porson off using a metaphor. It would certainly make life less colourful.

Joanna rang. 'Martin's called again. Hazlett. With some dates.'

'Oh?' Slider said warily.

'I know I said I would take the whole month off, but it's just two Saturdays, when you're usually at home, and I want to keep him on side. If he knows he can rely on me—'

'Or, to put it another way, take advantage of you.'

'Hey!'

'Sorry. But me being at home on a Saturday is rather the point. So we can do things together.'

'There'll be other Saturdays.'

'There might not.'

'That's very dark. Are you leaving me?'

'Of course not. But you never know what my job's going to

throw up.' He was deliberately not thinking about Rhianne, who doubtless had thought there would always be other Saturdays. 'If I have to go in—'

'So you can work Saturdays, but I can't?'

'You don't *have* to.'

There was a brief silence, then she said, 'Look, I don't want to quarrel about this. If it's that important to you, I'll tell Martin I can't do it.'

He sighed. 'No, take the dates. I know you need to work. I'm not going to come the heavy husband on you.'

'Well, you never know your luck. See what happens tonight,' she said with a grin in her voice. 'The concerts are in Bedford again, so I won't be late. I promise I won't go for a drink with the lads afterwards.'

'You can go for a drink. But be in by midnight, young lady,' he said.

'Yes, Dad,' she said. 'Did you hear the one about the Roman who went into a bar, held up two fingers and said, "Five beers, please"?'

I have got to get this case closed, he thought as he put the phone down. *It's turning me into a monster.*

You can work yourself cross-eyed, and then someone else gets the break. That's how it goes. Swilley had trawled Rhianne's Instagram postings until she knew every last stupid pointless picture by heart. It was after four o'clock and she'd been at it all day when the unmistakeable crackle of a crisp packet – Walkers, she thought, different sound from Kettle – and a whiff of salt 'n' vinegar on the air told her that McLaren had come up behind her.

'Making a cuppa, Norma – want one?'

'Yeah, thanks,' she said. But he didn't move away. His heavy breathing stirred her hair as he leaned in.

'Here, I know where that is,' he said of the latest image up on her screen.

There was a pizza on a plate, on a table with the usual white undercloth and a dark red smaller overcloth laid cornerwise. Beyond the pizza was a tiny vase holding a single white rosebud and a sprig of rosemary and beside it a tealight, unlit, in a square glass holder, and beside *that*, a small wooden rack for holding menus, the sort that usually had special promotions, cocktails and upcoming events in it.

The caption was, 'This new Italian we've found, the food is uh-maz-ing!!! (Face Savouring Food emoji. Thumbs Up emoji. Heart emoji.) Wish I could tell you where it is, guys, but we're keeping it to ourselves!! For now!! (Winking emoji.)'

'It's a pizza place, Maurice,' Swilley said. 'There's about ten thousand of them in West London.'

'No, but look at the menu thing,' he said. In the rack was a slim, upright, laminated card on which the words Signature Cocktails could be read at the top.

'Very good. An Italian restaurant that serves cocktails. That narrows it down.'

'Don't be so snarky, Norm. Look, above "cocktails" – see, the logo?'

'Yeah, I've seen it; it's no help. I've tried enlarging it, but there's no name on it. It's just a stupid drawing. A *bad* drawing.'

'I know, it's the Fountain of Neptune in Florence.'

'Is that what it is? I thought it was a bloke taking a whizz.'

'Well, you can't get a lot of detail on a logo that size. I asked the manager one time I was in there. The owner's son did it, so they had to have it. He wanted just them pillars with the triangle on top, what d'you call that?'

'I'd call it, "I could kiss you, Maurice, if you didn't stink of vinegar." You know this place?'

'Yeah, Vale Pizzatoria. In Uxbridge Road. I used to go there a lot with Nat. We haven't been lately because we've found a better Italian nearer to us. And she's trying to lose some weight, so she's staying off pizza. I said you could always *not* have the pizza, but it's their speciality and she says it's too much temptation.'

'Stop wittering, you twonk! Maybe a lot of places have the same logo? Is it a chain?'

'No, the bloke who owns it, Demarco, he only has the two, that one and the Santorini in the High Street – but they don't have the logo, just the Italian flag.'

'Does Vale Pizzatoria have CCTV?'

'I dunno, I've never looked. I was off duty whenever I went there.'

'Never mind, we'll find out,' she said, shoving her chair back. 'Wanna come with?'

'Yeah, course! They do these cannoli; they dip the ends in chocolate chips—'

'We're not going there to eat.'

'And they do these lemon pistachio cantucci, and you get a glass of this wine, Vin Santo, with it, and you like *dunk* them . . .'

The manager, a tall, thin, melancholy man with a drooping moustache and hair that was slipping backwards from his head like an elderdown in the night, turned out not to be Italian, but Croatian. His name was Jakov Horvat. He greeted McLaren as a former customer and looked at Swilley with slight puzzlement. If it was on the tip of his tongue to say, 'Wife not with you today?' discretion overcame it.

Swilley wondered why he was running an Italian restaurant.

'Lot of Italian influence in Croatia,' he said. 'Nearest neighbours.' He shrugged. 'In any case, food is food, service is service. I was a waiter at Santorini for five years and Mr Demarco asked if I wanted to manage this place for him. There aren't too many Croatian restaurants in London looking for a manager.' He smiled at Swilley, who was tall and glamorous and blonde. 'I don't even like Italian food,' he confided roguishly. 'I like a curry, me. But don't tell Mr Demarco.'

Swilley promised blandly that she wouldn't and produced the pictures of Rhianne and Denton. 'Have you seen these people in here?'

'Pretty girl,' Horvat commented. 'Yes, I remember her. Always notice a pretty girl. She's been in two-three times maybe. With an older man – not her dad, not old enough for that.'

'Is that him?'

He hesitated over the picture of Denton. 'He's the right age, looks a bit like. But the man she was with, he seemed nice, smiling and charming. This looks like—' He paused, frowning.

It was a custody photo, so Denton wasn't looking at his best. Certainly he wasn't smiling.

'I think it's the same,' he said at last, 'but I can't be sure. If you show me him smiling . . .'

'Can't do that at the moment,' McLaren said. 'When were they last in?'

Horvat shook his head. 'Couple of weeks ago, maybe.'

'Have you got CCTV?' Swilley asked.

'Yes, on the front door and back door,' he said promptly and then realized why she was asking. 'But it records over after a week. Sorry. It wasn't last week they were here – maybe the week before.'

'Maybe some of your staff might remember them,' Swilley said. 'Maybe they could identify the man more certainly?'

'Of course, you can ask. They'll be arriving soon for the evening session,' Horvat said.

But McLaren took Swilley's arm and said, 'We may not need that. You know what's next door?'

'A bank, isn't it?' She had noticed automatically on the way in. 'And a dry cleaners the other side.'

'A bank,' McLaren said. 'And they keep their footage at least a month.'

Swilley thanked Horvat and said they'd be back and followed McLaren out. The visible camera on the bank's façade was angled towards the ATM, which meant it was angled towards Vale Pizzatoria, and there was a good chance it would catch the door.

'Or at least if they turned right when they came out, they'd pass the ATM and you'd get them,' McLaren said.

'Thirty days here on the premises and ninety days in the cloud,' the manager affirmed when they had got access to her office, looked at the monitor in question and seen that the camera did in fact cover the Pizzatoria's door very nicely.

'Thirty days will be enough for our purposes for the moment,' Swilley said.

But the manager didn't want to give them the footage and was inclined to refer it to head office for advice. 'Or perhaps if you could get a warrant,' she dithered. 'If you could come back in a few days . . .'

McLaren could be intimidating in certain circumstances and to certain kinds of people, but Swilley could freeze and burn at the same time and her corn-gold hair and flax-blue eyes were disheartening to any woman with bog-standard looks. She followed piercing insistence with kindly reassurance, and the manager, frostbitten but comforted, and after ringing the station to verify they were who they said they were and that the footage was essential to a major inquiry, allowed them to download the whole month onto a firestick.

Rhianne had not deleted any photographs from her phone, so they were able to get the exact date of the Vale Pizzatoria picture and go straight to it on the bank footage, which saved a lot of time. They would have to trawl through the whole thirty days for any more sightings, but for the moment they had their confirmation.

'This is more like it,' said Porson, who had come in to see the results on Swilley's monitor. 'That's Denton all right.'

'Even if you couldn't see his face, you'd know him by his walk,' Slider said.

'Yeah, the turkey strut,' LaSalle said. 'But his Christmas is coming now.'

Denton came out of the Pizzatoria's door, followed by Rhianne, turned right towards the bank and were clearly identifiable as they passed the ATM and walked out of range. In case there was any doubt that they were together, Denton, though not ushering her through the door first, did at least pause and wait for her, and when she fell in beside him, she took hold of his hand, though he quickly freed it.

'Poor kid,' Lœssop said. 'Not even allowed to hold his hand in public.'

'She should have taken that as a hint that she was with the wrong guy,' Jenrich snapped.

'She was only just eighteen,' Lœssop said reproachfully.

Porson straightened up. 'So, putting this together with the stuff from Barney's, we can prove he was seeing her. We've still got to prove he killed her.'

'I think it's time we searched his flat,' Slider said.

'He'll never give permission,' Gascoyne said. 'Would we get a warrant on what we've got so far?'

'The flat's in Jenda's name,' Slider said. 'We arrest her for benefit fraud and suspicion of theft from her employer, and then we can search her flat without a warrant.'

'Good thinking, boss,' Swilley said, 'And if we—'

'—wait until tomorrow, when Denton's at work. We can do it without him knowing,' Slider anticipated. 'We don't want him to have any warning. We'll pick her up at work and make sure she doesn't ring him to tip him off.'

'That's what I was going to say,' said Swilley.

'And it was a very good idea of yours,' Slider said, straight-faced.

FIFTEEN
Lock, Stock and Two Barking Spaniels

'You seem more cheerful,' Joanna said. 'Have you had a breakthrough?'

'A little of one. A crackthrough maybe,' Slider said, shedding his suit jacket while three cats did their best to trip him up. It was oppressively hot this evening, thunder weather – though several times recently it had looked as though a thundering downpour was imminent, but it had moved away again, so he wasn't banking on anything. He went to the sink, got a glass of water and gulped. 'Kids in bed?'

'Just. Teddy was out like a light, but I said George could read for half an hour, so he might be still awake.'

'I'll go up and see them and get changed. Then I'll come and tell you about it.'

She glanced at the clock. 'He's had his half hour. If he's still awake, take the book away and turn the light off when you leave him.'

'Will do. What's for supper?'

'Cold chicken and salad again. Too hot to eat hot food.'

When he came downstairs again, he found she had laid supper outside on the patio. It was perhaps half a degree cooler out there.

'I wish it would rain and get it over with,' she said. 'It's hell playing with sweaty hands. So what's the crack in the saucer?'

He told her the day's news while they ate, the cats lurking casually in case anyone should misplace a fragment of chicken.

'So what are you hoping to find in his flat?' Joanna asked.

'Ideally, I'd like to find the scarf. It was taken from the scene, so it must be somewhere. Otherwise, my hopes rest mainly on the laptop that Lœssop and LaSalle saw when they visited her.'

'Hmm. But you said he was very cautious, wouldn't let her

take any pictures of him for instance. Would he leave incriminating evidence on his laptop?'

'Not very cautious. He avoided the checkout cameras but got caught on the door cameras. And, of course, he could never be sure what Rhianne would tell people about him, even if she promised him she'd keep him a secret.'

'Yes, that was risky. She was only a kid really.'

'I think in pursuit of his latest obsession, everything else becomes secondary to achieving his aim. He probably was aware subconsciously of the risks but let other things take priority.'

'You think he did it, then?'

'I'm sure now that he did. It's proving it that's going to be difficult.'

'Unless he does something stupid. Or has done something stupid.'

He smiled faintly. 'We always rely on that.'

'Hmm. So our holiday at the end of the month is still on?'

'I hope so.'

'You'd better do more than hope, because I've booked somewhere,' she said and produced some sheets of print-out. 'It's a cottage on Exmoor. Well, they call it a cottage, but it's a bungalow really. It's got a garden with views, and a little terrace to have drinks while looking at them on fine evenings.'

'If any,' Slider said. 'Exmoor didn't get so green for nothing.'

'And a conservatory for the kids to play in if it rains nonstop the whole fortnight.'

'It looks nice.'

'But? Bill, it's getting close – I had to book somewhere, or there'd be nothing left.'

'I know, but I haven't closed this case yet.'

'It's two weeks away. If you haven't closed it in two weeks, you'll be in the grind stage and someone else can run it for a bit.' Her eyes were bright. 'Honestly, you're a nymphomaniac when it comes to the Job. You booked this time off months ago. We have to have a proper family holiday, and if you don't put your brain in neutral from time to time, you'll blow your big end.'

'You don't know what a big end is.'

'It's what goes if you over-rev the engine.'

'I'm impressed.'

'Having this to look forward to will be good for you. And I was thinking – there are two double bedrooms and a twin. How about inviting Jim and Stephanie for one of the weekends? It might be good for them to see what family life is all about.'

'Good for them how?'

'One way or the other,' she said.

They got the plans in place early. Observers saw Jenda and Andy off to work and checked that they arrived there. Once they were safely inside, McLaren and Fathom in an unmarked car, settled down to watch D&K in case Denton came out again, while the search team got ready in Gayford Road and Jenrich and Gascoyne went down to Uxbridge News to arrest Jenda.

Jenda became very agitated as soon as Jenrich got the first words out, and started screeching that it was not a crime, every-body did it, then tried to run out of the shop. Jarwar was very excited about the whole business, jumping up and down and urging them to 'jail her for stealing my cigarettes!' while Mrs Jarwar wrung her hands and wept and asked the heavens why these things happened to good people. Jenda struggled so violently they had to cuff her. Mrs Jarwar went to the back room to fetch Jenda's jacket and handbag, and they finally got the still protesting but no longer struggling arrestee into the car.

At the station they told her that her flat was to be searched, confiscated her house keys, and Slider and Atherton took charge of them and drove over to Gayford Road. In the car, Slider checked with McLaren that Denton was still in place. They all had Airwaves. 'Let me know immediately if he tries to leave.'

'Yeah, we know, guv. Good luck.'

The flat was as Lœssop and LaSalle had described it, sparsely furnished and unexpectedly tidy. Denton's habit caught in prison, perhaps – Jenda didn't look like an organized person. The first objective was the laptop, which was still in the tiny sitting room, and surprisingly was not password protected.

'Or perhaps not surprisingly,' Atherton said. 'Most people don't bother, unless they're living in a multiple-occupancy house.'

'Most people don't have anything to hide,' Slider said. But an initial scroll through suggested Handy Andy didn't have anything to hide, either. There was email, but very little of it, and nothing relating to Rhianne. Mostly it was official stuff, with some encouraging screeds from the Rev Kev and information emails about church activities. The browsing history was also sparse, mostly news sites, some shopping for clothes and make-up, presumably Jenda's. Snapchat, Instagram and X were all installed, but it was obvious that he did not post, only looked in. There was no photo file.

'This is either a very cautious fellow, or he doesn't bother with the web,' Atherton said. 'Did he get out of the habit while he was inside? Or did our visit spook him, and he deleted everything?'

'There's nothing in the recycle bin,' Slider said. 'But if he's deleted stuff, it'll be retrievable. We'll get this to Jason Adebayo.'

'You don't sound very hopeful.'

'Because he didn't seem spooked when we saw him,' Slider said. 'He seemed smugly confident. Enjoying himself at our expense. I don't think he anticipated any follow-up, so why would he delete anything? I don't think there was anything here to delete.'

The bathroom yielded a wrap of cocaine, tucked away behind the men's toiletries. 'Does he think Jenda won't find it if he hides it behind his Bulldog shave gel?' Atherton said. And in the bedside cabinet drawer on what seemed to be Denton's side of the bed (an Andy McNab paperback with a corner turned down halfway through), two spliffs wrapped in silver foil, and a glass straw.

'We can get him on the drugs, anyway,' Atherton said.

'But it doesn't get us to Rhianne's death.'

'That spliff – wouldn't you say it was rolled the same way as the one found in Rhianne's room? I wonder if he supplied it? Could we match saliva from the paper?'

'Good thought,' Slider said. 'Still doesn't—'

'I know, but it brings us closer. How much evidence do we need of intimacy between them before it's enough?'

'You know the answer to that,' Slider said. 'Keep looking for the scarf,' he said to the team.

Jenda's side of the wardrobe and her clothes drawers looked

more promising – she was only tidy as far as shoving everything out of sight, probably Denton's requirement, but in all the tangle and jumble of clothes and underwear, there was nothing resembling a silk scarf.

'I can't see her wearing that sort of thing,' Atherton said. 'Anyway, nothing here you could choke someone with, except tights.'

'And if it was tights, it would have left a pattern,' Slider said. 'It looks as though – wait a minute. What's that?'

'What's what?'

The searcher turned enquiringly to Slider with what he had in his hand. 'It's a scrunchie,' Slider said. 'A pink scrunchie.'

'Most women have them,' Atherton said. 'Young ones, anyway.'

'Engage brain before using mouth,' Slider said. 'You've seen Jenda – she practically has a Mohican. She has nothing to use a scrunchie with.'

'She might have had longer hair once and it's left over from then.'

'But her hair is dark, and the hairs caught up in this are fair. So unless Handy Andy is a cross-dresser—'

'Rhianne's hair was loose,' Atherton remembered.

'There were – let me see – five scrunchies in her room, so we know she used them. All different colours. But there was no pink one. She was interested in clothes; she probably would have matched the scrunchie to her outfit. And she was wearing pink that day.' He looked at the searcher. 'Bag that. If the DNA matches, we've got him.'

McLaren called him. 'Denton's just come out.'

'Leaving?'

'No, he's just standing there.' A pause. 'He's lit up.' Another pause. 'Looks like he's just come out for a ciggie. He's just standing outside the door, smoking.'

'All right. Keep an eye on him.'

Slider called Jenrich.

'Jenda still under wraps?'

'Yes, guv. We're taking a long time processing her, as agreed.'

'Good, make sure she doesn't contact Denton.'

'Yes, guv.' Slider could practically hear the eye roll. *This is*

*what we discussed and agreed on. D'you think I've forgotten
already?*

'Carry on,' he said hastily and clicked off.

'What's he up to now?' McLaren asked.

Denton had come out again. This time he looked briefly round,
then set off across the lot, walking briskly.

McLaren got out. 'There's only a pedestrian exit that way, an
alley into the main road. I'll follow him. You might have to take
the motor round,' he said.

But Denton didn't head towards the exit. McLaren, threading
between parked cars so as not to be obvious, muttered,
'Where's he going? He's not got a motor.' Denton seemed to
be heading towards a green Ford Fiesta, and McLaren picked
up the pace. 'What's he going to do, break in?' But then he
saw him point something at the car, which blinked. 'He's got
someone's car keys,' he reported to Fathom and started to run.
Denton got in the car, started it and backed out at speed, almost
knocking McLaren down. McLaren made a futile grab at the
rear door handle as it accelerated away and started running
back, shouting into the Airwave, 'He's had it away! He's got
wheels!'

Fathom had the department car started but was not quick
enough to intercept Denton. McLaren reached it running and
managed to get the door open and himself inside without it stopping, and they were out of the parking lot and in pursuit, while
McLaren slapped the bubble on the roof and called it in.

'Damn and blast!' Slider said. He spoke to Jenrich. 'Someone
must have tipped him off.'

'Not Jenda,' she said. 'She's not had her phone call yet. She's
still with the doctor. He's having a long chat with her, to assess
her mental state, given she's off sick with bad nerves.'

'All right, well, make sure she doesn't call him. And send
someone over to D&K to find out what happened. I'm coming
back.' To Atherton he said, 'You finish up here, then come back.
This is the last thing we needed, a car chase.'

'He can't get far in West London traffic,' Atherton said.

* * *

You couldn't have a proper high-speed pursuit through the crowded outer-urban streets of Acton, but Denton could be more reckless of public safety than the police could, and he knew his back streets. All Fathom could do was keep in touch, while McLaren kept reporting and they waited for other units to join them.

'He's heading for the A40,' McLaren said as Denton hurtled onto Horn Lane, clipping a car coming the other way as it screeched to a halt. There was a shower of headlamp glass, but all the traffic had stopped in both directions and Fathom was able to whip the car through the gap and catch up some yards. There was a slip road onto the dual-carriageway A40 at the end of Horn Lane, and Denton took that, accelerating, and joined the main road without stopping, causing several cars to swerve violently, jamming all three lanes. Traffic was fairly light at this time of day, and Fathom gave a grunt of satisfaction as he put his foot down and swung out onto the dual carriageway. He ought to be able to catch up now. They were heading westwards, and the heavy clouds ahead showed a chink of declining sun fire for an instant before it closed down.

Gascoyne, with Coutinho – on loan from uniform and hoping to join the Department – reached D&K to find half the staff lurking around the entrance deep in enthralled speculation with the few customers who were around at that time of day. The manager was in the staff room with the deputy manager, comforting a female staff member who was slumped on a chair, red-eyed and red-nosed, and presumably responsible for the snow-drift of soggy tissues around her feet. Gascoyne's identifying himself and Coutinho as police elicited a fresh burst of tears.

The manager told them that Denton had come back from his cigarette break and had walked straight through to the staff room, where Lisa Munney had been alone, taking her break with a cup of coffee and a well-thumbed copy of *Bridal Guide Magazine*, May–June edition.

Munney, taking up the story through hitching breaths, said Denton, with 'an awful look on his face' had grabbed her handbag, which had been on the coffee table in front of her, and thrust it at her, saying, 'Give me your car keys.' When she had, under-

standably, hesitated and said, 'What do you want them for?' he
had opened the bag and started rummaging through it.
'I said, "oy!" I said, "What you think you're doing?" I tried
to grab it off him, and the next minute, he's grabbed me, he's
pulled a knife on me, he's got it against me throat.' She looked
at Coutinho as if waiting for the indrawn breath of impressed
horror and was forced to continue without. 'He says, "Gimme
the car keys, bitch, or you're dead."'
Gascoyne, taking notes, said, 'Are those his exact words?'
She looked defiant. 'More or less. He sounded like a madman.
I was scared to death. I thought me last hour'd come. So I found
the keys and give him them, and he grabs them, and he's gone.
I couldn't catch me breath. It took me a minute before I could
even scream.'

From the assistant manager, they learned that Munney's scream
had had the unfortunate effect of diverting all attention and unoccupied staff in her direction, while Denton had walked calmly
out.

The manager said, 'I saw him, and I called out after him,
"Where are you going? Your break's over." He called over his
shoulder, "I'll only be a minute." He seemed quite calm. He
wasn't running, just walking briskly, and there was the to-do
going on in the staff room, so I went that way.' He looked apologetic. 'I wasn't to know, was I?'

Gascoyne asked Lisa how Denton had known which car was
hers and where it was parked.

'The staff have reserved bays,' the manager replied to the
second part. 'He'd know where it was.'

And Lisa admitted that he knew her car because they had had
'a bit of a thing' a few weeks ago, and when they had dated she
had picked him up in her car because he didn't have one.

'Did he break it off or did you?' Gascoyne asked.

They hadn't actually broken it off, just they hadn't sort of
gone out together for a couple of weeks, Lisa said, looking
embarrassed. She hadn't been sure where she stood with him.
He'd been just as nice to her at work but hadn't made a new
date with her. She'd thought she'd have to ask him at some point
what was going on, but she didn't want to push him. 'You know
what men are like. They run a mile if they think you're being

too possessive.' But after pulling a knife on her and stealing her car, well, he was going to have some explaining to do before she'd go out with him again. She liked him, but, well, you didn't do that sort of thing, did you? And if he so much as scratched it – well! He could forget it.

Outside, it was getting unnaturally dark. 'It's going to rain like stink any minute,' said Coutinho.

'We've got plenty on him now,' Porson said. Everyone was in the CID office, waiting for updates. 'Common assault, taking and driving away, dangerous driving, breaking parole.'

'And the cocaine and marijuana in his flat,' Atherton added. 'We've sent the spliff off for analysis and comparison with the one from Rhianne's bedroom.'

Slider came out from his office, having spoken to Rita about the scrunchie. 'She says Rhianne was wearing one when she left for work. She often wore her hair tied back with one. She can't say what colour it was but says she did have a pink one. And we know there was no pink one in her bedroom when we searched it.'

'We've sent that off as well,' Jenrich confirmed, 'for DNA analysis on the hairs.'

'But no scarf,' Porson said. 'That's the fly in the woodpile. Wonder what he did with it.'

'Thrown away somewhere,' Slider said with a shrug. 'Could be anywhere. But now we know who to look for, we can get on with looking at all the local area CCTV images. If we can get him on his way to Rhianne's or on the way back, we can assemble a proper timeline.'

'Got to catch him first,' said Porson.

Car chases were a pain, but the felon was almost always caught. And it wasn't as if he was fleeing in a high-performance BMW or similar. Once the highway patrol was in pursuit it was like a leopard chasing a Shetland pony.

'It's as black as Newgate knocker out there,' Slider said. 'I hope they catch him before there's a downpour.'

Two highway units had joined the chase now and were looking for a safe place to bracket the Fiesta and bring it to a halt. Without superior speed, the motorway ahead was not in his favour. Perhaps he realized that, because at the Target Roundabout intersection, he veered off the A40 at the last moment and onto the Hayes cross route, which at the other end joined the M4.

'He's not heading for Heathrow, is he, the pillock?' McLaren said.

'What's wrong with that?' Fathom said.

'We know he's not got a passport. You can't even get a domestic flight without a passport. Or a driving licence, and he's not got one of them either.'

'How d'you know?'

'Never passed his test. It's all in his file.' He grabbed the rider's handle as Fathom whipped round the Ruislip Road roundabout in the wake of the jam sandwiches. 'He's no better off on the M4 than the M40.'

'Maybe he knows some more back streets,' said Fathom.

One of the highway cars saw its chance and overtook the Fiesta, then started slowing as the second car closed off the outside lane, blocking the object car in. Denton pulled right as if hoping to overtake, then veered off sharply left down a side turning, the second patrol car following closely.

'Got him now,' McLaren said, as Fathom took the turning in their wake. 'It's a housing estate. He can't get back out onto the main road except through here.'

The chase ended as it so often did. The patrol car overtook and slewed across the road, blocking the way, and Fathom did the same behind. Denton abandoned the car and ran but was quickly brought down by a muscular young officer from the highway patrol who, it turned out, ran half-marathons in his off-time for charity. In any case, he was ten years younger than Denton and six inches taller, most of it in the leg department.

'Here it comes,' said McLaren, as the first heavy drops fell through the untimely twilight.

'Got him,' said Atherton, from the telephone. 'They're bringing him in.'

At the same moment, Coffey, one of the uniforms, appeared in the doorway and said to Slider, 'Sergeant Nicholls sent me, sir. Mr Willans is downstairs kicking up holy hell and demanding to see you. Something about wrongful arrest of his son. He's got his solicitor with him and the skipper wants to know what you'd like him to do with them.'

'Oh, not now!' Slider groaned.

Porson said, 'You stay and deal with this. I'll go and sort him out.' He rubbed his hands. 'It'll be a pleasure. Coming in here with his brief, threatening us! I'll trim his nails for him!'

'I feel almost sorry for Willans,' Atherton remarked when Porson had gone.

Outside, the rain drummed down. The relief inside was palpable.

Reality had not yet caught up with Denton when Slider went downstairs. He was at the custody desk, hands still cuffed, looking a little tousled by the experience but still evidently 'up' from the adrenalin of the chase. He lifted his head defiantly as Slider came into his sightline and gave him a cocky, spit-in-your-eye look. 'You'd never have caught me if I'd got decent wheels, instead of that fart-box. Why do women drive cars like that? They shouldn't be allowed on the road.'

'Do you mean the cars or the women?' Slider asked.

'Guess,' Handy Andy spat.

'Has he been cautioned?' Slider asked.

'Yes, guv,' said McLaren.

'Suspicion of murder,' Denton affirmed, with a 'duh!' jerk of the head. 'You people are unbelievable! I'll be out of here before you can count to twenty – if any of you *can* count that high without taking your shoes off.'

'Talks a lot, doesn't he?' said Bright, the officer behind the desk. 'My aunt had a budgie like that once. Chattered away all day long.'

'It wasn't even murder,' Denton said scornfully. 'I read it on the internet. Drug overdose it said.'

'You shouldn't believe everything you read online,' Slider said mildly.

That seemed to rile him. 'I'm sick of being persecuted by you lot! Every time I turn round, there's some gormless plod trying to finger me for whatever crime you've got stuck on your books. And let's face it, there's plenty of 'em. Detectives? You couldn't detect a cockroach in a trifle! Well, I'm not going to sit here and let you use me for target practice. I want my phone call. And my brief.'

'All in due time, my lad,' said Bright, large, calm and fatherly – if your father had a core of tempered steel. Slider always thought of him as the ideal copper. Street incidents about to kick off often didn't kick just because Dave Bright had appeared. He was the AFFF on the fire of human aggression.

'Oh, I've got time,' Denton said. 'I've got all the time in the world. You lot are going to look stupid in a couple of hours' time when you have to let me go. I should say, *more* stupid. If that's possible. You've got nothing on me. I barely knew the girl.'

'That's an improvement on "I've never met her", which was what you were claiming last time we spoke,' said Slider. 'By the way, what made you do a runner? Did somebody tip you off?'

'Tip me off? Tip me off about what?' Denton sneered.

'That we had enough evidence to arrest you?'

Denton snorted. 'In your dreams.'

'So why did you have it away if you're not guilty?'

'I thought I might as well get a bit of fun out of it, before you wrongfully arrested me. I saw your monkeys, of course I did! Went out for a smoke and clocked 'em right away, sitting there in an unmarked car watching D&K like a couple of ventriloquist dummies. You people are pathetic. D'you really think I don't know the filth when I see 'em, just because they're not wearing the uniform and the big tit hat? They didn't know I'd made 'em, though, did they? No, thought not. Not till I started driving away. If I'd got a real motor instead of a bloody sewing machine, I'd have been away before they'd got their feet untangled.'

'Well, we've got you, anyway,' Bright said, 'singing away like a little bird in a cage.'

The cockiness didn't diminish, but for a moment there was a coldness underneath it, perhaps at the mention of a cage. Denton didn't want to go back inside – who would? Fear expressed itself as anger. 'I'll give you little bird!' he said. 'You're gonna be sorry for this, I promise you. I'm gonna sue your arses off. You'll be lucky to get a job delivering pizzas when I've finished with you!'

* * *

Later, in the tape room, with a solicitor at his side – from the
legal aid pool, one Kevin Swan, a brief Slider had dealt with
before, a stocky man with a thick head of black hair, liberally
sprinkled with grey, and the wrinkled skin of a lifelong smoker,
so that his face looked like a bag of walnuts – Denton had not
sunk, like most captured suspects, into sullenness. You would
think he'd had a cheeky toot of his own idiot dust, because he
was elated and talkative, despite Swan's efforts to calm him
down. He watched the security footage from Barney's without
flinching.

'So I chat to sales girls. When did that become a crime?'

'When you start grooming them,' Slider suggested.

'She needed bloody grooming from the look of her! No dress
sense, no style, these girls. Just throw on the first thing they pick
up off the floor.' He gave a derisive laugh, then looked at Kevin
Swan and said, 'Oh, cool it! They've got nothing on me. So I
knew her, so what? Half of bloody London knew her, from what
I've read. For the record, I saw her at the garden centre where
she works, and she came on to me. I can't help it if I'm attractive to women, can I?'

Slider ignored that and went on in a clerical manner, as one
reading facts from notes. 'And, very cleverly, you made all your
arrangements with her there, face to face, so there was nothing
written down that could come back on you – no emails, texts,
phone calls, letters.'

'Letters? What are you, PR for Royal Mail? Who writes letters
these days?'

'Not you, that's for sure. A nice, clean operation you ran. No
written evidence. No photographs. Knowing what teenage girls
are like, photographing everything all the time, how did you stop
her taking pictures of you?'

'If the occasion arose, I'd have just told her not to. I'd have
grabbed her wrist and twisted it hard to make the point. The way
I do it, once is enough,' he said, and the dark menace of him
was briefly visible for the first time. 'You've got to show them
who's in charge. A little bit of pain up front guarantees obedience
later. Nicer for everyone.' The cocky smirk came back. 'But of
course I never met her outside Barney's, and since you've admitted
there are no photographs, you can't prove I did.'

'I didn't say there were no photographs. Only none of your face.'

'Well, she never got a camera near my dick, so I don't know what you're talking about. Oh, relax, Kevin. I just said she *didn't* photograph it, didn't I? I never said I gave her the chance. You see,' he turned to Slider, 'this is where your case falls down. I was never at her house, and you can't prove I was.'

'When you roll a spliff,' Slider said casually, almost dreamily, 'how do you make the end of the paper stick down?'

'Me? I never do roll them.'

'There were two in your bedside drawer.'

'Must be Jenda's,' he said without hesitation. He chuckled. 'How many times have I told that woman not to leave her gear around? Criminally careless, she is!'

'How does someone who *does* roll a spliff stick the paper down?'

'Same as with a roll-up. You wet it.' His eyes narrowed. 'What's that got to do with it?'

'So if we analyse the saliva on a spliff found in Rhianne's bedroom, we won't get a match with your DNA?' He took that well, but Slider could see him thinking hard. 'It's quite a personal thing, rolling doobies. Each person has their own style. Funny thing, Rhianne's was just like Jenda's. I wonder how that happened.'

Denton had recovered his mojo. 'Buggered if I know. Maybe her and Jenda were pals. I've told you, I was never at Rhianne's house.'

'Yes, you have said that,' Slider said.

'Never saw her outside of Barney's. Not that she didn't beg me for a date. They can't get enough of me, the *lay-dees*.' He put on a joke voice.

'Your flat is nice and tidy. I suppose it's Jenda who tidies everything up, keeps it all clean and ship-shape?'

'Huh! Shit-shaped it'd be if it was left to her. I can't stand a mess; I make her shove everything in her drawers. Women! They're all sluts, basically.'

'I suppose you preferred to take women to your flat – nicer for you. But did Jenda know?'

'Jenda's got cement between her ears. She doesn't know anything about anything.'

'So she didn't know you had other women there? What if she'd come home early and caught you out?'

'She knew better than that. I told her when she went out when she could come home. It only took a bit of a slap the one time she didn't listen to drive the lesson home. You got to show them where they stand. And believe me, they thank you for it. They need someone to tell them what to do. Choices just confuse them.'

'Rhianne was another one, wasn't she? Terrible state her bedroom was in. Must have made you sick.'

'Vomiting on it would have improved it,' Denton agreed.

'So you admit you've been in her bedroom.'

'Nice try, Sherlock, but I admit nothing. I was never there.'

'You always had sex with her at your flat?'

'She never came to my flat. I didn't go to her house. Got that straight now?'

'So how did you get hold of the scrunchie she was wearing last Tuesday? We found it in your flat. There are always a few hairs caught in a used scrunchie for DNA matching, so there'll be no doubt it was Rhianne's.'

For once he had no answer. The look returned of furious thinking. 'No comment,' he said at last. It was an admission of weakness from a man who loved to talk. Even Kevin Swan looked sideways at him.

'It puzzled me, you see, why you took it home with you. How could someone as careful as you make such a mistake?'

He was riled. 'I don't make mistakes!'

'So what was it then, a souvenir?'

'If you found it at all, and you're not just mouthing off, you must have planted it there. I know how these things go. I've done time already for a crime I didn't commit.'

'Three women said you did.'

'That Marly wanted it. It was all consensual. She was gagging for it. They all are – they're all slags, bloody women! And the other two I'd never even met. That bitch of a lawyer just wanted to make a name for herself, get a big eye-catching case into the papers and get famous, never mind that it ruined an innocent man's life. They're all bitches, all of them. Man-haters. Probably closet lesbians as well.'

Kevin Swan said, 'I think we need to take a break. I'd like a word with my client.'

Slider wasn't inclined to stop when he'd got Denton on the ropes, but at that moment the door opened and Swilley appeared with an urgent look that said something important had happened. 'All right,' he said. 'We'll take a short break.'

'Tell me it's good news,' he said when he and Atherton were out in the corridor.

She grinned. 'The best,' she said. 'We've got the scarf.'

Slider felt such a surge of relief his knees went weak. The scrunchie was proof that Denton knew Rhianne and possibly that he had been at the house but was still not proof he had strangled her. Without that, they were relying on getting him to confess – not impossible, but not certain, and a long process.

'How? Where?' he demanded.

The search team had continued at Jenda and Denton's flat all this while, pretty much taking it apart. 'Found a hidden drawer in the kitchen,' Swilley said. 'Above the washing machine. It looked cosmetic, just a fill-in panel for the gap between the machine and the worktop, but when they levered the front off, there was a drawer behind it. All sorts of things in there. A lipstick, bits of underwear – looks as though he liked to collect souvenirs of his conquests. There was a photo of Marly Potillo in the nude. And a pink silk-type scarf.'

Atherton crowed. 'His 'n' hers DNA! We've got him now.'

'I sent it off straight away, boss,' Swilley said, her eyes bright. 'I wonder why he took the scrunchie as well.'

'I think that was a mistake,' Slider said. 'He didn't put it in his victim drawer, did he? Probably he stuffed it in his pocket without thinking, and when he got home it fell out somehow and Jenda picked it up and shoved it in her drawer without thinking. You could see it shook him – he said no comment for the first time. He couldn't account for it.'

Another long time later, Slider and Atherton went up to the canteen for a cup of tea and a bun. It was quieter at this time of day than the office. Outside the rain had almost stopped. Someone had opened some windows, and there was a fresh smell and the sound of water gurgling down the gutters. A gleam of dark gold light showed around the cracks in the clouds like kintsugi.

They sipped in silence for a while, then Atherton said, 'They wear you out, people like that.'

'Thank God for criminals who talk,' Slider said automatically.

Denton had remained defiant, and having, it seemed, acknowledged inwardly that the scarf was evidence too far, he seemed actually glad of the audience to boast about his exploits – even an audience as stupid as coppers. He was high as a kite on his own cleverness.

He admitted to having groomed Rhianne, though objected to the word 'groomed'. She was of age, he maintained, and what she chose to do with her body was her own affair. He had courted her, then seduced her, then gradually acclimatized her to the power and domination games he liked. He grew expansive through the details of his campaign. 'You've got to work with the grain,' he said, more than once. 'Make them want it as much as you do. It's a kind of hypnotism.'

'Like a stoat with a rabbit,' Slider suggested.

'The fun is seeing how far they'll go. Getting them to accept their own degradation. Mind you,' he added with a disdainful look, 'most of them haven't got any morals these days, so it's not the challenge it used to be. And I was just getting little Ree-Ree to the best part when the silly cow went and dropped down dead.' He shrugged. 'I shouldn't have gone to her house. That was more risky than it needed to be, when I'd got my own flat and Jenda safely out at work. But she wanted me there for some reason. To prove to herself that she'd got a real boyfriend, maybe. But she was nervous as hell all the time that her mum or dad might come back unexpectedly. I reckon it was the nervous strain that made her conk out. Not my fault, you see.'

'Except that you were strangling her at the time. You like to strangle them until they pass out, then have them while they're unconscious, don't you? Gives you a special thrill, doesn't it? Sort of like necrophilia.'

'I've told you a dozen times, I never did that! They lied to make themselves out as victims – and that bitch lawyer told them what to say. Coached them. Of course the worse it looked, the better for her career – making a name for herself as a fricking warrior queen. They're all at it. They were never unconscious. I just strangled 'em a little bit – they liked it. It got them excited. *You're* supposed to have all the resources – look it up! Pressure on the neck raises the libido. The girls are all into choking these days.'

'I know boys see it when they watch pornography and want to try it out, and girls feel they have to go along with it to please them. I don't think any of them like it.'

He shrugged. 'You write your own story, if it amuses you.'

'Then you ran away.'

'Well, I wasn't going to ring 999 and wait to be picked up, was I? A dead body is an embarrassing thing to be found in the company of. So I hooked it.'

'How did you know she was dead, not just unconscious?'

He rolled his eyes. 'Oh, please! It's not difficult.'

'And why in the kitchen and not upstairs?'

'Just a little taster, to get her primed and in the mood. I'm telling you, it was all consensual. You've got nothing on me.'

'I'm afraid the "rough sex" defence won't help you this time,' Slider said. 'The judicial system is coming down hard on this sort of thing. You were strangling her when she died, and you've got form. Manslaughter for certain, but I think they're going to slap you with murder this time. You're going down.'

Denton's reaction was a flood of profanity.

Slider didn't blink. 'You think you're the great master criminal-stroke-genius, but you made too many mistakes. You got lazy. You're past it, Andy.'

His eyes contracted with anger. 'You'll find out who's past it, copper.'

'I'm afraid you really will be past it when you come out. You'll be an old, old man, too old to attract young girls. If you ever come out.'

'He's still convinced that we can't touch him,' Atherton said to Slider later, as they sat in the canteen drinking tea. 'And the CPS is going to have terrible doubts about that congenital heart defect.'

'Manslaughter or murder, without any mitigating circum-stances, and with his previous record, he'll get the book thrown at him. I don't think in the long run it'll make much difference to his sentence. That drawer full of souvenirs? Prosecution will love that.'

'But how will her parents feel, I wonder?' said Atherton, absently picking currants out of his bun. 'I think they'd like to know he went down for murder.'

'I'm not sure by this stage it will make much difference to them,' said Slider.

'What about you?' Atherton said shrewdly.

'You know me too well,' Slider said. 'She was exploited and abused and died as a direct result of that. Freddie Cameron said it was a minor heart defect; she might have gone all her life and never known. So it was murder in my book, as much as if he'd strangled her to death.'

He offered Atherton a bed for the night, since Stephanie was away and his place was closer than Atherton's artesian cottage. Atherton was glad to accept. Without the cats there, his home was not welcoming.

Joanna had waited up for them. 'You poor things. You must be exhausted. Can I get you something to eat?'

'We've had sandwiches all through. Relays of them,' Slider said.

'How about a cup of cocoa? Recommended for shock, weariness, frayed nerves and so on. Very comforting.'

Slider smiled tiredly. 'Thanks. I'd like that.'

'Got any whisky?' Atherton asked.

'Oh, you're too grown-up for cocoa, are you?' Joanna teased.

'Not at all. I'll have some, just with whisky in it. But you can leave out the cocoa.'

She sat with them while they talked.

'Family liaison said that when she went to Acacia Avenue, Morgan wasn't there,' said Slider. 'Rita said he's moved out. Gone to the Holiday Inn at Gypsy Corner.'

'She threw him out?'

'I understand it was by mutual consent. Apparently she told Linda – that's the FL officer – that she could never forgive him for being preoccupied with another woman while Rhianne was being lured to her death.'

'But she didn't do anything to stop it, either,' Atherton said.

'She knows that. She said she'll never forgive herself for not knowing what was going on. She says she ought to have realized how withdrawn Rhianne had become, but she'd assumed it was to do with A levels and so on. And probably Rhianne had got good at concealing everything from them. That poor, troubled child! Lost her real father that she adored, fixed herself on her new father, then found out he had feet of clay. And went looking for another new father in all the wrong places. When I think of her begging Corey to tell her he loved her . . . Corey Willans, of all people! Handy Andy, all mature and charming and sympathetic, must have looked just the ticket.'

'It's horrible,' said Joanna. 'And all this going on under her mother's nose. What must she be feeling?'

'Yes, you'd expect a mother to be more in tune with her daughter's state of mind than a father,' Atherton said. 'She must be tearing herself apart.'

'And she can't forgive herself for not knowing about the heart defect. But obviously David's sin is the greater.'

'Linda says she was talking about selling up and going out to America to be with her sisters. But all she and David have now is each other,' Slider said. 'It's not as if he abused Rhianne or anything. If they split up, they'll each have to mourn alone.'

'Maybe they'll get back together down the line,' Joanna said. Then, after a pause, 'You think you've got enough to put him away?'

'DNA from the spliff proves he was providing her with drugs, the scrunchie proves he was in the house that day, and DNA from the scarf proves he did the strangling. I think it's enough.'

'How *did* the scrunchie turn up in his flat?'

'I can only think it must have been lying on the floor, and Jenda tidied it away without noticing,' Slider said. 'Apparently Denton's always bitching at her for being untidy, so when she knows he's coming home she reflexively grabs everything loose and jams it into a cupboard or drawer. Denton's still not clear how it got there. He remembers pulling it off Rhianne's hair because he liked to see girls' hair loose. I think he must have stuffed it into his trouser pocket without thinking, and then pulled it out without realizing when he emptied his pockets to hang his clothes up in the wardrobe. The perils of tidiness.'

'Do you mind?' Atherton objected. 'If everyone hung their clothes up in the wardrobe every day, the world would be a better place.'

They had the usual celebration at the Boscombe on the Friday. Atherton brought Stephanie, who ended up having a very long talk with McLaren's Natalie, to Slider's surprise. 'I wouldn't have thought they'd have anything in common.'

'Stephanie's throwing "save me" looks at Jim,' Joanna said. 'I think Natalie's asking her about plastic surgery. Maybe she wants a free sample?'

'What on earth would she want plastic surgery for? She's perfectly pleasant-looking as she is.'

'Perhaps she wants it for Maurice.'

'She'd have to catch him first. He's got an aversion to doctors.'

'He doesn't seem to be flinching away from Stephanie.'

'She's a gorgeous-looking piece of totty. That trumps an MBBS any day.'

'Chauvinist!'

'I didn't say I agreed with him.'

'Has she given Jim an answer yet?' Joanna pursued, watching as Atherton slithered up and surgically removed Stephanie from Nat's clutches.

'Don't think so,' said Slider.

'Boss!' Swilley called across the bar. 'No sitting with Significant Others! You can do that at home.' Her own husband Tony was tateytating with Gascoyne's Karen. 'Come and talk to us. We want you to tell us how clever we are.'

Later, Slider and Atherton found themselves temporarily alone together at the bar. It was Slider's turn to get a round in. For something to say, Slider casually put forward Joanna's idea of his coming with Stephanie to Exmoor. Atherton didn't say anything, and Slider glanced at him, afraid he had been embarrassed by the invitation. Atherton was looking bemused. Urgh, was it a step too far? Eating together, out or in, was well established, but they'd never holidayed together. 'No pressure, of course,' he went on hastily. 'Absolutely understand if you don't fancy it. And probably you'd want to wait until things are sorted out between you and her anyway. Until she's given you an answer.'

'Oh, she's given me an answer,' Atherton said. 'Just a moment ago. I think she's been overcome with excitement at seeing me in my milieu.'

'Your what?'

'All you lot.'

'Hark, hark, the dogs do bark?' Slider said doubtfully.

'Oh, I come out well from the comparison,' Atherton agreed. 'Given that several of our dogs are rabid.'

'Well, we're not everyone's cup of tea.' Slider was afraid that being earoled by Natalie, plus seeing McLaren put a whole Scotch egg in his mouth at one go, might make Stephanie judge Atherton by the company he chose. 'So what did she say?'

'She said maybe,' said Atherton.

'Maybe?'

'Actually, she said let's live together first and see how it goes.'

'Well, that's a horse of a different colour. What did you say?'

'I said, hell, yes,' said Atherton.